"He is suggesting surrender," Alba said, glowering. "He does not wish to fight to preserve the cargo."

I bit my lip. Of course, this tub couldn't stand against the Galatine ship; I was foolish for even trying to buffer us, to raise the possibility of victory. Charms couldn't make the impossible possible.

Quickly, without considering the ramifications of what I was doing, I spun darkness from the ether. I pulled black luck and death and misfortune, drew it tight around itself like a ball. With my fist clenched and my heart pounding against my ribs, I hurled it toward the Royalist ship. More specifically, toward a gunport and the maw of a cannon inside, its crew in the middle of loading the gun.

The black sparkling orb collided with the black cast iron of the gun and enveloped it. It didn't press itself into the metal; I hadn't expected that, and before I could decide if I should try to embed the curse in the unmalleable iron, the crew fired the gun.

It exploded.

Praise for
The Unraveled Kingdom

"Miller places immigrant ambition and women's lives at the heart of her magical tale of politics and revolution. I was utterly enchanted by this unique, clever, and subtly fierce fantasy."

—Tasha Suri, author of *Empire of Sand*

"One of the best novels I've read this year! *Torn* is masterfully written—full of fascinating politics and compelling characters in a vividly rendered, troubled city."

—Sarah Beth Durst, author of the Queens of Renthia series

"Strong research, moral ambiguities, and an innovative magic system....A well-executed historical fantasy debut whose author has a sharp eye for detail."

—*Kirkus*

"Fantasy fans, especially those who grew up reading Tamora Pierce's Circle of Magic series, will adore Sophie....Exciting and page-turning."

—*Booklist* (starred review)

"A delight, woven through with rich detail. Magic, sewing, and an achingly good romance—what's not to love? A deeply satisfying read. I'm dying for the next one!"

—Alexandra Rowland, author of *A Conspiracy of Truths*

"Miller weaves a fresh, richly textured world full of magic-stitched ball gowns and revolutionary pamphlets. The vivid, complex setting and deeply human characters make for an absorbing read!"

—Melissa Caruso, author of *The Tethered Mage*

By Rowenna Miller

RULE

The Unraveled Kingdom: Book Three

ROWENNA MILLER

www.orbitbooks.net

Copyright © 2020 by Rowenna Miller
Excerpt from *The Obsidian Tower* copyright © 2020 by Melissa Caruso
Excerpt from *The Ranger of Marzanna* copyright © 2020 by Jon Skovron

Cover design by Lisa Marie Pompilio
Cover art by Carrie Violet
Cover copyright © 2020 by Hachette Book Group, Inc.
Map by Tim Paul
Author photograph by Heidi Hauck

Orbit
Hachette Book Group
1290 Avenue of the Americas
New York, NY 10104
orbitbooks.net

First Edition: May 2020

Orbit is an imprint of Hachette Book Group.
The Orbit name and logo are trademarks of Little, Brown Book Group Limited.

The publisher is not responsible for websites (or their content) that are not owned by the publisher.

The Hachette Speakers Bureau provides a wide range of authors for speaking events. To find out more, go to www.hachettespeakersbureau.com or call (866) 376-6591.

Library of Congress Cataloging-in-Publication Data
Names: Miller, Rowenna, author.
Title: Rule / Rowenna Miller.
Description: First Edition. | New York, NY : Orbit, 2020. | Series: The unraveled kingdom; book three
Identifiers: LCCN 2019042374 | ISBN 9780316478694 (trade paperback) | ISBN 9780316478687 (e-book)
Subjects: LCSH: Magic—Fiction. | GSAFD: War stories. | Fantasy fiction.
Classification: LCC PS3613.I55275 R85 2020 | DDC 813/.6—dc23
LC record available at https://lccn.loc.gov/2019042374

ISBNs: 978-0-316-47869-4 (trade paperback), 978-0-316-47867-0 (ebook)

Printed in the United States of America

LSC-C

10 9 8 7 6 5 4 3 2 1

For Eleanor and Marjorie, who are still small,
a book about beginnings

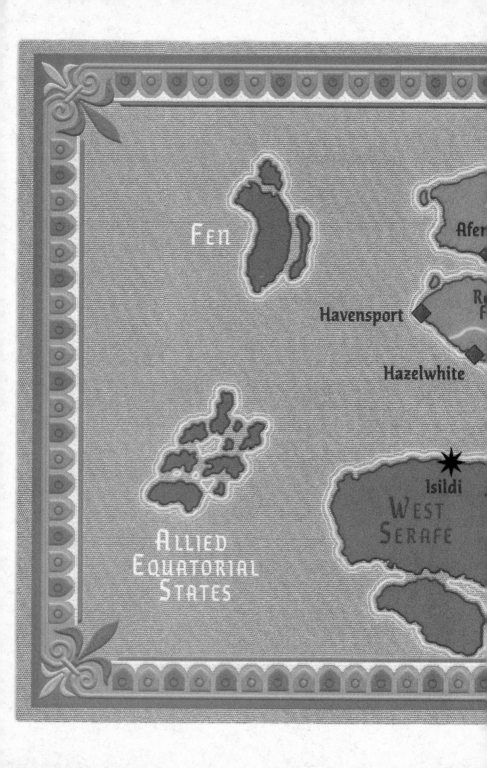

1

THE SUMMER SUN HAD RIPENED THE BERRIES IN THE HEDGEROWS of the Order of the Golden Sphere, dyeing them a rich ruddy purple. The juices, a red more brilliant than even the best scarlet silk, stained my fingers as I plucked them from the deep brambles. Within several yards in any direction, novices of the order filled baskets of their own. A wheat-haired girl with pale honey eyes had a smear of berry-red across the front of her pale gray gown. She sighed and adjusted her starched white veil, leaving another red streak.

I stifled a laugh, then sobered. A war waged some hundreds of miles south of us, the sisters of the Golden Sphere were deep in study at the art of casting charms under my tutelage, Sastra-set Alba was making final arrangements for an alliance-cementing voyage to Fen.

And I was picking berries.

I snagged my thumb on a large, curved thorn; nature made needles as effective as any I had used in my atelier, and the point produced a bead of blood almost instantly. I drew my hand carefully away and wrapped the tiny wound in my apron, letting the red stain sink into the linen.

Picking berries. As though that were an acceptable way to

spend my afternoon, now of all times. I flicked the corner of the apron away with a frustrated sigh. My basket was already nearly full, but the bushes were still thick with purple. I knew what Alba would say—winter cared little for our war, and all the members of the community fortified the larder against that enemy. I wanted to rebel against that pragmatic logic. The ordered calm of the convent mocked me, the pristine birchwood and the gardens all carrying on an unconcerned life and inviting me to join in.

It infuriated me. Probably, I acknowledged as I resumed plucking fruit for the basket, because the pacific quiet was so inviting. Here I could almost forget—had forgotten, in horrifying, brief instants—that my country was at war. That my friends in the city could be killed under bombardment, that Theodor and my brother in the south could be overrun on the battlefield.

Letters were painfully delayed, coming weeks after they were sent, if at all, as the Royalist navy poached ships off the coast and the overland routes remained treacherous. I had learned to cope by pretending that nothing happened between receipt of one letter and the next, that the events Theodor and Kristos described unfolded in the instant I read them. The possibilities that a single day could bring—a crushing defeat, mass desertion, my brother captured, Theodor killed—overwhelmed me if I allowed myself to think about them.

Which was especially difficult when the last letter had come weeks ago, sent weeks before that. Kristos wrote to both Alba and me, carefully penning his letter to avoid betraying any vital specifics should it come into the wrong hands. Still, the message was clear. Volunteers—mostly untrained agrarian workers and fishermen—gathered in Hazelwhite, and Sianh had to prepare them for future large-scale battles while engaging in skirmishes with the Royalists still holding territory in the south. The ragtag

army made up of both radical Red Caps and moderate Reformists had coalesced effectively enough to take several small fortifications, but I sensed from the letter that these were positions the
Royalists were willing to give up.

The real battles remained at a hazy distance in the future,
just soon enough that the thought of them left a swirl of nausea
in my stomach and a sour taste in my mouth. I wanted, desperately, to do something, but teaching the "light-touched" sisters
of the convent how to manipulate charm magic was plodding,
redundant work, removed from the immediacy of the war for
Galitha.

The novice with the berry-stained veil motioned me over.
Many of the novices took temporary vows of silence, and though
it was not required, there were some sisters who maintained the
vow for life, on the premise that silence made communion with
the Creator's ever-present spirit easier. Despite long hours of
silence, on account of having no one to speak with here, I was
no closer to any such communion.

I dropped the last few berries from the hedge into my basket
and joined her. I raised an eyebrow and pointed to her veil; she
flushed pink as she noticed the stain, and pointed toward the
narrow road that carved a furrow through the forest.

Still too far away to see through the trees, travelers
announced themselves with the rattle of wheels. She looked to
me with baleful curiosity, as though I might know anything. As
though I might be able to tell her in the stilted, limited Kvys I
had picked up in the past weeks if I did. The other sisters along
the hedgerow noted the sound and gave it little heed, turning
back to their berries as though the outside world didn't exist.

To them, perhaps, it didn't.

Alba crested the little rise behind the convent and strode
toward me. Her pale linen gown, a more traditional Kvys design

than she had worn in West Serafe, more traditional even than most of the sisters, floated behind her on a light breeze. The yoke was decorated with symbols of the Order of the Golden Sphere embroidered in blackwork, circles and crosshatches and thin dotted lines I now understood to be references to charm magic.

The berry-stained novice bowed her head, as did the other sisters, to a Sastra-set, but Alba wasn't looking for them. "The *hyvtha* is gathering," she said, using the Kvys word that usually referred to a band of threshers at harvest or a troupe of musicians. "Let's see if anyone has made any progress since yesterday, shall we?"

"Don't tell me we're disappointing you," I said, deadpan. Trying to teach adults who had been suppressing any inclination toward casting since they were children was nearly impossible. Of our *hyvtha* of eighteen women and two men from the order's brother monastery, only ten reliably saw the light, three could maintain enough focus to hold on to it, and one had managed a shaky, crude clay tablet. Tantia was proud of her accomplishment but had yet to repeat it.

Alba expected a battalion of casters capable of the exquisitely fine work in the order's basilica, and I had one caster who struggled with work a trained Pellian girl could churn out at eight.

The travelers appeared on the road, a comfortable carriage drawn by a pair of gray Kvys draft horses. "And those are the Fenians."

"Which Fenians?" I asked, craning my neck as though I could see past the lead glass windows in the carriage.

"The foundry owner. Well, his son who handles his negotiations, at any rate." Her smile sparkled. "Your cannons are forthcoming."

"So we'll go to Fen—when?"

"I'm still working on the shipyard, and I've two mill owners on the string, each trying to underbid the other for the fabric." She grinned—she enjoyed this game of gold and ink. It made me feel ill, betting with money that wasn't mine. My business had been built carefully, brick by precisely planned brick, and these negotiations with Fen felt like a house of cards, ready to topple under the breath of a single wrong word.

More, anxiety gnawed at the periphery of everything I thought, said, or did, fueled by the persistent fear that the war might be lost before I could even properly contribute. That I could lose everything, including everyone I loved, for want of quick, decisive action. Alba didn't seem motivated to act quickly as I did, and there was nothing I could do to prod her from her insistence on the time-consuming propriety of negotiations.

I bit back the argument I'd made many times, haste before all else, as she continued. "Given the meeting with the Fenians, then, I will not be joining the *hyvtha* this afternoon. See if Tantia can explain her methods to the others."

"I don't think the problem is my Kvys," I protested.

Alba ignored my suggestion—that her plan for a small regiment of charm-casting sisters and brothers of the order was next to impossible—and strode toward the gates to greet our Fenian guests. I rinsed the berry juice from my hands at the pump in the courtyard of the convent. Stains remained on my fingertips and palms.

2

—m—

"*Pra-set*," I said in poor Kvys, the words sticking to the roof of my mouth like taffy, hoping that my meaning, *very good*, was clear to the struggling initiate. Immell's hand shook as she drew her stylus across a damp clay tablet, dragging ragged charm magic into the inscription.

Tantia, who had managed to craft another charmed tablet, laid her hand on Immell's arm, reassuring her in a stream of quiet, almost poetic Kvys. I couldn't follow more than a few words, so I nodded dumbly, what I hoped was a comforting smile plastered on my face. Immell's hand steadied, and the pale glow around her stylus grew stronger, brighter. "*Pra-set!*" I repeated.

Immell finished the inscription, a word in Kvys whose meaning, *Creator's mercy*, stood in for *luck*. The charm magic receded from her hand as she lifted her stylus from the clay, but the charm remained embedded in the tablet. "*Pra-set*," I said again, examining her work. It was uneven and one letter was barely legible even to my unschooled eye, but it was done.

We were still a long way from what Alba hoped for, a phalanx of charm casters who had mastered what I could do. A complement to the Galatine army, she suggested. A safeguard for her house's authority, I read between the lines. And a challenge to the laws prohibiting magic in Kvyset.

A few simple actions, a few stones tossed into a pond infinitely larger than myself, and the ripples were still reaching outward, trembling and new, but intent on fomenting change wherever they went.

Tantia and Immell were speaking in rapid Kvys, gesturing at the tablet. Another novice, Adola, joined them, and the three linked hands. *"Da nin?"* I wondered aloud. *What now?*

Tantia slapped some fresh clay from the bowl on the table, forming a sloppy disk with her free hand. I was about to chide her—orderliness was supposed to cultivate the mind for casting, especially in new learners—but she picked up her stylus and pressed her lips together, squinting into the blank space in front of her.

Light blazed around the stylus and all but drove itself into the clay, sparkling clean and pure in the gray slab. *"Da bravdin-set! Pra bravdin olosc-ni varsi!"* she exclaimed.

"How did you make such a strong charm?" I asked, correcting myself swiftly to Kvys. *"Da olosc bravdin-set?"*

"Is hands holding," Tantia replied, bypassing attempting to explain to me in Kvys. "Hands. I put hand on Immell, she cast."

"And the three of you—you joined hands and your charm was much stronger."

She nodded, smiling. "Easy cast, too. Than before." She thought a moment, then added, "Easy than alone."

"How have I never come across this before." I sighed through my nose. Pellian charm casters worked by themselves, except when an older woman was teaching a novice. "You would think," I began, but stopped myself. My time in the Galatine and Serafan archives had taught me that precious little had been recorded on the subject of casting at all. One *would* think something important had been written down, but that didn't mean it had.

The other sisters and the one brother who had joined us drew closer and Tantia explained what had happened. "We practice," she announced.

I nodded, overwhelmed by their near-accidental discovery. Surely a mother held her daughter's hand while teaching her to cast. But perhaps the process of learning was so different in adults that we noticed the effects more, realized that they were amplifying and not only teaching or steadying one another. More research. In the convent archives. In Kvys. I sighed.

I fled to my room, the only place I was ever alone in the compound. It was clean and bright and spare, with pale wood furniture carved in woodland animals and starbursts on the posts and rails. White linen and cherry-red wool covered the bed. A Kvys prayer book and hymnal lay on a shelf over the window. I couldn't read any of it.

A light scratch on the door, and a dark gray paw shot under the slim crack. Its black claws searched for purchase.

"Kyshi." I laughed and opened the door. The dark gray squirrel scurried into the room. A thin circlet of hammered brass around his neck glinted as he clambered up my bedspread and began to nose around my pillow as though I might have hidden a trove of nuts under the coverlet.

I opened my trunk and produced my secret larder—a handful of cracked chestnuts. "These are mine, little thief," I chided him. He burrowed under my hand and swiped a nut. "Don't take all my good chestnuts. They're almost fresh."

His sharp teeth made quick work of what was left of the shell, his nimble paws turning the nut over and around as he chewed. He had been abandoned in his drey and hand raised by Sastra Dyrka, who worked in the kitchens, where he had developed an astute palate for nuts of all kinds, as well as pastries, sugared fruits, and ham. Now he was a communal pet and quite nearly a mascot for the order.

He settled onto my lap after his snack. I stroked his fur, rich and warm as the finest wool. I wanted to bury my fingers in his thick tail, but he chattered disapprovingly every time I tried.

I felt useless. I thought of a time that felt longer ago than a single year, when my brother was staying out late in the taverns and drumming up support for change, before Pyord solidified their plans with money and centralized violence. Before I had realized I couldn't escape the questions that nagged my brother, before I understood that, for all I had built with long hours and tiring work, it was on a cracked and crumbling foundation. I had resisted participating then, had rebuked my brother for even asking. Now I craved action. Picking berries, petting the squirrel, teaching novice charm casters—it all felt unimportant, artificial, and distant.

My place was with Galitha. My place was fighting for a better country, a better world for my neighbors and my friends and thousands of people I didn't know.

Kyshi started as the door opened, darted up my shoulder, and settled against my neck. "Alba." I acknowledged her as she entered.

"The Fenians are quite amenable to our terms," she said. "Ah, I do like having a freshly inked contract in hand."

"It's done!" I sat upright, dislodging Kyshi, who protested with a profane squirrel screech and his claws in my hair.

"Cannon barrels. Three-, six-, and twelve-pound guns. In the proportions Sianh recommended." Alba smiled. "And of course we will oversee the process for at least a portion of the run on-site at the Fenian foundry."

"Of course," I said. I chewed my lip.

"We'll finish talks with the mill owners and the ship build-ers and then—Fen!" She grinned. "You look less than pleased."

"I'm just tired," I lied. "And I admit, I'm a bit nervous about Fen." That, at least, was the truth.

"Fen is dull and they'll ignore you like they ignore anyone who isn't in the process of paying them or bilking them." She shrugged. "Fenians."

"But the law."

"'But the law!'" Alba mimicked my hesitation with a good-natured laugh. "What, you're going to hang out a shin-gle, 'Charms Cast for Cheap'?" Kyshi trailed down my arm and settled in my lap again, serving Alba a stern look for the volume of her voice.

"No. I wasn't. But if anyone found out…" I let my fin-gers tremble on Kyshi's soft coat. The Fenian penalties for even illusions, simple trickster's street magic, included transporta-tion to their cliff colonies, desolate places scoured half-dead by the northern winds. And actual crimes of attempted magical practices—execution, all of them. Galatine gossip pages some-times carried stories of Fenian women—always women—tried for buying or selling clay tablets, sentenced to drowning in the deep blue waters off Fen's rocky shores.

"No one will find out. Remember, they don't have any idea you can even cast a charm without your needle and thread. And we'll keep it that way. You're quite confident in your methods once we reach Fen, correct? The looms will be set up for our orders and running swift as a sleigh on new snow, just as soon as money has been exchanged."

"Yes," I said. It had taken little practice to embed the charm in lengths of cloth.

"And you can be…subtle?"

"Of course I can." To prove my point, I pulled a stream of

light from the ether and sent it into the blanket, spreading it thin and sinking it into the fibers, all without more than a twitch of my fingers. "See?"

"Yes," Alba said with a slowly growing smile, "I do. And you believe that doing so while the looms are running—"

"It will be fully integrated into the cloth. Woven into warp and weft, not just burrowed into it like a stain."

"Good, good. And the cannons—"

"I don't know what to do with the cannons." I shook my head. There was no way to predict what charmed or cursed iron guns would do. "I think it's best if we do nothing. If I charm them, they might protect our men but also fire ineffectually on the enemy. If I curse them, they might blow up and kill our own crews."

"It seems such a waste." Alba sighed. "Are you quite sure that even the shot couldn't be cursed?"

"It might foul the whole gun," I said.

"Too bad. But you see, there's nothing to worry over. You've everything quite well in hand."

"It's only . . . I didn't expect to be threatened in Isildi, either."

Alba laughed. "I assure you that the Fenians are not the Serafans. They aren't hiding anything, and you're bringing them significant investments. And in Fen, nothing speaks louder than gold." She caught my free hand in hers. "Trust me. The Fenians are a strange people, to be sure, but not indecipherable."

3

THE LONG DINING HALL OF THE HOUSE OF THE GOLDEN SPHERE was always cramped at the dinner hour, the simple tables and benches lined with novices and initiates and full-fledged sisters. I had expected the house of a religious order, and a Kvys one at that, to be a quiet place, but aside from morning and evening prayers and daily services in the basilica there was nearly always laughter and chatter echoing through the halls and gardens. It served to remind me, constantly, that I was an outsider here, speaking too little Kvys to converse easily.

I took my trencher of bean soup and a wedge of bread, flecked at the top with yellow cheese. The sisters may have taken an oath of simplicity, but that couldn't be confused with poverty here. Small indulgences like good cheese, wine, and rich desserts weren't uncommon. The sisters were expected to work for their keep, however, all contributing to the gardening that filled the larders and the cleaning that kept the pale, spare buildings shining.

Tonight Tantia doled out baked apples stuffed with spiced nuts; it was her turn in the kitchen, and even hours of study with me didn't excuse her from that duty. She smiled and gave me an extra-large apple. It smelled like the roasted chestnuts laden with mace and clove that street vendors hawked in the fall and winter in Galitha City.

I sighed, my appetite not matching the size of my dessert. Did Theodor have enough to eat, or had the Royalist navy blockaded the southern ports and cut off supplies? Was Kristos safe, or had he been injured or captured in a skirmish? I stared at the caramelized juices pooling around my apple, an ache no food could fill spreading in my stomach.

"Tantia likes you better than me," Alba complained, sitting next to me. Her apple was half the size of mine.

"You can have mine," I offered, and Alba swapped our fruits. "Shouldn't you be entertaining Fenians?"

"They left already—you didn't see them leave? No, that's right, you were cleaning the library."

"It hardly needs it, barely a speck of dust in all those shelves."

"Books are treasures, we take good care of ours." Alba savored a spoonful of the soup, and I wordlessly ate some of mine. The broth was rich with smoked ham hocks. "Of course I had hoped that you would spend some more time there with Altasvet to dig into the old volumes of the order's history. There might be something there that—"

"There isn't," I replied, short. We'd been over this. The logbooks, the diaries, the transcribed prayers—none of it included pragmatic applications for Kvys casting. The construction of the basilica, which was imbued with layers of charm magic, had not even been described beyond a few notes on the timing and the costs of materials.

Alba sighed. "We must use our time here wisely," she said tersely.

"I am." I stared at the shreds of smoked pork on my spoon

and forced a few more bites. I couldn't make myself sick worrying. The war in Galitha felt so far away, but it needed me. "The best use of our time," I added, "is elsewhere."

"In good time," Alba said. "The Fenian contracts are complete, and soon—"

"Soon!" I nearly shouted, drawing eyes from nearby nuns. I swallowed hard and shoved my trencher away. "They need us," I whispered. "They could be dying. Waiting. It's been weeks. Months, now, since we left West Serafe."

"I understand that this is difficult," Alba said. "But the business of negotiation is delicate. I can't simply barge into a Fenian factory and make demands."

"I can't just sit here any longer!"

"You can," Alba said evenly, "and unless you'd like to set off by yourself, you will." Perhaps she expected more argument, but I stood and left. I walked toward the basilica, candles already winking through the windows as the sisters set up the space for evening prayer service. Alba didn't understand. She couldn't. This was a gamble for her, too, of course, but no one she loved was waging war hundreds of miles away. Her betrothed wasn't risking death. Alba had her order, her sister nuns, but she was not, from what I could tell, bound in the kind of close kinships I had. If she loved, it was silently and secretly.

But she strategized and planned for the advancement of the Golden Sphere and, I allowed, protected her order. To the extent that I served that goal, she protected me, too.

I entered the basilica by the main door. The long aisle opened in front of me, benches of pale wood almost shimmering under candlelight. I didn't have to attend all of the services here the way the sisters did; novices were only required to attend morning prayers and the weekly services, as well as the long services on Glorious Holy Days, which peppered the Kvys calendar heavily. Still, I liked the quiet here, and I liked the order of the service, the way it moved in such a carefully orchestrated rhythm that it appeared organic, the way it repeated and circled. It reminded me in some ways of my sewing, of the peace that can come from familiarity and repetition.

There was far less ornamentation here than in the Galatine cathedral in Fountain Square. Instead, the beauty was in the purity of the arches, the gentle curve of the beams, the orderly, symmetrical windows. It was perfect with the same pale tranquility as fresh-fallen snow. I felt that I might mar it, somehow, as I found an empty bench in the back. All was still and silent.

Until the sisters began to sing.

In the music archive of the great West Serafan university, Corvin had told me about the choral music of the Kvys orders. Even so, the intricate, haunting beauty of the harmonies had stolen my breath the first time I came to evening services. I was in awe of the precision of the voices, strands of sound like thread weaving over and under one another. If I closed my eyes, I could lose myself as the music filled the basilica. I had no idea what the words meant, but it didn't matter, because I could feel the depth of the meaning.

If the Order of the Golden Sphere had ever cast using music, they had not retained any of that practice, even by accident. The magic of the choir was something else entirely, the magic I had experienced when Marguerite played her harp in Viola's salon. Even if war tore my country apart, beauty still existed. It always had. I clung to the belief that it always would.

The choir finished their piece with a resonant chord. Sastra Altasvet sat beside me as the cantor, a reedy sister with wiry red hair sneaking out from under her veil, began to lead the prayers.

"You look for answers in many places, eh, Sastra-kint?" Altasvet was the primary caretaker of the library. Her Galatine

grammar was nearly perfect, but her pronunciation was difficult
to understand; she had spent far more time with Galatine books
than Galatine people. It was probably fair to guess that she had
spent more time with books than with people of any sort.

"I do, Sastra," I answered honestly.

"There are most probably better answers here than in any
library," she said. "Our books, even our best books, are imper-
fect reflections of the Creator."

I smiled politely. I quickly found myself in over my head in
theological conversations with the sisters, our language barriers
aside. Galatine worship focused on the Sacred Natures, Pellians
on their ancestors, and I had not been a strict adherent of either
faith. The concept of a vague and distant Creator was strange
to me.

"There are very few places we have not looked in the
library," she said quietly. "I am afraid any hint of magic may
have been removed years—centuries—ago."

"It is not the sort of thing your leaders wish to hold on to," I
acknowledged.

"No, nor many of our people. It is a dangerous business,
Sastra-kint." She sighed.

"Indeed it is." Alba stood behind us. I started, but she maintained an expression like ironed linen. "I do not like to interrupt
your meditation on the Divine Creator, Sastra-kint Sophie, but
I must ask that you come with me. A carriage has arrived with
visitors."

4

—ɯ—

"WE WERE NOT ANTICIPATING GUESTS TODAY," ALBA SAID AS WE left the basilica and skirted the courtyard of the convent. She didn't intend it, but a faint tremor of fear slipped into her voice. We had plenty to hide. "That's the device of Nater-set Kierk painted on the carriage door. Of the Order of the Lead Scale—humorless fellows, all of them. *Tashdi*," she cursed. Nearby, a novice's eyes widened. "Get some berries from the larder," she instructed her in Kvys. "Tell Sastra Dyrka to make a berry pudding, it's Nater-set Kierk's favorite."

The novice meekly scurried off, no doubt effectively led to believe that any concern was over the reception of the high brother, given Alba's focus on the pudding.

"Berry pudding?" I said with half a smile.

"It's one of Dyrka's specialties—ah, and you learned the word for pudding. Very good," Alba teased. Then she straightened and sighed, smoothing the precise box pleats of her pale linen overdress. "Kierk is a pompous ass, and most of the order doesn't think much of him, but he is on the Church Assembly Council for Spiritual Discipline." Her mouth puckered as though she'd bitten down on an unripe berry. "That's code for investigations of blasphemy. Blasphemy of the theological, the liturgical, and the practical, of which casting is of course included."

"You said yourself that it would be impossible to keep my presence here a secret."

"Yes, but your presence here is not against any rule. Any person can seek sanctuary in our order, and that is protected under Kvys law. Just as any person can seek medical intervention with the Order of the Holy Well or orphans are always welcomed at the Order of the Blessed Dove."

"So he's checking in on me," I surmised.

"Possible. Possible he's just making his rounds. Or possible he's somehow found out that I've made contacts in Fen and wants to inquire more." She shrugged. "Or he knows it's berry season and remembers Dyrka's pudding. He's got a sweet tooth like a deprived child."

Alba insisted I accompany her to greet Nater-set Kierk. There was, we both agreed, no purpose in trying to evade him if he was indeed here to investigate my presence. The less we behaved as though we had something to hide, the less he might assume that we did.

Kierk already waited beside his heavy coach, his dark robes of fine gray wool picking up stray leaves from the cobblestones.

"Sastra-set Alba." The tall Kvys bowed slightly, from the waist, though he did not take his eyes off Alba. She did not bow; as high sister in her own house, she didn't have to. And she chose not to, not for the high brother of the Order of the Lead Scale, elevated by the priesthood's assembly far beyond merely managing a house of his order.

"Nater-set Kierk." She greeted him with open, outstretched palms, which she swiftly folded together lest he actually decide to embrace her. I made myself small against the shadows of the courtyard arbor. She continued in Kvys, and I made out *inside* and *refreshments* and *pudding*.

He shook his head with grave authority and a torrent of Kvys. Alba raised her eyebrows slightly, in controlled surprise, but didn't give anything else away. My palms, meanwhile, grew damp as I clutched my simple gray wool skirt, and my heart echoed hollow in my chest. What could he want? Was he, even now, scanning for my face among the Kvys sisters? I couldn't hide here; my sun-touched skin and dark hair stood out among these women with complexions of moonlight and birchwood and flax.

Alba beckoned him inside, leaving me in the courtyard with the rest of the order who had assembled to greet the high brother. My relief lasted only a few minutes before a novice in cream wool dashed into the courtyard to fetch me.

My throat clenched closed, but I forced myself to remain calm. If Alba felt I was truly threatened, I reasoned, she would have sent the girl to tell me to run.

I collected myself and joined the two in Alba's private study, a loft bathed in late setting sunlight over the communal reading room of the library. Four chairs sat in a circle. I sat next to Alba, leaving a space between Kierk and me.

"In the Galatine, yes?" Kierk's courtesy was rote and unsympathetic.

"Please," I replied, composure buttered thin over raw nerves.

Kierk spoke to me, though he barely met my eyes. "It is no secret, miss, that you are a purveyor of sacrilege." Alba's mouth tightened into a thin line. "Such practices are, I have no doubt you are aware, forbidden here."

He waited for me to reply. I didn't deign to answer. Alba nodded, ever so slightly—let him spool out his speech without any admissions, suggestions, or evidence from us.

He sighed. Gold rings on his middle and smallest fingers glinted; one held a ruby the size of my thumbnail. "Forbidden, and yet you are given safe refuge here. Why, Sastra-set?" He turned abruptly to Alba.

"The rules of our order are clear, and the law does not interfere with sacred rules."

"Ah. Yes. But I did not ask if she had invoked sanctuary here. I asked why." He glanced at me. "Perhaps *how* is the more apt in Galatine—*how* is it that she came to seek sanctuary here?"

"I made Sophie's acquaintance in West Serafe, at the summit," Alba answered deliberately. "When the civil war broke out in Galitha, she was stranded without a safe place to return, and so I—"

"Her, without a place?" He tutted softly. "The betrothed of the Rebel Prince, the sister of the Midwinter Quill?" I had a feeling these nicknames were common in Kvyset; spoken in Galatine, they made those closest to me sound like characters in an old legend.

"It was not so simple to return," I replied quietly. Kierk looked at me, surprised that I finally spoke. Surprised, or feigning interest well. "We feared capture if we returned."

"Yet your betrothed and your brother did return," he pressed.

"And were nearly captured," I retorted. "We decided—it was better that I wait somewhere safe."

"So you sought sanctuary here, where you no doubt were apprised that your...aberrant practice would not be welcome."

"Are you accusing Sophie of something?" Alba said.

"As a matter of course," he said, drawing something thin and square from his pocket, "yes." He unfolded a length of wool and deposited a gray clay tablet on his knee.

Tantia's tablet.

I maintained a neutral face, as best I could. Practice with the Galatine nobility and at the summit had trained me to hide my reactions. But how would we play this?

To my relieved surprise, Alba laughed. "Kierk, really. The woman's reputation precedes her—does she make clay tablets?" She had her strategy well in hand already.

"I do not know what manner her perversion takes."

"She's a seamstress, you old bear. A seamstress. Cloth and needle and thread."

"But this is a charm tablet. Or a curse tablet," he added, the word darkening his voice.

"Yes, it appears to be," I said. "May I see it?" I asked, hedging. The thin clay was inscribed with Kvys lettering, the words for *Joy* and *Felicity* marked in letters marred by shaking hands. I looked up at Alba, making my play. "I'm afraid I can't read it."

"Let me see that," Alba said. "Of course you can't—it's written in Kvys. Kierk, she can barely speak Kvys."

"So you say."

"Try her," Alba countered. "No—this must have been a cruel joke, someone sending you here on this pretense—"

"No joke," he said, taking the tablet back. "This came from your house, Alba. Someone here has been tampering with the dark arts." I held back a derisive snort—the tablet was a charm, imbued with light, and a badly done one at that. The precise opposite of dark anything, and it sure as the sun wasn't art.

"I'll make a full investigation. It is possible," she said with a resigned sigh, "that Sophie's presence here caused some . . . curiosity." She pursed her lips. I wanted to ask the question, too, but I knew she was weighing the risk even as she voiced it. "How did you come by it?"

"One of your servants loyal to the faith," he said.

"I would be remiss if I did not reward—"

"Do I look a fool?" Kierk snapped.

"I won't answer that," Alba said with a smile so sunny it cast a shadow. "Now you will stay for berry pudding, won't you?"

He blustered out of the study. I opened my mouth to speak, but Alba shook her head. Someone—many someones—might be listening. Loyal servants to the faith.

While Kierk made free with the pudding in the common dining room, Alba led me to the kitchen gardens. Fragrant herbs in lush rows and tangles of squash and pumpkin vines filled the space between the kitchen and the wall bordering the convent.

"What I would give to know who tattled to the Assembly Council," she said, following florid Kvys cursing. "It couldn't be one of the novices, one of the underlings. It must be someone who has access—pah."

"Does it matter who?"

"No, it matters why. Some blind devotee, that's not so dangerous. Not in the long-term, that is. Too late for us to get out of it so easily. Kierk has his eye on us now, we'll have to leave for Fen sooner rather than later. I'd hoped to cement these agreements first, and for you to make more progress with—yes." She pinched her mouth closed. "You're getting your way after all, leaving sooner than I had planned."

"Will he try to prevent our leaving? Does he know, do you think? That we're working with Fen?"

"I'm sure he knows, or could guess, that Sophie Balstrade is in fact still working to help her beloved Rebel Prince of Galitha." She sighed. "It's not subtle. But he can't prevent our leaving, even if he wanted to."

"Who would prefer a Royalist victory here? I thought Kvyset stood to gain from a new Galatine government."

"Kvyset does. But the individual houses—the individual houses are another story from the country as a whole. If Kierk suspects that my house would be more favored, that irks him. If he suspects that my house may be seeding power in high places to maneuver into a more influential position among the orders, that concerns him. And if Kierk thinks we may soon have a weapon he can't match? He's shitting himself."

"I thought you religious types would be more . . . pacific."

Alba snorted. "All to the glory of the Creator, but the Creator has been silenced by men like Kierk far too long."

And if your house rises, so do you, I thought.

Alba ran her hand through some waist-high rosemary. "Have to get this in soon, before the frost nips it." She snapped the tip of one stalk off and rolled it between her fingers. "And we shan't be here. We must leave before Kierk can make any move to detain us. We will leave tomorrow for Fen."

5

—〰—

I HELD MY HAND BY MY SIDE, FINGERS STRETCHED TOWARD THE Fenian looms clacking and whirring in industrious cacophony as they produced yards of gray wool. I clutched delicate threads of charm magic, spooling them into the fibers on the looms below. Already golden light shimmered in the drab fabric.

"Lady Sophie." My fingers constricted, nearly cutting off the charm, but I relaxed and kept the bright thread intact.

"Yes?" I smiled politely for Abus Hyrothe, the mill owner, a corpulent Fenian with a nose like a radish. He tolerated my presence here, and that of Sastra-set Alba, with the terse courtesy of a businessman who would have preferred to be left alone. That we were foreigners, and that I was rumored even here to be a witch, didn't help. Still, throughout the week since we arrived he had been patient with our persistence.

"Have you concluded your observation?" He pursed his lips, gazing out over his small empire of new looms and thinly clad workers. "We're nearly ready to shut down. This run is complete."

"Certainly," I said. I drew the gold threads thinner until they broke and embedded their ends in the weft of the woolen fibers. I had grown so comfortable with the casting that it looked as though I was merely watching the lift and fall of the looms through the thin haze of lint. If, of course, one didn't pay too much attention to the tension in my right hand.

Abus Hyrothe did not pay attention to much of anything aside from his sparkling new machines and their potential for earning.

"We'll bundle these up for shipment," he said. "Same place?"

"The same," I replied. To the port at Hazelwhite, still held by the tenacious grip of the Reformist army. There it would be cut and sewn into uniforms.

As I left the looms, I passed the stark mill offices. Alba debated the finer points of Fenian currency exchange with the cipher clerk in charge of our account. I had nothing to contribute to that discussion, and so I slipped outside, immediately drawing my pelisse around my shoulders to ward against a damp and determined wind. Galitha stayed warm well into autumn, sometimes slipping back into summer's cloying heat, and the trees took on a golden cast before losing their leaves. Here, the few trees that clung to life inland were thin and bent, their needles the same dark gray cast as the rocky cliffs. The northern ocean sapped the warmth from the rock, and the wind painted the coast with cold salt spray. Our crossing from Kvyset, in a tenacious ship whose captain pushed her into the waves like a tailor gliding a needle through coarse wool, had taken three miserably cold weeks, pushing all the while against that dogged wind.

"Miss." The voice, a hushed hiss. "Miss." I jumped and whirled around.

The mill worker was a short, skinny Fenian, a scab of beard crusting an angular face. "Yes?" I said, stepping toward him, uncertain. It was clear to me that trusting anyone in Fen was a risky endeavor. They all knew I was a charm caster, if they knew who I was at all.

"You are Galitha?"

I almost laughed—in a symbolic way, in this strange little del-egation to Fen, I did represent Galitha. But I knew a good-faith attempt at my language when I heard it. "I am Galatine, yes."

"No. Yes, I mean that, you are *the* Galatine woman? The Sophie?"

"Yes," I replied carefully. "I am Sophie Balstrade."

"Good! Yes. You will—for minute?" He beckoned with his fingers, folding them back over his hand, the terse Fenian motion for *come here.*

"What is your name?" I asked, out of politeness more than anything, but also ready to file it away in case of trouble later.

"Beryk Olber." He was nervous, glancing over his shoulder, and he made me nervous, too, even though I stood a head taller than him. "My friends waiting." My nerves ratcheted up, and then calmed. He wouldn't announce a mob ready to maul me, would he?

He led me past the benches and through the low doorway that opened into a workers' cloakroom. Several other mill work-ers waited, all in nondescript gray wool trousers and jackets. One reached into a pocket, then another, and pulled something out. I backed up, fearful of hidden weapons, but they each drew out something more dangerous than a knife or pistol.

Each had a red cap that he solemnly pulled on over tow-bright queue or shorn dark hair.

"You are Miss Balstrade?" A taller man with cheeks scoured red by the bitter Fenian wind held out an honest hand. "I am Hyrd Golingstrid, and am the leader of our group."

"Your group?" I asked, keeping my tone as polite as possible as I took his massive calloused hand in greeting.

"We are inspired by revolt in Galitha," Beryk said. "That a man will stand up to his overlord, there, means we can stand here, too." He pulled something else from his pocket—a thin, very worn pamphlet, and handed that volatile weapon to me.

It was a new title, one I had not yet seen, but it clearly bore my brother's name across the bottom in confident, block-printed ink.

"Oh," I said, very softly. *Tenacity and the Breaking of Chains*, the title traipsed across the page. I flipped it open, quickly, and read a few lines, falling swiftly into the familiar cadence of my brother's writing. A date on the inner cover confirmed that it had been printed only shortly before I had left Kvyset for Fen. Kristos was still writing—it was reassuring in its bittersweet familiarity.

Of course, I hadn't expected his work to reach Fenian factory workers. I forced myself to hand the pamphlet, clearly prized by these men even if few of them could read it, back to Beryk. "I had no idea, that is—I know very little about Fenian politics. I . . . forgive me, but I thought that your government was elected."

"Fenian politics, Miss Balstrade, is money." Hyrd shook his head. "We elect governance, yes, but it is only those willing to— how to say?—to stand on the back of his fellow Fenian who have the money to be elected. And meanwhile, our work is danger, our pay is poor, and our families go hungry when the mills shut down."

I swallowed, not sure what to say. Our fight in Galitha felt quite different, for a change in governance, for representation. Still, it stemmed from the same place—from a disrespect for the common people.

"We mean not to give alarm," Beryk continued, misreading my reticence.

"I'm not afraid—certainly not of you," I said with a reassuring smile. "But I'm not sure I understand—that is, why did you bring me here?"

"We know that our work for your cause is of great import, though it lines the pockets of the *rylkfen*—that is, the factory and mill owners, there is not a good translation." Hyrd leaned toward me. "We will finish our assignments to the best of our ability, but do not be surprised to hear of trouble."

I stepped back, almost involuntarily. "What sort of trouble?"

"The *rylkfen* care for profit. We will deny them their profit," Hyrd said. "We know the balance of task and time that produces their gold; we will upset that balance."

"Couldn't you simply...quit?" I asked.

"Yes, but then they would replace us. No, we will cut them where they bleed and they will not know—who is the beetle in the salt cod?" I suppressed a laugh at an expression that didn't work well in Galatine. "They know we are discontent. How discontent, they will learn."

"But our order will be unaffected."

"That is my hope." Hyrd smiled. "As soon as your run is finished, the looms may break."

"I see." I considered this. They weren't asking my participation or even blessing in their endeavor. In pragmatic Fenian custom, they were alerting me to a problem, or at least the potential I would perceive one.

"You should return to your companion."

"You told me and not her," I said.

"You are Galatine, you are part of the Reform." Hyrd shrugged. "She may be, or she may be angling for profit herself."

"One never can tell." The quip fell flat. "I trust her," I clarified.

"That is well. But do not reveal anything to her that might compromise us, out of courtesy. Our names, that sort of thing."

"Of course," I murmured.

"And one other thing." Hyrd cleared his throat. "There may come a time your new government can come to the aid of the Fenian worker. I hope you will remember our courtesy then."

I nodded, agreeing to a tenuous alliance as the unofficial delegate of an as-yet-unfounded government.

6

I RETURNED OUTSIDE, SOBERED EVEN MORE THAN USUAL BY THE conversation with Hyrd, Beryk, and their silent but earnest comrades. Alba waited in the square yard bordering the front of the mill. The dark stone and scoured wood of the buildings made for a stark backdrop, but her strictly starched veil and dour gray gown provided little contrast. "He says that run is finished," she said.

The wind bit my cheeks and made my eyes water. "The sooner we can leave Fen," I added, "the better."

"For your constitution or for the continuation of this war?" Alba led us out of the mill yard and onto the road.

"Both," I replied.

"We will leave Rylke for the Pygmik shipyards once the cloth is all milled, and then onward to Galitha in good time. I've written to several contacts in the Allied States to see if they wish to invest, but I doubt they will reply before we have to finalize our finances with the shipyards."

"I thought the Equatorials were stalwartly neutral in all this?"

"Perhaps they still are. I did not want to assume, given that the entrance of the West Serafans as at least tacit political allies of the Royalists may have changed their minds." She raised an eyebrow—we both anticipated Serafan magical support even if they did not commit troops. "The latest news," she continued, pulling a creased Fenian newspaper from her cloak. It was printed with cheap, smudging ink and was devoid of the flourishes and illustrations that spattered Galatine newspapers. "The Fenians care for foreign affairs enough to note that the harbor of Galitha City remains blockaded by the Royalist navy, interfering with regular trade."

"I suppose that gives them all the more motivation to work with us," I said. "Have we enough…motivation to keep them happy?"

"Quite sure." She smiled. "The Order of the Golden Sphere is well-known for, well, gold." She paused. "Which was never actually the intention of the nomenclature."

"I think I understand the naming convention a bit more now," I replied drily.

"You do, indeed." Alba slowed her walk as we approached a curve in the narrow road that took us close to a sheer drop-off, gray stone plummeting to cold sea below. I thought at first she was slowing for caution's sake, but no—she threw back her shoulders and inhaled the bracing salt wind. "All is going so well, but I would feel better, I admit, if we had some more recent word from Hazelwhite. I can't imagine it's easy for you to be away from your brother and Theodor."

I opened my mouth, then clamped it shut again. Of course separation from Theodor was difficult. There was, however, a strange relief being apart from Kristos. I had never expected to see him again, not after his betrayal during the Midwinter Revolt. In the mess of emotions that seeing him again brought on, I had not found forgiveness among the relief, anger, joy, and continued grief at losing our once-close relationship.

"I don't know how to feel about my brother," I finally said. I could still see his name on the pamphlet Beryk had shown me, could almost hear his voice reading it. I could also see his face framed by firelight in Pyord's study, fully committed to betraying me.

"Who would?" Alba said bluntly. "If my understanding of your relationship is correct."

"I'm sure it is," I said with wry assessment of Alba's observations of my spats with Kristos. She gazed out over the gray cliffs, not at me. I was grateful she couldn't see my reddening face. "He did try to kill me."

"To be fair, he never did try to kill *you*, precisely."

"Allow me some hyperbole," I retorted. "His actions could very well have gotten me killed—and worse, he made me compromise my ethics."

"Ah, well. Pyord had a good hand in that, too, didn't he?"

At the mention of her cousin, I felt the blood rush from my face. "Yes, he did."

"I do not quite know how to feel about my cousin, if we are being honest," Alba said. "To play at politics, one need not deal in blackmail and extortion."

"Well, good to know those are optional."

"He died without any chance of my forgiving him," Alba continued, ignoring me. "And, of course, without any remorse from him. And I suppose that is a significant difference between Kristos as I read him and Pyord—I do not believe I ever saw my cousin admit he was wrong."

I swallowed. "Kristos does," I said. "But still. What he feels and what I am willing to do aren't the same thing."

"Of course not. But you do have to put up with him for the time being. As an ally if nothing else."

"Sianh said something similar," I acknowledged, not adding that he had said it about Alba. "That we needn't be friends to be allies."

"Quite so." Alba clasped her hands and gazed out over the choppy sea fighting with the cliff face below us. "It's lovely, isn't it?"

"If you like watching birds," I replied, watching a teal-breasted cormorant dive for the waves.

"And do you like watching birds?" Alba's mouth twisted into a quizzical grin.

"I can't say that I do." I dodged a loose cobblestone. "Are there any albatrosses here?"

"Albatrosses? No, not this far north, not this time of year. Why?"

"Something Theodor said once," I replied. "I was just curious." Alba shook her head. "You two are a strange pair."

Like a pair of albatrosses, I smiled silently. If there was any decision I was confident about, anything I felt deep in my bones that I had been right about, it was my engagement to Theodor. Separation from him proved that, absence revealing the ways in which I had molded a vision of life around the shape of him and me together. Apart from one another, the shape felt wrong, hollow in vital and unexpected places.

We rounded the curve in the cliffside road that led into town. Alba made a face as we approached the neat, ordered, and entirely predictable Rylke. "Fenian towns—they're all alike. Except maybe Treshka, there's at least a concert hall in Treshka. And chocolate cafés."

"We're not going to Treshka, though, are we?"

"Of course not, that would be too fortunate for the likes of weary pilgrims like us." Rylke opened before us, with its ordered streets, beige brick buildings, and in the town center, a statue of some dull Fenian historical figure. I wondered if there was a different man captured in bronze in every Fenian town, or if they all had the same dour-faced effigy. "But I say that we spend a bit of time at the foundry. See how the order is progressing."

Even though I preferred the cold comfort of our sparse rooming house to the fiery heat of the foundry, I followed Alba, walking to the other side of Rylke from the woolen mill. Alba peppered the foremen with questions about every step of the process and nagged the foundry owner's son—assigned, to his chagrin, to accompany us—about the quality of ore used in various applications. We weren't to go near the blazing ovens and yawning maws of red-hot iron, though I didn't need any encouragement to follow that rule.

The heat in the foundry made me feel like a loaf of bread baking, but Alba showed no signs of waning in her enthusiasm. I slipped away, tiptoeing down the narrow stairs and stepping out into the biting Fenian autumn air.

The cliffs were lower on this side of Rylke, and tapered toward a small harbor where waves lapped a craggy black sand beach. I considered walking down to the strand, but I knew that might be foolish. I didn't know the tides—perhaps the water would rush up and leave me trapped, clinging to a sea stack.

I sat instead on the long benches that the foundry workers used for their tea and lunch breaks when the weather was clear. Now that I had spoken with the mill workers, I felt the eyes of the Fenian foundry workers on me. Instead of keeping my face turned toward my scuffed boots, I began to look at them, noticing their curiosity and silent determination. As a group of foundrymen passed me, dinner pails in hand, they clasped their left fists in their right hands, a gesture I was sure held deeper meaning than I knew but that I understood as solidarity.

I felt, suddenly, much less alone.

7

I SAID NOTHING TO ALBA OF MY CONVERSATION WITH THE MILL workers or the contact with the foundrymen, and we spent another week ricocheting between the foundry and the mill. Another order of wool, this time a rich madder red for the coat facings and cuffs. It was more expensive than the plain gray, but I had suggested and Alba agreed that the impact sharply made uniforms could effect, on both our own troops and on the enemy, outweighed the cost.

We watched the last of the red wool leave the looms with quiet satisfaction. The wool was finished, the cannon barrels well underway, and Pygmik and its shipyards our next stop on the long tour back to Galitha and her war. Alba chattered about the prospective shipyard bids we would entertain until we reached our rooming house near the center of Rylke's town square. Our accommodations were as luxurious as anything in Fen, which was to say that they were spare, stark, and coldly but beautifully made. The woods and woolens of the paneling and carpets were of the finest quality, but there were none of the bright colors that Galatines or Serafans favored in their decorations. My room had exactly one frivolous item, a starburst inlaid with mother-of-pearl that hung over the doorway. Alba said it was a half-defunct religious custom.

I flopped gracelessly on the bed, kicking at my boots. Under Alba's direction I had been given clothing favored by Fenians, dour gray and blue petticoats, jackets cut narrow and laced over plain stomachers, and a pair of heavy boots. I hated them. Compared to the pert latchet shoes and lightweight silk slippers Galatines wore, the calf-high boots with their tight laces felt like weights. I tore at a knot that had managed to work its way into the lace, finally getting the wretched things off my feet.

There were a pair of red silk slippers in my trunk, an incongruous find in the storehouses of Alba's order, and when I discovered that they miraculously fit my large feet, I claimed them. Slipping into the lightweight silk and leather soles induced a sigh.

Alba rapped on my door and swept in before I could answer. "Good, you're still dressed." She glanced at my feet. "Mostly."

"Supper already?"

"I'll bet you'll never guess what's on the menu." The scent of fish wafted thick from the inn's kitchen. I'd never had so many iterations of fish in my life—fish stews and baked fish and thick slabs of fish seared brown on the outside and still raw in the center.

Tonight was golden haddock, which flocked to the waters off Fen in the late summer and autumn, braised in butter and spices. "Do Fenians eat any other kinds of meat, aside from fish?" I asked the innkeeper's daughter, who worked in the kitchens.

Alba translated, chortling quietly as the girl answered my question. "By midwinter the ruby sailfin are running, and those are just delicious. And cod and silver herring and all sorts of mackerel—oh, and shark in midsummer. They gather to eat the seal pups," she said, via translation through Alba.

I turned back to Alba. "Did you not translate my question correctly?"

Alba suppressed a laugh. "My translation was perfect. You have your answer."

I wasn't ready to sleep after dinner, and the sun still hovered far from sunset. Nights were shorter here in summer than Galitha's were, though I understood that winter days were truncated and the nights long. The inn's windows were hung with thick curtains to block the light for the benefit of weary summertime travelers. Fenians, however, seemed to revel in the full length of the autumn days, at least as much as Fenians reveled in anything. From my window overlooking the sparse garden outside the inn's back door, I saw late evening picnics and fishing parties, and the occasional wagon loaded with young foundry workers and laundresses, rattling over the uneven roads.

They seemed happy, I thought wistfully, as I watched a gaggle of young men and women with baskets over their arms, traipsing toward the center of town. It was no Fountain Square, I thought. No public gardens. I sighed. The gardens would be beautiful as late summer turned to fall, roses in their final blooming and a blaze of zinnias and weeping hearts and purple fireflower. Even in the midst of war, I thought, nothing would stop the gardens from blooming.

Unless, of course, they'd been burned to the ground or razed or shelled out by artillery fire. I blinked back sudden tears at that thought, at the catastrophe that destruction of the gardens meant—that the city had been overrun.

I pushed the panic back, as I did every day. Galitha was an ocean away, and since I couldn't know any better, the Reformists and the Royalists simultaneously had the upper hand. Kristos and Theodor were alive and dead, the possibilities balanced in tandem. *No,* I thought firmly. *They are alive. The Reformists hold the city, they hold fast in the south.*

Hold fast, I repeated to myself.

Though the sun still filtered through the garden and into my window, I was exhausted. I drew the thick curtains closed in our room, stripped off my boots and wool clothes, and burrowed my head under my pillow to drown out the light and the thoughts barraging me even as I fell asleep.

It was black and silent when I woke again.

"Get up!" A firm hand jostled my shoulder into the thick featherbed. I reached out and gripped the wrist, twisting it in a newfound instinct of self-defense. "Let go, mercy of the Creator—Sophie, it's me, but get up!"

I released Alba's wrist and swung the covers away. Cold air buffeted me instantly, and my teeth began to chatter. "What is it?"

"I don't know. But someone is throwing rocks at our windows, so I presume there is either something of import about to happen, or something already has."

"Do we open the window?"

"Is there a better alternative?" Alba snorted, and drew her thick woolen bedgown tighter around her shift.

I was already wearing a quilted bedgown and petticoat to sleep in—I couldn't shake the damp cold of Fen even between featherbeds and wool blankets. I padded to the window and cracked the shutters, just a sliver.

A figure stood in the middle of the garden below, another rock primed to toss in his hand. I squinted into the pale moonlight, threw wide the shutters, and opened the window.

"Hyrd?" I whispered.

"Bad news, must hurry."

"I'm coming," I said.

"Wait," Alba hissed. "Who is he? What if he means you ill?"

"Now you're cautious," I countered, throwing my cloak around my shoulders. "He's one of the mill workers. He...made my acquaintance, he and several of his comrades."

"Comrades. Like-minded folks, then?"

"Indeed."

"Then I'm coming, too." We made as little noise as we could tiptoeing down the hall and outside. The night air was bracing, and I started shivering almost immediately despite the heavy wool cloak.

"Hyrd, this is Alba," I whispered quickly. "Alba, Hyrd."

"I am aware of the Kvys holy lady." He nodded once in greeting. I would have laughed at his title for Alba if his eyes hadn't been so serious. "You are in grave danger, Lady Sophie."

"What's the meaning of that?" Alba asked crisply. Her manner was efficient, businesslike, but I could sense the tremor of fear behind her clipped words.

"Some of the *rylkfen* talk. They say you spread unrest."

"I'm sure I do, but I promise it's entirely unintentional," I said with a forced smile.

"This is true enough. They know that they will find no proof of their fears. But they want their factories running smoothly again. They do not believe we are—how do you say?" His brow creased. "Capable, yes. Capable of resisting on our own. They think you are causing it, even though they have no proof. But they know, as well—you cast charms."

Deeper cold than even the damp Fenian night seeped through me.

"What does that matter?" Alba asked, even more clipped than before.

"They will bring charges. Tomorrow."

"False charges," Alba said. I bit my lips together, clamping my trembling jaw shut.

"It may not matter. If enough of the *rylkfen* are against her."

My teeth chattered when I tried to speak. "How do you know this?"

"A servant in Master Hendrik's household. They met there, tonight, the *rylkfen* of Rylke. They talk very loudly while she served the wine."

"Men like that never consider that the people they keep under their thumb don't like being squashed," Alba muttered. "Very well. I believe you. Go, get away now, before you raise anyone's suspicions being here. Wouldn't do to get caught conversing with some local revolutionary, would it?" She shot me a knowing look and dragged me back inside before Hyrd had turned the corner.

"Well then. Get dressed. Something to travel in. Boots. Not those damn slippers."

"Alba—"

"Trust me." She whispered through clenched teeth, and I could barely make out her face in the dim lamplight. "I have an idea."

8

I DRESSED QUICKLY, FOR ONCE THE COLD OF THE MEAGERLY HEATED inn supplanted by a deeper, more invasive chill. My throat tightened and my teeth clamped around my tongue, finally ceasing their chattering. To be accused of casting here in Fen—accused of sorcery and witchcraft and abomination—would mean immediate imprisonment and a very serious trial. Though I couldn't imagine how any accusers intended to prove my magic without using and admitting to use of magic themselves, a guilty verdict meant execution—drowning in the waters off Fen's dark cliffs.

The thought of the white crests closing over my head and the cold deep swallowing me whole prompted me to move quickly, and I plucked fresh stockings and a wool petticoat from my trunk, dressing in the dark without a thought to whether the ensemble matched. As I laced my jacket closed, the bodkin caught on an unraveling eyelet and tangled with the silk floss; I simply forced the dull-pointed needle through the fabric like a pin through a cushion to finish later.

"Where?" My whisper was too loud in the silence, stark and bright in the dark.

"I have an acquaintance who can help us." Alba shouldered

a small pack and handed me a coarse linen market wallet. "Bring spare socks."

With haphazard haste, I threw spare shifts and stockings into the market wallet, swept my correspondence and notebooks into the bottom of one side of the sack, and, knowing Alba wouldn't waste time arguing, tossed the slippers on top. A thin, nasal exhale was her only comment on the choice.

Nothing else in my trunks was of any particular value to me—some lucky chambermaid would, I hoped, claim the drab clothes for her own wardrobe. I glanced once more around the room, ensuring that I hadn't left anything incriminating. No letters, no notes on charm casting, no logbooks detailing charmed yardage of wool. Then I drew my thick wool short cloak around already shaking shoulders and followed Alba into the night.

Alba didn't speak as we cut through the inn's sparse kitchen garden and slipped down a narrow alley that reeked of yesterday's fish. The ruts in the bricks were indiscernible from shadows in the cold moonlight, and more than once I tripped, earning terse exhales and a firm hand from Alba, who somehow managed to sail over the uneven terrain without so much as a stumble.

The alley widened into a road and sloped downhill, toward Rylke Cove. Ships bobbed in the moonlight, cold water lapping their sides. One of these, then, to retreat.

"Alba, where . . . ?"

"Tsk!" She clicked and shook her head. Silence, then. Silence, and trusting that she knew what she was doing.

I saw why—a Fenian Night Guard patrolled the street ahead. In a thick gray greatcoat and miter cap, carrying a halberd, he kept watch over the intersection of two major streets near the center of Rylke's wharfside district. Strict decency laws kept the Fenians from carousing in taverns all night, or gambling, or even being out without official business past midnight. The Night

Guard ensured compliance and watched over the rich storehouse of merchants' goods near the wharf, as well.

He turned on his heel, crisp and deliberate even though surely he believed no one was watching. Alba's exhale was white mist in the moonlight. The cloud of her breath said what she couldn't: We were trapped here as long as the Night Guard patrolled this intersection.

She turned to me, eyebrow rising into a question. I bit my lip and tried to calm my thoughts into coherence, knowing what she asked. What could I do? My casting wasn't like the magic in a folktale, with sorcerer's invisibility spells or fairy sleeping dust. I spun some good luck from the ether, the bright gold winding around my fingers like yard. Alba squinted; I knew her vision for the charmed light was poor, and I drew more, stronger magic into the charm. She saw it and nodded.

I unspooled the charm, looping it around us as though tying us together with good fortune, forcing it to nestle into our cloaks.

"Now," Alba said. She strode down the street as though she belonged there, absurdly, in the middle of the night in a silent Fenian city. I matched her stride if not her self-assured gait.

The guardsman saw us approach—we were impossible to miss—but didn't shout or threaten. I breathed some relief; Alba's bluff and the charm were working so far. I kept a tight handle on the charm in my right hand, clenching my fist into my skirt.

"*Drats-kinda,*" he said as we moved closer. Something like *halt* or *who goes there*, I guessed, but the delivery, though official, was not threatening. Still, the moonlight glinted off the blade of his halberd.

Alba prattled off a few lines in Fenian, which sounded to me like indecipherable Kvys. He nodded, then squinted at me. Alba chattered again, drawing his attention.

Still, he glanced back at me, eyes curious, searching. A Pellian woman in Fen—a curiosity, certainly. Perhaps more.

He quizzed Alba, questions tilting the cadence of his voice, his eyes still on me. Alba smiled broadly, and I intensified the charm. Luck for us, safety, swirling in a ring around us.

It wasn't enough. I knew it wouldn't be, as the guardsman kept scrutinizing us. Darkness built at the edges of the charm, the sparkling black deeper than the night. Curse magic. I hadn't asked it here, but I wasn't entirely surprised to see it, like an unwelcome but familiar acquaintance at the door. I pushed it back, keeping it carefully away from the pale glow of the charm, then pulled at it as though pulling yarn into a ball from a skein, looping and turning, but it fought me.

The charm had perhaps kept him from arresting us at once, but I sensed it was reaching its limits even as Alba remained calm and resolutely patient with the guard's questions. I hesitated, then tied off the charm, letting it continue to pulse around us unbound. Out of my control and poorly anchored to the wool of our cloaks, it would quickly dissipate, but I turned my attention to moving the curse away from us, keeping those loose tendrils of darkness from encroaching on Alba and me.

I pushed the ball of curse magic away from Alba but, in my struggle to control it, cast it toward the guardsman instead. It collided with him like a blob of jelly enveloping a bit of toast, seeping into his greatcoat with tenuous hold on the fibers.

His eyes clouded, and his sharp questions ceased. Alba's eyes snapped to me, widening. The guardsman began to speak, but his voice looped on itself, as though his mouth were full of overcooked porridge, and he tripped as he stepped toward us.

"Go," I said to Alba. "Now."

Her face blanched but impassive, she grabbed my arm and we ran toward the harbor. She navigated between warehouses and crates in teetering piles to a small office, more a shed of weather-beaten clapboard than a proper building. A shingle with a Fenian name and an anchor was nailed beside the door.

"Foolish girl!" she hissed. "Now they've all but proof you're a caster—and casting curses beyond that!"

"We were going to be arrested," I answered. "And I didn't mean to use a curse."

"Didn't mean to?" She banged on the flimsy door. "For all the—How long will he stay muddled?"

I swallowed dry air. "I've never exactly experimented on humans before."

"Then best to presume he's already recovered his facilities." She smacked the door with her open hand, growing, for the first time, visibly desperate. "Erdwin! Erdwin, get up!"

A frowsy-eyed, diminutive man answered the door moments later. He squinted at us, recognized in me a non-Fenian, and cursed in Galatine, "What in the depths of hell—oh, Alba!" He beamed. "Evenin', dear. Fancy a drink?"

"Enough of that, Erdwin, move," she ordered, shouldering him aside and yanking me through the door after her. "I'm going to need that favor now."

9

———∿∿———

ERDWIN TYSE WAS A FENIAN MERCHANT. HE REFERRED TO HIMSELF as a "private vessel operator." Alba called him a mercenary. Either way, he had a ship headed for Galitha with space for us.

"A contract load of iron ore and shoes and various sundries for the glorious cause of Galitha," he said as he showed Alba the ship's license.

"Which glorious cause?"

"Does it matter?"

"It does to us," Alba replied. "We're not exactly welcome in some ports."

"The glorious Reformist cause," he replied. "The common men and their Rebel Prince." I winced—I didn't like the term, which made Theodor sound more like a usurper than an adherent to the law. Alba shook her head at me. Erdwin hadn't guessed who I was, and she preferred to keep it that way.

"Very good," Alba said.

"She leaves tomorrow morning." He raised his little finger as he sipped his tea laced with Fenian whiskey. "I take it you're not precisely on the up-and-up with the local authorities?"

"Am I ever?" Alba winked. She tasted her tea, then added

another splash of fire-like whiskey. "It's nothing to concern yourself over."

He laughed, then burst into a spate of coughing. "Do I want to know? Better you not tell me. Then when the Decency Police drag me up by the thumbs, I can solemnly swear I knew nothing about your underground brothel or gambling ring or the fifteen pounds of Equatorial dimweed you smuggled in—Creator above, don't tell me you smuggled in dimweed."

"I did not smuggle in dimweed." She sipped her tea. "This is better than your usual swill."

"I've been making good profits lately," he replied, ever so slightly defensive.

"War increases your business, I suppose?" Alba set her cup down. "At any rate, best we board tonight. The Night Guard hasn't come sniffing around down here yet, but at some point they may decide to make a search—"

"You miffed the Night Guard, too? Creator's arthritic kneecaps, Alba."

"It was unavoidable."

"This one doesn't talk much," he said, switching subjects so abruptly that I sloshed a bit of tea onto my saucer. The porcelain was finer than I would have expected, with gaudy gold vines painted on it.

"She doesn't have to talk to you," Alba said. "Seems to me we learned that lesson last time I came here, didn't we?" She drummed a finger on the scratched table. "Sastra Orvline still insists we should have levied charges."

"I only talked," he grumbled.

"And the courts would have believed that." She shook her head. "It seems to me you tried to sell her shares in a ship that didn't exist."

"Speculation, Alba! Shares on speculation of a purchase!"

"I don't think she saw it the same way. I didn't report you for shoddy business practice, and you're going to do me this one small favor."

"Favor that could land me a ticket to the cliff colonies."

Alba shrugged. "In your line of work, transportation is always a risk. Now. To the ship?"

Erdwin threw back the last of his tea, and we followed him into the wharf's narrow alleys. His ship, moored in the middle of a long dock of small vessels, was a thick-masted schooner with a gull carved into the prow. "The *Buoyant Gull*," he introduced her, smacking her thick sides with an open palm.

"I presume she has your usual...modifications?" Alba said.

"Of course. And payment?"

"You can expect payment when we arrive in Galitha with our hides intact," Alba retorted. "Payment. You should be so lucky."

He tossed our wallets over the side and helped us up the rough rope ladder onto the deck. "They'll be boarding before dawn and leaving Rylke Cove as soon as the port authority opens up to stamp their paperwork." He nudged aside a barrel with his boot, and prized up a thin sliver of wood. Underneath was a cord; he tugged it, and a trapdoor opened. "Until then, hide out down there." He stopped. "Don't light any candles, fair?"

"Fine," Alba said. "You're going to let your crew know you have passengers, right?"

Erdwin paused. "Of course. Of course I am."

"And that they won't be paid unless we remain unharmed?"

"The usual precautions, all of that, yes." He scanned the wharf, nervous. "Now let me get back to my usual habit of late rising lest I rouse suspicion of the Night Guard, eh?"

Alba acquiesced and we descended into the hidden hold.

I waited until the echo of his boots' tread on the dock faded, then turned to Alba in the thin glow that a sliver of moonlight granted us. "Where on earth did you find him?"

"He found us. Thought that the good sisters would be an easy mark for one of his shills."

"And you trust him?"

"He's a businessman. In a sense," she amended. "This is business. Besides, I know he won't go to the port authority or the Night Guard or anyone else to report us."

"How can you be so sure?"

"He said not to light any candles," she replied. "This hold is stuffed with black powder, like as not, off the books. He's probably trying to skip paying the export taxes on it."

I shrank away from the crates pressing into my back. "Comforting."

"Not quite as upsetting as whatever it was you did back there with the guardsman. Care to explain?"

I recalled with some trepidation how I had encircled the man, how he had reacted with the confusion I had cast on him. "There isn't much to explain."

"What made you think to try it?"

"I didn't think to. I drew the curse accidentally along with a charm for us—it happens sometimes, ever since—" I sighed. Ever since the Midwinter Revolt, ever since I learned to cast curses, ever since I thought my brother was gone forever. Ever since my life had grown tangled and complex. "It happens sometimes. Sometimes when I'm startled or tired, more often than when I'm focusing."

"And the charm for us? You drew that rather quickly." I couldn't see Alba's face well in the soft blackness, but her voice had the cadence of a patient, long-suffering teacher. "I've never seen anything written about directly cursing or charming another person."

"It's what the Serafans do."

"With music," Alba countered. "And you didn't use music. Or a needle and thread. I didn't see you writing anything on a clay tablet, either."

"You know that I don't need those things," I snapped. "I still have to use some kind of medium to embed the charm. It's in your cloak. Not incorporated very well—it's already almost gone." The faded golden haze clung like thin lint to our shoulders, quietly slipping back into the ether.

"In that case," she said slowly. "There are opportunities here—I ought to have thought of this before. You could develop casting to its logical conclusion." She paused, waiting for me to pick up the explanation. When I didn't, she sighed and continued, "If you don't need to use anything to create the charm or the curse, why would you need a medium to transfer it?"

"Because it fades as quickly as it's cast if it's not anchored to something." I thought of something else. "The light or dark, it wants to go back where it came from, whatever that means. Like the Serafan musical casting. It only lasts as long as they're actively pouring magic into the music."

"But you can pull it directly and embed it that quickly. The curse magic. That is something. Something, perhaps, to counter the Serafans if it comes to it."

She sounded delighted. I felt slightly nauseated.

"Have you ever tried it before?"

I chewed my lip. I had embedded curse magic in the water of a vase and accelerated the death and decay of the flowers in it, but only once.

"Not on people," I answered. Maybe it was wrong to withhold some of what I knew from Alba, since she was an ally—but she was an ally with her own motivations, too.

"Until tonight."

"And as you said, I don't think it was a wise idea." I had no idea if the man was still muddling in a cloud of manufactured confusion. I didn't think so—my casting had been sloppy, meant to control rather than embed the curse, so I guessed it would melt away fairly quickly. But what did the aftereffects of a curse feel like? When I began casting curses, I felt ill every time. Guilt gnawed at me for the guardsman who might be experiencing something akin to a nasty hangover.

"Perhaps so, perhaps not. It unsnarled that particular snag for us." I heard her settling against the crates. "Best to try to sleep a little," she said. "We'll be underway before long."

10

~~~

IT TOOK ALMOST A FULL DAY BEFORE THE CREW OPENED THE HOLD to check the cargo and found us. Erdwin, apparently no stranger to smuggling human as well as explosive cargo, had outfitted the hold with some jugs of stale water, a large package of indestructible sea biscuit, and a bucket. By the time the full sun bore through the ceiling above us in narrow slivers, I was grateful for all three.

When the ship's mate cracked the hold, Alba was ready with a calm smile and her hands folded as though in complacent prayer, like a Kvys meditation statue.

The mate cursed loudly, and Alba quietly addressed him, explaining her arrangement with Erdwin. At the mention of money, the mate grudgingly allowed us on deck.

"Does he know about the black powder?" I asked.

"Most certainly, though the rest of the crew, perhaps not." Alba watched with laughing eyes as he slipped into the secret hold. She glided away on silent feet to the rail and settled her gaze on the far-distant smudge of gray that was the rim of Fen's outer islands.

I, however, was tired of ships. Tired of the slow passages and the miles of open ocean, of the bracing wind and scent of salt. Each voyage meant time out of commission, time I wasn't helping the efforts of the Reformists, time I had no chance of hearing from Theodor. Miles and days stretched on ahead of us in the inky-blue northern waters.

I could practice casting, but I was tired of rote maintenance of my skill. What I had done on the streets of Rylke suggested that I had the potential to develop new skills, but I wasn't quite ready to touch those possibilities yet. At any rate, my charms' contribution had ceased when we'd left Fen. I might cast superficial charms on equipment already at the Hazelwhite encampment, but the bulk of our charmed investment was en route now, from Fen.

Instead, I rested. I hauled a small barrel to a tucked-away corner of the deck, even though the salt spray was biting cold, and watched the waves beat ahead of us and the sea birds fight the wind above us. I sewed, mending tears in my petticoats, knowing that these two worsted wool skirts and the jacket I wore would have to serve for a long time. I took a length of linen from the hold—it was, I reasoned, for the Reformist army and I was part of that army—and sewed a spare shift for myself. I sewed long seams, turned raw edges over and felled them carefully against fraying, hemmed in narrow, tight lines. No charms, even if that might have been wise. Just the rote motions of sewing soothing me until my hands grew too cold and my fingers too stiff to continue.

The sailors noticed me, quietly sitting for long hours every day, often with a needle in hand. One wearing a dark blue jacket carefully patched with red-striped linen finally approached me with a length of torn sailcloth and a thick needle. I assessed the damage and accepted the unspoken and likely unpaid commission. He sat next to me and took up a rip on the other end.

Exactly like a morning in the atelier, except on the deck of a ship with a ragtag sailor and a length of heavy linen sailcloth in hand instead of silk. Still, it felt strangely right.

The meditation of needle and thread ended abruptly as the mate shouted something in Fenian and the sailor dropped his end of the cloth like it had burned him and rushed toward the rigging behind us. I gathered the cloth and carefully worked his needle into the weave, ready for him to pick up again when whatever urgent task he had been set to had been completed. Then I noticed how every sailor around me had jumped to attention, not only my sewing companion, and stowed my needle, as well.

Alba intercepted the captain, who forcefully shoved her aside before remembering himself with a senior member of the Order of the Golden Sphere and tersely barking a few words of explanation. She set her mouth in a thin line.

"We've a bit of trouble with what may be a Galatine ship, I fear," she said.

"Galatine?"

"Royal Navy."

"Royal*ist* navy, you might say." I peered across the waves toward the ship, and could just barely discern the blue and gold of the Royalist battle flag.

"In any case. They're intercepting vessels bound for Galitha."

"Fenian vessels?" I asked, shocked. "Couldn't that lead to an international war?"

"War is international," she snorted. "But yes. Anyone carrying cargo for Galitha, boarded and searched and questioned, and if the vessel is bound for the Reformist army, the cargo is captured as a prize."

"Why am I only hearing about this now?" I exhaled through my nose.

"I ought to have guessed. But I hadn't gotten any reports

from Galitha, and neither had you. The captain seems aware of the problem, though, and didn't deign to tell us. Neither did Erdwin, that rat. And we can have a nice long talk over tea later if you'd like, but for now I'd like to avoid capture."

"Back in the hold?"

"I'm debating. You see, if we're in the hold, we're certainly hiding. What sort of people hide? Fugitives, spies, highly valuable enemy passengers."

"Yes, I see," I said. "So we stay on deck? Hope for the best?"

"If we're boarded, they may only take the valuables. They may not bother with the ship itself—they probably won't bother hauling this broken-down old barnacle back to port." She softened. "If we were recognized and caught, it's you who stands the most to lose. They might send me home—they probably would. You..."

"Captured most certainly, probably executed." The salt air I inhaled was cold and painfully bracing.

"And so much for what you can do for Galitha." She hesitated. "Not that I don't value you, very much so, but I know you undervalue yourself. You are most certainly not expendable. Still. It is your life. So I won't pretend to make the choice for us."

Alba had made most of our choices thus far, guiding me past my inexperience and ignorance. I took one slow, steadying breath—the last time I could be slow, deliberate, until this ordeal was over, I acknowledged. "If we're on deck," I said, grudging the words I knew were necessary even as I said them, "I could cast."

11

DESPITE THE FENIAN VESSEL'S ATTEMPTS TO MANEUVER AWAY FROM the privateer, we were not nearly as swift and maneuverable as the Galatine ship. Alba was right—the Fenian ship was old, and though her broad belly was a pragmatic hold for goods, it made her slow under sail.

"She's maneuvering to intercept, I think," Alba commented, almost conversationally. Meanwhile, my heart was racing. "Not necessarily a position to destroy us—that is, I believe her priority will be capturing our cargo, which is good for our chances of survival. She won't much want to damage her prize." She could have been chatting about the weather, or choir rehearsal, or hedgeberry pie.

"How are you so calm?" I demanded. "We could be dead within the hour."

She barely flinched. "I suppose I'm quite assured of my mortality," she replied.

I blanched. "That is not helpful."

"How so? It is only logical to be aware that this corporeal vessel of mine will rot away—not unlike this ship already appears to be doing. The creation is mortal, the Creator immortal, and there is nothing unnatural in that."

I swallowed against a dry mouth. "I really didn't need the reminder of my own, potentially very rapidly approaching, death."

"You asked," Alba said. "Death is merely the natural outcome of life."

"Can we stop talking about death, please?" I eyed the Galatine ship, sails taut and prow now turning her nose in course to meet us.

"Of course." She faced me. "Are you going to cast?"

I nodded. My strategy was only half-formed; had I known that we could be intercepted by enemy ships, I could have considered my options better. I could have, but perhaps I wouldn't, I acknowledged. My understanding of shipboard tactics was shallow at best, and I had thus far resisted every thought of militarizing my magic.

If I was going to survive to help the Reform, I was going to have to let go of those niceties now.

Charms first, I decided without thinking very deeply at all. Charms were what I was comfortable with, and where I knew how to predict the results. I drew quickly, long threads of thick golden light from the ether. They rushed toward me strong and fast, the practice honed by the long hours in the Fenian factories. I twisted them into rings, huge rings as big as the ship, my fingers making the motion of the glowing discs in miniature. I cast three of them tight around the ship, hovering over the hull below, the deck surrounding me, and above, the sails. I drove the magic first into the willing fibers of the sails and then, with effort that made my forehead bead sweat, into the wood. It was barely etched into the surface and I saw the pale white light leaking into the water and dissipating as soon as I'd tethered the magic to the hull.

Sailors ran past, either not noticing or not bothering about me, though I might well have been in the way, interrupting their precise and vital movements. Alba stood, a silent sentry, beside me.

There was a complement of swivel guns on the deck, a pitiful answer to the full broadside of cannon the Galatine vessel could deliver, and I let the charm magic dance over them as I considered them. We had questioned how a charm might affect the accuracy or safety of a gun; now was not the time to test the theory. A sailor pulled a crate of ammunition from the hold; I wondered, briefly, if I could ward off damp powder and ensure clean firing if I charmed the black powder. I might also render the explosive inert.

I shook my head and turned to the sailors themselves. I thought to charm their clothing, but stopped. They would have refused, and there was something unsettling about charming them against their will. I would charm the ship or its supplies, but not them, not their personal items, without their consent. The Galatine soldiers and their charmed uniforms were different; some of them simply didn't believe, but Galatines didn't, as a rule, have moral compunctions against charms. Not so the Fenians. Instead, I turned back to the sails, imbuing more charms into them, plying it in thick strands around the rigging as well.

The captain stopped briefly to speak to Alba. From their exchange I knew he had tried to insist we go below; from his red face I knew Alba's refusal had been final. He shouted something in Fenian, and she asked a quiet question. I tried to focus on the sails, but the deafening report of a shot from the Royalist ship broke my concentration.

A warning shot only, but I shuddered.

"He is suggesting surrender," Alba said, glowering. "He does not wish to fight to preserve the cargo."

I bit my lip. Of course, this tub couldn't stand against the Galatine ship; I was foolish for even trying to buffer us, to raise the possibility of victory. Charms couldn't make the impossible possible.

Alba argued with the captain, while the Galatine ship was close enough now that I could see them readying to fire again. Likely this shot would be aimed for us, aimed for the sails and rigging to incapacitate us and make us easy to board. When that happened, I could be discovered. I had to assume I would be.

Quickly, without considering the ramifications of what I was doing, I spun darkness from the ether. I pulled black luck and death and misfortune, drew it tight around itself like a ball. With my fist clenched and my heart pounding against my ribs, I hurled it toward the Royalist ship. More specifically, toward a gunport and the maw of a cannon inside, its crew in the middle of loading the gun.

The black sparkling orb collided with the black cast iron of the gun and enveloped it. It didn't press itself into the metal; I hadn't expected that, and before I could decide if I should try to embed the curse in the unmalleable iron, the crew fired the gun.

It exploded.

Orange fire erupted in the side of the ship, and though several other guns fired shortly after, the shouts and chaos reached us from across the water. They were, for the moment, incapacitated. One gun crew, maybe more, injured. I shook off the guilt—they would have killed me. They still might. We had bought time, nothing more.

Then I saw the bright tongues of flame licking the interior deck of the ship, tracing the wood and lapping up one mast. The first explosion that followed shocked me, but the others I began to anticipate, one after the other, as casks of powder exploded and ignited more of the ship.

Alba took a tiny step forward, mouth open, surprised out of her pious complacency for perhaps the first time in years.

She turned to me as the captain gaped next to her, clearly congratulating himself on his good fortune.

This was only the beginning, her bright eyes promised while my knees buckled and darkness like that I had hurled at the ship seemed to dig into the pit of my stomach.

12

~m~

WE LANDED NEAR HAZELWHITE WITH NO FURTHER INTERVENTION
from the Royalist navy. The weather hadn't turned completely
toward autumn this far south, and balmy sunshine bathed the
shore where we landed longboat after longboat of supplies. The
Fenian captain grumbled about the lack of proper docks, but he
made haste unloading the crates. The black powder came last,
barrel after volatile barrel.

I had gotten my feet wet alighting from the longboat, and took
off my shoes and socks to try to dry them in the sun. It was already
weaker sunlight than the height of summer, but I wrung out my
socks and hoped for the best. In the encampment, near Hazelwhite
village, there would be fresh socks and, far more important, Theodor. But for now I had to wait, with wet feet and poor patience, for
the wagons that would take us and our supplies inland.

In truth, I was nervous. My role had been clear while abroad
with Alba. I had felt a certain usefulness, necessity even; the
army needed supplies and a boost against the better-equipped
Royalists, and I could provide that. Now my role was unclear.
Was I rejoining the Reformist army as anything aside from Theodor's consort, Kristos's sister, and a pair of willing but unhelpful hands?

I turned the socks over, though they were still clammy and cold. Even rejoining Theodor—what would that mean? I had grown used to being together, to working alongside one another. Now I had grown used to being apart again. Surely he had changed, under the weight of leading one side of a civil war. Would he see me the same way as before, or I him?

The wagons crested the hill above the shore, and I watched them eagerly, but the sun had shifted westward and I squinted. I sighed. I would have to wait, then, to even see if I recognized the wagon drivers. I doubted I would.

My socks were still damp when the wagons reached us, stopping before the sand, the oxen drawing them slowing obediently to a halt. I drew my socks over unwilling feet, making a face at the damp wool clinging to my toes.

"Sophie!" A familiar voice echoed across the strand and a figure ran toward me. I gasped, though I couldn't see past the angle of the sun. I knew that voice.

Theodor.

He careened toward me and sank to the ground beside my crate, knees in the sand and hands finding mine. He laid his head on my lap and for a long moment neither one of us moved, shocked and overwhelmed by the realness of it, that we were both truly here, able to touch, able to speak. I lifted a tentative hand and laid it on his hair, overcome by the familiarity of the honey-brown queue under my fingers.

I finally found my voice. "I didn't think you'd come yourself."

He looked up. "Of course I did! The messenger said you were here, nothing could keep me away."

"Not even a war?"

He waved a hand. "Not even that. Well, maybe if we were actually fending off a Royalist incursion. But we're not."

I took his hands in mine and lifted them from my lap,

drawing him up beside me while I finished putting on my sodden shoes. "Not yet, anyway."

"It's coming," he said. "But now we can face it. We're outfitting the soldiers at a rate you wouldn't believe—maybe don't pick on the craftsmanship of the coats too much," he added. I stifled a laugh. "And shot and powder—cannon coming, too. You did this."

"Alba did most of it," I countered. "And I'm afraid we're bearers of some disappointment about the ships."

"Don't worry about it now," Theodor said. "You'll debrief everyone at the officers' headquarters as soon as we're back. But for now"—he smiled gently—"for now I could breathe you like air."

We climbed into the back of a wagon and settled next to one another on top of a bale of linen, drinking in all the courage and fortitude that simple closeness could offer us against the unknown. My tension melted into the comfortable silence. For now, we could be Theodor and Sophie, in a moment stolen from war.

We drove inland, the farm fields growing golden and some already harvested. Farmers in an apple orchard, picking early fruit, waved to us and cheered, recognizing the red and gray of Theodor's uniform coat even if they didn't realize at a distance that he was their Rebel Prince. The pastoral harvest scenes we passed were busy but calm, not the picture of a nation at war, an autumn not so different from that at the House of the Golden Sphere hundreds of miles away.

Then we crested a hill and I saw the encampment. Tents lined the gentle rolling field in rows like pale haystacks, one after another. The effect was impressively orderly until we grew closer and I could see that their sizes and dimensions were varied and their state of repair haphazard. More regular were the lines of men drilling in the open parade ground, wheeling and turning in movements that were, to my untrained eye, as precise as the soldiers who marched through the streets of Galitha City on the king's birthday.

Some were even uniformed already, smallclothes of unbleached linen and coats of gray wool with red facings. Seeing the uniformed men march on the open plain, I was confident in that decision to spend a bit more on the bolts of red wool.

"How are you deciding who gets the uniforms first?" I asked as we passed more soldiers in their civilian clothes, moving through a bayonet drill. I flinched at the sight of the cruelly sharp, triangular blades on the ends of their muskets.

"The First Regiment is getting the first run of coats," Theodor said. "For the most part, they've all been quite amenable to the formed-as-they-joined organization Sianh has devised. As they joined, we formed regiments—the First, Second, so forth. That way there's respect in having been here longer, and some incentive to join sooner."

"How many regiments?" I asked.

"Four. Each of ten companies of eighty. More coming every day—we'll have the Fifth formed before long."

I ran the math quickly. So many to outfit, and yet so few in the face of the established Royalist army.

"Quartermaster's Division," Theodor said as the wagons came to a stop by a ramshackle barn surrounded by wall tents and rapidly constructed canvas lean-tos. "And that's the end of the line for our ride, I'm afraid—headquarters is that way." He pointed to a two-story stone house on the hill, brick-red shutters and doors open and almost cheerful.

"Whose barn is this?" I asked suddenly. "And the house?" I stopped. "Did you...requisition these, from the nobility?" I thought of Niko, taking over full city blocks that he deemed necessary.

"No, not exactly."

"Not a non-noble!" I protested. "That wouldn't look well at all, the Reformist army tossing poor farmers off their land."

"Hardly a poor farmer," Theodor said, gesturing to the more-than-modest house with its fieldstone walls and thick panes of glass in the windows. "It's the residence and fields of a farmer, non-noble, who believed he owned the land. Some story of being granted land generations ago after some war, for meritorious service?" I waited. "I don't know, at any rate, it's on the books as belonging to a lesser member of the Pommerly family, so of course we figured it would be ideal to take it over. Until we got here and discovered poor old Rufus in quite a sour mood about that."

"I would think so! He didn't own the land after all? But surely you won't displace him?"

Theodor cracked a smile. "He was amenable to let us have the space given that he'd far prefer we win this war and grant him permanent, legal ownership. It's a cruel trick that the southern nobility has been playing at for some time, I think—telling locals that they're giving them land to ensure their loyalty, but they could snatch it back anytime."

"No more of that," I said confidently. "And we'll be good caretakers of his house and crops."

"Bit late for that, we trampled his pumpkin patch and accidentally burned a decent bit of the corn."

"Theodor!"

"Accidentally! I paid him for it. Sianh was angrier than he was; we could have used that corn. Kristos!" he called as we went inside the house. "Look who I found."

13

THE COZY WHITEWASHED KITCHEN OF THE HAZELWHITE farmhouse was perhaps the most incongruous place I could imagine for a military commanders' headquarters. A fire burned low into hot coals on the broad hearth, centered by a large iron pot simmering with onion soup. The smell was delicious, nostalgic, and comforting—the precise opposite of the formal, meticulous debriefing unfolding at the scoured wood table.

"The regiments are currently divided according to the Serafan model," Sianh said, quickly ticking off the numbers as he added, "so that each regiment includes a light infantry company and a company of grenadiers in addition to the regulars."

"And this is better than the Galatine model?" Alba seemed to understand the brief review Sianh gave us covering our numbers, troop strength, and training better than I had thus far. I sat cross-legged on the soapstone ledge of the dry sink, trying to understand the martial situation as best I could.

"In my opinion, yes. It gives us greater flexibility in moving troops, which we can hope we will be doing quite soon.

"The arrival of our cannon barrels means we will formalize artillery regiments, as well." Sianh paused. "I am unsure how to recruit. Thus far our entire troop strength has been trained as infantry."

"Volunteers?" Kristos asked, uncertain.

"I suppose. Their sergeants and officers will need to be at least marginally competent in mathematics, for the range and angle calculations necessary."

"How are you selecting the officers now?" I asked, piping up from my perch on the sink.

"*We* are not selecting them," Sianh said flatly. "Your bookworm brother's idea, they are elected."

"It's not *terribly* stupid," Kristos countered with a smile. "It's not as though any of them has any more skill with a musket than the others, for the most part, and they tended to arrive in groups that already had some poor sod herding the others along."

"It shows," Theodor said evenly, "a commitment to democratic ideals. Eventually the governance of the entire country should be at the will of elections. Might as well practice now, right?"

Kristos grinned. Clearly the two of them had come to a détente of sorts, either a comfortable working alliance or, perhaps, even a friendly rapport. "It made for excellent fodder for a pamphlet on how we intend to translate the successes of our army into a stable government. Printed by the distinguished Hazelwhite print shop."

"Someone with a printing press in their shed?" I guessed.

Kristos nodded. "Widowed, bakes an excellent egg-and-onion pie, and sets type faster than a squirrel in a candy shop. That pamphlet, on democratic methodology in martial practice, has had four printings so far and we've distributed it all the way up to Rock's Ford—I'm given to understand that it's wormed its way into the Royalist encampment there."

"It makes for good press, which we need if we're going to

keep pulling in recruits," Theodor said. "And we didn't have a better way to go about it, honestly. The companies elect their NCOs and company officers, we select the regimental officers from that pool."

"Sianh is just a crab apple about it because a couple of the lieutenants need improvement." Kristos shrugged.

"Need improvement! They need to be demoted. They are *ouajin crai*." He responded to our silence by adding, "It means a cup with a hole in it. Translated literally. An item meant to do a single task but unfit to do that task? You understand?"

"Ah! In Kvys we say a pastry crust made of custard." Alba laughed.

"A sieve can't hold much soup," I added.

"And in the spirit of democratic ideals," Theodor interrupted, "we will ask for volunteers for artillery regiments. Which we only have thanks to Sophie and Alba."

"And a navy?" Kristos asked, smile creeping across his face. "We're harried on our supply line by the Royalist navy, and it puts us at a disadvantage—on our ability to move our troops, we can't blockade their ports—"

Alba held up a hand. "We negotiated contracts for the cannon, shot, powder, and cloth. But there is some unrest in Fen, workers' strikes. The factory owners laid blame on us—"

"Figures," Kristos snorted.

"And a nasty little caucus of them was ready to accuse Sophie of witchcraft," Alba continued. "We had to leave."

"Before you could complete the contracts for the ships?" Kristos's lips pressed together into a thin line. "We need those ships."

"We did the best we could," Alba protested. "I couldn't wait to finalize the arrangements before leaving for Fen, and then we had to leave Fen before we could go to the shipyards and entertain bids."

"You did enough," Theodor said, pulling me closer to him as though he could absorb me. "More than enough."

"Not really," Kristos retorted.

"What would you have us do?" I asked. "You got your charmed cloth and your cannons. If we were arrested, we wouldn't be getting your ships in any case."

"But we need ships!" he exploded. "We need some way to counter the blockaded ports and the ships that keep sniping our supplies. You should have started with the shipyards."

"We agreed to start with the mills," I said tersely. "It was the lowest-hanging fruit. We got the charmed cloth quickly. You agreed to that," I reminded him.

"I expected that the ships would still happen!"

"Enough," Sianh said. "Enough. We will not make ships materialize by fighting, and what is done is done. We did agree to begin with the fabric, for the very reason that it would be completed and shipped if any interference prevented completion of the mission in Fen."

"I'm just thankful you weren't captured," Theodor murmured. He cleared his throat. "Both of you. It was dangerous, I surprise myself I ever agreed to it."

"It wasn't your place to give permission," I chided him gently. He closed his eyes, suppressing an argument.

"So you have cloth. And you have cannons. And the rest of the Fenian contracts are well in hand—the supplies will not be charmed, but you'll have powder and shot and linen for shirts and everything else this outfit needs." Alba glanced around. "And food? You are well supplied?"

"Well enough for the time being," Sianh said. "I worry about winter, but an army always worries about winter."

"Tentage? Firewood? Drums and pennants and flags and— oh, what all does an army need?" Alba pressed.

"Brush shelters to supplement the tents, plenty of firewood, requisitioned a few drums when we took the Royalist fort at Herring's Wharf." Kristos grinned. "But flags. We could use one, actually." He raised his eyebrows at me with a look I knew too well.

"Last year you were asking me for red caps," I said. "Who would have thought it would come to flags? I'll see what I can do."

"I suggest we dismiss and reconvene tomorrow morning," Theodor said. "I am sure you're both exhausted."

Alba raised an eyebrow. "Yes, exhausted." She shared a flippant smile with Sianh while Kristos pretended to ignore the insinuation.

"You'll share my room, if that's all right," Theodor said.

I suppressed a smile as Kristos pretended to be very busy with a stack of maps. "That's fine."

I followed him upstairs, the narrow stairwell opening to a hallway brightly lit by twin windows facing one another. Four doors stood sentry, and Theodor opened the one nearest the landing, held the door for me, closed the door gently behind us, then fell into my arms. I stroked his hair with my fingertips. There was no pomatum or powder in it, and his usually carefully dressed queue was tied sloppily with a bit of leather. "It's all right," I said. "I'm all right."

"I almost couldn't—I couldn't believe you would be," he said, his voice strained with what I realized were badly suppressed tears. "Not when we didn't hear from you for weeks."

"Damn sea travel." I smiled faintly.

"And Fenians."

"And everything. Everything keeping us from what we could have been." I traced the thin gold chain on my wrist, still bright, still there. My fingers traipsed over Theodor's hand and found the chain's match on his wrist.

"No." He straightened. There was determination in his red eyes, but his face looked thinner and tightly drawn. "No, this is what we are supposed to be. I'm sure of that."

I hesitated. "How are you holding up?"

"Me?" He cracked a smile that looked like it might break his face. "I'm fine. Turns out I remember enough from my tutelage to be useful in training troops, and the men elected me their general, so the Rebel Prince cachet must be worth something. I've proven useful despite myself."

"I meant more...you." I traced the faint line between his taut brows.

"I'm fine. You're here. I'm fine," he repeated. He held my face in his fingertips, brushing wayward hair away from my cheeks, melting my months of anxiety into a single sigh.

Then he kissed me, strong and full of anticipation. I pulled him toward me, wanting to envelop him in me or let myself be absorbed into him, not quite sure if there was a difference. His fingers moved over my hair, my neck, prickling my skin with the promise of his continued touch. I pulled at the lacings of my jacket, corded linen catching in the poorly stitched eyelets.

"Let me," Theodor whispered, and pulled the lacing from the jacket and then the cord from my stays, as well. "Ah, and here is my Sophie, under all that Fenian wool."

"And my Theodor, still looking ready for a full military parade," I said. He shucked the coat, the wool far less fine than any of his old clothes. No embroidery, no gilt, no lace. The smallclothes beneath were even coarser, made of the unbleached gray linen I knew the poorhouse bought in bolts, but it suited him. He wasn't a prince any longer, I wasn't a seamstress, and all of the layers that had separated us were gone. I unbuttoned the plain brass buttons of his waistcoat, finding underneath them one of his old, fine linen shirts, now much patched and growing yellow for want of a proper laundering.

We fell silent, words too much like paltry shadows compared to the sheer presence of one another, and he lifted me gently onto the rope bed and its lumpy mattress. I leaned back, pulling him onto me, closer, ever closer. I shut my eyes and surrendered to that closeness, and let our bodies bind us like strong cords or the gold chains that had bound our wrists when Theodor had proposed.

I fell asleep wrapped under thick wool blankets that smelled of hay and Theodor's arms swathed in linen that smelled, faintly, of his clove pomade.

14

WE WERE UP BEFORE THE SUN HAD FINISHED RISING, THE RAPID tattoo of reveille rattling the windows and jarring me from the warm comfort of Theodor's arms. A pitchy fife joined the cacophony like a soprano rooster, demanding everyone begin their day.

"You start to hate that song," Theodor said, buttoning his waistcoat quickly against the early morning chill.

"I think I might hate it already," I said. "Where did you find a fifer?"

"He plays the tin whistle, I think. The fife is still a bit of a stretch for him. He's trying to train some others." Theodor winced as the melody scraped flat. "Fortunately the bayonet drill is improving far more rapidly."

I had little enough in the way of clothes, and no bedgown or wrapper to put on, so I snatched Theodor's spare waistcoat, identical to the one he wore, and buttoned it over half-laced stays.

"I had to leave all my clothes behind. I'm going to need some wool at some point for a gown," I said as Theodor raised an eyebrow at my ensemble.

"Lucky for you we have a wide assortment. As long as you

like gray and red," he said. I hesitated—the broadcloth that made regimental coats wouldn't work well for a gown. "I think you can make an exception for wearing one of your charms given that it may be your only option," he added gently.

"No, you mistake me," I said. My old qualms about wearing my own charms had faded, given that I could draw and use one anytime I wished. "That weight of wool will be difficult to work into a gown. Though I suppose I could work up a riding habit."

"Make it gray wool with red facings, just like the military coats," Theodor suggested eagerly. "It will be a symbol of your importance here."

Though a riding habit was a practical solution, it would take long hours of careful tailoring and—I sighed just thinking about it—rows and rows of neatly made buttonholes. "I can't help but feel there are better uses for my time than sewing something so—frivolous."

Theodor paused as he fastened his knee buckles, met my eyes, and burst out laughing. "I'm sorry, but it's just—last time this year, what were you doing?"

"Probably stitching some frivolous trim onto a frivolous silk gown," I said, between hiccups of laughter, "with a frivolous love charm sewn into it!"

In echo to the drums outside, a fist pounded our door. "We're up," Theodor called. "Getting dressed."

"Don't want to know," Kristos said. I laughed and lazily pulled stockings over cold feet, imagining his reddening face as he talked through the door. "Come downstairs as soon as you can. Messenger from Niko Otni." I quickened my pace, and Theodor threw his coat on without finishing with his waistcoat buttons.

We crowded into the kitchen, the warmest room in the

house, with its expansive hearth pouring heat from coals banked overnight and roused into flames first thing in the morning. On a squat three-legged stool by the hearth sat Fig. Someone had given him a mug of tea and some bread and butter; he looked more like a farm boy having breakfast before feeding the chickens than a wartime messenger in an army's headquarters.

"Why, Fig! I shouldn't be surprised," I said. His tired face drew itself into a smile and he sat a little straighter.

"You know this one?" Sianh said.

"Alba and I made his acquaintance in Galitha City," I answered.

"Then I suppose you're vetted," Kristos said.

"He wasn't one of yours?" I asked. "From last winter?" There had been boys and youths, always, hanging on to the Red Caps when they could.

"Ma said I was too young to run round with the Red Caps," Fig said. "But that was before the war."

"And now no one is too young," suggested Alba.

"We were not sure if he was truly from the army in the city," Sianh said, "as he does not bring any seals or signatures or any sort of verifiable written messages."

"Written messages can get captured," Fig announced proudly. So, I thought to myself, could thirteen-year-old boys. I didn't want to consider what the Royalists might be willing to do to a Reformist partisan to gain intelligence, regardless of his age.

"What's the news?" Theodor said, voicing the same question I had.

"The city holds," Fig said first, adeptly sensing the tension in the room. "We're still open to the river and they haven't started a siege or nothing yet."

"Yet?" Alba said.

"We anticipate a siege being their eventual strategy," Sianh said, his brow knitting and pulling at the pale scar along his cheek. "Unless the troops in the city surrendered or made a very foolish mistake, there is no other way to take Galitha City by force."

"The terrain just outside the walls is uneven and heavily forested on most sides," Theodor said. "It's extremely defensible— artillery can't get a good purchase without excavation and building entrenchments, and that, of course, takes time. But if they focus on the city . . ." Theodor sighed. "They would eventually breach the walls if a siege goes unchecked."

"That's right." Fig glanced at his half-eaten bread and decided that now wouldn't be a good time to tear off a hunk. "Niko says now's the time to cut them off. He wants you to move your troops to the city. Has to be overland. Port's thoroughly blockaded."

"Damn it." Kristos threw his cap on the table. "I'd hoped they'd be busier patrolling our coast—shit, I'd hoped that maybe more of the crews would mutiny and take some of their force out of commission."

Alba quietly took Fig's cup and refilled his tea. "They pay 'em too well," Fig said, accepting the hot tea. "A few defected to us, but sailors are a strange lot. Loyal to their captains. And their captains are treating them right—paying them bonuses, sharing out the prize money on captures."

"How very democratic of them," I said.

Theodor cracked a smile. "If only more of them understood how to apply it to politics, we wouldn't be in this mess." His smile faded. "I don't think we can give Niko what he's asking for."

"It would be a foolish maneuver. Even if we could move thousands of troops overland and aid the city without being challenged, a large contingent of the Royalist army is at Rock's

Ford. They would cut us off from behind and swiftly undo our work—and put us in position to force our surrender," Sianh said. "If they did not annihilate us before we even arrived."

"So you're going to leave the city to fend for itself?" Fig said. His fingers drew tight around his mug of tea, the knuckles whitening. "Niko was worried you'd be selfish."

"This is not selfishness," Sianh said. "The Royalists still have superior numbers of trained soldiers, not to mention they are still better supplied. Time—building our numbers and training, and draining the Royalists of supplies—will even our odds. The city has time, and we will use that time to weaken the Royalists. Every small fortification we take here, every supply train we dismantle, moves us closer."

"We don't have that much time," Theodor cautioned. "Once they commit to a siege, what do we have—weeks, months?" Theodor shook his head.

Sianh nodded, acknowledging the point. "Then we move more quickly here. I had wanted more time to build our troop strength and train more thoroughly, but if we lack that time, we are ready."

"Ready?" I said. Foolishly, I hadn't considered military strategy beyond massing troops in Hazelwhite—but of course they had to be sent to do something, to take territory and hold it against the Royalists.

"Moving toward the Rock River," Sianh said. "If we can defeat the Royalists at Rock's Ford, or at least sever their lines, we have a chance at moving on the city. We do not have that chance if they can simply resupply from Rock's Ford."

"Bad news for Niko, he's going to have to hold out," Kristos said. "But I agree. Taking the south step by step and holding Rock's Ford, we may actually be able to pull it off."

"And you'll send a message back?" Fig said.

"Of course. One of our men will go," Theodor said.

"He'll expect *me*," Fig argued, his chin jutting out in a portrait of childish defiance.

Theodor glanced at me, and I understood his meaning immediately. Niko may have sent Fig with good reason—if the city fell, the Royalists might not care who was young, who was barely more than a boy, if they wore the red and gray. Even if he didn't, something maternal flared in me, wanting to protect him even if I didn't have the power to protect anyone else.

"It will be faster if we send someone on one of the horses," I suggested. "And, Fig, if you can't ride, that many miles at once is not a good way to learn."

He sucked in his lips, unable to debate that very valid point.

"Besides, we could use you here. Perhaps even more than Commander Otni," I said, forcing my mouth and my mind around the still strange combination of Niko's name and the title. "If we're beginning a campaign, we'll need a seasoned messenger. A sort of an aide-de-camp—that's the term, isn't it, Sianh?"

"Yes, that is the term," he replied curtly, shooting invisible darts at me. "You come with me, *vimzalet*."

"*Vimzalet?*" I asked, wondering what new curse word this might be.

"Little mosquito," Sianh answered with raised eyebrow. "I have a feeling he shall be just as persistent and just as annoying."

15

~m~

"IF YOU WANT A FLAG," I SAID AS THEODOR AND I OBSERVED A marching drill on the parade ground, "I am going to need silk."

"Wool won't cut it?" Theodor teased. "Linen? That we have in bolts."

"Linen could work, if we could get it to hold color for more than a month out in the elements. Or if you like brown or blue, those seem to hold up well enough."

"Let's avoid blue," Theodor said. "Damned Royalists have ruined blue for me for quite some time. We've established red and gray rather nicely, though. Gray was always a favorite of mine, and red is growing on me."

"You want a red device on it, it must be silk. Linen will go pink or brown within a few weeks." I laughed. "Even scarlet doesn't hold on linen."

"Well, then, we shall have to make a foray into Hazelwhite to see if there is anything to be had," Theodor said. "The artillery pieces have started arriving, and Sianh will be starting to establish the artillery units. Necessary, before we can hope to take Rock's Ford. I'm sure he wouldn't begrudge me an afternoon's walk into town."

Sianh supervised the drill on the parade ground. He was

fluid, almost, in his movements through the camp, gliding
between mentoring the green officers and berating a unit whose
muskets had begun to show rust with seamless transitions.

"You look well," I said to him.

"If you mean overworked, then yes."

"You seem to like overwork, then."

Sianh cocked his head with a conspiratorial smile. "So you
have noticed. You, as well. The riding coat suits you."

"Thank you," I replied. With some shoddy work on the
buttonholes and a few long days with little else to do, I made
myself a gray-and-red riding habit to match the uniforms of the
Reformist army, down to the unbleached linen waistcoat. I felt
a bit too conspicuous, at first, as though I was trying to force
myself into a place here.

"We're going into Hazelwhite to see if the draper or the
haberdasher still have any silk on the shelves," Theodor said.

"Very well," said Sianh. "Do be back before evening. I need
a bit of help working out the artillery officers." He opened a
thick leather-bound notebook full of pen scratches. "And this—
another twenty new recruits joined us last night out of the southern coast. Trouble with those fellows is that their accents are so
thick the others are unable to understand them half of the time."

"We'll make sure to assign a corporal with some facility in
both the northern and southern dialects," Theodor said. "I'll
finagle that when we're back."

The distance from the cliffside encampment to Hazelwhite
itself was less than a mile, on a hard-packed red dirt road. An
early morning shower had settled the dust, and the noon sun
was gently warm as we followed the old ruts of oxcarts and hay
wagons. The town settled itself onto the plain below a low pair
of hills, both covered in broad fields of wheat and rye.

"They still have their market every week," Theodor said,

"but the shops have half shuttered. The draper is still open, but I've no guarantee on his wares."

I nodded. The orderly town center, branching out like spokes from a circular green where a small flock of sheep balefully tore at the grass, was quiet. Several tidy little storefronts had apologetic signs hung in their windows—the proprietors had fled or closed shop due to lack of business. The milliner and the haberdasher were both closed.

"I'm sure no one would fault the local army general for a little breaking and entering, but we'll try the draper first," Theodor said.

"I doubt either of those stocked fabric in enough quantity, anyway," I replied. I looked at the little shops with a sense of loss. Shops like mine, proprietors like I had been, their livelihoods overturned by war. "What will they do, the shopkeepers?"

"Not every townsperson or farmer is in support of our aims, Sophie," he reminded me gently. "There was a bit of a row here, when we first arrived and began massing. The Pommerlys had been run out by the local Red Cap contingent already, but it wasn't tenable any longer for anyone with Royalist sympathies, not after we showed up."

"So they were run out of town," I said. That was an inevitability of a civil war, but seeing how it played out in a picturesque town that still had sheep grazing on the green sobered me.

"Some have followed the Royalist army, some have holed up in Rock's Ford or other Royalist-held territory. Those with enough money have fled to West Serafe. There's a regular expatriate community at this point, Royalists who plan to return at the first sign of the king's glorious victory. Here's the draper."

The draper's small store tended toward linens and wools, with heavy broadcloths and fine worsteds on display in his front window, similar to the drapers who served the working classes of Galitha City. The ones I had frequented had taffetas and bro-cades proudly swathed across the windows, but no one in Hazel-white needed anything so fine now.

"To be honest," the draper said when Theodor inquired about his silk, "it's been months since I could get a shipment of Serafan silk in, and this bit of Equatorial cotton is the last I expect to see for a good while. Shipping's all sorts of cockeyed."

"There is a war on," Theodor replied with mild humor, which made the draper chuckle. "Anything at all?"

"Gray I've got—follow me," he said, beckoning. "Here, take your pick."

"We will, of course, pay," Theodor said, pulling a cipher book from his pocket as I perused the limited selection. I ran my fingers over several bolts of taffeta, thin Serafan silk, and satin weaves in various shades of gray. I pointed out two whose weights were correct—the colors were different, but that didn't matter now. The only red silk was a tissue weight Serafan silk in a hideous tomato red, but I reasoned that might work, backed with some linen.

Shouts and the unmistakable sound of shattered glass inter-rupted our tabulations. Theodor's hand was on his sword as he moved toward the door, a utilitarian officer's broadsword that replaced the flimsy ceremonial rapier he had carried as a duke and then a crown prince.

"Some trouble at the haberdasher's," Theodor said.

The draper snorted. "Man was a damned Royalist. Smash his windows and his nose for good measure, for all I care."

I stiffened. Maybe the haberdasher had been a patent Roy-alist, and maybe he had been throwing in his lot for survival with whoever he thought might keep him from starving this winter. I couldn't bear the weight of hating my enemy any lon-ger, not when he could have been my neighbor. But I had, I acknowledged, been removed from these fights during my months abroad.

"There's a group of—hold on, now." Theodor glanced at me with half a smile working its way into a grin. "They're coming here."

"Not to worry, then?"

"You needn't worry over nothin', Miss Sophie," a husky but definitively feminine voice asserted from outside. I followed Theodor to the door; the draper's tinny bell jangled as we left. Before us, a small army of women in red kerchiefs tied around their heads in lieu of caps waited for us.

"I—thank you?" I said. "I confess I'm confused as to the purpose of this assembly," I added.

The woman who had spoken, with broad shoulders and tow-bright hair, grinned. "We're what's left of the Red Caps of Hazelwhite," she said. "The menfolk mostly all joined up, so keeping the order here is up to us."

"I see," I said. There were young women barely older than girls and women with gray hair visible under their kerchiefs, and several had babies on their backs.

"And so's requisitioning supplies. Bring it out, Sukey." From the open door of the old haberdasher, a woman tugged a crate toward me. She cracked it open—it was full of scarlet silk, neatly hemmed in squares a yard across. "When Mr. Finney realized we was buying the red kerchiefs for political-like reasons, he stashed 'em. But we figured they was still there, so when we heard you was looking for silk." She shrugged.

"Thank you," I said. I hesitated; this Finney was certainly a Royalist, but the part of me that was still a shopkeeper and not a military strategist felt as though I was stealing.

As if sensing my reticence, the woman standing by the crate

added gently, "He was old Lady Pommerly's man through and through."

"Old Lady Pommerly is—was—Lady Floralette Pommerly, dowager of one of the estates near here. Her son was technically lord of the family estate, but he lived much of the year in Galitha City," Theodor supplied.

"She was a mean old bat," added the woman with the blooming kerchief. "And Rafferty Finney did whatever she wanted."

"What happened to her?"

"Dunno. Heard she ran for Serafe. Heard she maybe didn't make it." The tow-haired woman shrugged. "Anyway. These are yours. With a couple requests."

I knelt and felt the silk—good, brilliant scarlet. "Of course."

"First, we've got a regular corps here sewing and doing laundry for the army. We're getting paid, but we want assurances of winter rations from your stores. All our men are in your army, and we're working for your army, and your army has bought our crops at a pretty scraping-bottom price. We're glad to do it." She paused. "But we have to eat." As if on cue, a baby began to fuss. So did their children, I added silently.

I glanced at Theodor. He nodded. "Done. Send your numbers to our quartermaster. With my promise you'll be included on the ration rolls."

"And another thing. We're on your side because it's not right that people should get to rule other people on account of how they were born. Nobles were just born lucky, that's all." She squared her shoulders and levied a hard look at Theodor. "But we don't much fancy anybody being born lucky. Men included."

I stood, hedging my response carefully. "I can't promise what precise rules will govern us after this war ends. But I can say I will advocate for the very thing you ask for." I didn't meet

Theodor's eyes—on this, we did not need to agree. "If we can run our businesses and our farms and our towns, why should we not have a stake in running a country?"

Behind me, Theodor shifted uncomfortably, and I knew I was edging close to promising too much. But the women surrounding me grinned and tied a red kerchief in their signature knot over my cap.

16

THERE WAS LITTLE TIME TO DESIGN A COMPLICATED FLAG, AND no one skilled enough to paint an elaborate device on the silk, so I pressed Theodor's cipher book into service and divided the red and gray as carefully as I could to avoid waste, resulting in a simple gray banner with a red diagonal bar as our ensign. The regimental flags were copied from that design, adding additional thin bars of scarlet on the right-hand edge, one for the First, two for the Second, and so on.

Sianh admired the first completed flag as I finished the hem in the warm stone kitchen. "It will serve well," he said. "The design is not as complex as the Serafan flags typically are, but there is something quite fitting about simplicity for this home-spun army."

"If we had Viola here, we could have created a painted device," I said. "But I hadn't any silk to waste and didn't trust anyone green with it," I said.

"They are, I assume, fortified with your abilities?"

"But of course," I said. "A bit of extra luck stitched into each."

Theodor joined us. "Looks lovely, of course, Sophie." He turned quickly to Sianh. "Have we heard from the raiding party we sent northward yet?"

"They came back this morning. They ran afoul of some guards near—oh, what dull name do you have for it?"

"The fort at Dunn Creek," Theodor replied.

"Yes, the Dunn Creek fortification. They did not manage to return much in the way of supplies, so I confess my disappointment. They were supposed to be on a raid to capture muskets from the magazine there. Instead they got caught up in an exchange of fire—"

I exhaled with near-motherly concern, and Sianh raised an eyebrow as he continued. "Which happens with fair regularity, and which they handled well enough to assuage my confidence in this rag-and-bones army, but I did not wish to risk manpower on sniping at a few Royalist guards."

"They're all right?" I asked.

Sianh snorted with almost aristocratic grace. "They are on latrine duty for disobeying my orders to avoid engaging with the Royalists at—what was it—Dunn Creek. We must fight like foxes," he added. "Swift, flexible, and utilizing the supplies in other people's chicken coops."

"I'm sorry to interrupt." Fig tapped the door frame, shifting his weight in a pair of too-large shoes.

"Go ahead," Theodor said.

"Something Commander Balstrade and Sastra-set Alba think you need to see. Right away."

I glanced at Theodor, whose face remained impassive, but newly etched with taut lines of worry. "Very well."

We followed Fig to where the others waited, at the crest of the hill overlooking the ocean. "Lookout post spotted them about fifteen minutes ago." Kristos handed Theodor the glass. "It's a West Serafan vessel."

"Then they're showing their hand. Finally!" Alba said. "That's a relief."

"You have a strange idea of relief," Sianh said.

"We assumed that they would be coming into this war on the side of the Royalists. We had all but a writ of guarantee. Now we can see what, precisely, they intend to do." Alba folded her hands and watched the ship maneuver closer to the harbor, though the artillery placed on the shore and on the high bluff next to us countered any possibility of landing.

Kristos didn't look relieved, no matter what Alba might say. "From what I can tell, there's no soldiers on board—at least, none above deck. Just musicians."

I felt myself go cold, right down to my fingertips. "Musicians." I took the glass Theodor offered. Three Serafan women stood on the deck of the ship, one harpist, one with a recurved Serafan violin, and one holding a sheaf of paper. Sheet music. "What do they expect to do from there?" I handed the glass back to Theodor, hand trembling.

Theodor looked to the horizon, sweeping his glass in a broad arc. "There's no one else out there." Eerie calm stretched on the sea, silent and punctuated only by this one bobbing Serafan vessel.

"This isn't right," I murmured. "Sianh, this isn't how you said the Serafans used casting in battle."

Sianh grunted in uncomfortable agreement, and Theodor squinted at the ship. "They're too far out. Anything they're doing—it can't reach us." He looked to Sianh and Kristos. "Right?"

Kristos nodded. "It must be some sort of...rehearsal."

"No," Alba said, plucking the glass from Theodor's hand. "It's too great a risk to come within range of our cannon for a mere rehearsal."

"But do we even fire?" Kristos replied. "It doesn't look well, firing on a civilian ship. And," he added, countering Sianh's immediate argument, "there's nothing we can see that suggests it's anything but."

Sianh's mouth tightened. "I would make the guns ready in any case."

Theodor sent Fig with the message to the artillery emplacements along the cliff. "Still. What do they expect to do? We're too far away for their casting to work."

"What's that?" Kristos's question was simple, but it dropped a weight into my stomach. Silently, we passed the glass from hand to hand. I looked through the opening like a keyhole into a door that led to an answer I wasn't prepared for.

Sailors set panels around the musicians—no, not panels, I understood as I squinted through the glass. Convex shells made of taut canvas on frames. As they worked, the square of the deck began to look more like the front of the cathedral in Fountain Square, or the basilica in the House of the Golden Sphere.

"Acoustics," Kristos said. "They're going to project the sound toward us. Amplify it. Using those shapes."

Fear rose like bile in my throat. Shot and shell I'd been prepared for; this was something different, an unknown horror. I remembered the strange manipulation of my emotions in the Serafan magic show at the summit, the insidious creep of reactions not wholly mine coupled with heightening anxiety. That was what the casters had intended us to feel then; what could the aim of this manipulation be?

Theodor chewed on his lip. "We need to get back to the camp. To warn everyone."

"And say what?" Kristos ran a hand through snarled hair. "We don't know what this is, what to expect—"

The musicians began to play.

The melody, thin and sweet like a slow-oozing line of treacle, flowed toward us. It was simple at first, not complex or layered, but almost pretty. Repetitive. It grew stronger, and my head began to throb. The harpist and the violinist played together while the third woman—some sort of caster-conductor, I surmised through the growing haze behind my eyes—directed them as they deftly drew black curse magic into the strains of music. It glittered in a sickly black fog, and I could see the path of the sound in its billowing folds.

"Back to camp, now," Theodor said. Kristos didn't argue. As we climbed away from the lookout point, the syrup-sweet melody intensified, plucked on the harp strings and echoed by the increasingly aggressive strain of the violin. Kristos narrowed his eyes, fighting the same dizzying whirl in his skull that I felt. Like turning too fast, like falling, but without moving at all. Next to me, Alba leaned over, face paling and beads of sweat glistening at her temples. She stumbled and gripped a tree for support, then doubled over, heaving.

Nausea gripped me, too. Theodor held my arm and helped me toward the officers' tent even as his lips grew pale and he swallowed, hard. I bit back bile.

Sianh stumbled toward the officers' tent. I thought he might have some plan, but instead he fell to all fours in the grass and vomited. I turned away, already sick.

"How—how can they do this?" I trembled. "They can make us feel—not only emotions but—" I stopped, overcome by a wave of nausea. This was a vertigo of confusion and fear, heightened, made visceral and sustained.

Up and down the rows of canvas, soldiers gripped their bellies and upended their stomachs, burrowed heads in hands and closed their eyes. Those who tried to stand promptly stumbled and fell or were overtaken by the persistent, rolling nausea. I sank, shaking, to the ground. It helped to avoid movement, to hold perfectly still. I closed my eyes. Better yet, gazing into nothing, into velvet darkness. I started—was this what they wanted? For us to all choose oblivion? Could I drive myself into a self-chosen death this way?

I forced my eyes open and moaned faintly at the brightness, at the shifting world around me that plucked the nerves in my head like a harp. In time with the harp—yes, I could still see the dark curse magic around us, its glitter and shift in time with the music.

Fortunately, it didn't get any worse. Soldiers realized the same thing I had—that stillness helped—and settled into the grass, leaning against trees or lying flat on their backs. Theodor pulled himself closer to me and reached for my hand. I pulled away—even his touch intensified the vertigo. I recognized my fear that I could kill myself under the direction of the magic for what it was, an illness-induced anxiety. Induced by the thrumming waves of the curse itself.

"There must be a reason for their timing," Sianh said. He forced the words through a grimly set mouth. He was still trying not to be sick again.

"An attack," Alba murmured, "and we're unable to fight."

"No," I whispered. "Not now. Or here." The words tasted like bile, and forming thoughts, let alone the words themselves, through the vertigo made my head swirl like leaves in a stiff fall breeze. "Their own soldiers can't, either..." Nausea rose too quickly and I clamped my mouth shut.

"Right." Theodor breathed, carefully, through his nose. "Right. Wait."

No one argued with him. There was nothing else we could do.

Finally, the music faded. The glittering black cloud dissipated, and the fog over my brain lifted, slowly. My stomach settled back into its usual uncomplaining silence. A vague headache remained, like the ghost of yesterday's migraine.

"At the ready!" Sianh was up and shouting before I could regain my balance. He hauled a drummer up by the collar. "Beat to quarters!"

The camp erupted into life around me, drums sounding the urgent call to arms, men layering on coats and cartridge boxes and haversacks, tightening bayonet belts and shouldering muskets. Some took swigs from their canteens on the run as they formed their companies.

"If they hoped to catch Sianh off his guard," Kristos said with a lopsided grin, "they miscalculated." He rubbed his temples. "They may be preparing to attack. That may have been some kind of diversion."

"But diversion from what?" I asked. "If they planned an immediate attack, and had troops nearby, their soldiers would have been hit as hard as we are."

"Or they are attacking somewhere else," Sianh said, "and we are supposed to be tricked into staying here, anticipating."

"Damned Serafans," Theodor cursed through clenched teeth. "Without knowing where or how they're planning to take advantage of that tactic…"

"We will wait," Sianh said. "I do not like it, but we cannot react against what we do not know."

17

THE SILENCE FOLLOWING THE SERAFAN ATTACK CREPT IN EERIE waves over the encampment. We waited, increased patrols and pickets guarding the camp, but no incursion came, and no messengers arrived to bring news of attacks on other Reformist-sympathizing towns or ports.

"I don't like waiting like this," Kristos said as we ate our dinner, pea soup with thin shreds of ham and heavy brown bread. The quartermaster, a thickset butcher who had known both Kristos and Niko in the city, had built ovens and his battalion of bakers churned out loaves of coarse bread from the local oats and wheat and rye. "It's making the men nervous."

"They are indeed wary," Sianh said. "Some of them do not even believe that the Serafans could effect such a thing, but even they are worried. Illness is as much a danger in a military encampment as shot and shell."

"The Serafans have kept the secret of their particular kind of casting for centuries, perhaps," I mused. "You said that there have been sorcerers at the court for centuries, right?" Sianh nodded. "Why let the secret out now?"

"They think you already have," Alba said quietly. She daubed the last of her soup with her bread crust. "They know that you discovered their casting," she added. "They were quite keen to have you dispatched in Isildi, to keep the secret from escaping, but now? It's loose."

"So they may as well unleash it to its full potential," Theodor murmured. "That's not a comforting thought."

"Then how do we fight back against this?" Kristos said. It wasn't a rhetorical question, I realized, as all eyes in the room settled on me.

"I don't know!" I said. "I—well. Start with the soldiers who were wearing charmed clothing. Let's see if it affected them less."

"Very scientific," Kristos said. "But if it didn't do anything, or not enough—what then? They can drive us mad, make us ill, render us unable to fight, anytime?"

"Not quite," I said, thinking out loud. "Unless they've got an antidote I don't know about, there's no way their own soldiers wouldn't be just as badly affected."

Kristos nodded, clearly not satisfied with that answer. "I confess I am entirely underprepared for this kind of thinking. We all are, excepting Sianh, I suppose. But it seems wrong, making these decisions for everyone. Like we're a troupe of nobles. Like we're exactly what we're fighting to stop."

"Someone must take leadership," Sianh scoffed. "Especially in the midst of a war."

"It doesn't have to be only us," Theodor said slowly. "Kristos is right. We are quite literally fighting for an established form of representation that's been denied."

"The Council of Country, from the Reform Bill," I said.

Sianh shook his head at his pea soup. "We are not able to pause a war and hold elections. Do not let your ideals compromise your ability to win a war."

"Who has a better stake than the men who are already here,

fighting? Who more than they deserve to confirm some vision of Galitha?" Kristos smiled, an idea growing. "The Reform Bill promised a Council of Country. Our first one is sitting right out there," he said, gesturing toward the wavy panes of the kitchen window. "They already voted on their officers. They chose their leadership already. We could formalize that structure, and begin establishing government procedures, too, for after the war."

"They chose men who they thought could lead them in battle the best," I cautioned. "That doesn't mean they are the same people who would best write, I don't know, court martial procedures or rationing orders." I paused. "And what about the women? They may not be fighting on the field, but they have a stake in this, too."

Theodor inhaled slowly. "At any rate, the needs of an army are different than the needs of a civilian government. Not to mention," he added, "there's precious little agreement about what, precisely, the nation will look like after the war. The Reform Bill retained the nobility in much of their authority and simply added elected councils."

"The Red Caps never wanted to retain the nobility," Kristos said. It wasn't an argument for or against the nobles; rather, he looked tired. "But it's one or the other."

"I don't think it's up to us to decide," Theodor said. "And I'm not at all sure that simply instating our officers in government positions is ethical. It has a rather despotic taste, doesn't it?"

"You're right." Kristos grimaced. "That does complicate things."

I gazed out the window over the sloping field toward the main encampment. Who knew what those men were thinking? Surely they were shaken. The skirmishes had been small thus far, but men had died, and now Serafan curse magic cast a shadow over them, too. "What about new elections? I think this army needs a bit of optimism. And it needs to be unified. We have Red Caps and reluctant Reformists alongside one another. They need some kind of promise of what this country will look like." I paused and tried to smile. "When we win."

"When we win." Theodor couldn't help a small smile. "So we could hold new elections and form a Council of Country—our first."

"Why, you could hold your elections tomorrow and have your council within two days," Alba said, faintly amused, like a mother watching her children inventing the rules to a game.

"No, wait." Kristos drummed his fingers on the big kitchen table. "Not tomorrow. Let me publish that we're doing this. Any man enlisted for the duration of the war has a vote, provided he gets here by Threshing Market."

"You're having a market?" Alba asked.

"Galatine harvest festival," I explained. "That gives you less than a month to get the word out," I said to Kristos. "Is that enough?"

"It will have to be," Kristos said.

The fierce tattoo of drums interrupted us. Sianh ran to the window, with Kristos jostling beside him. Drummers beat to assemble at the center of camp, and troops rushed to fall in, muskets in hand. I turned to Theodor, who was sliding his arm through his sword belt. He met my eyes and nodded, once. Whether a full-scale battle or a skirmish, we were ready.

18

FIG BURST THROUGH THE DOOR OF THE KITCHEN, THE ECHOES OF the drums amplifying his urgency. "Word from Hazelwhite village. A troop of horse under—oh, one of those Pommerly bastards you all talk so much about."

"They're not," I said, unable to resist a bit of moral guidance despite my shaking hands, "actually bastards. Mind your language."

"Sophie, report to the surgeon," Sianh said. "Perhaps you can be of some use there. It is too unclear what is underway in Hazelwhite for anything else."

I nodded. I knew that I needed to discover how my charms and curses might affect an active battle eventually, but that could wait. Something more familiar—health charms in fabric— waited for me at the field hospital. The surgeon and a complement of surgeon's mates and nurses occupied a sagging marquee tent on the far end of the camp. Theodor had studied proper layout of a military camp with his tutors, along with botany and ornithology and fine penmanship and dozens of other subjects far less useful at the moment. The placement of the medical corps away from the main body of camp would, he ascertained, limit the spread of disease.

The head surgeon was a stout man, shorter than me, with a barrel chest and thick, competent hands.

"Don't need more nurses," he barked as I ducked under the drooping door flap. He had a wooden chest open in front of him and inventoried the supplies inside. "Ration quota's full."

"I'm not a nurse," I said. "I won't need rations, either."

He looked up, still holding a bottle of some kind of cloudy tincture. "My apologies, you're the prince's—what exactly are you? Can't keep up on wedding gossip."

The honest lack of deference was refreshing. "I'm nobody," I replied. "My name is Sophie."

"Ha, Sophie Nobody—but your last name is either Balstrade or Westland and either has quite a bit of cachet around here."

"It's Balstrade. For now." I paused—who knew when I might formally marry Theodor? Not now, that was for certain.

"Don't really mind either way, they're both honest fellows." He shrugged. "I'm Hamish Oglethorpe."

"I'm sorry." I reacted to his comically awkward name before thinking, but to my relief Hamish burst out laughing.

"It's true, my parents were cruel old skunks. But why are you here, if not to apply for the nurses' corps?"

"No interest there," I said, "but if you've heard gossip at all, you probably know that I cast charms. For health, if it's needed."

"I'd heard that," he said, noncommittal. "I'd heard you were coming with wagons full of charmed gunpowder or some such, too, going to make this war an easy win. But here we are, ready to fight a battle, perhaps, the old-fashioned way." I thought for a moment he was serious, that he blamed me, but then he winked.

"Give me some credit—the uniforms are charmed. Not the gunpowder," I said with a faint laugh. "We weren't sure how that would turn out."

"Ah, might blast out of the guns and turn into roses, pepper the opposing forces with perfume, is that it?" He chuckled and put a few bottles back in his trunk, then pulled a few others out.

"One never does know," I said. "I can, however, with your permission, lay a health charm on—oh, the bandages would be best."

"My permission? You may be nobody, so you say, but you outrank me."

I hesitated. I had the authority of the men in command who had sent me, if nothing else. "No, this is your surgery. Your surgical theater," I amended.

He choked on a phlegmy laugh. "Ha! Like the fine university! Except mine is built of canvas that reeks of old cheese."

He wasn't wrong. "Do I have your permission?"

"You have it and more. My stock is there," he said, pointing to a stack of linen, and I put out of my mind thoughts of torn flesh and blood.

"Do you need anything in particular?" Hamish asked, but I was already pulling charm from the ether, smoothing it into the fibers of a bandage.

"Someone will have to roll these back up again," I murmured. "I'll do it when I'm finished." I fell into the quiet rhythm of charming, so much like sewing yet different, my materials not physical but ether itself. The gold thrummed in the fibers of the linen, the warp and weft infused with charm magic as I pressed it into the fabric.

Working took most of my concentration, so when I had finished I was not surprised to see that one regiment had marched on Hazelwhite—the First, the only regiment already completely outfitted in gray uniform coats. One of the nurses had rerolled all the bandages. "Now what?" I asked Hamish.

"Ah, that's the worst part of this job. We wait."

A thick purple dusk had fallen while I'd worked, tucking

shadows into every corner of Hamish's tent and rapidly dropping the temperature outside. A cool dew spread across the grass; it would be frost before long, I thought, and after that—after that, winter, and an army to feed on meager rations. I didn't harbor much hope that we would conclude this war quickly.

I turned back toward the house, not sure where to go, what use I might be. If fighting came here, perhaps I could weave a defensive net of charm over the troops, as I had done in the collapsing ballroom at Midwinter. Or perhaps—I swallowed. The curse magic flung at the Royalist navy cannon had produced death and destruction exponentially greater than what I had envisioned or, I thought, actually cast. The chain reaction of an exploding cannon on shipboard was, perhaps, a unique circumstance. Or perhaps not.

The cold dew seeped through the seams of my shoes. There was no going back now—if this camp was attacked, I would have to do what I could. And that would mean learning, as I experimented with life and death, what utilized my talents most efficiently.

It was a far cry from stitching charmed gowns in my atelier.

"If you've nowhere better to be," Hamish said, ducking under the doorway of his tent, "I've some port somewhere."

"Should you be drinking before—" I stopped myself.

"Before my kind of work, seems appropriate." His smile was grim. "But it's a cold night. A drop of something is sustaining."

He made it sound like health advice, so I accepted. He had a small table in the corner of the tent, set with a pair of battered pewter candlesticks and a green glass bottle shaped like an onion. He fished a pair of thick-stemmed glasses from his personal trunk and poured a few fingers of tawny port into each.

"I thought you said a drop!" I laughed.

"It's port, not whiskey," he countered. "Now you tell me— how do I expect these charms of yours to work?"

"They'll better a man's chances," I replied. "It's not fail-safe. Not a magic spell that heals someone or anything like that."

"Figured that would be too good to be true," he said. "So I do my usual butchering and your bit just...gives me a boost, is that it?"

"Exactly."

"You were a seamstress before, is that right?" He waved his half-empty glass. "A seamstress and, what have you, sorceress."

"Yes, I was a seamstress. And what have you."

"Quite the change to this. At least I'm still in my line of work—was a barber surgeon in Havensport." He had the look of a professional—he could have just as easily been my neighbor in Galitha City, the gruff but capable barber surgeon a street over from my old shop who could pull a tooth before the patient had finished opening his mouth. "You could probably learn to stitch wounds, you know."

"I thought you didn't need any more help." The port was warming my chest and settling my stomach.

"Ha! I hadn't considered your qualifications." He pressed his lips together. "I'm not a proud man. I'm not one of the noble's physicians, riding on a reputation. I hung out my shingle, I earned my pay. Never made enough to put on airs about it. If you think you can do anything else here, you're welcome to stay. I don't know your trade, but it seems it might be you can do more than work a little magic into bandages." He tapped his empty glass on the table. "And if you don't want to, I don't fault you. If there's a true battle out there, this place will be hell for a while."

I took a steadying sip of the port. I had seen the face of men's brutality imposed on other men in Galitha City twice already, at Midwinter and under Niko's command. It still wove a knot of nausea in my stomach, but if I could do anything to help, I had some obligation. "If I'm needed elsewhere, I'll have to go," I finally said.

"Fair enough. I wouldn't press your services on the wounded when those still fighting might need it more."

A tall blond surgeon's mate thrust his head through the door. "They're coming back," he said.

"What happened?" I asked. "Did we push them back, is Hazelwhite still ours? Were the horse—"

"I don't know anything but that we pushed them back." He hesitated. "It wasn't a large troop of horse, or infantry after them, and they pulled back without much resistance. As though they were testing us and found us a tougher fight than they anticipated."

"After the Serafan curse," I said. Hamish raised an eyebrow. "It makes sense. They were testing our strength, seeing if they could overpower us easily, after the curse."

"Didn't work," Hamish replied with a snort.

The wounded arrived shortly after, and I kept myself out of the way, pressed against mildewed canvas that leaked dew at the seams. Most of the wounded weren't bad off. Nurses and mates cleaned and bandaged wounds outside while the more serious injuries were brought in to Hamish.

Even those weren't what I had feared, at least not at first. Hamish stitched a slash wound from a saber while the poor First Regiment corporal averted his eyes and bit his lip. I pushed health charms into the thread Hamish used, the stitches themselves charmed to stave off infection. Then I wove a cloud of charm magic around him, calm and healing and a bright white light that I sensed was purest charm, and let it settle on him. Of course, I couldn't tell if it made any difference; I couldn't set a twin of the man next to him with an identical wound. Still, he seemed more hale than I would expect after seeing the glint of the curved needle the surgeon used.

I settled into my spot in the corner, unnoticed by the men brought in needing stiches and, for one swearing sergeant, a broken arm set. I laced golden charm magic around all of them; it wouldn't last, not long. Not as long as the bandages or the sinews stitching their wounds shut. Yet it seemed to help; the sergeant stopped cursing shortly after I settled the charm on him.

Then a loud commotion broke out from outside and a man, wan as death, was carried in on a stretcher. Hamish roughly helped the sergeant to his feet, pushing him outside to the care of the nurses in a neighboring tent. His operating table cleared, he directed the man to be set down.

I caught my breath. He had been shot in the abdomen, the wound seeping blood and his shifting body revealing things I was sure I wasn't supposed to be able to see. He was pale, nearly gray, and his eyes lacked focus. Yet I could tell, looking closer, that he was young. Probably sixteen, seventeen.

And he wore the silver-braid-trimmed blue uniform of a Royalist army officer.

"Well, then," Hamish murmured as he peeled layers of blood-soaked wool and linen away from the wound. The fibers had shredded and torn, and I wondered how much of the young officer's waistcoat and shirt Hamish had left inside him. The thought nearly made me gag, so I pushed my mind back into work, into the repetitive and nearly meditative motions of drawing charm magic and laying it around the wounded man.

Hamish didn't seem to treat the man any differently on account of which uniform he wore; he examined the wound, prodding it despite the man's strangled cries of pain, even bending down to sniff it.

"Too bad." He sighed, lowering his voice to near-gentle tones. I wasn't sure that the young man could even hear, let alone understand, the surgeon, but he spoke as though only to him. "There's no point digging round for the musket ball that caught you. If you'll be a good lad and take a dram, it will ease the pain."

Hamish gruffly ordered the mate nearest him to fetch a bottle—an oily-looking amber tincture. He considered a gill cup and poured out a larger glass instead, one of the port glasses filled not quite halfway. "Help with his head," he barked, and the mate obliged.

The young officer swallowed, coughing. "Now don't hack it back up again, it's rather dear stuff," Hamish said. "Haven't much time now before it kicks in—your name?"

"Elias Hardinghold," the young man murmured. I started— he was of the same family as Pauline, from Viola's salon. He wasn't just a Royalist officer; he was a son, a brother, or a cousin to someone I knew. A hollow ache opened in my chest, an awareness of someone else's pain I could hold at bay when the man was a stranger to me.

"And have you any affairs you'll need settled?"

My charm magic snuffed out, retracting as I recoiled. I had thought Hamish only waiting to treat the man, taking care of his pain before addressing the wound. No, he was a dead man, lying on the table in front of me.

"I'm yet a minor. Lately fostered by my aunt. Lady Rynne Hardinghold. Please inform her. Don't tell her—don't tell her..." His fingers trembled toward the gaping wound, and Hamish laid his hand on them.

"Of course I won't mention the unsavory details," Hamish replied. "You were wounded fighting in admirable fashion and died with little pain, how's that for a story? Ah, feeling tired now, then."

Hamish strode back toward the chest nearest me, digging for more bandages. "Why...?" I asked.

"Gut shot. Could smell the shit already—nothing to be done. That size dose of tincture of nightbloom spares him several hours of agony." He glanced at my drawn face. "Common enough practice, to let them die dreaming instead of howling."

I watched the young man's eyelids flutter, dipping into a placid sleep. I wove a thick blanket of pure gold and laid it gently over him.

19

MORNING BROKE ON A CELEBRATORY MOOD AROUND THE CAMP. An incursion of Royalist troops had been rebuffed from Hazelwhite, leaving the town Reformist territory. Sianh returned to the farmhouse kitchen after reviewing the morning inspection. "Casualties?" Theodor asked immediately, pouncing on him as he walked through the door.

"Very limited. Forty wounded, mostly minor. All but a couple will be back on service before the week is out."

"Then why do you look so grim?"

Sianh's jaw was set in a firm line. "It was a foray. As Sophie has suggested to me, probably testing our strength after the casting. They would have taken the town had we yielded easily, but they did not press us. Those men on parade, all puffed up like parrots?" He shook his head. "I am afraid they think that is all there is to this war. That it was easy."

"So now the Royalists, and we, know how long the casting lasts. Not very," Alba said, appearing with an earthenware cup of musty tea.

"And Sophie is right," Sianh said, "that they would require some kind of antidote if they were to try to occupy the same space while the casting was active."

"As far as we know, none exists." I had taken an inventory of which soldiers wore my charms and which hadn't during the attack. Though my charms had alleviated the worst symptoms and those wearing them recovered quickest, no one felt battle-ready during the casting itself. "That evens our odds significantly. As far as I know, they can't pinpoint their casting the way I can."

Alba finished her tea with a flourish. "Well! If that's the Serafans' great secret weapon, and it barely dented us, I think we're in fine shape. No need to grouse." She nudged Sianh with her foot. He glared back at her. "I could make you some coffee if you like, would that wipe that sour look off your face?"

Sianh had discovered a penchant for Galatine-roasted coffee. "I suppose," he conceded. "They will still use their casting, make no mistake. The Serafan military does not waste its resources, and casting remains a resource. They will recalculate."

Alba snorted. "You tried to make coffee with only a third of the water you needed yesterday morning. Don't tell me about impeccable Serafan calculations." She pulled the crane over the hearth toward her and hung a kettle of water. "Does anyone want tea? Or am I only making coffee for the Serafan bear?"

"Where did you find tea?" Theodor asked Alba. "I thought we were out."

"It's foxwort. Mint family. In the hedgerow outside. It's not very good," she added, sipping. "But it does help settle the stomach, which, after that Serafan stunt, was helpful."

I sniffed the foxwort tea—it smelled like mint left in a trunk of moldering linens for a very long time. "Coffee," I said. "If we're out of tea, how long will we even have coffee?" I wondered as she handed me a cup, chipped at the side but filled with richly scented brew.

"We didn't have much tea to begin with," Alba replied.

"Coffee, flour, salt pork and fish, dried peas and beans—we have an abundance of those. Not much sugar."

"You made quick work of memorizing the quartermaster's inventory." I smiled as she flushed—first she had herded supplies into Hazelwhite, and now she was shepherding them.

"What good am I here otherwise?" Alba replied. "I can't fight, I don't know tactics well enough to be of any use in planning, the good soldiers have no reason to trust a Kvys nun so I shan't hang about the surgery, and I hate laundry. So, I assigned myself to the quartermaster."

"What she does not say," Sianh said, "is that she improved his inventorying systems, suggested better storage methods for the fresh produce, had a root cellar dug, and reworked the ration rolls. All of that will prolong our stores by at least four months. I am less concerned about winter than I was."

Alba flushed. "I am only making myself useful."

"Sounds like you've done a good job of it," I said, sipping the coffee she'd handed me. It was quite good.

"We'll need more than foxwort tea and reorganized supplies," retorted Kristos. "We're stagnating here. We need to move forward." I knew what goaded him, perhaps more than anyone else in our cadre of leaders—the thought of siege on Galitha City, of our home under bombardment, the eventuality as uncertain as how much time we had to stop it.

"And so we will," Sianh said. "You have put out your pamphlet for elections. And we have seen a significant influx of volunteers from it."

"Elections, then, and boost their morale with a formal government, and then we move north," Theodor said. "I need to work more with the artillery officers on range calculations." He grimaced. "Wish them—and me—luck. Arithmetic was never my strong suit."

Sianh sent Fig to summon the artillery officers while Theodor set out books and charts in the long, sparse parlor that ran
along the other side of the hall from the kitchen. I noticed Sianh
didn't complain about Fig, his little mosquito, tagging along
with him any longer, though he did box his ears once for leaving
a map out in the dew.

"Your impatient brother is right. We'll be pushing north
sooner rather than later," Alba said. "I'm working to prepare our
supplies for that—we'll need to talk, rather seriously," she said to
Sianh, whose shoulders slumped. "But I wonder if there is any
preparation Sophie ought to undertake." I knew she was thinking
of the Royalist ship and my curse casting, and what effect it might
have in battle. I stiffened as she hesitated. "But how, precisely?"

I shook my head. "I certainly don't know enough about tactics to make any plans." I turned to Sianh, and saw Alba was
pressing him with a pointed look, as well.

"Not you, too." Sianh turned his back to the fire and audi-
bly sighed at the comfortable warmth. "I have had nothing but
nagging from your brother and your lover over tactics, tactics."

"That is in fact why you were hired," Alba said, plucking a
mug from the shelf and filling it with coffee.

"Yes, but it is impossible to plan a pitched battle without
knowing the Royalist troop strength, how they deploy their
cavalry, the placement of their cannons." He accepted the coffee
from Alba with a slight bow. She sniffed and rolled her eyes. Yet,
for all her disdain of the Serafan, I noticed that she had dosed
his coffee with a liberal spoonful of the sugar she knew was limited. "Much of tactics is reaction. And that—I can only teach so
much. Basic principles that must be applied, weighed against one
another, when the situation presents itself."

"And what," Alba pressed, "of adding magic to those tactics?"

Sianh sipped his coffee, carefully choosing his next words.

"The uniforms are charmed. I believe I have seen an improvement among those wearing them. You could employ additional charms, though, yes? Is it helpful to have more than one charm?"

"I don't know," I said. "It's not a science like chemistry, you can't pour two things in a glass and watch what happens every time."

"Is that what you think chemistry is?" Alba interjected. "We need to spend more time in the convent archives."

"Anything but that," I said. "But Sianh—what do we need? What could help us most, in a battle against the Royalists?"

Sianh sobered and set his coffee on the table. "Our liabilities on the field are significant. Our army will be undertrained and outnumbered when we come to a full-scale battle with the Royalists at Rock's Ford. Do you know what an undertrained army does in the face of a highly skilled professional fighting force?"

I shook my head, numbness creeping through my limbs.

"They forget what they have been taught. They fumble with their muskets, they load slowly, they panic under bayonet charges. They turn tail and run. Fear becomes their enemy before they even come to blows with the opposing forces. And even if they fight perfectly, under immaculate command from their green officers and their unseasoned noncoms, even if they do not flee or fumble, we will require luck beyond luck to defeat the Royalist army at Rock's Ford."

I sucked in my breath. I knew our position was tenuous, but no one had said so quite so bluntly.

"And then," Sianh continued, "we must march immediately on Galitha City, and push the Royalists there into a position of surrender, as, if they can utilize their navy to evacuate and muster elsewhere, we may well be chasing them for years."

I could tell from Sianh's tone what he thought of the chances of accomplishing this. Still, it gave me some direction. If our army needed to be bathed in good fortune, I could do that. I could conjure clouds of confidence around them to drive out fear, I could wash them in courage and surround them with luck. "That I can manage. I can cast a charm over our troops," I said. Alba slowly turned in front of the hearth, ostensibly warming her hands, but she listened.

"Much as the Serafans did, with music, when I served with them." Sianh considered this.

"Yes, but I can control it better than music. I settle it around them, nestle it into any willing fibers. It doesn't last long, but it's there. Your musicians could only follow so far before the casting would affect your enemy, too, yes?"

"This is true." He set his empty cup on the table with the finality of a judge's gavel. "And if you can control it that well, you could cast a curse over the Royalists, too. As the Serafans did. But only over the Royalists."

Alba turned and stared at me, waiting. The entirety of the Reformist army, it felt, seemed to be waiting, hanging on my decision.

"Yes," I said. "I believe I can."

20

THE MORNING OF THRESHING MARKET DAWNED COLD BUT BRIGHT, and I knew that the sun would burn through the thin frost on the ground quickly enough. Alba had quietly gone to the barn that housed the quartermaster's stores before dawn, and had apples and russet squash sorted and ready for distribution right after morning formation. The extra rations were small but offered a celebratory token for the holiday. I hovered behind her as the quartermaster's mate, a thin youth who had worked in his father's gristmill, doled out fruit and small gill cups of sugar with exacting precision.

Some of the men recognized me; even with only one man sent per mess to retrieve the extra ration, plenty knew who I was, and who the reedy nun next to me was, too. They whispered to one another, and for perhaps the first time in my life, the whispers didn't make me feel like the subject of threats or vile gossip but something closer to a celebrated figure, like Viola or Princess Annette had been.

"You ought to do the handing out, miss," the quartermaster's mate said shyly, motioning me toward a pile of apples.

"You've got it well in hand," I argued, but Alba shoved me forward.

"Do the smile and wave routine," she said. "They've little cause for confidence, but you're giving them some."

I awkwardly stood by the apples, a particularly round and red variety called Banshee, though I wasn't sure why it had earned such an imaginative name.

"Thanks, your ladyship," one corporal stammered, taking the six apples for him and his mess mates.

"I keep telling everyone, I'm not a ladyship," I said with a laugh.

"Yes, ma'am. Miss?" He blushed as red as the apples.

"Titles matter less than good, honest respect," I said. "And anyway, the time is past for *ladyships* and *your lords!*"

The line of men laughed, but I realized what I'd said. There was no treading backward on my ill-considered joke, even if it could and likely would be read and repeated as an endorsement of stripping Galitha of titled nobility entirely. What system of governance would follow this war? Would any threads of the nobility be salvaged? Were they, I thought doubtfully, even worth salvaging? The question hung over us like underripe fruit. The elections were set for the next day, with Threshing Market the final opportunity to join the army and gain a vote— or a position in the Council of Country.

I finished distributing apples, and by noon they were roasting merrily in the thick-walled camp kitchens dug from what had been a turnip field.

"I think that's gone rather well so far," Theodor said, joining me outside, watching the units joke and talk, almost like a large threshing party after a field had been cleared. A very large party, I considered with restrained confidence. More uniforms arrived from the seamstresses in Hazelwhite regularly, and I looked out over a scene populated nearly entirely by gray-and-red uniformed men.

Theodor set a case on the barrel next to him and I started with surprise. "Your violin!"

"Not mine," he replied. "Mine's somewhere in Galitha City still—probably matchsticks by now, poor lad." He pulled the violin from its case and I saw that it was different—older, scratched, and with replaced pegs in the neck of varying colors of wood. "I picked this up in Hazelwhite, a secondhand shop selling bits and bobs."

"You spent Reformist army money on a fiddle?" I asked with feigned horror.

"The shopkeep gave it to me—said he'd give the Rebel Prince and the Reformist army anything they asked for."

"And all you asked for was a violin." I laughed as he tuned the instrument.

"No, all he had of any use was a violin. And some shoes. I took him up on the offer for shoes." He struck up a lively tune— a harvest tune, I realized. One of the songs we danced to in taverns and in the square in Galitha City for Threshing Market.

Several of the men nearest us recognized the song, and began to clap and call to one another. A pair of women, camp followers married to soldiers, sat on the edge of the camp kitchen with their feet hanging into the narrow trench that ran around it. They jumped up and caught another three women carrying russet squash back to their kitchen.

Laughing, the five beckoned to a couple of messes of men, who happily joined them. With no dance caller but the formations well-memorized, they stepped into a simple country reel. I liked the easier dances common in the taverns at Threshing Market and at Galatine wedding parties, and I recalled the name of this one.

"Wedding Morning," I said. "They're dancing Wedding Morning."

"Now to see if I remember it well enough to play the right amount of time," Theodor said. He kept playing, and more lines of dancers formed in the parade ground.

Kristos and Sianh followed the commotion to the field. Sianh raised an eyebrow but smiled tacitly, and Kristos laughed out loud and caught my arm. "You know this one, Sophie!"

"I do, but Kristos—should we?" I glanced at Theodor and Sianh—was it improper for us to dance with the soldiers?

"Hang it all, who cares? They ought to see us having some fun once in a while, lest they decide we're a bunch of sour old barn owls."

Sianh shrugged his acquiescence, and I let Kristos drag me to a line just forming, short by one couple. Next to us, a corporal and his partner, a plump and red-cheeked farm girl in a faded gown of purple sprigged cotton, gaped at us until Kristos laughed at them and half shouted, "I promise we won't trod on your feet!"

"I promise no such thing," I added as I counted eight steps in a circle and then eight steps back. I had never been a graceful dancer, but the bright music and the dancers' inevitable mistakes made for a merry time in the taverns; it was no different here.

Theodor finished the reel and began another tune, also one of the harvest songs. "Sheaves' Return!" Kristos shouted, calling the name of a dance that moved in a circle, plucking first the women and then the men into the middle like sheaves of wheat. All around us, the dancers fell into step, forming circles that expanded and constricted with the music.

Suddenly a piercing whine cut through Theodor's fiddle playing. I dropped the hands of the women in the circle with me, our sheaves of wheat broken as I searched for the source of the sound.

"Sianh!" I called. His face bore the same fear—could this

be a Serafan casting trick? Some far-flung Royalist artillery? Around me, dances broke apart and Theodor finished a bar of music with an abrupt halt, leaving an eerie absence as the melody stopped, unfinished.

The whine intensified, droning as it took on multiple pitches, and was soon accompanied by hisses.

"It's the kitchens!" Theodor called, and several soldiers ran to investigate. My stomach clenched—could someone have sabotaged the kitchens with gunpowder, with fuses? Were there grenades hidden in the squash? That was absurd, I thought—but I couldn't convince myself anything was outside the realm of possibility. It could even be a Serafan curse, somehow.

The soldiers hesitated by the edges of the trenches, then steeled themselves and dropped inside. A moment later, one man shouted back.

"What did he say?" I asked Kristos.

"He said—it's the apples?" Kristos asked the corporal next to him.

"He said apples," the man replied with an incredulous shrug.

"Apples?" I shouted back to Sianh.

After a brief conference with the men who had investigated, Sianh joined us. He fought to keep a straight face. "The apples— that variety—they appear to have a very thick skin. Most apples will split when roasted, but these do not easily rupture. So the steam building inside eventually rents a spot near the stem and the result is not unlike a scream."

"Banshee!" I grabbed Sianh's arm. "They're called Banshee apples."

His lip quivered, and for a moment I thought he was angry, that he was going to blame someone for what now appeared to be less of a mistake and quite possibly a prank. Instead, he laughed.

He sat down hard on the ground, his legs bent under him,

and roared with laughter. Kristos began to laugh, and soon I bubbled over with laughter, too.

"Alba..." he managed to say between fits of laughter, "did you know?"

Her shocked face answered for us, and I wasn't sure if she was going to laugh or go box the quartermaster's ears for him. She blinked dumbly as Sianh began laughing again, so hard tears slid in bright trails from the outside of his eyes.

Then she began to laugh, too.

Theodor began his music again, and the dancing resumed. I caught Kristos's hand and squeezed it.

"The two of us haven't had this much fun in—it's been years, I think," Kristos said.

"It only took a war," I laughed ruefully. He was right. Even before he'd grown invested in the Laborers' League and become a leader of the Red Caps, I had pulled away from him, pouring myself into my business. I had told myself it was for us, and it was, at its heart, about security for my little family. It was about more, too—about my identity and my passions, and Kristos had never had an easy place there.

For all the time we had spent living in close quarters and relying on one another for our rent and our coal and our bread, we had grown distant. Here, with a common goal, we felt like family again.

"What's that little scamp up to?" Kristos said, raising an eyebrow as Fig came barreling toward us from the far side of the camp.

"I'm surprised he's not filching roasted apples," I said with a laugh, which I stifled before Fig joined us. He took his role as messenger and errand boy seriously, and I remembered feeling very important when I sold thread buttons on the street at his age.

"Spotted off the coast," Fig said, panting. "Fenian ship."

21

———❦———

KRISTOS GRINNED AS FIG TROTTED OFF TOWARD THE DANCING. "Excellent—it should be a shipment of cannon, not to mention powder and shot. Just the thing to celebrate Threshing Market."

"And linen," I reminded him. "Your army's shirts are getting a big ragged."

"They're supposed to be mending those. You want to give a lecture on sewing patches?"

I laughed. "I suppose many of them need it—they don't have their wives or their mothers here to mend their clothes any longer."

"It's one of the few military skills Sianh hasn't taught them," Kristos said. "You know that the regular army expects every man to carry a housewife." He winked—the term meant a small sewing kit, but I laughed as I envisioned a beleaguered soldier's wife riding piggyback.

"Want to go watch our ship come in?" I asked.

"Of course," Kristos said. The day was mild, and between the new arrival of troops and the impending arrival of supplies, I felt that we were bathed in luck as well as warm sunlight.

The squat Fenian cargo vessel was still far out to sea, outlined against blue sky paling against the horizon. "Remember waiting for Da's boat to come back? In the harbor?"

"No, because I was always helping our mother in the house while you ran off to watch the boats." I jabbed Kristos in the arm with a pang of long-buried loss. Our father had made a living fishing for someone else's profit on someone else's boat, and he had made his death out of it, too. One day a storm had churned the water dark and that little fishing boat didn't come back.

"I knew his boat—well, not his. Thatcher, the man's name was, who owned it?" I shook my head—I didn't remember, even though I'd been old enough to have known the name of my father's employer. "I knew it by sight, though. Even though it looked like most of the other old tubs in the harbor. It would come trundling up to dock and I'd see Da start unloading crates of fish."

"He smelled like it when he came home," I remembered. "Mama hated it."

"He kept a cake of soap in his bag," Kristos said. "He went to the well down the street every day before he came home and tried to wash up as best he could. He knew Mama hated it."

"I never knew." The Fenian ship drew closer, turning toward the inlet, and I was about to point out the Fenian flag I could see curling in the wind when Kristos tightened next to me.

"What's that?" He pointed to the south.

I squinted, the sun slanting into my line of sight. "A ship, isn't it?" My stomach sank. There was only one kind of ship patrolling the coast of Galitha—the Royalist navy.

"I thought so." Kristos looked at me, fear in his voice pleading for him regardless of which words he chose. "Can you do something?"

Farther up the cliff, drums rolled a sharp tattoo near the battery of artillery pieces. The sentries stationed there would be joined by artillerists, but the ship was too far out. We could prevent its landing here—Sianh had chosen a highly defensible position for our encampment—but we couldn't stop it from intercepting the Fenian ship.

I was already pulling light magic into my hands, weaving a net of protection and pushing it out, quickly, toward the Fenian ship. It spooled thin and loosely woven from my hands, but it was too late to worry about craftsmanship as I pushed it out over the sea. It glimmered over the nearest waves, but its tendrils began to unravel and curl over themselves.

"Is it working?" Kristos said.

I clenched my jaw, determined not to lose concentration. "If you think we can do anything, get back to camp and muster troops."

Kristos yelled toward the sentries, running toward them, but I ignored him, shut out the words and the fear in his voice, shut out the pounding of the waves below and the racket of a flock of blackbirds roosting in a nearby tree. I focused everything I had on the wavering net of magic, and pushed it farther toward the Fenian ship, building more magic behind it and sending it with greater and more fervent force.

It surged ahead, and, heartened, I pushed more protection and courage into the net. But it stalled again, my control over the farthest threads waning. They unraveled and spooled back into the ether, fading in a golden glow over the distant waves.

"It's too far," I whispered in dismay. I could control it over a field nearby, over a battalion of troops lined up a few hundred yards away, but not a mile out to sea.

I turned my attention instead to the Galatine ship. If I couldn't control charm magic over a distance, how could I expect to control curse magic any better? I thought quickly. I didn't need a net or a wall or embedded curse magic; I could throw a ball of black at the ship and see what happened. The

Galatine ship was maneuvering into position to fire a broad-side at the Fenian ship, who had little recourse built into her sparse decks.

I mustered a curse, black fortune glittering in my hands, lay-ered and thick into a projectile only I could see. I took a breath and sent the curse and my breath out in a steady, straight line, willing the curse to move in a rapid, sure course toward the Galatine ship. And it did, rolling in a ball through the air like a cannonball careening downhill. Faster and faster it moved, but as it did, it unraveled.

I pressed my will on it, to hold together, but as it moved out over the sea, it spent itself into a black cloud, fading to gray and eventually dissipating altogether. I stifled a yell and tried again, but this curse was weaker than the first.

The report of the Royalist navy cannons shook my concen-tration and I let the curse fade. The Fenian ship was already run-ning up pennants of surrender, fluttering pale. Anger welled in my chest. I was helpless again, as helpless as I had been when Pyord had me under his bidding during the Midwinter Revolt.

I hated it. I hated the Royalists and their cannons and their damned navy, but I hated even more standing on a cliff watch-ing it all unfold, clenched fists that might as well have been tied hands.

Theodor ran toward the cliffside as the Galatine ship approached the Fenian. "Damn it!" He joined me and exhaled another curse. "Damn it. There's nothing we can do." He looked to me. "Is there?"

I shook my head. "I tried. I tried both charm and curse and—they're too far. I can't do anything."

"Shit." He trembled, his hands barely controlled. "There's nothing we can do without a navy. All the work you and Alba did—all of it—at their mercy."

"We have supplies," I reminded him. "Plenty of them got through. We've cannon, shot. It's enough, for now—"

"No, it's not. It's not enough against the entire Royalist army, not if we're going to march north, not if we're going to break the siege on the city."

I shrank back into myself. I was useless. The only thing I had to offer I had tried, and it was too weak. All we could do was watch the Royalist marines board the Fenian ship and take possession of a sizable portion of our cannons, powder, and precious months of work.

22

"It wasn't the remainder of our supplies," Alba said with calm stoicism, tracing a slim finger through her logbook. "That shipment would have been—let's see—"

"We can't afford any losses!" Kristos thundered. "We needed a thrice-damned navy."

"Do not blame them for what we do not have," Sianh cautioned in a low growl. "I am as frustrated as you—"

"You don't look it!"

"You do not control your emotions well," Sianh countered. "Do not mistake that ability in others to be a lack of feeling."

Kristos clamped his mouth shut, seething.

"A goodly portion of the powder, unfortunately," Alba continued calmly, "but nothing on board that ship was charmed."

"Thank the Divine," I breathed. "If they've Serafans working with them, and captured charmed supplies, they'd know exactly what we've done."

"Best we assume they've guessed we're doing something already," Theodor cautioned. "But the charmed supplies are irreplaceable."

"And we've another two dozen cannon tubes coming," Alba

said. "And more linen and powder." She closed her logbook. "Well?"

"Well what?" Kristos snapped.

"How can we protect our investment?" Alba enunciated in frosty tones. "I cannot undo the lack of ships."

"It was your damn job to get us ships!" Kristos exploded.

"Perhaps if they landed elsewhere," I suggested. "Or...or if we stopped shipments for now?"

"None of that gets us a damn navy," Kristos said through tight lips.

"Enough," Alba said. She clutched the logbook as though it provided some sort of lifeline. "We can't produce a navy in the next five minutes."

"Sastra-set Alba is correct," Sianh said. "Nothing will be decided right now. And it is a holiday, yet, is it not?"

"The apples are all eaten already," I said with a rueful smile. "I'm sorry you didn't get any."

"Not all," Alba said. She pulled a crock from next to the fire. "I took the liberty of stewing a few with a mite of sugar and some nutmeg."

"Where did you get nutmeg?" I asked, incredulous. Our spice supply was worse than our sugar stores.

She pulled a case from her pocket and produced a whole nutmeg and a tiny silver grater. "It's for emergencies," she said. "I thought this counted." Theodor shook his head with a laugh, and even Kristos cracked a smile. "I should like," Alba added to Theodor, "to hear more of your violin."

Theodor's lips twitched into half a smile, but his eyes were still tired. "I don't know—"

"I would like it, too," I said, laying a hand on his knee. He softened and his smile broadened. As Alba doled out spoonfuls of apples in juices cooked to a thick spiced syrup, he retrieved his violin and tested out the strings.

A shuffle of sheet music lay in the bottom of the case. "This is your music from home," I said, thumbing through them.

"They were in my portmanteau. I carried them to Isildi by accident, and then they've come with me ever since."

"This is Marguerite's composition," I said. "The one she played before Midwinter, at Viola's—the one that sounds like a winter snowstorm."

"Play that," Alba said. "I should like to hear some snow; it would remind me of home." Sianh laughed, but he didn't tease her as he usually did.

Theodor set the bow to the strings and drew a few tentative notes. The song started distant, cold, and gentle, the quiet of winter settling over even the bustle of Galitha City. Nothing would quiet the city now, I imagined, not even snowfall. But for a few still moments, I let the winds pour from Theodor's violin and the driven snow scour the bloodstains from the streets, cover the scars and burns with pure white winter.

Then the drums punctured the cocoon of Theodor's music.

Sianh was on his feet in an instant. Afternoon had slipped toward evening, but the last thick sunlight still bathed the camp. A surge of pride buoyed me as I saw how quickly the men leapt to their feet, spiced apples and rum rations abandoned as they slung bayonet belts and cartridge boxes over uniform coats. I was surprised to feel tears swelling at the back of my throat— their shabby holiday, abandoned in an instant for their duty.

Theodor settled his violin back into its case and sighed as he closed it, then we followed the others to the parade field where men formed into units and those units into companies.

"He's sending the First," Theodor said, nodding toward

Sianh on a bright bay mare. She wasn't a warhorse, but she was the best mount in Hazelwhite, according to Sianh.

"That's good?" I asked. "Or that's bad?"

"It means he thinks it's quite serious," Theodor said. "They're the best trained."

"I should go, too," I said. "I should help."

Theodor gripped my arm. "We don't know where they'll be, how to keep you safe."

"None of us is safe if we're overrun by Royalists. Me least of all." I didn't shake off his grip, but turned to hold him even more firmly. "This is why I am here. If I am of no use besides charming bandages and sewing coats, send me back to Alba's convent."

Theodor inhaled. "Fine, go with the First. Not on foot. Fig!" He waved him over. "Fig, saddle the dappled gray for Sophie."

"The gray? For—oh." He nodded quickly and ran for the stable.

"You will keep well behind them," Theodor said. "Absolutely avoid—any kind of danger. Don't even be seen—"

"I know," I said. "I won't act a fool."

"And at the first sign of—if things aren't going well—if." Theodor's mouth clamped into a firm line. "You run."

"Of course," I said, annoyed. I knew, full well, my limitations. I turned to follow Fig.

"Wait." Theodor pulled me back, and for a moment I thought he would stop me from going. Instead he kissed me, rough and desperate. "I love you."

I held on to him for a moment longer, returning that kiss with equal fervor despite a crowd of gawking soldiers nearby. Then I ran for the stable, where Fig had a stablehand readying a placid-looking gray mare for me.

Sianh had already ridden out with the troops, and I had little chance of catching up to him with my poor seat and uncertain skill at higher speeds. Instead, I fell in behind the lines of marching men, keeping a safe distance but sure that, if we arrayed into lines of battle, I could weave a charm over our troops. And, I thought through the possibility clearly, if my view was good, cast a curse over the enemy.

I hadn't seen our men deployed on the field before. I wasn't sure what to expect—but if I had been worried about the panic or fear Sianh had warned me about, it wasn't evident here. At least, not yet. Their lines were orderly, their bearing military. Farm boys and dockworkers and fishermen, stoic and ready. Faintly, embedded into the very fibers of their coats, charm magic glowed protection for them.

I began to pull a charm, a simple and easy one, knowing that it would be more difficult to cast with the fray of battle and the troops moving in rapid order. The light built around me and I spread it like thick butter on warm bread over the marching columns, letting it sink into their coats and cling, tenuously. I held the charm, testing the concentration and energy required for its maintenance, pleased to find that it wasn't taxing at all to hold the cloud of light. I built it, added to its intensity slowly, and tested holding it again. It was easy, like keeping a kite aloft on a pleasantly breezy spring day.

We moved across a wide plain, and quite suddenly, the Royalist troops crested a hill like a sunrise. There were hundreds—no, I amended. There could be thousands of them.

I felt a collective breath, a moment of pause, and then Sianh began shouting, the drums beat the orders, and the ranks began to move—not forward but out into long lines of battle. My charm constricted as I reacted, but I swiftly regained control of it, and spread it over the ranks as they fell from columns into lines of battle. Before the men the farthest back had joined the formation, the first units to fall in had their muskets loaded and ready. Meanwhile, I urged the horse toward a copse of trees near a bend in the road and dismounted. I couldn't cast and control even a placid beast who might turn fretful when the gunfire started.

I tied the horse's reins to a tree, hands shaking, and moved a safe distance away in case she decided to try her luck kicking or bucking. Then I began to draw bright white from the ether, adding it into the cloud over the troops, spreading it diffuse and thin to cover all of them. It settled in a film on coat shoulders and hat brims. I didn't know if one section would advance first, how to gauge who would need it the most, so I tested sending some of it forward, pulling some back. I steeled myself for the report of the muskets, not wanting to break my concentration.

But the report never came. Sianh rode out in front of the lines, accompanied by a quartet of riflemen. Hastily, I looped charm magic around him, too, fearful that he might be in some danger. Instead, as I followed my line of light out alongside him, I saw something else—a party of Royalists, marching toward us, muskets upside down and pale kerchiefs tied to the locks of each.

Surrender.

I didn't allow my charm to fade, not yet, but I watched as a Royalist officer saluted Sianh, who returned the salute. They spoke a short time, Sianh's demeanor not changing in the slightest, but the Royalists visibly relaxing, even from my distance.

Then, in a flurry of orders and movement, our men secured their arms, split their ranks, and reformed their lines so that they could escort the Royalists back to the encampment. The Royalists marched past me, their muskets all upside down in the position I had heard Sianh call *clubbed* when drilling our troops. They weren't all of the same regiment, I noted with some surprise—their regimental coats were of the varying colors of the Galatine army, from the standard blue of the regulars, to the pale blue of the northern outpost infantrymen, to brown of the eastern artillerists to, in small numbers but still impressive, the dark rose of the elite riflemen.

Sianh brought up the rear, allowing the officers of the First to take charge of the front of the column. He noticed me struggling to mount the mare, and laughing, he joined me. "We have had a windfall and no doubt," he said. "And I do not think you even got a chance to cast much of a charm."

"You're right," I said. "So we made this bit of luck some other way. What exactly happened?"

"They are defecting," he said. "All out of Rock's Ford." He didn't say much, but his mouth twitched toward a real smile. He tossed a pamphlet at me.

"Did Kristos write this?" I asked. I hadn't read this one, and the language, though not directly aimed at the enemy troops, was pointedly martial and vaguely mutinous.

"Yes, and it has clearly been read by many." The pages were dog-eared and soft at the edges, the ink smudged and, in some places, almost indecipherable. "He wrote it intending for its distribution among the Royalist troops. It was not easy to smuggle copies into the Royalist camp at Rock's Ford, but the effort has, clearly, paid its dividends."

"I should say," I breathed, watching the column march on ahead. Another piece of paper fell from the pamphlet—the announcement of the election of a Council of Country at Threshing Market.

"Perhaps this pushed them over the edge," I said.

"It seems so, indeed. Do you need help with your mount?" Sianh asked kindly, returning the pamphlet to the interior pocket of his coat. I nodded.

"It seems," he continued as he boosted me into my awkward seat on the saddle, "that there has been much discussion and discontent among the ranks of the army. Even," he added, "among their officers. Fighting their own countrymen is distasteful, even to those who agree with the Royalists."

"Then maybe they're not such formidable adversaries?"

"All men will fight when faced with death on the field. Do not doubt that." He mounted his own horse beside me.

We rode behind a column of new Reformist soldiers in the varicolored uniform of Galitha.

23

IT TOOK MOST OF THE NIGHT TO GET THE INCOMING DESERTERS OF the Royalist army into some sort of order, and I felt as though I had only just fallen asleep against Theodor's chest when the morning's reveille reverberated through the thick panes of glass in our bedroom.

"Tell dawn to wait an hour," I mumbled into the rough linen bedsheets.

"Not today," Theodor said, clambering over me to pull his stockings on and comb his hair. "Today we elect a new government." He barely winced as his comb caught a snarl, and the time it took to button his waistcoat made him tap his foot with impatience.

I sat up in bed, raking fingers through tangled hair, and smiled. This was what I had hoped to see, as soon as we had settled on holding elections—optimism. Though the framework for the Council of Country had been a collaboration between Theodor and Kristos, Sianh organized the actual election in precise military clockwork, from the quartermaster distributing sheaves of paper to a ballot box under guard at all times. Theodor didn't bother to stop for porridge in the kitchen, but I couldn't resist the scent of freshly brewed coffee.

"Do you know," Alba said, pouring me a now-familiar

earthenware mug, "that coffee beans look just like deer droppings when you dump them outside on the path?"

I raised an eyebrow as Sianh glared at Alba from the doorway. "Uncommonly like deer droppings," he confirmed, scraping something off his boot that I quickly identified as used coffee
beans. "I will be having a conversation with *vimzalet* about appropriate refuse disposal."

"Don't be too hard on him," I said. "I doubt Niko taught
him any manners."

"Of that," Sianh said, "I am sure. I wonder what our
co-commandant would think of our elections?"

"Thought's crossed my mind," Kristos said, joining us long
enough to shovel some porridge into his mouth. "More salt next
time," he said through a mouthful.

I made a face. "Kristos has no manners, either." I nudged
Sianh, and we both laughed privately. "Whether Niko likes it or
not, he's not here. And most of the army is."

"A fair point." Kristos had a bit of porridge on his upper lip.
I didn't say anything. "I imagine he'd have different ideas about
who earned a vote."

"And our Royalist deserters would not make the list?" Alba
said, tone pleasant but a sharpness in her eyes.

"I doubt it. He said once that the only people who should
have a say are the ones who fought from the beginning—the
'real' Red Caps, he called them." Kristos shrugged. "Maybe he's
changed his mind. But we disagreed on that, that I saw the Red
Caps as serving the Galatine people and handing their liberty
over to them, not keeping control for themselves."

"That reads better in pamphlets, at any rate," Alba said,
earning a sour look from Kristos. "What! I'm in earnest."

Shouts echoed from the parade ground, where the ballot box
was stationed under all the pomp that Sianh's personally selected

guards could offer. "Am I surprised or am I not surprised that our first elections are starting with fisticuffs?" Alba mused as Sianh and Kristos both took off for the field.

"I hope that's all it is," I retorted, following my brother down the hill.

Theodor already stood before two men, held by guards from the First Regiment Commanders Corps. One had a split lip and the other a swelling eye that would be purple by sundown. Before Theodor could speak, the man with the bleeding lip wrested his arm free of his guard and yanked a scrap of red from his uniform pocket.

"You see this?" he shouted as he threw his cocked hat to the ground. The pale gray cockade that marked his membership in the Third Regiment tore free against a rock. He yanked the red fabric down over his ears. A red cap, like those I'd made for Kristos. Like hundreds—thousands—that had sprung up all over Galitha. "I'm a real Galatine. Been fighting since the start. So how come his vote counts same as mine?"

The other man straightened his shoulders. "I have as much right to be here as you."

The Red Cap snorted. "Son of a noble, hardly! Get some damn calluses first."

"I have more than my fair share after six years as an officer in the Fourth Royal Light Company." The man wore a poorly tailored red-and-gray uniform, devoid of rank. "I took a demotion to be here. You didn't need officers so I stood aside. But I have a vote."

"Who is your family?" Theodor asked quietly.

"Pommerly. Fourth son of Jerem Pommerly of Lark's Hill."

"I remember your father," Theodor said evenly. A small crowd gathered, keeping a respectful distance, but they could still hear everything said.

"What does that matter?" The first man crossed his arms in disgust. "But what do we expect from a prince?"

"You will show respect to your general, private," Kristos said, steel in his voice. He shared a brief glance with Theodor. "Galitha is a country of her people and will, by our victory in this war, be governed by her people. All her people."

"With permission, I would like to cast my ballot," Private Pommerly said.

Theodor nodded briskly. "Both of you will be allowed to cast your ballots. Then you'll both be sent up for court martial for fighting."

"I was only defending myself." Pommerly had the tactful control that noble governesses must have ingrained in him from toddlerhood.

"Save it for the court martial," Kristos answered sharply. "Our regulations are clear, and match the Galatine army for centuries before us—no fighting with fellow men-at-arms."

"I'm fighting for Galitha!" the Red Cap shouted. "Not for pricks like him, who would take it back from us inch by inch!"

"Then vote for representatives who will advocate for your interests!" Kristos shouted. "That's the point of all this. It's not just some charade—" He stopped, realizing how large the crowd had grown. Sianh stepped forward, ready to disperse them, but Kristos held up a hand. "You are deciding the fate of Galitha. Today. With these slips of paper. Just as much as you will decide her fate on the battlefield."

He turned on his heel and marched back up the hill. I followed, leaving Theodor to direct the guards where to take the Red Cap and the Pommerly. Who would have imagined, I thought ruefully, that the two would wear the same uniform at all? But I had another matter to consider.

"You never did anything about the women," I said, catching up to Kristos.

"About what?"

I sighed, heavy exasperation forced into a single exhale. "Votes. For the women here. If they're here, with the army, shouldn't they get to vote?"

He turned and threw his arms in the air. "Damn it, Sophie! What, you want a vote? Go vote, I don't care."

I felt like my brother had hit me. "I want everyone to have that consideration! What, that whole speech about Galitha being governed by her people—*all* her people—was that just for show?"

"What do you want me to do? Now is not the time to have that fight." He ran a hand through his hair, tugging at the thick waves in frustration. "I know what you're going to say, and I—I don't have a good answer. Damn it all, Sophie. If I'd known how much of gaining liberty is negotiating compromises and spending political capital, I would have stayed a dockworker."

"No, you wouldn't have." I sank down on the overgrown grass and pulled him down alongside me. "I know you better than that."

"Despite everything I've done, yes, you do." He sighed. "I promise I'll take it up. Women's rights. Once we have a country to exercise them in, I'll do what I can. You know it's going to go over like a cat in the dairy as well as I do, and I can't risk tearing this fragile army apart over it."

I didn't answer.

Theodor stood next to Sianh, deep in conversation. Next to me, Kristos let his head sink into his hands. "What's wrong?" I asked. "Isn't this—today, elections, an army of thousands ready to take Galitha—isn't this what you've been fighting for?"

"Look at the two of them." Kristos's voice was soft, wistful, even. "They're so much better at this than I am."

"Surely you're joking." I punched his arm. "You just gave an impromptu rousing political speech. Sianh could never do that."

"Theodor could. Theodor just—he walks into a room and

people shut up. It's that crown prince thing—not just the title, he embodies this natural, solid authority, and shit! He earned it, coming with us. They love him for it. And Sianh is a genius on the field. One of the raids I was on with him—Divine Natures, Sophie, he's so decisive. And brave. He rode into enemy lines like it was nothing."

"It was his job for years. He trained for this."

"But what am I? I can string words together and I've got some good ideas once in a while. But Sianh is our military leader and Theodor is our figurehead."

"Are you honestly worried you don't have a place here?"

Kristos gazed out over the field, units from the Fourth Regiment lining up to cast ballots electing their peers to the council. "Maybe I don't."

"You're an idiot." He started, surprised. "Sianh says we gained two thousand troops. Yesterday. Because of a pamphlet you wrote."

"Because they were promised a voice." He shook his head. "It's the draw of liberty, and that's not my doing. That's a natural right of man. It pulls him." He cocked a smile. "And her."

"See? I couldn't say that. It may be a natural right, but you put it to words. You make it clear, you make people see how they can have a part in it. That's not going away. I have a feeling..." I watched a few men in the Fourth shake hands as they deposited their ballots, grins spreading over their faces. "I have a feeling this is going to get much harder before we have a victory. You're going to have to keep reminding them of why they're here."

Kristos took my hand in his. "I hate to say it, but you're probably right."

At that moment, Fig crested the hill and nearly careened into us. "One of the sentries posted on the seaward lookouts," he panted, out of breath. "He spotted Serafan vessels. Sailing this way."

24

I sent Fig for Theodor and Sianh, and Kristos and I joined Alba already gazing out over the cliffs to the deep blue water below. The sun pierced the choppy waters and reflected in almost painful, dazzling light, but Alba had sighted the ships easily.

"There are three of them," she said, "proper military vessels, or I miss my guess."

"Guns?" Kristos asked.

"They appear to be fully equipped," she replied, handing him her spyglass. "But ask Sianh, I've no good gauge on naval weaponry."

Sianh confirmed what Alba had guessed as soon as he arrived, snatching the glass from Kristos. "Serafan *an-thentai.* Exact translation is sea falcons, but they are the rough equivalent of your frigates." He passed the glass to Theodor. "If they are being used as troop transport, they may be intending an incursion here. Our artillery will barrage and likely prevent landing. We will also assemble infantry to prevent their movement up the shoreline road if any are able to land."

"I may be able to do something. If they're close." My mouth pinched. If they were close, and only if they were close, could

I effect any change in their fortune. And if they were close, we were in danger.

The three ships grew nearer, aided by the swift winds bearing the bracing scent of salt. Their imposing rows of guns leered at the coastline from open ports. "They're not close enough yet," I said. The First Regiment assembled and marched toward the steep cliff road at a quick rate.

"At least they already voted," I joked weakly.

Sianh nodded. "That will not do much good if these vessels are only the beginning of a larger invasion here."

"Ever the optimist, Sianh." Theodor's voice was strained. "None of our intelligence suggests that the Serafans have committed to a full military alliance with the Royalists. Just tacit support."

"That appears to be more than tacit support," Sianh retorted.

"And they did send martial magicians," I added. The ships grew closer. I began to pull dark curse magic. I could try for a ball of bad luck on their guns, laying destructive will on them as I had the Royalist ship on the way from Fen. It was the best idea I had; layering bad luck on the vessels would be difficult as they were still so far out.

I didn't like how comfortable it felt even as I readied a fistful of curse magic.

"Wait." Sianh squinted. "Those are not Royalist flags."

I looked down at the ships, but didn't see any flags I recognized at all. No Serafan banners, no Fenian commercial markings. But run high was a simple flag of red and gray stripes.

"Those are our colors," I said, holding the darkness steady but not loosing it. Not yet. "Not our flag, but—"

"But intentionally those colors." Sianh shook his head. "Have we a navy we did not know about?"

"I—I don't know." Theodor shook his head. "They're not Royalist or Serafan."

"Unless this is a very nasty ruse," Sianh said. "Unbecoming of the Serafan Navy, but I would not put it past your Royalists to engage in such tactics."

"Only one way to find out," Theodor said. "Sophie, you should stay here. Just in case."

"No, I should come with you. Just in case." The ships drew closer to the bay below. "The closer I am, the more effective I am."

He hesitated. "Sianh?"

"Wherever she is most effective. If this is a ruse, we will have very little time to react and our troops will be bottlenecked at the cliff road. Which is why I am going to remain here to direct the artillery and reinforcements." He pressed his lips into a thin line, and I knew that there were a dozen scenarios unspooling behind his focused eyes.

"Good enough. We'll go greet these—shall we optimistically call them a delegation?" Theodor said with a strained smile that Sianh didn't return.

We moved quickly down the cliff road, its winding, slow descent particularly frustrating at this moment. I scuffed my boot on a rock and sent a loose torrent of gravel down the side of the cliff face.

"Easy," said Theodor. "They'll have to lower boats, and row them to shore, and that takes some time."

"You're assuming that they—whoever they are—are here for something nice, not Royalist marines worming their way past our artillery cover to pitch grenades through our defenses or some such."

"You have the loveliest imagination," Theodor said.

"Don't tell me you didn't consider it, too."

"Of course I did. Not the grenades, I don't believe that the marines employ grenadiers," he added with a grin.

My breath pulsed against my stays, my lungs burning. If I

was going to march north with the army, I chided myself, I was going to need to be in better condition.

We reached the bottom of the cliff road where it opened into a sandy harbor beach. Rows of red-and-gray clad soldiers lined the bottom of the road and the bay, making an impressive show of force with their muskets ready and bayonet hilts glinting in their belts. Already the ships had anchored in the bay and were preparing to lower boats.

"That's a good sign," I said, cautiously. "If they intended to fire on us, they wouldn't be anchoring, would they?"

"Doubtful," Theodor agreed. "I'll get the opinion of the men down here—maybe you should find a place to cast from... just in case." He strode toward a nearby officer, a captain of the First Regiment, and conversed with him in low tones.

The bay was wide and open, and the beach offered very little cover. Still, I spotted a rocky outcropping behind a company of the First where I could comfortably slip out of sight—and out of the way—if need be. I squinted at the boats, each outfitted with rows of oars manned by sailors. No uniforms, I ascertained, even on the man in the bow of one longboat, standing with hand on the hilt of a sword and, I guessed, either the captain of the ship or an officer of the landing party.

I looked harder, and my eyes widened. "Theodor!" I called, ducking out from my half-hidden spot and dashing toward him.

He turned, panicked, and I slowed my pace. "Don't worry, it's good news!"

The longboat scraped ashore as Theodor joined me. "Is that—no."

"It is!" the officer called, and made a nimble hop into the shallow water, wading the last few steps to us, then drew Theodor into an exuberant embrace.

Annette. In a simple gray coat and with a dainty rapier slung over her chest, her dark hair clubbed and her cheeks ruddy with the sun.

"And you! Sophie! I'm so glad—I wasn't sure if you had made it here." She flung her arms around me, and I stood half-dumbfounded.

"But how?" I finally managed to ask. "How are you—with a boat—is that yours?" I asked, pointing to the sword.

Annette laughed, and the last of the tension holding the First Regiment behind us melted. "Yes, it's mine. It's a Serafan blade—pretty little thing, isn't it? A captain of a ship needs a sword."

"Captain of a ship!" Theodor exclaimed.

"Admiral of a fleet, if you prefer," she said. "I'm given to understand you're in need of a navy."

"Desperately," Theodor said. "But how is it you've come by one?"

"Oh, it's a long story and involves too much time talking about bank transfers." She turned back toward the boats. "So might we repair to your headquarters—I presume you at least have a marquee with a chair or two? I've someone on board who won't wait another minute to get to the main encampment."

"Viola?" Theodor guessed.

"Afraid not. She's managing the finances out of a counting-house in Pellia—a navy uses so much money, you know. No, someone to see Kristos."

The last longboat landed and a woman clambered over the side. "Penny!" I cried, and ran to her. She grinned and caught my arms, jumping up and down like a little girl who had just sighted the table of desserts at a wedding. She turned and I gasped.

She was pregnant, her apron hiked high over a burgeoning belly.

I clasped her hands as she grinned. I bit back my first

thought—that she shouldn't be here, that it wasn't safe. "Does Kristos know?" I asked. "If he knew I was going to be an aunt and didn't tell me I'll slap his ears back!"

"No, he didn't know. It felt so impersonal to write it and I wanted to come anyway—we agreed I would, once he was settled—and it took longer than I'd expected. I look like a barrel, don't I?"

"You look lovely," I answered. "And he'll be so delighted," I said, even though I couldn't be sure. The dangers here were real, and he might not be pleased at risking even more with Penny and a baby in tow.

"Back to camp, then," Theodor said, taking in Penny and her unspoken news in one long glance. "Annette has some explaining to do, and it seems Kristos has some news, as well."

25

SIANH GREETED US AT THE TOP OF THE CLIFF ROAD AND, UPON
seeing Penny, sent a runner for Kristos immediately. Not to be
deterred, Penny dashed ahead as soon as she saw him, unmistakable with his mess of dark waves even in his Reformist uniform.
I held back, keeping Theodor and Annette on either side of me,
as the two met behind the camp kitchens.

Kristos stood stock-still when he saw her, and I could see
him blinking stupidly even from fifty yards away, and I almost
cried when a slow smile spread over his face and he lifted Penny
into the air with a whoop. She laughed brightly, the sound cas-
cading over the camp, and they hurried away to the relative privacy of Kristos's room in the farmhouse.

"I don't suppose she ought to stay here," I mused.

"Wives travel with the regular army," Theodor said with
a shrug. "And wives mean children, too. Ever increasing children." He laughed.

"It is not unusual in the Serafan army, either," Sianh said.
"It is doubtful she has anywhere better to go, at any rate, though
Kristos is already as distractible as a young colt." He raised an
eyebrow. "At the same time, Penny may be a good influence on
him. She always was, before, in Isildi."

I considered this—I had known both well, but I hadn't known them together. "They got on well, then? I always worried, with Kristos's stubbornness and Penny's temper—"

"You are thinking of them as brother and employee. They know one another's faults well, and they tolerated them. But more, Kristos never wanted to disappoint Penny. He would leave a lively debate and concede it as a loss if he had planned to make her dinner."

"And to think, I couldn't get him to keep his dirty laundry away from the kitchen table at home," I said.

"People show different faces to their lovers than their sisters," Sianh reminded me. "I am sure you would be appreciative if Theodor did not compare notes with Kristos about your habits."

"Too late," Theodor joked. "It's a shame, too, because Kristos swears she darned his stockings, but she never offered to repair mine."

"Oh, you had a bevy of servants to attend to that," I said.

"How times change. Shall we have tea, Annette?" Theodor said, turning to the admiral of our fleet, who had watched our exchange with brightly smiling eyes.

Annette laughed. "Very proper, Theo. Will we take tea in the powder magazine or on the artillery emplacements today?"

"I suggest the kitchen. It's quite cozy."

"Very well," she sighed with mock disappointment.

Alba already had the kettle boiling when we packed into the kitchen, gathering around the hearth and holding our damp soles up to the heat radiating from the coals. "So I am given to understand we have a navy," Sianh said once we had settled onto the rough benches and stools.

"At your disposal," Annette said. "I'd sent several letters—a bit coded, though I knew Theo would catch onto the references. I assume none arrived, from your utter and complete surprise?"

"No word from you or Viola," Theodor said, passing Annette a small pitcher of milk. "Though I wasn't surprised by that. The Royalist navy is intercepting anything coming toward Galatine ports."

"Which is why I didn't say anything outright in those letters." Annette dosed her tea with milk. "We should have realized when you first came to us the...gravity of the whole situation," she said. "And for that blind spot, I'm sorry. I think—Viola and I didn't believe that your father would side with the nobility to the extent he did. We thought he'd return order to the city, and quell the violence. We expected a return to safety."

"There is no safety without change any longer," Theodor said quietly. "I didn't realize it for a long time, either, Annette."

Annette shook her head, her rose lips pulled into taut chagrin. "No, you saw it sooner than most of us."

I cleared my throat. "If Kristos were here, he would remind you that the common people have been quite aware of it for some time."

"We believed in the Reform Bill," Theodor said.

"And it was worth believing in," Annette said. "I...I underestimated many of the nobility. Or, rather, I overestimated them." She sipped her tea and gave Alba an approving nod. "But when the reports began coming in, that Pommerly and Merhaven had taken control of government—there was no denying it any longer. And we began to try to decide what we could do."

"And you decided...navy?" Theodor asked, eyebrow raised.

"We decided to try to get money to you, first off. But that's when we realized what trouble you were in."

"You may wish to be more specific on that point," Sianh said with a grin. "We are in all sorts of trouble here."

"Getting anything to a landlocked army from overseas when

they have no navy! We thought to buy powder and shot, but then we heard the Royalists were boarding and requisitioning anything bound for you. Landing supplies anywhere was going to be a logistical nightmare, least of all Galitha City, which we understand is completely blockaded."

"It is," I said. "They're holding for now, but at some point..."

Annette gestured with her mug of tea, agreeing with me. "We thought to simply transfer money, but. Well."

Theodor nodded. "Yes, the nobility unfortunately had a good handle on the banks, didn't they?"

"So we decided, since most of what we wanted to do was thwarted for want of a navy, that we ought to build a navy." I imagined Viola and Annette, discussing the pragmatics of founding a wartime navy in their genteel white garden, wearing their silk wrappers, hair still dressed from some evening's entertainment. Strangely, it suited them perfectly.

Annette continued after a draught of tea. "We finally got what money we could claim as ours out of the Galatine banks. And not just us." She grinned. "You have more friends in the nobility than you may realize. They're in hiding, some of them, but we collected donations from the Mountbank family, the Clareglens, the Rock River Cherryvales, so many others—even a few Pommerly offshoots.

"That's why Viola is in Pellia—we found an exchange there that would accept the money in our names. That's another story entirely, and you should consider banking reform at some point in your next council session," Annette said with a wry smile. "It still wasn't nearly enough, especially as the Serafans were not going to be willing to sell us naval vessels on any kind of open market, knowing where we intended to deploy them."

"The Serafan black market is quite expensive," Sianh agreed.

Alba burst out laughing. "'Quite expensive'? As though

you were talking about the price of button mushrooms at the market!"

"At any rate," Annette continued, "I wasn't sure what to do. And then I heard from—well he isn't really an old friend. Do you recall Prince Oban?"

"That intrepidly dull East Serafan you were supposed to marry?" Theodor said. "Of course."

"He sold me fifteen ships, at what must have been a loss. Fully outfitted with cannon, and rigging and sails so new you can smell the hemp."

"Why would he do that? Still madly and hopelessly in love?"

Annette snorted, somehow dainty. "It probably comes as no surprise that the East Serafans are less than thrilled with the West Serafans' involvement in the Galatine Civil War." She passed her mug to Alba for a refill. "Oh, yes, you have an official name abroad now. The Galatine Civil War."

"It's not very creative," Alba said.

"It will have to do," Annette replied. "As for Oban. The East Serafans don't have the money or influence of the West Serafans, and rely quite heavily on Galatine grain exports. War means more uncertainty and fewer rewards for them. But they're rather dragged into the whole thing by virtue of being neighbors. Oban saw a way to make some money to lay aside for the inevitable increase in grain prices, and some insurance in case we happen to win. Won't we be grateful?" She inclined her head with a conspiratorial smile.

"Makes sense," Theodor said. "Though I can't help but worry that they're ready to spring leaks at any moment or that the cannons aren't sound, if it was such a bargain."

Annette rolled her eyes. "I know more about ships than you do. If Ballantine is here, maybe he can settle any argument about their quality." Theodor's face went ashen.

"Ballantine was captured by the Royalists," I said quietly. "We presume he's been executed, as we haven't heard anything from or about him."

"Oh no," breathed Annette. Tears sprang into her blue eyes. "Theo, I—I'm so sorry."

Theodor swallowed, forcing back the thick pain I knew rode with him all the time. "I am, too."

"Damn. I had so hoped—he would have made a far better admiral than I."

"You seem, my lady," said Sianh, "to make a fine sea captain. But is it not unusual for a lady to do so? Or do I presume Galatine custom too similar to our own?"

"You presume nothing incorrect," Annette replied. "We've recruited along the southern coast, and they've been accommodating to the, shall we say, inconsistencies of this armada. Serafan vessels with all of their quirks, a former princess assuming the role of admiral. With all of *her* quirks," she added. "But I had hopes of giving this all off to someone with better expertise than I have."

"It seems it's on you, at least for now," Theodor said, "but what I want to know is, now that we have a navy, what best to do with it?"

"Protect our ports, of course," Alba said. "We've supplies incoming. We can't afford to lose any more to the Royalists."

"A prudent course of action," Sianh said, but he looked unconvinced.

"What are you thinking?" Theodor asked.

"I am considering," said Sianh slowly, analyzing the idea even as he spoke, "the methods by which a navy can grow itself."

26

"What do you mean, 'a navy can grow itself'?" Kristos asked even as Sianh and Annette exchanged a conspiratorial glance. "I figured you'd just—patrol the coast or whatnot."

Annette drummed her thin fingers on the table. A pink garnet ring on her right hand caught the light and winked at me. "There is no point in patrolling unless you're going to do something about anyone you happen to come across. Tomcats patrol their territory to tear the ears off any feline intruders. Ships?"

"Ships patrol to chase off incursions or to take prizes," Sianh interjected.

"Exactly," Annette said.

"We are undersupplied. Still." The kitchen went quiet at Sianh's simple statement, the only sound the muffled pops of the settling coals in the hearth. "If we are to succeed in taking first Rock's Ford and then Galitha City, we are in need of more powder and shot. Particularly for the cannons."

Theodor sighed. "I know. But we can procure more from Fen, now that we have some lines of finance coming through, with Viola managing the funds in Pellia. It will take time to run the money through and send messages, but—"

"We do not have time," Sianh said through gritted teeth.

"Beyond that." Alba's voice was quiet but cut through the argument instantly. "The factories and foundries of Fen are... shall we say, understaffed at the moment?"

"What's that supposed to mean?" Annette leaned back in her chair, her narrow shoulders in her perfectly tailored coat nestled into the high back.

"The workers," I said. "They're in a proper revolt now?"

Alba nodded, then dug a creased letter out of her pocket. "Just received this from Erdwin Tyse. He's offering to sell another load of powder, along with some bayonets and muskets, at exorbitant prices—but recommends we take the deal given as he foresees difficulty in any manufacture in the near future." She paused, waiting for the rest of the group to follow. "The workers are striking."

"That can't go on forever," Theodor said.

"No," Alba agreed, "but it can go on a good long time— long enough that your war will be over and lost for want of powder and shot. Besides, do you realize how volatile the production and storage of black powder is?"

"I've a good guess," Kristos said.

"So you can understand how difficult it would be to prosecute anyone for arson in such facilities." Alba's mouth twitched into a smile. "Funny, but all three large manufacturers experienced 'accidents' just before the workers went on strike."

"Then if we want more supplies," Theodor said slowly, "we are going to have to capture them."

"And one excellent method," Annette said, "is to take ships."

Sianh smiled. "There we are. And. We could use a larger navy. How does one grow a navy?" He was enjoying this almost too much, I thought as he waited. "One cannot plant a longboat and harvest frigates. There are three options. One may build ships. One may buy ships. Or one must take ships as prizes."

"I think we've only got one option open to us right now," Annette said. "What money we still have in the coffers won't cover much in terms of buying ships, but it can buy that powder from this—Tyse fellow."

"Oh, I'm not sure I advise that," Alba said. "Personal assessment of his character and motivations," she replied to Annette's raised eyebrow. "I don't believe he'd lie about the state of Fen, but I do think he'd gouge us for every penny he can. I would advise, instead, keeping a good reserve of funds."

"Very well," Annette said. "My fleet will leave a small contingent here to patrol near your waters, and the rest will go out on the hunt to see what we can see."

The first task to tackle with the small but intrepid navy Annette had supplied us was to set protection spells over it, as I had planned to do with the ships we had intended to buy from the Fenian shipyards. Annette was willing to help, although curious and cautious, as though approaching a strange animal for the first time. I resisted reminding her that there was nothing to be afraid of—after all, she had been willing to wear charms I had made at Midwinter.

"I'm not sure," she said as we walked to the cliff to overlook her miniature fleet of three ships, "of the best way to go about this. You'll have to tell me."

"What do you think these ships need most?" I asked. "Protection, luck, strength?"

"Protection, certainly. Good luck, yes. Can you make them impervious to cannon shot?" She was still wearing her men's coat and a pair of petticoat breeches, but her impish grin was just as I remembered it from Viola's salon.

"Afraid not. Though—do you anticipate that the Royalists will fire on you to sink you or to tear up your rigging and disable you for boarding?"

"Look at you, learning naval strategy like a wee cabin boy on his first cruise!" Annette laughed. "We have cannon and powder and shot, and those are worth taking, not to mention the ships themselves. But these are not Fenian ships ferrying supplies—the ships themselves are our assets. I wouldn't put it past the Royalists to want to simply sink them. They've a large navy—they would use our ships, if they could capture them easily. But I doubt they'll take any risk to do so."

"Then it would be best if the hulls as well as the sails were charmed." I assessed the three ships at anchor with a thin sigh. Embedding charm in wood was harder than in cloth, and the expanse of dark, weather-hardened wood stared back at me, daunting.

But I had to. "It will be easier if I'm closer," I said.

"Want to come aboard? I'll give you the grand tour."

Within the hour we had returned by longboat to the largest of the three ships, a Serafan frigate with lower, sleeker lines than a Galatine ship. "Ever climb up the side?" Annette asked. "It's a regular riot."

"Afraid I haven't," I said, staring at the rope ladder with trepidation. When we were children, Kristos used to climb trees, and drainpipes, and stacks of barrels, and anything else our working-class quarter could offer up for adventure. I preferred to stay on solid ground.

"Don't fret, we'll stay in the longboat as they pull her up. I'm not very steady on the ropes, myself." But I saw her glance at the ladder, once more, and I had a feeling Annette's lithe, nimble figure had found itself quite at home climbing among ropes and rigging. As she offered me her arm to clamber out of the longboat onto the deck, I felt the taut sinews of new muscles under her coat.

"Now. Should we get you a chair, or something to drink, or anything?"

"No, I'll have to move about the ship." I mapped its features, its construction and materials as I planned how to most efficiently lay a charm. I considered asking if there were specific places she was most vulnerable, if there were weaknesses or liabilities inherent in her design. But I knew that, in the end, I needed to cast over her entirety.

So I started with the bow and moved forward, weaving a tight net of protection and luck, nestling it over the seasoned wood of the ship's hull, and driving it into the grain. The wood resisted; it was sturdy oak to begin with, and then hardened from years of service in the water and sun and wind. I pressed, slowly, carefully, determined to write good fortune over each inch clearly and completely. No shoddy, half-completed charm from me, not with so much on the line.

It took well over an hour to complete the first ship, the sails and rigging taking the charm more easily than her hull, and I refused Annette's suggestion of joining her for tea in her cabin before moving on to the other two ships. She watched me warily. "What?" I half snapped.

"No one said we needed to finish today," she said. "And there's still the rest of the fleet, to the south."

"I'm doing a thorough job," I replied wearily. Annette couldn't even see the golden grid embedded in her ship; I didn't want to try to defend my diligence to someone who couldn't see the proof herself.

"That's not really what I meant," she said. "Go on ahead to the next ship, then. I've some ledgers to balance here."

By the end of the second ship, I was wishing I had accepted Annette's offer of tea. The sun was warm for autumn, I reasoned, and it had been a long time since that morning's meal of hot cooked oats. I pressed on to the third ship, using the short trip in the longboat to clear my head. I closed my eyes and was surprised when a strong arm yanked me back from sleep.

"You were 'bout to fall in the drink," the oarsman nearest me said. I flushed and abandoned the idea of a rest. My legs shook as I stepped onto the last ship, but I had pressed through work before; deadlines in the shop and of course the cursed shawl had demanded my full concentration and effort. It was time to dig into those reserves now, I resolved, and began to cast.

The threads of light I pulled wavered, strangely brittle under my manipulation. Before I could begin to weave it into a cross-hatched net, several threads snapped, springing back like Theodor's violin strings when they broke. I pulled at them, but the more I tugged, the tenser and thinner they became, until more of the threads snapped and recoiled.

I expelled frustration through my nose in a terse sigh, and tried again, but my knees threatened to buckle and my vision seemed, suddenly, two-dimensional and flat. I blinked, hard, and pulled at the light one more time.

Instead of light magic, blackness washed over me, and I felt myself falling.

27

I woke to a pounding headache and the kind of nausea that churns an empty and very hungry stomach. I struggled up on my elbows, surprised by the faint scent of damp canvas and a creaking cot beneath me.

I was in Hamish's field surgery. I pushed a coarse wool blanket aside and would have stood up if the bayonet of a headache lancing through my eye hadn't roared to life. Instead I sank back with a sigh.

I didn't need anyone to tell me what had happened. I knew—I had worked too hard, for too long. I hadn't tested my body's ability to keep pace with my casting capabilities, not like this. On Fen the work had been controlled, slow, and with malleable materials. The hard grain of the ships' hulls fought my casting, and the speed with which I had tried to cast had been too much.

I stared at the stained gray canvas ceiling above me, frustration building. If this had been too much, what use was I? I had produced the charmed uniforms, but I was beginning to feel, painfully, the limits of my casting. I always knew it wasn't a panacea, that it wasn't all-powerful fairy-tale sorcery. But I had allowed myself to forget, briefly.

And if I couldn't help by casting, what could I do? I was a

minor celebrity, or perhaps more accurate, an oddity, but not a figurehead like Theodor. I wasn't a visionary like Kristos, and I wasn't a military expert like Sianh. I certainly wasn't a leader like Niko.

"You ready for some tea?" Hamish shuffled into the tent. "Maybe a biscuit? I can get Lara to toast some of that brown bread on the brazier for you if you're keen."

"No," I said, pushing myself back onto my elbows, ignoring the roaring protest in my head. "I should get back."

"To the ship?" He snorted. "Not likely."

"To my own room, then," I argued. "I should free the bed for someone who truly requires it."

"A lugheaded tar rat carried you in here, with the former princess in tow, saying you dropped like a stone on their deck. No warning, no symptoms beforehand. Now what am I supposed to think, that you don't 'truly require' my expertise?"

"I don't," I snapped. "I know exactly what's wrong."

He didn't rise to the bait, didn't demand an explanation of my self-diagnosis. "And knowing exactly what's wrong means you're feeling better? All right, trot on up to the house, then."

I set my jaw and swung my legs over the side, but the headache flared like fat poured on flame, and I nearly heaved.

"Ah. So you're not feeling too chipper. Perhaps if you told me what ails you, I'd have something for it."

I swallowed hard on both bile and pride. "My head. It's as though there's a spike running from the back of my neck through my eye."

"Rather like a migraine or occipital inflammation," he muttered. "Either way, it's got your stomach in knots, too?" I nodded. "Then ginger tea for the stomach." He shouted something to one of the nurses outside—I assumed about the ginger tea. "And my headache balm."

"Balm?" I asked, unconvinced. The Pellian women I knew chewed catmint for headaches, and Galatines swore by a bitter powder some of the apothecaries sold.

"It's never failed," Hamish boasted. "And besides, worst it can do is make you smell pretty." He produced a tin of what looked like hair pomade from his chest.

He offered the open tin. "Just rub it on your neck and forehead. I'll be back shortly with that ginger tea." He paused, and added, "And toast. I'd like some toast, anyway."

I rubbed doubtful circles of the balm, which I had to admit did smell like a kitchen herb garden, into the knot at the back of my neck where the headache seemed to originate. Useless, I breathed in each exhale. I'm useless.

The tent flap opened, but instead of Hamish with the tea and toast, Kristos poked his head inside. "You're all right," he said in greeting.

"Of course I am," I replied, cross. "Annette overreacted."

"I have a feeling," Kristos said, crossing the tent with two strides of his long legs, "that the woman who commands our fleet isn't the type to overreact. You collapsed."

"I—" I intended to say something noncommittal, something vague about overwork. Instead, I half sobbed, "I'm of such little use here. I can't even cast effective protection charms."

Kristos pursed his lips. "You can't, huh? Well thank every corner of sweet hell, because now I can ditch this uniform. No, no, I don't look good in gray, and if the charm that's supposed to be woven in here is useless, why…" He cocked his head at me with a chiding look that he must have inherited directly from our mother.

"No, those charms are good. You know that, don't be an ass."

"I'm being an ass?" He snorted. "You make charmed uniforms for an entire damned army, then question your usefulness, and I'm being an ass?"

"I meant now," I whispered. "Maybe my part in this is done."

"You can still charm our ships. Just take your time?" he suggested.

I nodded, still miserable. "And when that's done?"

"You thought you could directly cast during engagements," he reminded me.

I sighed. "I don't know. It's difficult, maintaining direct casting, and I don't know—I don't know if I can do it long enough."

"Anything is better than not," Kristos asserted confidently. "Besides, you don't have to maintain curses, do you?"

My stomach sank. "That depends. But I also can't cast from a long way away. I'm afraid by the time we were close enough, my help would come too late."

"We'll find a way—"

"We might not," I retorted. "It's not witches with cauldrons and sorcerers with magic wands. There are limits, more than you realize."

Kristos fell silent, and I wallowed in the misery of knowing he knew I was right. My magic might not be the turning point he had hoped for. It might not even level the field with the Royalists and their Serafan allies. With more time, with years of development and research in the Serafan archive and the library of Alba's house, with an army of casters, perhaps, but I was alone.

"There's limits to everything," Kristos finally said. "But mark me, if we can do anything to help you work within these particular limits, you tell me."

I nodded. The only worth I had here was the light and dark I controlled; I owed everyone the full reach of what I could do. "Sometimes I wonder," I said softly, "that what frightened me the most about your protests and pamphlets, back before the revolt, was that I would end up useless."

"What?" Kristos said, brows constricting. "How do you mean?"

"I had a life with some purpose," I said, trying to pick the right words, "a vocation. I was learning how to use that vocation to the best of my ability, to help others. In a small way, maybe. And you admit, *you* needed me." I smiled wanly.

Kristos laughed ruefully. "I did. You kept food on the table and a roof over my head. I probably should have admitted a long time ago that I would have been living in a gutter if it hadn't been for you. And your shop," he added.

"All the changes you wanted—they could have meant the end of that vocation. And you wouldn't need me anymore." I stared at my hands, the calluses and the dirt under the nails.

"Ah, Sophie," he sighed. "I thought I didn't, maybe, before the revolt. But I do. You're the other side of me. My balance. My friend." He reached awkwardly for my hand, and I let him take it. "There's no apology sufficient for what I did. But I didn't realize I hadn't apologized for this—for not acknowledging how much I needed you then, and how much I still need you."

At that moment, Hamish stomped back into the tent with a tin mug of tea and a hunk of toasted brown bread. "Any better?"

I stopped, surprised. The headache was still there, but dimmed, quieter, no longer the rage of pain it had been. My stomach had settled. "I am," I said.

Hamish winked at Kristos. "That balm. Never failed yet."

28

"I WISH I COULD SEE WHAT YOU DID TO MY SHIPS," ANNETTE SAID several days later as we watched Sianh take the Third Regiment through their paces. I had finished the third ship, slowly, still disappointed in my plodding work. I had to add this to something I couldn't do on the fly—though sails and riggings could get a quick protective cast, ships' hulls, fortifications, and buildings would take much more time and effort.

Instead, I was practicing adding pointed charms to the men of the Third Regiment, spread across the parade field as they practiced open order movements. I could land a charm on an individual man, settling the magic into his coat or even his cocked hat. It wasn't well-anchored in the fibers, and so it didn't last long—Annette had her pocket watch out as I timed the unsustained boosts of charm—but I reckoned that it could be an additional dose of protection during the urgency of battle. Or, I acknowledged, a rapid system of deploying curses.

"Charm magic? It looks like sunlight on dust motes," I said. "Or candlelight reflected into a mirror. But on your ship, it looks rather like I swaddled the hulls in very loose cheesecloth made of light," I said.

"I can't even imagine," Annette said. "How fares the—charm?—that you're doing now?"

"Yes, it's a charm. Wouldn't want to curse our own fellows, would I?" I laughed. I could make conversation and cast, I could walk around and change position—which was good to know in the face of potential battlefield use. But the charm was far from permanent.

I pushed at the limits and I found them. Resolute and stubborn, waiting for me.

Annette watched them walk through the motions of firing in open ranks, the rank behind moving up like clockwork to outpace the front rank. "They seem to have learned the motions well enough," she said with approval. "Will they stand up to the battlefield, I wonder? In terms of their perseverance?"

"That's what I'm here for," I reminded her. "Some insurance on their moral fortitude."

She turned back to watching them, silent. "Dust on the road," she said. I followed her gaze to a small cloud on the road to Hazelwhite—a single rider, I discerned.

I allowed the charm to falter and fade. "I wonder who?" He was in a hurry, riding at full gallop, and didn't wear our uniform. Without a word, Annette and I half ran back to the stone farmhouse.

We arrived only seconds before the rider, a diminutive man on a dappled horse flecking foam. Or not a man at all, I realized, but a lad still on boyhood's side of adolescence.

"Jeremy!" Theodor pushed past the rest of us and half embraced, half hauled his brother from the horse. "What in the name of the Galatine Divine are you doing here?"

"I ran away," he asserted immediately. "Father has another think coming if he expects me and Gregory to commission in his army of Royalist whores."

I bit back a laugh at his salty language—the lad looked thirteen, but I knew he was nearing sixteen. He and his brother were at the military school in Rock's Ford, and sure enough, they were both set to commission into the army within the year.

"Call me an ass, Jer, but I didn't know your sympathies lay with us." He glanced at me, worried.

"I wrote enough letters," he said. "When I didn't get any in return, I figured something was happening to prevent them getting to you, or your responses getting to me."

"Never got a single letter," Theodor confirmed.

"And then Greg overheard our geography professor talking to our mathematics tutor about our early graduation—we didn't intend to graduate early. Father was going to put us in for commission to take charge of units on the eastern border."

"Putting you out of harm's way," Theodor said. "Which makes some sense, Jer, don't fault him too much for—"

"Could give us the choice! Over half our class is talking about refusing commission. There's been meetings, we share the pamphlets—is that Kristos Balstrade?" he asked suddenly, hushed, pointing.

This time I did laugh as Kristos flushed and gave the king's son half a wave. Kristos, a celebrity among schoolboys—it wasn't so absurd, rationally, that the predominant writer of the Red Cap movement and then of the Reformist army would be widely known, but he was my brother, not some folk hero.

Except, I allowed, he was.

"Refusing commission would be a grave choice," Theodor said.

"They can't make us sit through political theory and ethics and philosophy courses and then ask us to ignore everything we learned in favor of perpetuating an unjust war," Jeremy retorted, as though giving a recitation on a thesis in one of his classes.

"I could have written that," Kristos said with a lopsided grin. "And you're right. When can we expect this crop of cadets to arrive?"

"That's just the thing. They won't let us leave. Rock's Ford is practically locked down, a base of operations in the south. We're on house arrest at the school, for all intents and purposes."

"I don't want to know how you got out," Theodor said, holding up a hand. "If I ever end up in the same room with Mother, I don't want any complicity in whatever cockamamie scheme you and Gregory came up with—you did pull this off together, I assume."

Jeremy just grinned, but his smile quickly faded. "There are troops mustering in Rock's Ford now. They're ready to move south and, as they say, end this thing. Before winter."

Theodor sobered. "Very well. You and Sianh and Kristos and I are going to sit down and go over everything—everything— you know about the Royalist army in Rock's Ford. And then we make plans to move north and take Rock's Ford before they can move south on us."

29

—〰—

SIANH TRACED THE ROUTE ON A SPLOTCHED AND SCARRED MAP. Ink stained his calloused fingertips, and he smudged a bit near Rock's Ford on the map, where his index finger came to rest. The officers of all the Reformist regiments listened, intent on our next plans. Which of them would march north, which would stay here. Where we would move next. What we would do if we failed.

"They've left themselves open here, from this southwesterly direction." Sianh's thumb and little finger straddled the map to indicate two points on either side of Rock's Ford.

"Left themselves open?" Kristos asked, brow tightening.

"I should clarify. They've not left themselves open. There is a weak point we can probably exploit. If young master Jeremy is correct."

"Young master Jeremy had better never hear you call him that," Theodor joked. "How are we going to move past the fortifications at Falcon's Crest—here?"

"It is my estimation that a small force holds Falcon's Crest given the most recent reports." I backed away from the map as Sianh began to lay specific plans, troop numbers, ration arrangements, marching orders. The officers waited to hear more details. My breath shook; after months of preparation—flying, hurried, uncertain preparation—we were finally at the brink of action.

"We will move overland by that route," Sianh concluded. "Meanwhile, Annette will continue with the plans we already made to intercept and capture Royalist ships. We will rendezvous near the mouth of the Rock River to claim what supplies she may have earned us."

"My thought exactly," Annette agreed.

"And—quite sorry for your luck, Kristos, but in your case, you will have to prepare for staying put and holding Hazelwhite." Sianh inclined his head with an apologetic nod.

Kristos grinned. "At least I won't be all alone—Sophie's staying, right?"

I didn't answer right away. Instead, I followed Annette's fingers tracing the map, and met her eyes. "I don't think so," I said. "I might be of some use on board ship."

"A word," Theodor said through terse lips, "privately?" I acquiesced, sharing a conspiratorial smile with Annette as I left the kitchen.

"Absolutely not," Theodor said when we reached our small bedchamber. I opened the window. The last of the summer's marjoram and rosemary scented the air, punctuating odors of moldering straw and woodsmoke.

"They can probably hear us if you insist on talking that loudly," I said, nonchalant. "In case you wanted any actual privacy."

He glowered at me but lowered his voice. "What are you thinking? If I could stop Annette from taking this kind of risk I would, but given that she's the only thing we've got going for a naval commandant, I suppose I can't."

"You suppose?" I arched an eyebrow. "She's not dainty

Princess Annette any longer. Like it or not, she never really was dainty Princess Annette—that clever, strong woman has been there all along. For that, she ought to have your gratitude."

"Fine, my little cousin is now fighting in the topsails. I can almost wrap my head around it." He sighed. "But, Sophie, the risks of sending you, too?"

"The risks? I'm well aware of the risks. I'm aware of the risks of losing this war, too."

"And you think your presence on one ship is going to change the course of the war?"

I bristled. "No, I don't. But it might help, just a little. It might mean the difference between taking supplies and missing a chance. It might mean the difference between escaping with a bit of damage and being sunk. It might mean the difference between one small victory and part of a great loss."

"But we'll need you moving northward." There was pleading in Theodor's voice, a lost boy in a man's body.

"We'll rejoin you before you try to take Rock's Ford," I said. "But in skirmishes, in forays before that—I'd be in the way very quickly and quite useless, to boot."

"What about the wounded?" Theodor asked. "You've been able to help them. There will be more, you know."

"I'm well aware," I said, more sharply than I had intended. The suffering in Hamish's surgery—I didn't want to think of it repeated, multiplied. "I'll charm more supplies. If I can't be in two places at once, that's the next best thing."

"Damn it, Sophie!" Below us, chairs scraped the stone floor as officers rose to leave. Indistinct conversations drifted up the stairs. Theodor lowered his voice. "I don't want logic right now. I want to find some way to protect you—and Annette, and everyone else."

"You can't!" I drew closer to him, trying to be gentle but

fighting an overwhelming urge to shove him. "It's as though you still think that's your job, your duty as a noble, to protect all of us somehow. It's not any longer."

He steadied himself with a long inhale. "Even if it isn't my duty as a noble, I would do anything I could to keep you from harm. To keep any of my family, any of my friends, from harm."

"I know." I reached for his hand, but he didn't want to give it.

"But I can't anymore. I don't just mean this war—I mean after. Everything I relied on to help those I loved—it's probably going to be gone, isn't it? Nobility, if it survives, won't mean what it did before. I can't rely on the clout of my name."

"No," I said, measuring my words carefully, "it isn't the same. We'll all have to adapt." I slid in front of him, forcing him to meet my eyes. "This is adapting."

"It hurts," he said with a humorless smile. "This adapting business, it means watching you risk yourself for me. And I don't like that."

"No one says you have to like it." I slumped, leaning against him. "But I think this is just the beginning of what's going to change."

"You're most certainly right." He reached out tentatively and stroked my hair. I didn't like this feeling of distance between us, more painful in a way than when the ocean had separated us weeks before.

"Not everything will change." I pulled his hands closer, around me, asking him, begging him to envelop me.

"You'll still love me, even if I'm a landless, titleless nobody?"

I pulled back, shocked. "You loved me even though I'm a common seamstress and always have been."

"Yes, but—I was someone else, before. I was First Duke of Westland."

"And that almost stopped me from even speaking with you."
I shook my head. "I was never interested in your title or your
money."

"It's gone now, anyway. Or will be."

"Rock's Ford." It dawned on me, slowly, what was at the
root of Theodor's sudden insecurity. "Marching on Rock's Ford
doesn't mean only a pitched battle against the Royalists. It means
going home."

Theodor averted his eyes and stared at the bright blue sky
outside the open window. "It hasn't been home since I was a
child. I spent more time in Galitha City than Rock's Ford for
years."

"And yet." I waited.

"And yet it makes it all real, somehow." He turned toward
me. "This is my family," he said, voice breaking. "This is my
father. We're both willing to turn our home into a battlefield
over this. I have to give the order to fire on the house I grew up
in, if need be. I have to give the order to fire on my cousins, my
neighbors, my father." His voice caught on the words and he let
his head sink slowly into his hands.

"You're a very brave person to sacrifice all of that for what
you believe in."

"That isn't how I'll be remembered if we lose. That isn't
how my father and most of my family see me now. I'm a traitor
and a monster. I'm a stain on my noble name and an embarrassment to my title."

"You are no such thing, and you never have been. Do I have
to tell you why I was interested in you to begin with?" I asked,
voice low and thick with memory. "It was your inquisitiveness,
your gentleness, your humor. Your passion. The fact that you
could talk about Kvys lichen for hours, that you were earnestly
entranced by the process of Equatorial nut germination." This

drew a smile out of him. "It had nothing to do with names and titles, that's for damn sure. Frankly, all the money, the formality, the excess—that part always made me uncomfortable."

"You like this better?" Theodor gestured around our spare, damp room. As if to prove a point, a gust of wind rattled the bubbly panes of glass in the drafty windows.

"In a way. Here, we're—well, we're as close as we've ever been to equals. And we're working together, as peers. And we're—well, we might be risking an untimely death, but I can see my future with you more clearly than ever before."

Theodor looked up, pain creasing the corners of his eyes. "I don't know what I see when I look beyond tomorrow, beyond the next battle. I don't know who I'm going to be anymore. I need to know." He gripped my hands tightly in his. "What do you see?"

"In terms of titles and politics?" I leaned against him again. "I have no idea. But I see us standing together, our hands dirty with work, whether it's farming a field or planting rose balsam in the greenhouse. I see us laughing with our friends over dinner, whether it's in a cottage like this or a grand hall. I see us—" My breath caught, but I realized with a start that I meant it as I continued, "I see us raising children."

"That is a beautiful future," he murmured. I thought I saw the soft glint of tears in his eyes, but I wasn't sure as he pulled me closer. "I can understand why you'd risk everything for it. I would, too."

He buried his hands in my hair and drew me into the warmth of a deep kiss. I succumbed to the quiet comfort of his embrace, pulling his weight onto me, marveling at the thickening sinews of his arms, the roughness that a day without a shave had brought to his face. So much had changed, but we were changing together so that it was familiar, comfortable.

I drew my legs onto our bed, raising a haze of dust from the moldering straw, and the last of the day's sunlight pierced it, radiating through the motes in a cloud of sparkle. Like a charm, I thought as Theodor's kisses intensified and his lips pressed my neck, my collarbone, the half-ticklish spot beneath my ear. I raised my body toward his, the invitation he had waited for. The dust motes swirled around us like golden magic.

30

"Isn't she grand?" Annette twirled like a girl in a ballgown as her flagship sailed from the safety of Hazelwhite harbor. "She's the prettiest of the ships."

"You chose your flagship for looks alone?" I laughed.

"Hardly!" Annette ran a hand over the weathered wood of the railing. "She's the swiftest, too, because she's so pretty." She saw my confusion. "She's built well. Her lines are just perfection. And she cuts through the water like a porpoise." She grinned. "But she's also lovely to look at. That's why I rechristened her the *Nightingale*."

"What now?"

"Why, we patrol," Annette said with an impish smile.

Annette's plan was simple enough—in groups of three ships, our small navy sailed in separate directions, each assigned to a grid on the map. Each pod of porpoises, as Annette dubbed them, would be judicious in which ships they would approach, and were charged to outrun or evade any they thought themselves incapable of taking successfully, with minimal damage.

And minimal damage was what we needed—not only to our own ships, but to the prizes we captured. If we could take even a few large Galatine vessels, our firepower at sea would increase substantially, and we had a far better chance at pinioning the Royalist navy into the Galitha City harbor when we took the city.

On our fourth morning at sea, Annette called me to the deck. She pointed to a smudge of gray on the horizon.

"I want her," Annette said, handing me the spyglass. "She's a perfect little man-o'-war."

"I will never get used to the gender of naval terms," I said, peering at the ship through the spyglass. The Royalist man-o'-war was larger than any of the individual ships in our pod, but like a pack of wolves approaching prey, we could work in tandem to take her.

"And what do you need?" Annette snapped the spyglass shut.

"A place out of the way." I wasn't quite sure what, exactly, I would do once we engaged. The tactic I had discovered by accident on the Fenian ship might not be the best one to employ here—a chain reaction that ended with sinking our prize wasn't what we hoped for.

"Then find it. Once we begin moving, we move quickly." The refined princess was still apparent in the crispness of her movements, the precision of her commands, and her unflinching authority. But she was a confident captain, and watching her transform from my friend Annette to a formidable commander was nothing short of awe inspiring.

I hauled myself onto a raised part of the deck. At the stern, our signalman relayed Annette's orders to the other two ships in our pod. The *Nightingale* moved ahead in position, sails unfurled and straining in the wind. Annette was right—the ship did slice through the waves like a sleek little porpoise.

The next few minutes were all confusion for me, though Annette shouted orders in a clear, calm voice and the sailors on board carried them out swiftly. We seemed to close the distance between the Royalist ship and ours in the space of a few breaths, though I knew it took longer.

The *Nightingale* was already charmed, burgeoning with protection spells, as were the others in our pod, which left one clear avenue I could pursue—cursing the Royalist ship. I scanned her, not knowing how to spot inherent weaknesses in a particular ship despite Annette's tutelage. But I knew one weakness Annette would surely exploit, and that I could weaken further— the rigging and sails. Without maneuverability, the ship couldn't turn and outrun us.

I began threading dark magic out of the ether, weaving it into a messy net of black fibers visible only to me. We were close enough, I thought, to try to cast the curse onto the ship's sails. I forced the net toward the ship, and it stayed under my control as it slipped over the waves, as though borne on the same wind that filled our sails. My breath hitched in excitement—the black net hovered over the Royalist ship, farther away than any charm or curse I had managed to maintain.

I was getting better, I thought grimly as I pressed the curse into the canvas and ropes. I pulled more dark glinting curse and strengthened the spell, working rapidly as we closed the distance. It grew easier to manipulate the magic as we grew closer to the ship, but I knew that also meant my time was almost up.

As if on cue, the *Nightingale*'s guns opened on the Royalist ship, the reports echoing across the water as the first shots tore through the rigging. I blinked—either the gunner's calculations were impeccable, or the dark sparkle in the Royalist rigging had drawn the chain shot from our guns the same way the big magnet I kept on the worktable in my shop pulled at pins.

That damage done, I scanned the ship for my next move. Her gunports were still closed—I had a mad idea, and threw dark layers of curse across the ports themselves, gritting my teeth as I forced them into the wood. I didn't dare curse the guns themselves—not like I had while on board the Fenian ship—but what if a good number of cannons couldn't be employed because the ports wouldn't open?

Moments later, the Royalist ship's cannons showed their charcoal-dark maws. A few ports jammed, but I was swiftly reminded that my abilities weren't storybook magic. I couldn't close a door with a wink of my eye and a magic word. What next? I pulled more curse magic into a loosely woven mat. The nearness and sheer quantity of it was beginning to foul my mouth with bile and tease a headache at my temples, like it had long months before, working in curse magic for the first time. I forced myself to continue.

I laid the mat of magic on the side of the Royalist ship, holding it firm against the resistant wood. Not below the surface—I wanted any shots to wreak havoc on the decks and, I admitted, wound sailors and marines, not sink the ship with shots below the waterline. The ship had a sea osprey carved into her bow—I wondered, briefly, if that was her name. The *Nightingale* against a fearsome raptor—I didn't like those odds. I would have to weigh them in our favor. I pressed the magic against the sea-hardened oak of the ship's hull. The oak fought back like a living thing, stubborn and strong.

Even when I had time at my disposal instead of the life and death unfolding before me, working curses into wood was difficult. I pressed on the upper part of the hull again, feeling its strength rebelling against me, and revised my tactic. I sensed, beneath the magic, the grain of the wood, straight and true but stable. I didn't understand wood as I did fabric; that was my trouble. But as I felt it, sensed it, I discovered something— that though it lacked the openness of fabric's weave, it had a set pattern within the grain. It wasn't as easy as burrowing a charm into sailcloth, but sliding the curse into the grain of the wood worked better than pressing it.

I slid lines of dark curse into the grain of the hull, haphazard and resolutely unscientific. As I pulled back and looked at my work, it looked very much like the time Kristos had spilled ink on our kitchen table, the black winnowing its way into each point of weakness in the grain, spreading in unpredictable veins. Now all I could do was hope that the curse magic in the hull would draw the shot as deftly as the rigging had.

Almost without warning, we turned like a dancer in a reel and loosed a broadside on our foe. Annette had them aiming high, as I had assumed, for damage and death, not for breaching the hull and sinking her. The shots raked across the deck, and I turned away as I saw the wreckage wrought in an instant, a tangle of shattered wood and foot-long splinters and flesh and blood.

Within moments, it seemed, Annette was ordering the boarding party to ready, and the other two ships in our pod flanked the Royalist vessel. She had pennants of surrender out before the boarding party could even assemble on her decks, and I thought I saw a bit of disappointment in the faces of some of our newest marine recruits, though the older men were visibly relieved.

One older tar leaned against my platform as the negotiations began between Annette and the dour Royalist captain. "The *Sea Hawk*," he said, jabbing his thumb toward the name, painted in swirling scarlet on the captain's personal banner. "And to think I've sailed on a *Lioness* and a *Spearhead* but beat a *Sea Hawk* with a *Nightingale*." He grinned, showing me a few missing teeth.

I smiled back. "You don't mind that you didn't get to see much action?"

"A battle won without sweat or blood is still a battle won." He shrugged. "Just saves the blood for another time, eh?" He squinted. "You have something to do with that?"

"Maybe," I hedged.

He grunted and turned his attention back toward the ships' captains. The crux of the negotiation came down to whether the sailors and officers of the *Sea Hawk* would be free to go or be taken prisoner. Annette forged ahead with terms taking all of them prisoner, but I knew she would retreat to only holding the Royalist officers.

With the captain and his lieutenants secured in our brig, and the *Sea Hawk* outfitted with a complement of our own sailors and marines to ensure the loyalty of its temporary crew, we continued our patrol up the coast.

31

THE *SEA HAWK* YIELDED CRATES OF POWDER, BOTH MUSKET AND cannon shot, and an impressive stockpile of hard biscuit and dried beef, as well as a fine complement of Equatorial rums and the captain's private stash of Galatine vintages. After that, however, we didn't have any more luck intercepting other Royalist vessels before it was time to return to shore and meet with the north-bound army.

"Still a successful foray," Annette said as we watched the sun set over the hazy shore of Galitha's coastline. "And who knows—the other porpoises might have caught even more fish."

"What next, then?" I wondered out loud.

"I've got the coordinates of where Sianh expects us to meet up with them."

"Yes, I figured that," I said. "What about you?"

"Shore up and prepare for the naval side of the Battle of Galitha City," Annette said. "I'm hopeful we won't have long to wait." She shifted her weight and spread the tails of her pale blue coat behind her. It was nearly the same color as the court gown my shop had made her for the Midwinter Ball nearly a year ago. It suited her better than the structured gown, though I did, privately, think that it could use a bit of the same silver trim.

"Once we've won the Battle of Galitha City?" I asked, tentatively adding, "Will you be going back to Port Triumph?"

Annette's confidence faltered. "I don't know. When we bought the villa, we never expected that West Serafe would ally with the Royalists—we didn't even think there was going to be a war like this at all." She sighed, her delicate shoulders ratcheting toward her ears. "So it may well be that we won't be able to return at all. Especially not after this."

"And Viola?"

"Is understandably upset about that." Annette's smile was lopsided. "Galatine Divine, but I miss her. She would hate this," she added with a laugh.

"Which part?"

"The sailing, that's never been her favorite. All this lovely sun and salt spray would ruin her paints." Annette smiled ruefully. "And she certainly didn't want a war, and wouldn't want to be in the midst of one."

"Do any of us?"

"Well, of course not, but some of us seem to have taken to it better than others." She raised an eyebrow. "Your skills have certainly developed."

"What was it that Theodor said about desert plants and Taiga lichens—botanists think that they developed certain traits in response to environmental pressure." I drummed my fingers on the deck.

"Your Kvys friend would say they were perfectly created for the environment in which they grow," Annette said. "And I don't know which of those is true of you, but you fit here. Strangely and impossibly, but you're very badly needed."

"I hope it's enough. Can something be inadequate and too much, all at once?" I sighed. "I'm afraid, Annette. I can't take back what I've done, what everyone will know is possible."

"None of us can go back," Annette replied. "I can't go back to being Former Princess Annette, most desirable spinster in Galitha, not after commanding a ship and wearing breeches and causing all sorts of scandal. Galatine Divine, I can't go back to my family—wherever they are." She exhaled thinly through her nose, and I saw the pain that estrangement and uncertainty leveled at her.

"But you don't want to go back to being Former Princess Annette." I pressed my lips together. "For everything, I'm not sure who I'm going forward into being." I shook my head, trying to clear the intrusion of memories, of golden afternoons in the public gardens with Theodor and chilly mornings lighting the stove in my shop, of picnics at horse races with my brother and long talks over strong coffee with my Pellian friends. I couldn't go back, and the memories themselves began to feel like places on a map that were impossible to reach. Annette reached for my hand, and let me sit in the silence that I needed.

"Even if we win," I said, "what does life look like after a civil war?"

"Sweet hell, none of us know that!" Annette drew her knees toward her chest. "I know I'll be in it with Viola, and that helps a bit. And you lot, too, of course."

"Will we?" There was a fear, deep and bitter and usually buried, but I gave voice to it now. "What if—there are Red Caps whose hatred of the nobility runs deep. The institution, the people themselves. What if winning means..."

"Some sort of culling? Well, that's an unpleasant thought." Annette frowned. "But I think most of the Galatine people agree on that—it's unpleasant. That shiny new Council of Country will come up with a solution no one quite likes but everyone accepts, I'm quite confident. I don't anticipate being allowed to keep our lands or assets or any of that. But I can't imagine most Galatines would be keen on not letting us keep our heads."

"I hope so," I said. "I came through this with Theodor. That's the only thing I see clearly, when I look ahead."

"Oh, come now." Annette waved her hand like a vapid old countess at tea. "You're going to be the famed Galatine Sorceress Sophie Balstrade, Heroine of the Great Revolution, and there will be ballads and epic poems and portraits of you. You'll be invited to all the best parties."

"That's precisely what I do *not* want," I said with a reluctant grin.

"Speaking of things you don't want." Annette hopped up. "Viola wanted me to keep these as a surprise, but—well, I think now is a good time." She dragged me into her cabin, a spare, sleek little room with a bunk and shelves built into the walls. She tugged on a length of canvas, and it fell to the polished floor, revealing four petite portraits.

"Viola! She didn't!" I smiled, looking at perfect renderings of Kristos, Theodor, Sianh, and me. We each wore gray and red, though Viola hadn't known what our uniforms looked like. She had improvised, with Sianh in a gray-and-red imitation of proper Serafan military dress, Kristos in a workman's set of trousers and a bright red wool cap, Theodor in a dove-gray suit like a sober politician, and me—

"I don't live up to this." I laughed. I looked like an image of one of the Galatine Natures personified, as I'd seen in religious works in the cathedral. She had painted me swathed in pale gray fabric like a cloud, red woven through my dark hair, holding a bright red poppy. "It's ludicrous, is what it is."

"She made sketches as soon as you'd left Port Triumph. She said she wanted to be the first to paint the official portraits of the heroes of the Galatine Civil War," Annette said. "She didn't know what that Niko fellow looks like, and she wasn't quite sure if the nun was an official member of the cabal or not."

"Alba is—well, she's Alba." I had no doubt that she would one day have an official portrait of her own, hanging in a Kvys convent or basilica somewhere. "And Niko would be properly horrified at being excluded." I laughed again. "Which suits me fine, his head is too big already. But this. Please don't show the one of me around to too many people?"

"Can't promise that, sorry. It's going to hang in the National Gallery someday, just you see."

"We don't have a National Gallery."

"Well, that's something for Viola and me to do, once we get this war won." She grinned. "And by tomorrow we'll be one step closer."

32

SIANH AND A COMPLEMENT OF SOLDIERS WERE ALREADY WAITING AT the small inlet Annette navigated us toward. As we approached, another trio of our ships hailed us, signaling briefly that they had left several loads of supplies already.

"Now you can tell Theodor 'told you so,'" Annette said with a grin as we said goodbye on the deck. The longboat waited to row me to shore, where I could see Sianh's impatient foot tapping the sand already.

"I'll try to refrain," I said. "This suits you well. Even if I hope we're all settled on dry land again soon," I added.

"Viola hopes so, too," Annette said with a wry laugh. "I'll send a message to her, to join me soon whether she likes it or not. She can't stay shut up in a Pellian countinghouse forever."

"Certainly not," I said. "Good luck."

"Fair winds," Annette replied.

I joined Sianh on the beach a short row later. "I do not care for being exposed like this, with all these supplies," he said by way of greeting. "Even if Annette's *Nightingale* could protect us in a fight."

"You can be confident she could," I asserted, allowing the feminine pronoun to stand for both.

Sianh assessed me. "Very well," he said slowly. "Her leadership has yielded fruit thus far. Three ships captured and many crates of supplies."

"Did she send the wine with us?" I asked.

Sianh raised an eyebrow. "I do not believe that she did. Was it worth mentioning?"

"Oh, I'm sure it was common swill, not southern Pyraglen or oak-aged Norta or anything special." I suppressed a smile that told him the truth.

"Damn her eyes, the little thief!" Sianh laughed. "Ah, well. We could not enjoy it properly on campaign, and more is to the point, she earned it."

And Annette and the small navy she had delivered to us had certainly proven their value. Three wagons were already loaded, most with barrels of black powder. Sianh was nervous, if the speed with which he worked was any indication. The remaining crates and barrels were swiftly sorted, counted, and transported up the shore. I perched on one of the wagons, settled between a bolt of very ugly green wool and a barrel of black powder. I felt quite sure the wool was the more hazardous of the two.

"We have made swifter progress through the midlands than I would have expected," Sianh said, riding beside me on his favored mount, a cinnamon-bright bay with a lopsided ear. "But Rock's Ford still lies ahead. I believe the Royalists have determined it not worth holding these southern outposts."

"Is that bad?" I asked, confused.

"It is not bad. But it means they have shored up their men and their attention on Rock's Ford. It will not be an easy fight."

We stopped near a grove of trees, a thin trickle of an ice-cold creek running nearby and the full complement of the northbound Reformist army bivouacked in the open. I found Theodor overseeing the disbursement of firewood.

"Thank the Divine," he sighed as he gathered me into a swift embrace. "I had the worst nightmares about you sinking or being captured."

"I had a fine adventure instead," I told him. He raised an eyebrow. "And I'll tell you all about it later."

"I take it Annette's patrolling worked out in our favor, then." His shoulders relaxed a bit when I nodded. "There will be frost tonight," he said. "And the baggage train won't reach us."

"A cold night, then," I said. "Ah, I miss our moldy bed already."

"You joke, but you will miss it," Sianh said, dismounting and beginning to survey the site and direct the officers where to make their camp. "Welcome to campaign—it is uncomfortable."

I took charge of our rations and mess kettle and began to collect some of the drier and older wood I found. Fires bloomed around me, promising some warmth and a hot meal. Split peas, salt-cured pork, and some withered carrots—not bad, I surmised, given that a swift boil would produce an edible soup.

"Can I help with the fire?" A pockmarked young man offered a spade.

"Of course, please," I said. "Unless you're wanted elsewhere."

"Nah." He dug the blade into the sod, turning it over. "I mean, no, ma'am, I'm not needed. Vicks has got the fire under control and Helms says I'm not allowed near the food." He tried for a grin and missed.

"What's your name? And where are you from?"

"Harrel," he said. "Vernon Harrel. I'm from Havensport. I don't reckon you recall, but you were there, before Midsummer. I saw you at the packinghouse."

"Oh!" I said, louder than I intended. He started and grinned, a real smile this time. "Then you were there, with Byran Border and the rest of the Red Caps?"

"That I was," he said, producing flint and steel and some tow from his haversack. "And what you said—gave us all some hope we'd come out of this scrape better than before. That there was someone on our side, you know?" He struck steel to flint until sparks fell on the tow. He breathed it into full-fledged flame and tucked it into my firewood. "Were ready to give up on that until the prince came back with your brother and the Serafan—not on fighting, we were going to run ourselves into the ground if we had to. But we'd about given up on winning."

"Border wrote to me, it was how we knew about the outbreak of the war," I said. "Have you heard from him? I expected him to join us in Hazelwhite, I suppose, but perhaps he went to the city?"

Harrel shook his head. "He was captured, in a raid on one of the Pommerly outposts, before you came."

"Captured? Perhaps we can discuss prisoner exchanges—"

"No, ma'am. They don't—they didn't keep many prisoners, early on." He looked away and prodded the wood with his toe, maneuvering a log into a better angle to catch the flames licking at its underside. "That should do it, ma'am." He ducked his head and hurried back toward his mess mates.

I stared into the flames, sobered by his news. I hadn't known Byran Border, not really—only by a brief exchange over salted fish and by his letters. Yet he'd represented something for me, a foundation of common people ready and willing to fight, and ready and willing to work with Theodor, too. Before we'd left West Serafe, before I'd traveled to Galitha City and then Kvyset, Fen and then, finally, Hazelwhite, I had known that there were those willing to fight.

"Are you planning to cook those peas or are we going to eat them like pistachios?" Theodor said. "I imagine we need a tripod like those lads have." He cocked his head as though trying to calculate the exact angle of the branches they had used to suspend their kettle.

RULΞ   185

"I know we decided that we wouldn't do a formal officers' mess sort of thing, or outfit you with servants," I said, "in the spirit of democracy and equality. But you're either going to have to get more competent or I'm hiring you a manservant." I slipped inside his embrace and kissed his cheek.

"And you started this fire entirely on your own, in the past fifteen minutes, without a flint and steel! Most impressive." He kissed me back.

"I did," I said, "and you can't prove otherwise."

"I imagine that I could," Sianh said, carting with him a trio of thick branches from closer to the creek. "We ought to have gotten you a proper fire-starting kit, and for that, I apologize," he said. "Now—let me show you how this is done."

Theodor helped Sianh set up the tripod and looped a bit of hemp rope from the center for the kettle. We boiled the peas and ate without speaking much, heavy responsibility for this small army settling like a mantle. I felt a bit as I had when, as a child, our mother had charged me and Kristos with going to the market to buy fish and turnips. I knew, deep in my bones as much as from the warning Mama drilled into us, that if anything happened to Kristos, I was responsible. Even though he was older, I was the responsible child who could be trusted to remind her brother not to run off or get into any scuffles with the other ragtag boys in the market. I forgot to buy turnips, if I recalled correctly.

I looked out over the camp, a temporary mark on this quiet pastoral corner of southern Galitha. In a week, the trampled grass and broken branches would begin to settle back into the landscape, and in a month, one would never be able to tell that an army had bivouacked here, eaten a poor supper of dried peas, and shaken the frost from their blankets in the morning. And in a year, a decade? In a generation, how would they tell the story of this army, this encampment, the battle that would surely come within days?

33

WE STAYED ON THE MOVE FOR THE NEXT WEEK, TAKING THE ARMY
farther inland and farther north, toward the Royalist stronghold
at Rock's Ford. The Rock River came to a narrow and shallow
point, and there the Crown had built a military school nearly
two centuries before on the site of an old castle stronghold.
Nobles sent their second or third sons, the ones who weren't
set to inherit titles and land, to train to take commissions in the
army or navy. With the outbreak of civil war, the fortified location had become the stronghold of the Royalist army.

That narrow bend of the Rock River was also home to the
Westland estate. When he fled the capital city, the king had gone
home, like a loosed horse or a wayward dog, I thought with
some contempt. The largest and oldest Pommerly estate was not
far, either, and between the ancestral lands of two old, powerful,
and rich families, the Royalist army had bided its time.

"They were smarter than I might have hoped," Sianh said as
we huddled around a campfire, the final night before the push
to Rock's Ford and the anticipated battle. "They could have
attempted to hold any number of small fortifications or outposts
along our way, but they've given us very little resistance."

"Just a few skirmishes, and they pulled back quickly," Theodor agreed.

"Too quickly." Sianh sighed. "They learned. When we engaged in small skirmishes like that, they got the losing end too often. They know their strength. Their strength is in massed numbers like they will have at Rock's Ford."

"Cheery," Theodor said. "I wonder how Kristos and Alba are faring."

"No word is a good word," Sianh said. I smiled privately at his attempt to translate the expression—his Galatine was usually exceptionally precise, and employing better grammar than most Galatines. "I am going to review the rest of the camp." He stood and strode away, though I noticed that he made toward where the horses were tethered to their line, not toward the rest of the men.

"You think he's nervous?" I asked.

"Most definitely," Theodor replied. He swallowed. "I am, too. If we fail here, it's over."

"And if we win, we still have to march on toward Galitha City." I looked out over the scattered campfires, bright in the dark field like night-blooming flowers. "Are you all right? We're . . . we're so close to your house," I said lamely.

"It's not my house any longer," Theodor retorted. "That's clear enough. It's Royalist territory, my father's stronghold. There's no room for me there unless we make room." He bit his lips together. "Damn, but it gets cold out here."

"For us as well as them," I murmured. Bodies huddled close to fires, hands outstretched to coax life back into frozen fingers. There was no promise that tomorrow night, or the night after, would prove any more comfortable.

"They're here because they believe in what we're doing," Theodor replied, level. "Anyone who doesn't want to be here . . . isn't."

"What does that mean?"

Theodor unfurled his blanket roll and draped it around us. "It means that we lost a few men to desertion."

I started, displacing the thick wool from my shoulders. "How many? Are we—"

"It's all right," Theodor said, voice still level in what I now realized was terse control. "Not many. We had some cold nights and one of those skirmishes moving northward—to Sianh I suppose the engagements didn't mean much, but men were killed, and that was a bit much for some of the lads who hadn't seen action before."

"What did they think they were signing up for?" I tugged the blanket back around me, brow creasing with contempt. "Parades and uniforms?"

"Well, you're of the same mind as most of the fellows out there, then." Theodor moved closer to me. "They felt rather the same as you. I think—Sianh won't agree—that it's been a bit of a good thing. A few running off now, and being ridiculed by the others for their tender feet and delicate constitutions." He pulled my hand between his, warming my chilled fingertips. "Gave them some solidarity."

"I'm not sure how I feel about solidarity from vilifying other people. It doesn't always end well." I raised an eyebrow, recalling the angry words from broadsides translated into reality on the streets of Galitha City during the Midwinter Revolt.

"Your brother is working on that back in Hazelwhite," Theodor said. "We figured we could use a pamphlet or two extolling the virtues of the brave fellows sticking it out to direct the momentum a bit. And some celebration of the Council of Country, newly elected, in session currently at Hazelwhite."

"I'd say I was jealous of their warm beds," I said as I watched an army unroll blankets, bank fires, and bed down for the night, "but I seem to recall they were tasked with creating enlistment records and procurement policies."

"Under Alba's watchful advisement, yes." Theodor pulled me next to him, welcome warmth against the gathering cold. We layered our blankets against the night's chill and curled together.

"Whatever happens tomorrow..." I swallowed, burrowing closer to Theodor in search of both warmth and security. "Whatever happens, I know what you're giving up. Your home. Your family. You already had, but this—"

"I don't want to talk about it tonight, Sophie." His voice was heavy and rough, as though he was holding back fear or frustration or, I realized as I heard a few shuddering breaths, tears. I wrapped my arms around him and tried to sleep, ignoring the weight of the next day already pressing against us.

I woke in the pale gray before dawn, stiff and chilled. I slunk out from under the blanket, hoping not to wake Theodor. It was too early to be up; there was no promise of warmth from the dead campfire next to us, and the sun still a good hour from rising enough to make a dent in the frost. I looked over the sleeping camp, and tiptoed away, flexing frozen feet in unforgiving leather shoes.

I climbed a rise, stamping my feet and clapping my hands together to warm them as I got far enough away that I didn't risk waking anyone. My cloak was still cold, but I knew that if I kept moving, I could work some warmth into the wool. I had been cold plenty of times, running errands in the snow of Galitha City's winters or huddling next to the stove when we had to stringently ration our coal use. This was different, living in the open as the cold set in, not quite the bitter cold of winter, but unrelenting. There was no warm fire after the errands were finished, no bed piled with down feather mattresses and quilts.

I crested the hill and stood beneath a thick-trunked beech. It was nearly bare of leaves, which lay in a scattered golden carpet around me, the color almost pure enough to feel warm through the frost glistening on each stem and vein. Cold, but beautiful, and I admired the brilliant yellow that would have put the best silks in my collection to shame. Then I looked down at the valley below.

The Rock River sparkled like ice in the first rays of the rising sun. Beyond it were thick forests and, almost obscured by a gently sloping hill, the bend in the river where I knew the military school sat. I squinted—it almost looked as though, against the sparkling brightness of the river, there were people moving, fording the stream.

Drums beat behind me in the camp, not the steady reveille, but the rapid staccato of the call to arms. I looked at the river again. They were people, massing on the riverbank and, if I looked more closely, wearing Royalist army uniforms.

I turned and ran back, the cold forgotten. Theodor was just sitting up from under his rumpled blanket. "Where were you? I didn't see you, and the drums—"

"They're forming on the riverbank." I caught my breath, which formed a white cloud between us.

"The Royalists?" Theodor could be impossible in the morning, I remembered, frowsy and slow to wake completely.

"Yes! Wake up! Find Sianh, I'm sure we're under attack. Or whatever one would call it—it's happening, now."

"Indeed it is." Sianh strode toward us, purposeful and somehow impeccably dressed already, even his hair combed and clubbed. "They have grown impatient waiting for us and, I would venture, overly confident."

Theodor raked his fingers through tangled hair and gathered it into a messy queue. "But they're in position already? Doesn't that mean they've rather chosen the field for their advantage?"

Sianh grinned. "Their advantage was staying behind walls, and they have chosen to forgo that. No, they did not antici- pate a quick response from us and we will prevent them from asserting a position on the higher ground." As if on cue, a volley of musket fire echoed across the morning plains. "The pickets are already supported by several units of the First. I imagine the Royalists did not expect that. You will move the bulk of the Second toward a position on the front side of that hill."

"And you?" Theodor struggled to button his epaulet over his sword belt, slung across his shoulder. I pried his cold fingers from the strap and buttoned it for him.

"At the front, where else?" He grinned again. "The dra- goons will press them from the side so that we can keep them pinned against the river."

"And me?" I asked.

Theodor's sharp breath spoke objection, but he knew he couldn't prevent my participation. Sianh ignored him. "We will be moving swiftly at the beginning—this first part will be a mad shuffle, I imagine, and there is no use your getting caught between two colliding armies. We will be repositioning the artillery pieces on the other side of that ridge." He pointed to an outcropping. "If you move with them, there is little risk of your getting in the way or coming under fire."

"Then I'll find a spot on that ridge and work from there," I agreed.

Sianh nodded once, brisk. "Try not to be seen. We do not know what the Royalists might do to prevent your aiding us."

34

THE ARTILLERISTS ALREADY HAD ROPES ON THE CANNONS AND were moving them from their position with the supply wagons and oxen toward the river. I laid a hand on one iron barrel, the simple foundry marking raised in relief near the touchhole. Somewhere across the cold Fenian sea, the men who had made this gun were fighting for liberty in their own way. Thinking about them, about how they'd made sure our work was complete for us, about how the Red Caps and the Reformists had inspired them, in turn gave me encouragement.

The enlisted men were tasked with the actual pulling, though several officers, I noticed, joined them in the spirit of either egalitarianism or pragmatism. Though they were far from the heavy guns used on ships and in fortresses, the men strained at the weight and the wheels cut into the soft turf near the road.

"I miss the oxen already," complained one young man, maybe eighteen, with the insignia of his artillery company stitched into his wool forage cap.

"Damn it, Genrick, put your hat on. An ox would be smarter," muttered his sergeant. The private yanked his wool cap from his head and dashed for the black cocked hat still lying on the ground, red-and-gray cockade as bright as a beacon.

"Would have gone to battle in your shirtsleeves if we let you," the sergeant added as Genrick resumed his place on the ropes.

I hung back, silent, letting them tease and jest as the rate of volleys from nearer the river increased. This was good, I reminded myself. This meant our men were engaging the Royalists, not falling back or surrendering. But the echoes of gunfire hollowed my chest, and my heart skipped at every volley.

We waited well back from the fray—the cannons were too valuable to risk losing, so the first order was to avoid being overrun. Gently sloping hills blocked my view of the fighting itself, except for an all-too-brief glimpse of dragoons in Reformist gray and red thundering toward the river. Where was Theodor, I wondered, and how was he faring? The question itself was enough to tie my stomach in a thick knot, and I forced myself to stop asking questions I couldn't answer and, if I were honest, might not want to.

I was a bit jealous of the companies of artillery, gathered in hubs around their guns, joking, speculating, never still long enough to descend into fear and worry. Of course, they also knew their roles, and everyone had someone a rank above him telling him what was expected of him next. Even Genrick, his hat awkwardly perched on his head, only needed to concern himself about doing what he was told, whether it was hauling a rope or ramming a charge or running powder. He'd practiced, drilled, had the movement and the orders ground into rote memory.

I had no idea what to expect, and no one telling me what to do. My part in this battle was an experiment, and one with no testing or trial runs. I couldn't make a muslin to see if it fit before draping it on the field of battle. I didn't like the unknown, the variables.

"We're moving around now." I started. An officer with a bright metal spontoon reflecting the morning sunlight into my

eyes interrupted my thoughts. "We're moving," he repeated.
"The commander told me that meant something for you?"

"Yes, I—yes." I nodded. "It means I'm moving, too." I tried
a smile, failed, and left the artillery companies to their maneuvers while I climbed the hill.

I wasn't sure what I had expected to see—visions of a chess
game and a slaughterhouse had vied for prominence in my imagination. What was in front of me was neither. There was orderliness and chaos side by side, lines of battle shifting, yielding,
overtaking one another rapidly, and both sides asserted themselves with musket ball and bayonet.

I took a breath, trying to make sense of the action as I saw
it. As soon as I felt fairly sure of the Reformists' victory in one
section of the field, they were flanked by Royalist forces. When
I began to weave a charm of protection for the outmaneuvered
Reformists, a complement of three-pound field pieces on light
carriages appeared to assist them, swiftly turning the tide in that
section of the field.

I couldn't keep up, and I fought back the rising panic that I
was useless here, that we would fail for my lack of ability. What
would I have told anyone else to do? I imagined a full slate of
orders and an overwhelmed Alice in my shop, a bewildered
Emmi fighting with fitting a sleeve and sweeping the floors at
once. "Just pick something," I muttered out loud, "and do it."

One thing. One thing at first, I told myself. I couldn't do
everything at once. *No one ever can*, I reminded myself. I had to
cut a gown or sew a hem, tabulate expenses or copy receipts.
One thing at a time, and I chose the nearby and relatively static
artillery company that had just deployed onto the field. I pulled
a charm from the ether and focused on the properties I thought
they would be most in need of—protection, speed. I drew the
charm tight, strengthening it, and then unspooled it over the

guns' carriages. Protection and speed. I pressed into the grain of the wood, willing it to accept the offering I was giving it, and let a cloud of gold linger half-embedded.

More of our men poured onto the field. The Royalists reacted with surprise, at least it seemed so to me, and even I was shocked at the massed numbers of our men on the field, large companies moving together. I wove more charm magic and cast it toward the troops moving onto the field, but in my haste I didn't anchor it well to the moving men and it flickered and glowed in undulating patterns in the air.

Focus. I took a breath, realizing each intake had been shallow as I took a long moment to fill my lungs and then exhale. Nearby, cannon crews maneuvered heavier pieces onto the flat plateau that my hillside became before dropping toward the river below. A perfect emplacement for artillery. I pulled more charm, deliberately, efficiently but not in haste, to fortify their position.

The hillside twenty yards away from me exploded in clods of dirt and dead grass, and I lost my concentration entirely. The Royalist artillery, from across the river, had sighted and responded to the cannons near me too quickly, and were perfectly positioned to not only suppress our fire but turn the field carriages to kindling. Another round buried itself in the hill, still not quite aimed perfectly, but too close for me.

I knew what Sianh and Theodor would both say if they saw me—perhaps one or both did, and was resisting yelling at me to pull back. I pressed my blanched lips together and surveyed the field one more time. I could cast a charm over the advancing infantry, just one more quick net of protection—

A cannonball shattered the limbs of a tree behind me, raining sticks like greenwood shrapnel. I cowered with my arms over my head, instinct overriding any attempt at strategy. I tentatively peered at the damage. Fortunately, the ball had struck outermost branches, the thin stems and dead leaves making for an impressive scatter of what now looked like mulch, but at least it hadn't struck closer to the trunk, where I might not have been so lucky.

I took the order I knew Sianh would have been shouting at me if he had seen and retreated down the backside of the hill. I wasn't sure what direction to take—the main body of the battle had moved east, so I trotted down the road wending its way through the gently sloping riverside plains. It was quiet country, a placid, pastoral region that even now seemed vaguely sleepy, confused at being awoken by the gunfire echoing through its hills just as it was ringing in my ears.

A small trail opened toward the river. The grass was recently trodden down, and I knew troops had passed this way. Hills rose in both directions, so I hoped I could find another place to perch, a bird above the fray, and do what I could to cast.

The path opened into the field, and I had only begun to get my bearings when a large cinnamon-colored blur nearly ran over me.

"Damn it to sweet hell and beyond, Sophie!" Sianh's voice ricocheted over my head as I stumbled backward and nearly slammed into another horse, his charcoal-gray flanks quivering with excitement.

"Sorry, I—I'm sorry," I stammered. Horses and riders surrounded me like a flock of very large, very well-armed sheep. I backed myself into the safe corner created by a pair of trees.

"I was clear not to get in the way," Sianh barked. "So why did you leave your position and end up very much in the way?"

"I was fired on," I said. "Artillery. Well, not me, exactly, they were aiming for the cannons beside me—"

"Beside *you*! Of all the incompetent—that lieutenant will be a private by morning." He paused, directed a complement of dragoons around him to return to the field, and resumed speaking to me as though nothing had happened. "They were not supposed to be in that position. It was in clear view of the Royalist artillery across the river. Thrice-damned fool." He shook his head. "No matter at the moment. We are moving, and you will need to find a better vantage point."

35

Before I could ask where he wanted me to go, Theodor joined us, his horse's ears pricked as though waiting on orders, too.

"Well met," Sianh said with a hint of relief in his cordial smile.

"And the same," Theodor said, his eyes resting on me for a long time, his relief written far more plainly on his face.

"They are on the retreat," Sianh said. "It is clear they have sustained heavy casualties. But they are not surrendering, not yet, and I fear that they have a very good defensible position."

"But we press it anyway," Theodor said.

"We must." Sianh swallowed. "Their point of retreat is Westland Hall."

Understanding washed over Theodor's face. His family's home. His noble birthright. "Of course it is." He slumped, resigned. "It's better ground to defend than anything else near Rock's Ford, and Galatine Divine bless it, the old fortified cairn still stands."

Sianh nodded in agreement. "Sophie, the light infantry are moving quickly to cut off as much of the retreat as possible, or at least harry them on their way. Do you think there is anything you can do?"

I tested the edges of my concentration, checking my reserves.

I was far from fresh, but there was still energy left. "I'll do what I can."

"From this position," Sianh warned. "Just up this hillside. Any farther toward the fighting, and an unexpected flank or redirection, and you could be caught on the wrong side of the lines."

"Understood."

"Then I will ride with the dragoons to see if we can manage to cut off the rest of the retreating Royalist infantry. Theodor, direct the artillery in moving toward…"

"My family home. Yes, understood. I know the best ways to keep the guns from getting mired down."

I caught Theodor's hand, reaching up from the ground toward what felt like an impossible height, impulsive and yet necessary. "Be safe," I whispered as I began calling a charm for luck and speed over the dragoons, the hooves of their mounts already pounding the hillside. Energy surged through me and the charm intensified.

"What was that?" Theodor's hand stiffened. "It felt—as though I was casting, for a moment."

I dropped his hand. I hadn't meant to draw out his unwitting support for my charm. "It was me. I'll explain later, but you should go. You've an errand with some six-pounders." I essayed a smile, and he returned it with a grim nod.

The hill gave me a clear view of our light infantry, arrayed in formation to slow the retreat of a large segment of the Royalist forces. They fired rapidly, with deft timing resulting in near-constant volleys. The Royalists only returned fire sporadically, but I saw what I was sure Sianh noted, as well—units coalescing into companies and bayonets fixed on their distant muskets.

I pressed more luck on the dragoons. The only chance to stop the Royalist retreat and force these troops into surrender—and prevent them from joining their comrades at Westland—was for the dragoons to sweep their flank. Even then—I was no tactician, but I knew it was far less than certain.

Theodor barked the orders at the artillery on the rise of hill behind me, calling on them to begin the descent. The trail around the base of the hills to approach the east ford of the Rock River from the rear was longer than approaching it from the front, but it was also protected. We couldn't afford to lose our guns; capture by the Royalists would have been devastating. Companies of infantry remained with the guns, in reserve, though I knew how badly they might be needed on the field itself.

I held the charm strong, undulating golden over the galloping horses, and swept some onto the light infantry, as well. I felt as though I were watching a tapestry or painting, red-and-gray uniforms dotting dead-pale grass, the colors guiding my actions. Speed, accuracy, strength—I could pour all these into the charm, but the farther it moved from me, the more the golden light waned.

No farther—Sianh had been clear, and I had no intention of disobeying. The diffuse charm was as strong as I could make it. My fingers twitched, calling up something else, calling dark sparkle. What would be effective? I demanded. What would compromise the capability of the Royalist troops? I didn't ask if it was right; I didn't think about the men in the blue and brown uniforms arrayed below.

Most of all, I didn't think about how many might be very recent graduates of the military academy.

I reeled a curse as I held the charm, my dexterity at holding both surprising and even thrilling me. I could send it over all the Royalists on the field, a cloud settled over the troops. Or, I considered, it might do more good in a single, decisive impact.

I had more control over a small projectile of curse at this

distance. I surveyed the field; a unit of grenadiers guarded a redoubt near the ford itself, holding the route open for retreat. A company of our light infantry moved toward them. I manipulated the curse, imbued with inefficacy and weakness and deep, dark luck, into a loose ball of black magic like a clod of sticky mud and sent it sailing toward the mass of men inside the earthen fortification.

My control over the charm wavered for a moment, but I held it, weakened but steady, as I guided the curse toward the Royalists. The officer of the grenadiers was unaware of the curse even then settling around him and his men, drawing tight around them, sinking into their uniforms and, as I focused with urgent intention, into the fuses of their grenades.

I trembled—I didn't know what to expect next. If their hands slipped, if their footing grew unsteady, if their slow match flickered and waned, I was too far away to see it. For a long, dreadful moment nothing seemed to happen. I pulsed more charm over the advancing dragoons and the light infantry, who were still firing, and I fed more energy into the curse. My stomach clenched, from nerves or from the effort of keeping curse and charm magic distinct from one another, I didn't know.

Then I saw a flash like a streak of fireworks, and tongues of flame licked at the grass near the front line of grenadiers. My eyes widened—someone had fumbled a grenade and it had set an accidental fire. I held my casting steady, but my breath hitched. This was beyond my control, beyond anyone's control now.

The dead, dry grass caught quickly, consumed by rapidly spreading flame as the grenadiers fell back from the fire, abandoning the redoubt. The Royalist regulars fell back, as well, their retreat cut off. But there was no escape route—their path away from the fire led them back to the remaining force of the Reformist army still on the field. They began to exchange volleys with the Reformists, but even my untrained eye could tell that they were caught in a pincer and surrender was imminent. Even so, I spun a cloud of luck and suspended it over the infantry.

I exhaled in relief, but then red caught my eye from near the edge of the flames. The dragoons, a good portion of the detachment, was caught in a pocket and hemmed in by fire. The horses shied and pulled in fear; even the steady hands of the trained horsemen fought to keep them under control. Not only could they not aid our infantry in finishing the battle, but they were trapped, threatened on all sides by fire.

Though I was sure the infantry officers saw the dragoons' distress, there was nothing they could do to aid them. They ordered the infantry to fix bayonets, and began a rapid charge. The opposing sides grew too close and too tangled for me to try to charm or curse any side without plastering the other, as well.

I turned my focus to the dragoons, redoubling the strength of charm magic, pressing it as hard as I could on the hapless men and horses. I peered through the shroud of smoke; was Sianh among the trapped horsemen? I couldn't tell. I pressed more luck toward them, but my efforts were returned not by diminished flames or a means of escape, but by the unearthly, gut-twisting screams of the horses.

My charm faltered, and not, I realized, from broken focus. I shook, my energy spent. I could do nothing to help our trapped horsemen, nothing.

I sank to the ground, forcing my breaths steady and deep. Drums echoed across the field. Advancing Reformist soldiers halted, the sun glinting off hundreds of pointed bayonets as I squinted to make out their progress.

The Royalist troops held their muskets clubbed, and their ensigns inverted their colors. They were surrendering. I gripped the dry grass around me, sure I might tumble off the hill if I let go.

We had won the field.

36

WITH THE SURRENDER OF THE MAIN CONTINGENT OF THE ROYALIST forces at Rock's Ford, Theodor quickly turned his attention toward effecting a full surrender of the remaining troops fortified at Westland Hall. An ancient fortification still stood on the perimeter of his family's lands, overlooking the river, and he anticipated correctly, according to scouts' reports, that the Royalists would make their stand there. More, though we couldn't be sure, it was possible that Pommerly, Merhaven, or even the king himself might be at Westland Hall.

The full strength of our army was convened against Westland Hall, and its heir would lead the charge. "I wish Sianh were here," he said, mouth set in a grim line. "I know to array what artillery we can against the fortifications, and to attempt an incursion from the flank—but which flank?"

"Is Sianh—do we know . . . ?" I tried not to think of the fire, of the screams and the smell of burnt grass and flesh mingling on the wind.

"I don't know. We've moved quickly, but if he's with the dragoons, he ought to be able to ride—I don't know," he cut himself off.

I knew Theodor didn't only want Sianh's military advice; he

didn't want to be the sole supervisor of the siege on his family home. There was something too final, too bitter about directing troops to fire on the rolling meadows he had roamed as a child, collecting, I was sure, specimens of flowers and grasses. I didn't say anything. He wouldn't want to be reminded, to vocalize what he had to do.

"I'll come. At the rear," I reassured him. I kept my plans silent—he didn't need to hear how his betrothed planned to use her magical gifts for the siege of his home.

"I think—I can't promise, but I think—we will manage without help," he cautioned me. "If you're overtaxed, or if it's not secure."

I shook my head. "I'm coming. We have the opportunity for a decisive victory. We'd be fools not to leverage what we have."

Theodor inhaled slowly and gave me a brisk nod. "I have to go. Stay back and stay safe."

He mounted his horse and rode ahead, and I slipped back, far back, watching the movement of the artillery rolling on creaking carriages and the infantry in ordered lines.

Hooves pounded to a halt behind me. "Sianh!" I called. "You're all right."

"Better than can be said for many." He rode a different horse than he had set out with that morning, and his face and uniform were marred with soot. "I lost my mount," he added, and I knew he didn't mean the horse had run off—the flames had taken the loyal bay.

"Theodor moved ahead already."

"Very well. I will join him. But, Sophie—" He looked over my head, toward the stone fortification at the edge of Westland Hall's lands. "Be wary. There may be Serafans in the stronghold. And by now, it is possible that the Royalists have discerned your presence."

"I understand. Now hurry!" I said with a forced smile. "Best of luck!"

"We never wish luck on the field in Serafe," he returned with a cockeyed smile. "We wish fortitude and a quick engagement."

"Then fortitude follow you," I said. He didn't see me cast a thin veil of strength and endurance over him, shrouding his gray-and-red uniform with a fresh haze of gold.

The artillery was set to fire on the old cairns and a stout wall of stone that ran overlooking a shallow outcropping over the river. Wagons of shot and powder waited at a fair distance behind the guns themselves, and I found a spot near a pair of baleful oxen, out of the way yet with a clear view of the targets. One ox watched me warily, already annoyed and fretful at the scent of smoke and the deafening reports of the guns. I made sure I was out of range of his hooves and hard head even as the officers calculated the ranges of the artillery pieces.

I had never wanted to curse artillery pieces, or even the shot itself. Cannons could—as I had seen while on the Fenian ship—explode. A curse didn't care who it affected; it clung to the object or hovered in the ether and affected everyone near it. Cursed shot might have been more deadly to the enemy, or it might have injured our own men.

But once it left the barrel of the gun, its only effects would be on its target. I wasn't sure if I could cast rapidly enough to coat a moving ball in a curse, but I could accompany the shots downrange with a complement of curse magic.

First, I drew gold light from the ether and draped it around the artillery. Emplaced nearly in the open, with little cover, I knew that they were prime targets. I couldn't build them fortifications, but I could give them some silent protection. Then I turned my attention to the Royalist position.

Built of fieldstone, the cairns and the wall were a relic of a bygone era, one when the lords of Galitha presided over castles built for military purposes instead of manor houses, when they fought one another more frequently than foreign enemies. It wasn't an impenetrable fortress, not like the Stone Castle in Galitha City, but it was a strong defensible position. Persistent artillery fire might weaken the mortar and shatter the stones, but that gambit depended on the artillery, working under fire, sustaining an unremitting barrage. And if their cover disappeared, the Royalist forces inside would be susceptible to our musket fire, or a bayonet charge.

I swallowed, surveyed the stone, and began pulling streams of shadow from the ether. I knew I wouldn't have the time or strength to bury the curse deeply into the rock, or even to etch it on the unyielding surface, so I instead nestled it over the stones like a dark blanket, pushing it into the crevices and the curves of the stone. It was difficult to see, from a distance, but I followed the lines of the wall and structures as best I could, layering denser curses where—I tried not to think about it—denser clusters of troops seemed to gather. It wouldn't hold, not for long, but perhaps it could draw bad luck just long enough to pull a well-placed cannonball.

The first of our artillery pieces fired with an air-rending report. Then another, and another, firing in a ripple effect down the battery. By the time the last in the line had fired, the first was loaded again. Caught off guard by the rapidity of the reports, I focused for a moment merely on sustaining the curse on the distant stones. The first round of shot had left some pockmarks in the earth around the wall, and had cracked, faintly, a few of the more crumbling areas of stone.

Not nearly enough, I acknowledged as the battery continued firing. I mustered up more dark magic, concentrating it, curling it in and around itself like a pill bug tightening its hold on its own feet. I chose a gun three away from firing, and concentrated on readying my volley as they readied theirs. Two away. One.

I hurled the ball of glittering shadow alongside the report of the gun, imagining it melding with the cannonball. It lagged behind, and I saw it plaster itself against the stone wall behind the cannonball, seeping into the thin crater the ball had rent in the stone. The crack gaped a bit wider, and a thick shower of mortar crumbled away.

I readied another dark projectile, and timed its release with the firing of a gun better this time. I pressed it toward the cannonball even though I couldn't follow its progress with my strained eyes. Instead I focused on the trajectory, fixed and dead centered on a section of weak wall, made weaker with my layers of curse magic.

The ball collided with a spectacular, shattering crash and stone broke away from mortar, raining down the shallow hillside. The artillery commander shouted, directing the guns to fire on that weak point, to pound a wide swath of the now-broken wall into rubble. I sent another projectile downrange, but I could feel my strength waning. The cannon could finish their work without my help.

But as they fired, I saw something else. A thin man, not wearing the uniform of any of Galitha's regiments, surveyed the wall from the hill behind, a glass pressed to his eye. His robes were dark gray and pooled loosely at the crook of his elbow.

Serafan robes.

I sucked in a breath—he could see my curses. I knew he could. I suppressed panic—I was in no more danger now than before, no more likelihood of an attack here at the rear, on our supply wagons, past ranks upon ranks of Reformist soldiers.

But I felt as though I was laid bare and vulnerable. There was no undoing it. The Serafans and the Royalists knew, now, our capabilities. No more advantage of secrecy.

I turned my attention instead on the advancing ranks of our army. Sianh shouted across the din to the artillery—stop firing, I comprehended. A swath of infantry rushed toward the broken wall, bayonets fixed. I blinked at the sudden onslaught of blood, not believing how quickly men could butcher other men.

The foray on the fortified position was over before I realized I should look away, with our victorious forces holding fast. Another rush, flying feet and flashing steel, and the emplaced Royalist artillery guarding the river was subdued.

Then, eerie and thickly cloying, echoes of music rang across the field. Pipes. I felt suddenly uneasy, my stomach clenching in faint cramps, but the men in the fortification doubled over nearly instantly. Serafan cursing.

37

As soon as I recognized the strains of music and saw the dark, sparkling cloud over a section of the field, I began to look for Sianh. I stood and ran behind the supply wagons, earning judgmental glances from the oxen, trying to see where the casting was coming from. The music was fainter than the music we'd been cursed by from the ship, but I expected that. The Serafans didn't want to curse the Royalists still holding positions close to the manor house itself.

Sianh met me on the road toward the ford.

"We cannot locate him," he called. "There is a reason they are employing him. They have lost, even if he plays that damned song forever. But we cannot move past that section of the field while he plays."

"Covering someone's retreat?" I suggested.

"Very likely, and in that case covering the retreat of someone valuable." The king, we both acknowledged silently.

I scanned the hillsides, the forest edges, everywhere, searching for the telltale dark sparkle. Finally, I spotted a thin stream, which spread over the field but had, I realized as I squinted, a distinct point of origin under the cover of a large brush shelter.

"There," I said, pointing.

Sianh pulled out his glass. "And I spot a piper and another man." He nodded once. "Very good. I do not believe the riflemen will be able to aim effectively upon them, so we will press a foray toward them."

"Can you?" The curse would be stronger the closer they got, and those it affected would be hardly capable of standing upright, let alone fighting.

"Perhaps." He exhaled through his nose. "Can you do anything?"

"I've never tried," I confided. "Curse and charm don't like to be near one another, though," I murmured. I swiftly gathered a spike of bright white charm and drove it toward the stream of darkness. It severed through the line and the dark sparkle receded from it. The music faded, briefly, but there was a rapid if temporary effect on the men on the field.

"Very good," Sianh said. "Keep doing that." Before I could ask anything else, he spurred his horse forward. I kept driving spikes of pure light into the darkness as he thundered across the ford, and I realized—he meant to eliminate the threat himself.

As though the curse casters recognized what I was doing, or what the horseman bent on them intended on doing, or both, they intensified their efforts, the dark cloud growing thicker. But it pulled back, coalescing on a narrower and narrower part of the field.

Coalescing, I saw, toward Sianh.

I pulled all the light I could, with all my strength. The jabs and spikes of charm magic weren't going to suffice, I knew. Not now. And I couldn't sustain the same degree of magic that these two did, working in tandem and, I conceded, far fresher than me. I summoned a projectile of charm magic, and began to aim it at the base of their stream of dark curse, hoping, desperately, that if I cut it off at the source Sianh would have a chance.

"It's true, then." Theodor stood beside me, watching the exchange of light and dark in battle over his victorious field.

"Go back," I gasped. "The king—may be—"

"I sent light infantry to intercept him if he did. Too late for me to do anything."

"Except one thing." I could barely breathe. I grabbed his hand. Renewed energy rushed through me, and the charm magic under my control blazed with power. Now more than a ball, it was a miniature sun in my hand. I split it, sending one part swiftly over Sianh, hovering as a protective skin around him. The other I hurled toward the source of the dark magic, smothering its base with light.

I didn't see Sianh cut down the piper and the caster, because I had my head between my knees, charm magic sparking bright around my buzzing eyes.

"What happened?" Theodor demanded. "Are you—" He searched my face, lines of worry furrowing his forehead, too close to mine.

"Fine, I'm fine." I shook off the last of the charm magic from my hands and the dazed hum from my head. "I hadn't expected that much of a...surge."

"You'll have to explain this to me later," Theodor said. "For now, we have prisoners to secure. And Westland Hall to search."

He didn't mention the last item on his short but weighty list—determine which of the Royalist leadership we would capture, or had allowed to escape. Including, possibly, his father.

The process of securing the field, moving the artillery, and beginning to evacuate the wounded from where they had fallen felt stilted, a plodding pace after the rapid wash of movement over the field of battle. I felt drained, the beginnings of a headache pressing my temples, and was grateful, for once, to be useless.

Sianh found me sitting next to the oxen. I was beginning

to think one particular ox might even have warmed up to me after our day-long sojourn together. "Theodor would like you to accompany him at the house."

"Who did we catch?"

Sianh's laugh cut through air heavy with smoke. "Catch? Like a fish? We caught no one. Intercepted no one, took no one of import prisoner."

My shoulders drooped, but Sianh shook his head. "No, this was expected. The king would not allow himself to be taken prisoner, for he is too great a liability in the wrong hands. What if we threatened to execute him in exchange for surrender? What then? His nobles could neither let him die nor surrender. So they will protect him first."

"Fair point," I said. "So why does Theodor need me at the house?"

"Family business," Sianh said, with a strange, ominous humor coloring his faint smile. "You and two clerks are going with him to negotiate the terms of surrender."

Polly—Lady Apollonia—waited to receive us in the grand formal parlor of the house, which was mostly unscathed save a shattered windowpane from a stray musket ball. She wore a dark blue gown of thick duchesse satin, the color and the plain trim like mourning clothes. If the rigors of a military conflict in her backyard wore on her, it didn't show. Her hair was perfectly coiffed and powdered, and rouge stained the bow of her lips to doll-like perfection.

I slid next to an ornate cherry wood chair, knowing better than to sit and make myself at home, an unwelcome guest in this unwelcoming house. The clerks, also keenly aware that they were intruding on the private home of their vanquished enemy, quietly made themselves scarce at a card table in the corner and began setting up their paper and ink.

"Theodor," Polly said in greeting. "Is this to be treated as a formal surrender, or will you be ransacking the house?"

"I'll do no such thing. But why are you here?" Theodor moved toward her, but she backed away, subtly. Confirming the distance between the two of them.

"You did not expect Father," she retorted.

"No, I did not. Perhaps Pommerly. Perhaps Merhaven. Perhaps an officer I knew, perhaps one I did not. I didn't expect you, my dear sister."

Her eyes grew icy at the term of endearment. "You don't get to leverage family ties. Not now. I know that I am not valuable to the continued success of the Royalist army, so I stayed to confirm the terms of our surrender." She raised her pert chin, her rosy lips a thin line. She was beautiful, perhaps even more so than I remembered, mature bearing and serious countenance balancing the girlish plump cheeks and wide eyes. "Regardless of what you and your lieutenants decide to do with me after."

"You'll be free to leave," Theodor said, shocked. "What, did you expect me to confine my own sister to a prison barge?"

"Father would have done no better for you," Polly replied.

"Or would he have had me hanged, Polly? Drawn and quartered, perhaps?" Bitterness finally broke through his tempered speech. I realized that my grip on the blooming vines carved into the chair back next to me was turning my knuckles white, and dropped my arm. "What did he have done with Ballantine?"

Polly blanched. "Such is done with traitors, Theo." She sat on one side of a polished cherrywood table, her dark blue silk ballooning between chair arms built for a man, not a woman's full gowns. "Which you knew before fomenting this rebellion. Before you turned traitor to your father, before you sought his crown for your own."

Theodor closed his eyes for a long moment. "They've turned

you so far against me? Polly, you know me. Have I ever han-
kered after power? Is ambition my greatest weakness? Hardly."
He took two confident steps toward her, but stopped as she stiffened. "You may not agree with my politics. But I want the laws
of Galitha restored. Trust that. I don't want a crown."

She averted her gaze. "Yet the people, the angry rabble of
them who would kill Papa and me as surely as they have killed
so many of our friends, our cousins, our fellows—those people
would put a crown on your head." She looked up, eyes almost
as dark a blue as her gown meeting Theodor's. "You would
refuse it?"

He sighed in exasperation. "I've far less confidence than you
that they want a king at all. And I would do whatever the laws of
Galitha prescribed!"

"Laws you wrote, laws that break our natural order, laws
that turned this country upside down? And for what?" She
shoved the chair back with a jolt and a shuddering scrape, and
looked out the window behind her. "For bloodshed and pain
and turmoil."

"The nobility sowed that pain themselves," he answered,
low. "The people did not decide one day, under my tutelage or
any other's, to be discontent with the scraps we'd been feeding
them. Their grievances were fair—Polly, look at me! They were
just!"

She dismissed his speech with stony silence. "We ought to
discuss the terms of surrender."

"The terms of surrender, yes." Theodor sighed. "You know,
I am sure, that your position for negotiation is not strong. Unless
there is something further you are considering parting with?
Surrender of the king, perhaps?"

Her smile lacked all humor. "Not a chance."

"Then terms—your soldiers and officers will spend the

remainder of this war confined to a prison camp near Hazel-white. There will be no parole, and exchanges only considered between persons of comparable status."

"A prison camp. Better, I suppose, than ships—but oh, yes. You haven't enough of those to spare on incarceration."

Theodor continued as though she hadn't spoken. "Your supplies will be forfeit to us, save the individual soldiers' and officers' uniforms and personal effects, which they may keep."

Polly did not react. These were, surely, terms she had anticipated. We could not afford to send her troops back on parole, to fight another day. And we needed the supplies.

"They may march under their regimental colors, provided that they are not recalcitrant or disobedient." This concession had been one of the only ones we could afford, and Theodor was convinced it would confirm our civility and refute rumors of barbarism. "All weapons will be confiscated."

Polly lifted an eyebrow, and her hand slipped into her pocket. Before Theodor or I could react, there was a slim pen-knife with a mother-of-pearl handle on the desk between them.

Theodor exhaled in a controlled, thin sigh. "You can keep your knife," he said, terse.

"You said all weapons." She left the knife on the table.

"I did." Theodor paused. "I know this will be difficult, but Westland Hall and the lands surrounding it are forfeit as well. We will also occupy the military academy."

"I expected no less." She traced the polished russet wood in front of her. "I suppose there's precious little chance that much of this will survive."

"I'm not in the business of tearing apart houses for sport, Polly. Of setting fires to watch things burn."

"No, but plenty in your retinue are." For the first time, she glanced at me. "I presume that I have parole?"

"You do. Take anything you would like, take horse and carriage and—"

"And go where?" she shot back. Her pristine composure cracked, just slightly, and I saw her—a terrified young woman who had just lost not only her house and her security but her confidence that her way of life could continue. "Where can I go?"

Theodor paused. "You can go follow after Father. I'm sure he's either joining the rest of the Royalist army in preparing to siege the capital, or he's holed up somewhere that's safe. Safe for now, at any rate." He paused. "I would ensure you weren't followed, in case that was your concern. I won't use you as homing pigeon to find him."

"And I can be promised safety on the road?" She shook her head. "Even you, at the head of your army, can't promise that. Not everyone is Royalist or Reformist. Plenty are mercenaries in service to themselves alone."

"You can stay here," Theodor said abruptly. I started. This hadn't been discussed. "In an occupied house, which I imagine will be serving at least partially as a hospital, so it shan't be particularly pleasant. You will not get in the way or obstruct our operations here."

Her lips parted and her breath was shaky. "I—I had not expected to be offered any such concession."

Theodor swallowed hard as he watched her. "I hadn't expected to give it."

38

ONCE THEODOR HAD ARRANGED WITH SEVERAL SUBALTERNS AND Hamish how to divide Westland Hall into a field hospital, headquarters, and reserve a small apartment for his sister, my strength was fading fast. Too much casting, and the increasingly heavy burden of the part I had played in the outcome of the Battle of Rock's Ford, were tightening into bands of pressure around my head and causing a bone-crushing weariness.

I stumbled as I tried to walk toward the door and Hamish intercepted me. "Are you aiming to make yourself truly ill?"

"Hardly." I smiled weakly.

"Now, I know there's little enough scientific study on the effects of what you do on the human body. But from what this old physick can tell, it demands rest. Not more work, not even standing." He took my hand in his, as though assessing my pulse, but remarked instead, "And cold! Phaw, girl, you need a hot toddy by the fireside more than any other remedy I might offer."

"I can't take someone's place here in the field hospital..." I protested weakly, knowing that my chances at a comfortable fire and something hot to drink were unlikely in the still-organizing military camp outside.

"I wouldn't let you bed down among them, at any rate.

You'd be up all night listening to the worst cases. And a woman in her shift among those men? Not decorous, not a bit." He hailed the nearest lieutenant with a logbook. "Set this patient up in one of the spare rooms upstairs." He paused. "And build up her fire before you leave her." I had the good sense not to argue with Hamish Oglethorpe despite my conviction that someone else could have used a warm bed more than me.

I had stripped off my shoes and socks, soaked from the wet fields, and was hanging my petticoats near the fire to dry the hems when Theodor found me. "Good," he said as he surveyed the room and followed my lead in hanging his stockings and breeches by the fire. "If it takes the surgeon's orders to make you settle down for a rest, so be it."

"Ah, don't talk so loudly," I said. "My head is splitting."

"Then come here," he said, beckoning me to the thick wool rug in front of the roaring fire. I leaned against Theodor and dug a tin of Hamish's headache balm from my pocket. I handed it wordlessly to Theodor, who understood what I wanted, his fingertips massaging the scented balm into the hundred points of needling pain in my neck and skull.

He spoke quietly, honoring my request, though I would have preferred the comfortable rapport of silence. "If someday military tacticians write analyses of the Battle of Rock's Ford, I wonder what they'll make of the grass fire."

I closed my eyes. "I don't know what to make of it," I said. "I know what I did, and what it caused, but I can't work out what it means." I felt I should turn and face Theodor, to have a proper conversation, but my shoulders were a mass of worry and his hands on them were strong enough to work some of the tension away. "What it means for my participation with the army."

"The grenadiers were halted," Theodor reminded me. "They might have broken our line of infantry."

"But we lost almost an entire troop of dragoons," I whispered. "What would have happened if I—if instead—"

"No one ever knows for certain what would have happened," Theodor said, pressing his palm into a particularly obdurate knot. "Even the best scholars and analysts can't pinpoint those answers. And you've said a hundred times that there's no way of knowing, for sure, what happened because of a charm or a curse."

"That doesn't mean we shouldn't try. For next time, to know what to do, what not to attempt—"

"It does mean we shouldn't bury ourselves in it. Now. You warned us, time and again, that when you cast a curse, you can't control the outcome. Damn my eyes, but I understood it well enough and chose to ignore it." He paused. "I remember—I asked you if the curse on the queen's shawl would mean that *any* ill luck could befall her or those around her, be it assassination or bad prawns."

"I remember. And that's just it. The curse is just—there. I could try to control it better, hold it over just the enemy more tightly, but this—this proved to me if I ever doubted it that I can't have perfect control."

"If it's any consolation, the Serafans seem to be limited in similar ways. They didn't use their casting until they weren't going to affect the Royalist troops' progress. Until they were only holding us back so their leadership could retreat."

I sighed through my nose, headache still gripping my temples in a tight band. "It's precious little consolation. They could win without their damned casting."

Theodor's hands stopped their rhythmic pressure on my shoulders and he wrapped his arms around me instead. "Maybe they can't. Or believe they can't. Have we considered that?"

"No," I replied. "And it's a poor wager to lay, if you ask me."

"But it's worth considering, and I hadn't considered it before. Why indebt themselves to the Serafans and dabble in magic they surely aren't too keen on unless they've their doubts? We've proven those doubts right."

"This is quite nearly too comfortable," I sighed, leaning into him and toward the glowing coals of the fire. Complacency could settle into my exhausted bones here, the promise of warm food and a comfortable bed almost dangerous.

"It is too comfortable. Which is why I'm not staying. The men are encamped on the lawn for now; they'll be barracked in the military school eventually. I shouldn't have a feather bed and a fireplace while they shiver." He stood and tested his stockings and breeches with his fingers, judging them dry.

I gathered myself to stand. "Then I'll dress and—"

"You will not. Didn't Hamish say you needed rest?"

"I can rest as well as you can, as well as the soldiers."

"Which is to say not well at all." He sighed.

"I don't want"—I struggled to admit it, even now—"to be parted, even for one night. I—I'm scared," I confessed.

"No one will harm you here. The whole place is under guard, the estate firmly occupied—why, you can't be worried over Polly, she's more snap than blade—"

"I'm scared of what I did." I quaked. "I—it's become so natural, when it felt so wrong before." I folded my hands as I realized they were shaking. "What else might I do?"

Theodor set his breeches down on the chair by the fire. "What are you afraid of doing?"

"I've killed people," I whispered. "I was ignoring that, I suppose, somehow. The Galatine ship that sank, the men on the field under my cloud of curses. I didn't stab them or shoot them so I felt somehow removed…"

"This is war, Sophie, and it's not—"

"I know that! But I've become comfortable with it somehow, the thing that turned my stomach to even consider last winter. It's proved itself practical and I've made it my companion!"

I struggled to force words past the rising panic in my throat. "I caused people to die. At the very least, participated in their deaths."

"As did every soldier on the field. As did I."

"I know! I know, but I...there's no other use for a musket and bayonet, is there? It's not like that for me." I felt a hollowness yawning in me, a blackness staring me down when I considered, truly, my participation. "They died...so horribly. Truly, Theodor, to burn to death? To drown on a sinking ship? What kind of monster am I? The cartoons this summer were right about me. They were prophecy, not propaganda."

"They were no such thing!" Theodor's eyes blazed. "You wouldn't have chosen the manner of their deaths. But they are our enemies, and they would have us all killed."

"You needn't lecture me on the pragmatism. I'm an expert scholar in that." But I couldn't quite reconcile it, not with the screams of the horses in the fire, not with the bodies of the dead still awaiting burial outside. Not with the men downstairs, who, without their Royalist uniforms, looked identical to our own soldiers. "I know what has to be done. But I'm terrified of what it's making me into."

Theodor pulled a silk quilt from the bed and draped it over my shoulders, which were trembling with tears I couldn't quite manage to shed. "It was unfair," he said quietly, "to push you into all of this. No—I'm not saying it was the wrong choice or that you were forced. I know you made this choice and I know, practically speaking, it was possibly a very necessary part of our strategy. But no one—no one!—has ever done this before." He bundled me in the quilt, my shaking body beside his staid one. "You're bearing a greater burden than any of us. Your brother, me, Niko—no one knows what this is like. We can't pretend to try."

My strength went out of me and I wilted into him. His body, more sinewy with muscle now than before, still soft enough to accommodate my form, now racked with sobs.

39

THEODOR WATCHED ME CAREFULLY AS I UNFOLDED MYSELF FROM around him the next morning and began tugging my stockings over my calves. "I'm fine," I replied to his unspoken question. "Really."

"I usually feel better the morning after a good night's sleep," Theodor hedged, still not convinced.

I forced a smile. "And I slept like a baby."

"Have you ever been in a house with a baby?" Theodor laughed. "They're awake squalling every few hours."

"I'm afraid I haven't had the pleasure."

"Trust me, I remember all too well—Jeremy was colicky and screamed like he was being flayed." He paused, a strange smile shadowing his face. "Funny, that the next squalling baby in my house will likely be my own."

I dropped my shoe. "You're thinking about that now?" I said.

"I suppose. Being here—it brings back memories, happier times. My family was happy, Sophie. My brothers playing together, Polly ordering us around—I make no mistake, she was in charge—and two loving parents." He sighed. "Not every noble house was like that—unhappy mothers, philandering fathers, siblings who set to fighting early as though preparing for feuds over land or inheritance later."

I slowly buckled my shoe, the leather too stiff after repeated dryings in front of fires the past month. "You want a chance at having that again," I said quietly.

"I hadn't realized how much I'd lost. Polly and I were best friends for years when we were young. I didn't like the rough and tumble games the neighboring boys all liked to play, and she didn't like playing tea party with the Pommerly girls, so we would spend hours avoiding them when they visited, exploring the woods. She indulged my silly passion for plants when no one else did—she had this little sketchbook, and when I found a new flower or root she'd draw it and we'd name it together.

"They already had names, of course. We weren't discovering anything but cowslip and sow's ear. It was just...it was our way of pretending we were important."

"Pretending?" I almost snorted but stopped myself. "You were the children of the heir to the throne."

"But we never saw it that way, not as children." He shook his head and closed his eyes. "Now we can't avoid it. I had managed to forget, for a while, that I'd lost this." I knew he meant more than his grand family estate. "No more pretending for us now." He cleared his throat. "But yes, someday, I very fondly hope to have a new family."

"I'm not having six boys," I countered with a faint smile.

"I should say not!" He laughed in earnest now. "I—that doesn't frighten you, does it?"

"Once, it would have." I repeated what I'd said to myself, to my brother, to Jack, dozens of times. "Children would have meant giving up my shop, and my shop was who I was. My identity, my fondest ambitions. I have something more now. I've had it for a while."

Theodor grinned and struck a pose.

"Not you, you pompous ass," I joked. "I have a country."

"That we do," Theodor replied. "And now we have to move quickly, to push northward and finish this war."

"We'll have the capital by first snowfall, I can move into my old row house again, set the council up in the old Stone Castle?" I joked. There was little chance our luck would hold for such a quick victory.

"I'm not counting on it," Theodor said. "Given that we've secured Rock's Ford and this will become our primary base of operations for the time being, the council will join us here. Along with Kristos and Alba and more wagonloads of grain and dried beef than I care to think about." He finished dressing and hurried away to oversee the morning roll call and inspection on the fields in front of the military school.

In the following weeks, the troops that had been held in reserve and wagons of supplies poured into Rock's Ford, along with the Council of Country. The first decision put to the council was Kristos's idea, pitched before his horse had even been properly stabled. I waited for him on the broad lawn in front of Westland Hall as soon as our pickets reported that the caravan of wagons and men was spotted on the road from the south.

"Sophie!" he called as he swung down from the saddle with an awkward stiffness and a graceless thud. "I've been thinking about it the whole ride up—when I wasn't thinking of my poor ass. We need a new name."

Theodor joined us. "Good to see you, Kristos," he said, extending a hand, and as Kristos took it for a hearty shake, I was pleasantly shocked to see that both meant it. Kristos would never quite get over Theodor's noble upbringing, and there would always be the bitter memory of how my brother had used me, but the two had become comrades in arms and stood shoulder to shoulder as leaders. As they briefly discussed the events of the past weeks, cracking jokes and sharing moments of concern, I saw two friends.

"A name?" I prodded.

"Yes. The first thing the council should deliberate on—what ought our new nation be called?" Kristos grinned.

"Isn't it still just Galitha?" Theodor asked, brow wrinkling. "We aren't forming a new country."

"True," I said. "But I like this suggestion—that we ought to formalize the break with the old regime. Some minor change, perhaps, could have a significant meaning. And a significant effect on morale."

"I had thought to suggest the Democratic Union of Galitha," Kristos said, gathering me into a bear hug. "You've gotten thinner."

"It's all the peas porridge," I said. "The DUG? That's a terrible idea."

Kristos paused. "Fair point. But the first lesson of writing a country from scratch, there are no bad ideas in a first draft. One must trust one's comrades to provide commentary and editing."

"Duly noted," I said, "and edited."

"I'd say that our council's first session in Rock's Ford, not to mention Kristos joining us, is worth a celebration," Theodor said with a strained smile. Very little was yet worthy of celebration, but we had to elevate the moments that we could. "And all of us together, for a little while at least. I'll have Alba requisition us a chicken to roast and some wine."

"A chicken?" I grinned. "An actual, real live chicken?"

"It won't be alive for long," Theodor quipped.

40

———ᴍ———

THE NEXT WEEK WAS SPENT IN PREPARATIONS FOR THE PUSH NORTH. Sianh and Theodor were in agreement—with the Royalists on the run, now was the time to press toward Galitha City. Supplies made their way from Hazelwhite, along with messages from Annette. She was ready, she said, to engage with the Royalist navy at Galitha City, opening the port and, we hoped, cutting off a route of retreat for the Royalists. Alba tallied the northbound supplies, perched on top of wagons with a logbook as she ran calculations on the fly.

Meanwhile, detachments left Rock's Ford moving north, securing the routes we would use for the main contingent of the army. Sianh put Gregory, Jeremy, and the rest of the rebellious military school students to use, assigning the oldest, who had been ready to commission, as advisors to our untrained officers. The younger ones joined Fig as aides-de-camp and Alba as quartermaster's assistants, and served as runners. Sianh grumbled about his fleet of mosquitoes, but he was so attentive in his mentorship that I knew his complaints were more habit and show than truth.

I did everything I could to fill the long hours between dawn and dusk with useful additions to the war effort. I cast charms in the field hospital—and pushed a broom and ferried sheets and shirts to the laundresses when Hamish didn't notice me. I made sure any new recruits joining us, both the young military school officers and recruits from the adjacent countryside, had charmed uniforms.

It was inadequate, and I found myself with little to do too many long hours. Even when I was working, my mind was churning in a thousand unhelpful ways, and when I wasn't working, the feeling of inane uselessness folded itself into every crease and wrinkle of my worries. I wasn't helping. I wasn't doing enough. The march north could fail and I didn't even do anything to help. Finally, I set to making as many health-charmed rollers and bandages for Hamish as I could before the march north.

"You do realize what you've the opportunity for here, don't you?" Hamish interrupted me as I worked in the formal parlor, which he and the entire medical and clerical staff had adopted as an office. He sat next to me, marveling at the stacks of linen rollers.

"The opportunity?" I asked.

He swung one leg up and balanced it on the window frame. I imagined Polly's reaction at seeing his dirty shoe marring the woodwork and winced. "Real scientific study, girl!" When I didn't respond, he added, enthusiastically, "Study on your casting. You told me you don't know for sure when it's done some good, what degree it's affected the outcome."

"That's true, it's...it's influence more than anything," I replied carefully.

"And if you could measure the outcomes of those under that 'influence' against those who aren't, with time and numbers, you'd have some real statistics."

"Treat some of them and not others?" I asked, brow knitting. "But I—I couldn't. That seems positively unethical—presuming it's doing some good."

He huffed in frustrated agreement. "I suppose not. It is, I do believe, doing some good. My survival rate is far better than usual."

"You usually kill more people?" I teased with a lilting smile.

"I try to avoid killing people, though I could be persuaded to consider the habit if Grove over there doesn't quit squeaking his pen." He stared at the back of the clerk's bobbing head. "It struck me, though, that this is right fascinating stuff. I'm no scholar, I'm just an ordinary barber surgeon. But someone who was learned, who could write well—he'd have a book in him, most certainly."

"You can write." I laughed. "I've seen your logbook."

Hamish flushed. "Logbook, bah. That's not real writing. That's scratches about the day, what worked, what failed. What I tried for various troubles."

I raised an eyebrow. "And you may be no scholar, but I've also seen the books stuffed in between the bottles in your medicine case."

"Unbound pamphlets and treatises, all of them. Bought cheap or bought used," he deflected.

"I don't think that leather binding makes a scholar," I said. "My brother reads more than anyone I know—and I know quite a few people with libraries full of custom-bound books."

"Nonsense," he grumbled, but I noticed he began to make notes about my work, who I cast good health for, when I did my casting, and who got charmed bandages.

A year ago, I thought as I pressed health charms into lengths of linen bands destined to be bandages, I had been deeply uncomfortable when someone suggested studying my practices. It wasn't merely that Pyord was untrustworthy; I hadn't appreciated the attention on my gift. A year ago, I allowed, I wouldn't have been comfortable with most of what my casting was becoming.

The linen glowed with a deep gold health charm, and I rolled it. I never would have chosen to push the limits of casting like this, I acknowledged. Even knowing that the Serafans had employed casting to their gain, there was still something about what I had done with the charmed fabric and the charms on the ships that ran counter to the way casting had, to my knowledge, always been. It was rolled into a commodity now, as clearly as the good health charm was rolled up in the linen I held. What did that mean for the rest of the world, for how nations would interact? I shook my head. That was beyond me, at any rate. I gathered the bandages and delivered them to the ward.

"Miss Balstrade?" I started. No one usually talked to me while I worked in the surgery. Even when I sat within arm's reach of the nearest pallet while I rolled bandages, the patients seemed, somehow, to know I wasn't a nurse posted to fetch them water or change their wound dressings. "I don't know that you'd remember me," the young man on the nearest mattress said.

I tried to place him—he had a thick dressing over a shoulder wound, and another lapped over his forehead. "Victor. I don't recall the last name, but from Havensport, yes? And you helped with my fire, when we camped on the march north."

He grinned sheepishly. "Vernon. Vernon Harrel," he said. "But yes, I helped dig your firepit."

"When did you end up in here? I don't recall seeing you."

"I was on a northbound detachment. Sent back, wounded in a skirmish."

My heart skipped a beat. "Was anyone else hurt?"

"A couple cuts, they dressed those in the field." He paused. "No fear. Was a very small skirmish with some Royalist scouts. Trumped 'em thoroughly. I'm the only fool who took a damn bayonet." He blanched. "Pardon the language."

"You have a bayonet wound in your shoulder, you can say

whatever you like," I said. I knew the wounds were cruel ones, created by a triangular blade and seldom healed cleanly without painful festering.

"Nah, it's better already." He brushed the bandage on his forehead. "And this one is all my fault, I fell and hit my head on a rock just about as soon as I'd gotten poked. Because I'm a prize idiot."

"I think if someone drove a bayonet into me, I'd do more than trip." I laughed. "Do you mind if I—that is, I could cast a little extra luck for you. If you would like."

He paused. "I don't know that I would, miss, but thank you. It's just not been my folks' way, you know."

"Oh," I said. "I—you do know that some of the bandages… and the coats?"

"Yes, sure, we all know. It don't bother me none." He fiddled with the edge of his blanket, avoiding my eyes. "I don't—I don't mean to offend, but I don't really believe in it anyway. So for you to cast on me…look, it would be a bit like asking me to join you in praying to the Creator like a Kvys or lighting incense to the ancestors like a Pellian. It's just not what I believe."

"I understand," I said softly. If only everyone could see the light, could feel its gentle joy, I thought, then stopped. There was still plenty to not believe in. Someone could quite easily believe it wasn't to be tampered with—many of the Kvys certainly did.

"I don't mean to offend. What you're doing—it's real nice," he said awkwardly. "You don't have to be here."

I forced a smile. "I rather feel that I do."

41

I WOKE IN THE STILLNESS OF MIDNIGHT. EVEN THE USUAL BUSTLE OF activity downstairs was quieted. The majority of the army was encamped at the military school, but I knew that below, on the lawn and in the gardens, patrols still kept watch here, too. The picket lines of an army at war were never asleep, I thought wanly as I padded to the window and looked out. Sure enough, moonlight glinted from a bayonet point at the edge of the portico.

Reassured by the quiet sentinel below, I returned to my bed, but stopped before I slid under warm covers.

There was a footfall in the hallway.

I was sure of it, as I willed the bed to cease creaking and I slid myself back off the edge of the mattress. I shivered; the fire was low and it was too cold in just my shift. But I heard it again—a soft touch of foot on stone, certainly, bare feet or slippers, not army issue shoes or riding boots.

I swallowed. It was understandable, completely, for someone billeted in the house to be up at night, unable to sleep, perhaps checking the sentries outside, reassuring themselves that the night was still peaceful.

Still, something kept me wary, unwilling to succumb to my warm bed while someone waited in the hall outside. I moved against the wall, as the footsteps outside resumed, closer now. Feeling prickles of foolishness at the absurdity of it, I picked up a heavy candlestick and slunk against a thick decorative tapestry. I still glowed like the moon in my white shift, but I was half-hidden.

My door opened.

The figure was female, I was sure, in a dark dressing gown and pointed-toe slippers. Polly. It had to be, the only woman I might expect to see here, at night, who wouldn't have to slip by a sentry to get in.

Despite the absurdity, I drew charm magic around me and, at the same time, pulled curse into the candlestick, pressing darkness into the metal and holding it there. It felt heavier in my hand.

She didn't see me; the curtains of the bed blocked her view of my corner, and I saw where she was looking—a lump of pillows and blankets under the quilt that, had I not known better, I would have assumed to be a sleeping form. What Polly, surely, assumed to be my sleeping form.

What was she doing here? I demanded silently, fingers tightening on the pewter candlestick. The weight in my hand was reassuring, but what, exactly, did I intend to do with it?

She stepped inside, movement lithe and quick, and shut the door softly, a faint line of light showing around it where she left it cracked. Quieter that way, I thought.

She stepped toward the bed.

My heartbeat grew faster, pressing against my throat, limiting my inhale. What could she possibly want from me, at midnight, that she couldn't ask during the day?

Nothing good, I realized, eyes widening with horror as I saw the glint of silver in her hand. A blade.

In one movement, she flung back the top quilt and the knife lowered toward where my throat would have been, had I been asleep in the bed. Her movements arrested suddenly, and she stood upright, defensive, back pressed against the bed and knife at the ready.

I barely breathed. She would find me if she searched any more thoroughly. I was standing mere yards from her, and a single flutter of the bedcurtains or tapestry would reveal me. She was smaller than I was, but she had a knife—

I shook off the idiocy of that thought, of weighing who would win in a fight. I had never even been in a fight, save slapping and kicking my brother a few times. But surely Polly hadn't either, I reasoned. And further, what choice did I have, if she came at me with the knife?

She pulled the curtains nearest her aside, and all of the hangings moved. Her eyes snapped to me, to my white shift in the bare darkness.

Before I could reconsider, I flung the candlestick at her, a glint of dark sparkle tracing its flight across the room toward her. I winced; if I missed, I was without a weapon. And if I hit her, square in the head with a cursed, heavy candlestick?

I pushed aside the thought of killing Theodor's sister as the projectile collided with her breastbone at the base and her nose at the tip. The knife clattered to the floor, and I rushed toward it before she could recover it. Hating myself, I pointed it toward her, and she shrank away from me.

"Stand up," I said simply.

"I owe you nothing," she half spat. Blood poured from her nose onto the fine silk of her dressing gown, but she didn't make a move to wipe it away.

"I owe you less," I retorted. She stood, still edging away from me. In the clear moonlight from the window, I could tell that her nose was broken. "You'll want the surgeon," I said. "Let us find him, shall we?"

"What?"

"It's broken." My voice was flat. "Your nose. I'm sure of it. I presume you'll want it set."

Her hands hung lank by her sides. "You can't be serious."

"Quite serious. I've seen broken noses, in the taverns and such."

"I've no doubt you have," she said, scraping up an imperious tone despite her swiftly swelling nose and the beginnings of a black eye. She finally wiped her face with a wince. "But you can't be taking me to the surgeon. You wouldn't."

"I wouldn't?" My mouth tilted into a humorless smile.

"They left me behind for one reason," Polly said, delicate jawline set firm and angry under smeared blood. "To kill you."

"Why you?" I didn't question her willingness.

"Who else would be allowed close enough? The officers, some soldier—you wouldn't let them stay two doors down from the Rebel Prince's betrothed, would you?"

"I suppose not." I exhaled. Sianh anticipated that someone— many someones—might try to eliminate me, but he hadn't guessed at who. We should have, I chided myself.

"I knew what would happen if I failed," she said bluntly. Her deep blue eyes met mine. "You'll have me executed, I know. Not you, personally. Or is that one of your specialties now?"

"None of this is my specialty," I whispered. The thoughts came rapid and haphazard, and they were foolhardy in this situation, stupid even. Still, I caught them and turned them into a plan. "I'm not having you executed. No one need know this happened."

Her eyes flashed blue fire. "What, you would hide this from your own people?"

"Yes." I toed aside the bed curtains pooling on the floor, disgusted with her and myself. "Theodor was devastated by what this war did to your family. To know that his sister tried to kill his betrothed? It would gut him."

Pain crossed Polly's face, briefly, before the hard mask settled into its familiar lines again. "I cannot be responsible for my brother's choices."

"I never asked you to be. You're clearly too busy with your own," I hissed. "Come on now." I hesitated. "I'll put the knife away once we're out in the open."

"I wouldn't"—she swallowed—"have done this for you."

"I know full well," I muttered, losing patience. "Go!" She finally limped out the door in front of me, acutely aware, I made sure, of the blade in my pocket. "If anyone asks, you fell down the stairs."

To her credit, she didn't shriek or faint when Hamish set her nose, and to his credit, he didn't ask any questions, though I could imagine the outlandish scenarios Lady Apollonia, in her silk dressing gown with a broken face, must have conjured. It looked like we were in a brawl and she was on the losing end—a rumor I was sure I would hear repeated in the coming weeks.

Better that rumor than the truth.

42

Lady Apollonia of Westland left two days later for West Serafe, claiming she had only just gotten word from a distant cousin-by-marriage that he had offered to open his home to her as a refugee. I suppressed a snort—she was no refugee, but no one else questioned her decision to leave. I was suspicious, of course, of any connection to West Serafe, but I knew that Theodor's family was large and supplied with well-connected cousins, and in the end, it didn't matter. Polly had tried, and failed, at her mission in the Civil War.

She waited for an escort to the docks near the military school, and I waited with her. "Are you sure you want to go? As you said, no one can guarantee your safety," I asked. Her eyes were still rimmed in purple and her nose was wrapped under a linen bandage circling her delicate face. Alba was the only one who had questioned the injury, with a single, deftly raised eyebrow that I had answered with a shake of my head. Polly's secret went with her.

"I have no real choice, have I?" Polly said, gazing into the distance.

"No one is forcing you to leave your home."

"You'd let me stay?" She barked a laugh. "You cannot trust me. Even a common seamstress is not a fool."

"I lock my door now," I replied simply. We stood in silence a long, uncomfortable moment. I knew I didn't have to wait with her, not for propriety's sake or politeness, but I wanted to see, for myself, where she went. It was like having a spider in the room; I felt better if I knew where it was than if it scuttled out of sight.

"It will end badly for you. You do realize that, don't you?" Polly finally said. Not maliciously, but with a strange edge of curiosity.

"Perhaps you are too confident that your Royalists will win."

"I'm not. Not after what I saw here. I—I confess I believed Pommerly when he said you didn't have an army, and Merhaven when he said the Serafan casters would negate any influence you might have. I never believed them," she added with a slight crack in her voice, "when they said Theo couldn't lead. That he was too soft. I never believed that."

"Then perhaps," I said, "it will end badly for you, not me."

"It likely will." She shrugged. "But for you as well. It does not matter who wins this war. The country is split open like an overripe plum. It's going to rot now, don't you see that? If we win, it's rebellion and insurrection for decades, likely, that we'll have to keep suppressing. Bad enough. But if you win?" She bit her lip, then winced as it pulled the swollen skin around her nose taut. "If you win, it's chaos."

"Why do you all believe that?" I threw my hands up, frustrated. She shied away from my white gloves as though I might hit her. I calmed myself. "Why don't you believe that a change in governance could mean anything but anarchy? We can create a government that will rule Galitha fairly, and peacefully. We already are—the Council of Country is quite literally in deliberation now in your old ballroom."

She shook her head, hair rolled and powdered as though this was an ordinary morning out on the lawn. Perhaps going on a hunt, perhaps a picnic. She smelled like lilacs, cloying powdered lilacs. "You can't. You won't. You'll fight and fracture and make your own people suffer for a fool's dream."

"That's not true. You've convinced yourself it's true, but it isn't—you only believe it because," I said with dawning understanding, "because you want to believe it. If you believe anything else, that the common people can govern themselves, then everything you've lived for has been a lie. All your duty, all your honor, all your importance—your very existence doesn't matter."

"Our existence held Galitha in security—no, prospered her!—for centuries. And you think you can do better?"

"Security and prosperity mean nothing if they aren't shared. And yes. I do believe that the people can do better. We can prosper and secure this nation, too. But even if we don't surpass your ability to build deep coffers and stack up gold, giving the people the freedom to govern themselves is worth it."

She sighed. "We won't ever agree. But when this country is in anarchy, rotting from the inside out, split open by wounds you helped create—not me!—don't think you'll be safe. Just because you're one of 'them.' You won't be." She pursed her perfect pink lips as she spoke, like a spun-glass bottle full of poison. "They won't be satisfied, and they'll turn on you. Or they'll see you as too close to us—you, who spent so many hours with Viola and Annette, who gave herself up to a noble's bed."

"You underestimate their humanity," I chided her.

"No, I understand humanity quite well." Her eyes narrowed, as though remembering something painful, then she straightened. "I know this much, too. You're a woman. There's danger enough in that."

"I'm not your ally simply because we're both women," I said as the wagon pulled up the road, ready to ferry us to the docks.

"I never would have suggested it," Polly replied.

We rode in silence to the docks, and a corporal in Reformist gray and red unloaded her small leather trunk and portmanteaus. Scanty luggage for what might be a very long exile. I saw her on the boat myself, a barge moving toward the ocean and its ports.

I walked from the river docks to the military school, where Sianh stood with a few young—too young—newly minted Rock's Ford Academy officers, wearing gray and red that would have grieved many of their noble parents to the marrow. One of them was Jeremy, his hat cocked at a rakish angle over his eye. They watched the unit working through bayonet drills in front of them, the sun glinting off the metal even though the wind was damp and cold.

"Going well?" I asked as I approached.

"They are progressing," Sianh said, allowing himself a small smile. "I have created a few elite units by combining the professional soldiers who defected to us with the best of the recruits from this summer. If all goes well, these fellows will be their officers." He nodded to the young men who stood near me, looking too young, too green for this role.

"They're still too far apart," one of the young men said. "See? The blond at the end, he's edging too far away, he'd get the man next to him gored."

"His arms are longer than that man's by an ell," Jeremy replied with a laugh. "We should have them lined up using Maraun's Rule to minimize height and build differences."

"But we don't have the numbers Maraun was working with," a third said.

"Hey!" The first young officer trotted across the field. "Not like that." He took the musket from a soldier and faced off against his neighbor. "Not loose at the stock like that. Your control is coming from there, like—see?" He lunged forward like lightning and parried the bayonet of the neighboring man, who was so surprised he nearly dropped his musket.

I bit back any argument I had about the young officers not knowing their business well enough. I still wondered how they would stand up to the rigors of campaign life after their upbringings, or the thick horror I knew they would see on the field, but if Sianh was confident, so was I.

"I was just going to join the officers' mess for the midday meal," Sianh said. "Would you have time to join me, or are you returning immediately to Westland Hall? Theodor will be there, and I am sure he would appreciate seeing you." Sianh weighted his request carefully, but I heard it clearly—the time spent as head of an occupying army in his childhood home had been difficult. No one here, I was sure, understood quite like me—and even if they did, he was in no position to crack in front of the men he was supposed to lead. I knew I couldn't convince him to stay at Westland Hall, and he couldn't be convinced to let me barracks with him.

"I'd like that," I said. "I suppose I can walk back to Westland Hall after. It's not far—a mile, maybe? I'm on my own schedule."

"Very well. I suppose it is safe enough, you walking from one of our encampments to another." He looked around us. "In what I can only guess was some sort of game park."

"It is rather nicely manicured, isn't it?" I said.

"It is not a forest at all." He shook his head. "I hear all about the wilds of Galitha, the southern forests choked with brambles and great towering hardwood trees. And I am encamped here." He gestured with wide arms. "A picnic lawn."

"We marched through enough wildwoods," I reminded him as I matched his quick stride.

"We did indeed. It seems that the nobility of your country is much like mine—it has a curious habit of domesticating its countryside to suit its whims." He paused. "But I forget myself. I should not criticize."

"No, I understand what you mean. I think," I added with a laugh. "I lived in the city all my life. This—this is new to me."

"Ah, I see. And it is different? The people who live here, are they different from your city dwellers?"

I paused. "I hadn't considered it. I suppose they are." I slowed my gait, forcing Sianh to slow his, as well. "And they'll have to form a government, all of them, somehow. Agreeing to laws and taxes and—"

"I do not envy those men trapped in the Westland ballroom having such debates. That is where my role in your nation's play comes to a close," Sianh replied. "I shall have no dialogue there. I am not interested in politics, yours or any others. People speak as though war is ugly. War is clean compared to politics." He shook his head in disgust. "I will leave such concerns to your brother and your betrothed." He paused. "And you."

"If you can make an army out of field hands and dockworkers, and then fold in professional soldiers and noble officers, I think anything can be done."

He slowed to a stop and turned back, looking over the elites-in-training on the field. "Yes, anything can be done." His brow creased as he watched them.

"There's trouble?" I asked.

"Not in so many words. But there is...ah, how to describe. A new pair of leather breeches, sometimes they are too stiff, they chafe in uncomfortable ways."

"Sianh!"

He suppressed a smirk. "It is the same here. We had an army of common people, of volunteers, who learned together. Then we brought in the deserters. They are better soldiers in every technical sense, and everyone is quite aware of it. Despite my best efforts at keeping them from gloating." He shrugged. "And before, they voted on their officers from among their ranks.

Now?" He nodded toward Jeremy, who was correcting a southern Galatine man's stance with the bayonet. "They have nobles' sons teaching them."

"We can't waste any resources we have, people and knowledge included," I said.

"Agreed. And yet." He watched the men continue their drill for a moment, then began walking again. "And yet they are frustrated. It chafes. Beneath that, they are reminded—there was division and discord before the war, too."

"Plenty of those men were Red Caps from the start, but plenty weren't," I said. "Some joined because they want complete annihilation of the system of nobility altogether, others because they just wanted the reforms upheld."

Sianh nodded his agreement. "They fight alongside one another because they have a common cause in defeating a common enemy." He met my eyes as we reached the columned entrance of the military academy. "And yet they are not entirely sure what they have been promised any longer."

"The council will fix that," I said. "They'll draft a new charter, a new country in pen and ink."

"Indeed," Sianh said. "I hope they do not believe all of their deliberations shall be so simple as the first," he added pointedly.

"Picking a name? I thought that produced plenty of rows," I said with half a smile. "But the result—the Republic of Galitha." I gestured with open hands as though presenting a fine new painting or a long-awaited music premiere.

"It is a fine name. And has, I believe, inspired some renewed confidence in the soldiers." He returned my smile grudgingly. "Ah. And here is Theodor. Look who I found at bayonet drill."

"She's picking up some new skills, then?" Theodor's smile was half-hearted, but he took my hand and didn't let go for the duration of the midday meal.

43

GALITHA TOOK A SHARP TURN TOWARD WINTER IN THE FOLLOWING week, laying heavy frost on the ground each morning and buffering the sun in thick clouds that broke, frequently, into cold rain.

Theodor paced the colonnade of the academy as the Third Regiment lined up for a final inspection before we began the march northward. Tents, powder, and supplies were stowed in baggage wagons, the Fourth Regiment already held positions along the northward road, and Sianh directed the final preparations from the back of his new favored horse, gray and exceptionally tall.

"If only the weather had held," Theodor muttered.

"It's what it's always like in late autumn," I said. I watched him reach the end of the colonnade, turn, and repeat his steps. He'd paced this thin stretch of ground ten times if he had crossed it once, distracted and anxious. I caught his hand. "Do you remember where we were last fall?"

"We had just met one another," Theodor said softly. "At Viola's salon. I—I thought you were the prettiest lady I'd ever seen and was miffed she'd never introduced us."

"Joke's on you, I wasn't a lady. I was the hired help."

He laughed. "No lords and ladies at all any longer. The

council decided." My breath was sharper than I would have expected. "Disappointed?"

"No, hardly. Just...I didn't expect any of this last year. A war. A council voting to abolish nobility as a legal construct. Ever spending this much time at the Rock's Ford military school," I added.

"Are we having a garden party?" a voice interrupted us. I started, but it was only Jeremy. He stood a few feet away, laughing gray eyes crinkling at the corners as he tried to suppress a smile.

"Are you bringing a picnic, Jeremy?" I asked.

"I'm Gregory." He couldn't hold back the grin any longer.

"I'm so sorry!" I flushed pink, but Gregory just laughed harder.

"You have no idea how much fun we had as kids with that," he said. "Once I snuck out for a whole three days to visit one of the Pommerly boys at cider-bottling time to—ah, least said, soonest mended. On the off chance you someday meet my mother." He grinned, ignoring the distinctly slim chances that would happen in any circumstance that would include a polite chat about family memories. "At any rate, Jer covered for me and I promised to return the favor."

"And did you?"

"Nah, we got shipped off to military school."

"I can't imagine why Mother made that decision," Theodor said blandly.

"I could say it was entirely having to do with our futures and family honor and all that, but you're probably right—it got us out of the house for most of the year." His smile softened. "We were never easy on her. Not like Theo." It was impossible to ignore any longer that the conversation brushed against something painful, as both brothers fell silent.

I cleared my throat and forced a smile. "And here I had

hoped you would have good stories to blackmail him with later." I shrugged. "Too bad."

"I'm sure I could work up a couple. Ambrose might have one or two, but he was always crammed deep in a book." Gregory stopped abruptly—we hadn't heard anything from or about Ambrose, and I knew Theodor had begun to accept the jagged, painful knowledge he was probably dead. "At any rate, we didn't come along until Theo was almost done making a fool of himself." Gregory sighed. "And he was always looking out for us, making sure we were in line. He took his responsibility as the oldest seriously."

"And I certainly hope you're taking your responsibility seriously." Theodor tapped his foot on the stone pavers lining the colonnade. "Your company is ready to move?"

"Yes, sir. They're a little sore that they're leaving their lieutenant behind, though."

"You're their lieutenant now. Act like it." Theodor sighed. "We agreed—the council stays behind. And Lieutenant Davies is one of the most intelligent, well-read men in the council."

"Fair enough, but just so you know, they like that Red Cap better than my noble ass."

"Gregory! In front of a lady."

"Hey, now, we don't have ladies anymore, right?" Gregory flashed a cheeky grin at Theodor.

"Or," Theodor said through a firmly set jaw, "every woman could be treated with the same respect and gentility with which you would treat a noble lady. Let's try that. Given that we have the opportunity to engender some new social mores."

"Yes, Professor Westland." Gregory saluted. "Going to go round up the rest of us grunts now."

Theodor returned the salute. "And you and Alba will stay at the rear. Near the baggage. The quartermaster insists she's the best to take along to keep track of supplies—I won't argue."

"Kristos is not keen on staying behind."

"He...military strategy isn't his strong suit, Sophie. I'd like him kept out—that is, assigned somewhere he can be of the most use."

"Out of the way. You were going to say 'out of the way.'"

"Yes, I was. Not because I don't respect him." He watched me, askance, as he continued. "I didn't know how this was going to work, a split leadership like this. I admit my bias in comparing it to a kingship—could three men lead as effectively as one?" He gripped the hilt of his sword. "Three men lead better than one, as long as they all respect one another, and we do. Kristos is invaluable to us as a visionary, as a writer. He's invaluable to the council—just because they finalized a charter doesn't mean they don't have plenty to do in our absence." Theodor sighed. "But he's more liability than asset on the field."

"Don't say that to him," I said. "I've a feeling that hearing his sister is more valuable on a battlefield than he is would be a blow to his confidence."

"Confidence aside, he should probably be here for Penny, too." Theodor inclined his head toward Penny, who counted out barrels of dried beef alongside Alba as they were loaded onto a wagon. "You'll be an aunt before spring. Ready?"

I laughed. "Babies aren't military campaigns. They come in their own time, ready or not." I sobered as I watched the Third Regiment marching out of the front gate of the academy. "And ready or not, it's time for us to go."

44

—◊—

DAWN BROKE ON THE THIRD DAY OF THE MARCH COLD AND CLEAR. I uncurled myself from Theodor, bracing myself for the rush of cold air as I peeled the frost-stiffened blanket back. White rime coated each blade of grass and the bare branches and fallen leaves in intricate filigree that broke under my shoes as I tied and retied my short cloak. Even wearing the thick gray wool, wool mitts, densely woven stockings, and layers of petticoats, I was chilled.

"Once we start moving, everyone will warm up a bit," Theodor said as he hastily swapped the wool fatigue cap he'd slept in for his proper cocked hat. "That's my philosophy, anyway."

"As I recall, you required a bit more than philosophy to get you out of bed on at least one rather cold morning." I exhaled a cloud of white.

"You stole the covers, yes. In my defense, what was in bed was much more enticing than—what was that particular event? Lady Opaline's winter hunt?" Theodor grinned. "Cruel mercy, but my ears are cold. Now, I believe there's a dappled gray who's saddled and ready for you."

"I still don't think I ought to ride, not when the other women are walking." I glanced at the wagons of baggage, the artillery limbers hitched to draft horses and oxen, and the women accompanying the troops, all relegated to walk behind the marching columns.

"Yes, but those are laundresses and nurses. Not a high-ranking sorceress."

I snorted, but the elevation bothered me. I was just like them, following this army and throwing my lot in with the Reformist cause. Like them, I was here because of people I loved. Like them, I left behind a home and security and, Galatine Divine bless it, a warm stove. "Is it too much like what we're fighting against? Too much like nobility?"

Theodor slowed his walk and turned to face me. "Nothing like that. This is pragmatism. If we come under attack, we will need to deploy you quickly. That won't happen if you're hung up back there with the baggage."

I nodded, pacified but unconvinced. At any rate, riding was hardly my strong suit. The gray mare Sianh had selected for me was patient and slow, and responded well to my reluctant commands, but I felt ill at ease riding with Theodor, Sianh, and Alba, who acted as though they'd been born with riding crops in hand. At least Kristos's seat was as awkward as mine. I missed him.

"Any word from Annette?" Theodor asked Sianh as we rode next to him.

"Not since moving north. I do not expect updates from the admiral while we are on the road. She has ships scouting the coast—they will know quickly enough when we begin our attack on the city and will convene on the port."

"And hope she can prevent a Royalist retreat," I recalled. "So that we end it there." I didn't mention the crawling fear—that was if we prevailed. Despite Sianh's careful planning, that was far from certain.

"I had a few more questions, Theodor, about the composition

of the forests near the city. Are they dense, or rather more like your Westland game park?" Sianh flashed me a brief smile.

"They're thick, new forest near the river, lots of underbrush. I wouldn't want to move troops off the road through there. The southern portion is mostly old hardwood, less undergrowth, and—"

Shots echoed between the hills in front of us, the sound ricocheting and amplifying the report of musket fire. The rounds found their marks as my breath caught in my throat. A half a dozen men fell at once—not many, but a tremor ran through the entire length of the column.

"Creator preserve us," Alba murmured quietly next to me as line upon line of Royalist troops crested the hill. Our road snaked between it and another steep incline. We were bottlenecked here, underneath an onslaught from the high ground that had trapped us. "Why did we hear nothing from the advance scouts about this?"

Sianh cursed, and Theodor blanched, but both quickly recovered their composure as Sianh began shouting orders. I reined my horse back, grateful for her placid demeanor and hoping fervently that swift riding wouldn't be in order for me.

"They are over that rise," Sianh called, gesturing with his drawn saber. "Deploy the First in lines facing those hills, Theodor, go. I'll join you with the Third. Captain Frissett," he shouted, "pull the Fifth with a reserve for any flanking maneuvers and to reinforce."

"Artillery?" Theodor replied.

"No time. Perhaps later," Sianh amended, swallowing hard. "Sophie. Back."

"I can help," I squeaked.

"Yes. From behind us. Either fall back with the baggage or—"

The pounding of hooves interrupted him. As swift as a hawk

alighting on a ground squirrel, a troop of dragoons thundered down the opposite hill. They swept toward not the First Regiment, which was already deploying in neat and ordered lines to engage, but toward the Second, still in marching column. The officers of the Second struggled to untangle the columns into a fighting line.

"The rise behind you," Sianh shouted. I stared back, blank. "Your position! Forget the rear, you will not make it there. That rise!" He jabbed his sword toward a steep hill, covered heavily with brambles and squat bushes. I answered in movement only. I dismounted—the horse wasn't going to make it up that craggy slope—and looped the reins around the branch of a nearby tree.

"Do not do that," Alba said. "It will drive her mad, and she could be shot. Let them run away." She held the reins of her mount, her face pale and her eyes wide, but her voice impossibly calm. "They will make their way home."

I wasn't sure I believed her, but I didn't have any better options. I released the reins and the horse bolted alongside Alba's mount. Without speaking, I resumed climbing the hill. I found a vantage point where I could see the troops moving across the field, the influx of Royalists, and could appreciate with full, dreadful clarity the magnitude of our situation.

The Royalists had us pinned on the road between the hills, where the space to maneuver narrowed and our retreat was limited to one direction—back the way we had come. The baggage blocked a swift retreat, though the oxen already moved under the steady direction of their drivers.

"Is there anything you can do?" Alba whispered urgently.

"I don't know yet," I snapped.

"It's imperative that we deploy your particular weapons quickly. We don't know if they might have Serafans in their ranks."

"I am well aware! Don't harass me." I closed my eyes, centering myself, and then opened them again onto the scene as a volley rang out from the Royalists. They were in full lines moving down the hillside now, a gentle slope that still gave them the advantage of high ground. The horses still chewed through the badly prepared Second Regiment, but our men were drawing themselves into formation. I couldn't help them. They were clustered too closely together, the flashing sabers of the horsemen and the disciplined bayonets of our men clashing in close quarters. Any charm I settled over our men would aid the Royalists, too—and I certainly couldn't use a curse.

Instead, I focused on the infantry pressing hard against the First. Biting my lip, I drew dark lines of curse magic and pressed it toward the oncoming Royalists, trying to push it into the wood of the muskets. It resisted, as I had expected, and I pressed on it harder until the dark glitter permeated the oiled stocks.

It didn't seem to have much effect. They fired again, and the volley sounded no quieter than before. Dozens of men in our lines fell, but they returned fire quickly, by unit, in rapid succession. Pride rose in my chest even as the Royalists advanced—the First was working exactly as Sianh had said a disciplined unit should under fire.

But the Royalists were still gaining ground, and my strategy of cursing the muskets didn't seem to be making a dent in their advance as they fired again, and again.

I changed my strategy, settling layers of golden light on the First and, as they formed in reinforcing lines on the wing, the Third.

"We may not have to retreat," Alba said quietly. "And they would have surely utilized casting by now if they had it."

I didn't answer. Musket fire peppered the field from the hill opposite the Royalist advance. I thought at first that it was echoes, but my heart fell as I saw that thick lines of Royalist infantry moved into position on the opposite hill, as well. And then, with resounding clarity, the report of artillery pieces filled the small valley between the hills.

"No," I whispered. "No, no." I pushed more of myself into the casting, thicker gold, brighter light, but it was no use. At least, no discernable use—perhaps, I thought as my stomach clenched, it was helping the Third and then the First fall back in orderly, careful formation.

Then the horse troops wheeled and cut into the flank of the Third. It was close enough that I could see Theodor's shock and Sianh's rapid change in commands. I could see blood on saber edges, and carved limbs and red seeping into uniform coats. Even as the Third reassembled to refuse the oncoming onslaught from the mounted troops, the artillery thundered again and twenty men in the ranks of the First fell.

There was too much. I couldn't guess where to turn next. The drummers changed their cadence, and the flags on the field shifted suddenly. The Third split its ranks and the First poured through their lines, dragging wounded and pushing toward the rear.

Retreat.

I exhaled hard through my nose and turned my attention to the rear, to the baggage. It was still blocking part of the way, but all I could do was send broad waves of golden light to settle on the wagons as though blessing the backs of the great, hulking beasts as they trundled out of the way. The retreating troops pressed hard on them, the bottleneck an invitation for the Royalists.

"We should retreat, as well." Alba's voice beside me was pale.

"Just a moment." I pulled all of my reserves and sent a cloud of pure white charm over the retreating troops. Calm. Order.

Strength. If they panicked, we would lose more men, baggage, maybe everything. The retreat was inevitable. It had to be controlled.

I saw Sianh shouting even though I couldn't hear what he said, and the rear ranks of the retreating men turned and began firing in swift discipline. I let out the breath I hadn't realized I was holding. They were covering the retreat, in perfect military bearing. Gold and white layers of light clung to them, a cloud burrowed into their coats, bleeding into the air around them. The charm wouldn't last, but their stoic stand didn't have to last long, either.

"Let's go," I said, mouth dry. Any longer and our route to escape might be cut off.

Alba didn't reply. I turned to grab her arm.

She wasn't beside me.

Instead, Alba lay on the ground in a pile of gray wool and crimson blood. I dropped beside her with a choked scream, searching for the wound that had produced so much blood. She didn't respond as I called her name, over and over, and patted her hand. I took a shaking breath, pushing back panic, and pressed my fingers against the veins lining her inner arm.

Nothing.

"No, no, this can't be right." I shoved her veil aside, letting her ashy blond hair spill over her neck. "You can't be." I looked for a pulse under the curve of her jaw, but I quickly stopped.

A round wound marred her skull. Her white veil was soaked red; on the slope, the rivulets of blood had coursed down her body, but she had died instantly where she fell. I felt a low, instinctual cry of pain and fear rising in my throat and, more, saw the black curls of curse drawing close as I reached out in unintentional anguish.

I pushed both the magic and the tears back. The Royalists

pressed down both hills, convening on the road, but they might spot me at any moment. I couldn't let that happen any more than I could let the Royalists capture our cannons or ammunition. I was an asset. I had covered the retreat of our army and baggage, and now I had to save myself, too.

I had to reduce the calculations to rote metrics, because there was no other way I could leave Alba lying on the hillside by herself.

I turned and ran toward the baggage train, rolling out of the bottleneck as our soldiers formed in ever-improving ranks to refuse the Royalists trying to follow us.

"Sophie!" Theodor wheeled his horse as I reached the baggage wagons. "Are you all right?"

Blood stained my hands and my skirt. I nodded as I broke into tears.

45

OUR RETURN TO ROCK'S FORD WAS, AS SIANH SAID, A MANUAL-perfect example of orderly retreat. The baggage pushed ahead with the main contingent of the army at as rapid a pace as they could, with companies of each regiment in turn falling back to cover our race back to Rock's Ford.

The Royalists did not press us. They had set their trap and sprung it perfectly, effecting a demoralizing loss of life. Half of the Fourth Regiment had been caught in a pincer between the Royalist dragoons and had been captured. We had left behind many wounded, and we could only hope that the general conventions of war, which we had thus far followed, of providing medical care and quarter for enemies was respected by the Royalists. The only consolation was that our equipment and artillery had not fallen into their hands.

"It was Sophie," Theodor said softly as Sianh copied figures into the cipher books Alba had used. "She covered us with charms as we were retreating off the field."

I shook my head, numb. "They were well-trained and they did their duty."

Sianh met my eyes. "I am quite sure that your influence made some difference to their composure and in the enemy's aim. It is precisely what I would have ordered you to do," he added, giving me a long, steadying look. I averted my eyes. It was because I stayed on that hillside to cast over the retreat that Alba was dead. Theodor and Sianh agreed that it was a chance round that strayed far from its mark on the dragoons who had been engaged below us.

I didn't care how it happened. My friend was gone.

It didn't matter how often I had cautioned myself to think of Alba as an ally, not a friend, the loss tore at me. I saw a little squirrel outside my bedroom window who looked like Kyshi, and I went to tell her before remembering she was gone. I found several Kvys books and hymnals in her trunk and a black hollow ache spread through me realizing that the little prayer book she always carried in her pocket was gone forever, buried like she was in a nameless grave in the Galatine midlands.

"I'll write to the Order of the Golden Sphere," I said. "And send her things to them."

"Most of her things." Sianh pulled a crisp white handkerchief edged in Kvys blackwork from his pocket. "If it is not disrespectful, I would like to keep something of hers."

I nodded, fresh tears springing to my eyes. In their strange, sparring way, they had cared for one another. "She made her mark here," I said softly.

"She certainly did." Kristos ran a hand through uncombed hair. "I fired the quartermaster."

"What?" Theodor started.

"He was doing a shit job. Alba was the only thing keeping him from overextending our grain and letting the fall vegetables rot. His records were a mess." Kristos slammed a record book, whose thick pages were crisscrossed with corrections, closed.

"That is fair," Sianh answered through clenched teeth, "but with whom shall you replace him?"

"I don't know, the Second Artillery has a trained crow, maybe we could try that?" Kristos snapped. "It can count, so I'm guessing it would do a better job."

"There is enough to be decided, given the annihilation of our campaign strategy, without replacing personnel," Sianh replied, carefully controlled but terse. He gripped Alba's cipher book with white fingers.

"Not now," I said, weary. "Please." I laid my hand over my eyes. What now? The thoughts swam fast and angry and colored by a thick band of black grief. We had failed in our campaign northward. We had lost many men. We were weakened. Winter was coming on quickly, and there was no way we could remount the Galitha City campaign now.

"We have to make these decisions now," Theodor said, not unkindly but firmly. "And someone had better write to Niko, if anything can even get through."

"He got a letter through to us," Kristos said darkly, digging a folded missive out from the back of the ledger. "It came while you were gone. He—he rejects our charter and the council. He says none of this is legitimate until we include the Red Caps of Galitha City."

Theodor cursed. "He can demand legitimacy all he wants but we needed a damn government now! Damn Niko Otni. He's a mangy runt of a cur who thinks he can fight the wolf-hounds because he has a loud bark."

"We'll sort it out once we take the city," I said. "Even bringing the city's Red Caps in, with their votes, they can't undo what's already been decided."

Sianh huffed. "That means taking the city. And we cannot do that without rebuilding our army first. That must take priority."

"That could take months if it happens at all," Kristos said, his voice dull. "We can keep recruiting, but it's going to be difficult to write good, motivational, optimistic broadsides on the heels of defeat like this. Where are we going to find enough men for this army?"

Sianh heaved a sigh. "It is no matter. We would be unwise to undertake a campaign on the cusp of winter. We will overwinter here, and in Hazelwhite. It is likely the Royalists will do the same."

Kristos bit his lip. "What if they press us here?"

"Our position is quite defensible and we have the numbers for defense." Sianh let no emotion slip into his face or his voice.

"But if we don't? We can retreat south, and they could press us right to the cliffs of southern Galitha." Kristos relinquished the cipher book to Sianh's grip.

"The real problem," Theodor said, "is that they could keep bombarding the city. If they overwinter near the city, they could have it captured by spring, easily."

"If they breach the walls, they must still fight the combatants inside." Sianh exhaled through his nose, controlled, careful. "That could take a very long time." He didn't add what I knew was also true—it could be a bloodbath for the citizens of Galitha City, as well.

"They could very easily turn their focus toward us, and damn it, they could outmaneuver or capture or—"

"Those were always possibilities," Theodor said quietly.

"And if that possibility comes knocking? What then? We all hang!" Kristos threw his chair back as he stood.

"Then we'll all hang together!" Theodor roared. "Yes, this is bad. It's very bad. We played the best hand we had and we lost. But the game's not over, not yet. And I promise you, we all hang together."

"We will discuss strategy," Sianh continued, "for every

possibility we might encounter. Perhaps we should begin with our defensive strengths and liabilities."

At that, I stood and swept from the room. I couldn't think about our next steps, not now while I was buried in loss. I almost ran into Penny, who was carrying a load of linens from the laundry behind Westland Hall to the field hospital in its parlor. She almost dropped them as she gripped my hand.

"Sophie, I am so sorry—I know you and Alba were..." Penny paused. "*Close* is probably the best word, isn't it?"

I hiccuped something between a laugh and a sob. "Yes, close whether we would have chosen to be or not. We went through a lot together." Weeks of travel, months in foreign countries, a shared fondness for berry tarts and aversion to Fenian fish stew. How could I even begin to summarize our brief but profound time together? "I'll miss her," I said instead.

"Are the fellows holed up in there deciding our fate?" Penny asked.

"Yes, I—I fear we're stuck here for the winter. We need to recruit to replace the men we lost, we need to rework our strategy, we can't very well engage in a long campaign in winter." I sighed. "I'm sure they'll make wise plans for us." I maintained the optimistic words of a leader, but my voice belied my exhaustion and disappointment.

Penny bit her lip. "I—I'm sure you're really busy. And I have no right to ask. But maybe—do you think you could help me sew some baby linens? I haven't started and I only have a couple months now, before..." She smiled. "You know. Hamish said I could have some of these shirts, they've worn out at the tails and the collars."

Impulsively, I hugged her, dodging the growing bump under her apron. "Of course, Penny. You set me to work."

"Should we have a slate?" she asked with a laugh. "You

could write up the orders, make assignments. Tabulate numbers of tiny little shifts and gowns and caps and clouts."

I returned her joke with a rueful smile. "I think we're pretty far past that, now. I miss Alice and Emmi and everyone. I—" I stopped. Were they all right? Was winter already gnawing at the supplies Niko had hoarded in the city? What would happen if the city fell? I shook my head. "Let's start sewing those baby linens, Penny. I'll get my housewife; we'll sit in the family parlor like a couple of proper ladies."

46

—⁓—

IT WAS ONLY AFTER WE HAD PRODUCED A STACK OF TINY, CAREFULLY sewn shifts and petticoats of soft white linen and little gowns of red-and-gray wool that I comprehended that Penny's way of diverting me from the pit of grief I was tiptoeing toward was work—hopeful, familiar, and absorbing work. Work that went on regardless of a war raging around us. Work that was pointed and necessary because life, whether we won or lost, whether Galitha progressed or fell back into oppression, would go on.

"Are you planning on him being a mascot for the Republic of Galitha?" Kristos joked as he held up a baby gown of gray wool with red cuffs and facings at the hem.

"Him?" Penny asked with a laugh. "No, *she* is going to be the Republic of Galitha's first woman governor." The new charter replaced kings and even a single elected leader with a trio of three governors, nominated and elected by the council.

"Not so fast," a familiar voice lilted from the hall. "I'm not so sure that some other enterprising lady might not beat her to it."

"Viola!" I cried. She laughed as I nearly plowed into her. "I thought you were holed up in Pellia, counting...something."

She laughed again, crisp and clear like the bright early

winter sunshine outside. "I was moving funds from the relative safety of a Pellian countinghouse. I didn't have to do most of the actual counting myself, though."

Gregory darted into the room. "I was passing and I swore I heard—I did."

Viola assessed Gregory. "Greg, well met. You look like a gnome wearing something he found on the laundry line."

"Thanks, Vi." He made a face.

"It's just so...grown-up," she hedged, but I knew what she meant—at sixteen, Gregory was short and slender, his frame still more boy than man, and even tailored, the charmed Reformist uniform he wore was awkwardly proportioned.

"Greg, we're expected in an officers' meeting." Kristos met my eyes. Sianh had spent the weeks after our resounding defeat running numbers, tabulating losses, seeing how we could make the campaign for Galitha City work. The news was not good. There was no way we could do anything but overwinter in Rock's Ford and push—hard—for recruits. Kristos and Gregory, sobered by that disappointment, walked silently down the hall.

"But you—how did you get here?" I asked Viola.

"Boat. Then another boat. Then another—well, you get the idea." She shrugged. "I should have persuaded Annette to send one of her fleet for me, but I understand she's otherwise occupied."

"Bit of an understatement," I said, then bit back my words as worry creased Viola's face. "We need supplies, and she delivers them. She's been invaluable," I added, "and she's exceptionally cautious and sensible about our little navy."

Viola nodded, but the wrinkles drawing a taut line between her eyes remained. "I arrived in Hazelwhite first—last I had heard, you all were still there. I understand I'm woefully behind on the news—well done taking Rock's Ford."

"Not so fast—we had a rather large setback when it comes to taking Galitha City. I'm sure Theodor will tell you all about it." I swallowed, hard. *Then we'll all hang together*—his words to my brother echoed in my thoughts, frequently. "But you! Why did you come now?" I asked.

"That," she said with half a wry smile, "is a very interesting story. I've a traveling companion who prompted me to leave Pellia in the first place. She's eager to talk to you."

"She? Who is this mystery guest?"

"Oh, let me have my fun! I deserve it after however many days of seasickness, don't I? On that, Annette and I will never agree—sea travel is wretched, no matter what the purpose. But my traveling companion rather wanted to surprise you."

I narrowed my eyes, not sure if Viola was teasing or in earnest, and decided it was all in jest for her. Still, the mystery envoy she had brought with her wanted to meet me with no preparation on my part. I had seen enough of the dance of diplomacy and negotiation at the Five-Year Summit that I knew surprise and lack of expectations could be, in the right hands, useful tactics.

I had developed a keener sense for politics, schemes, and betrayal in a few short months, every installment in the war from Isildi to Rock's Ford providing opportunity for instruction. Before I could decide if I would press her or not, Sianh strode into the parlor. The floorboards creaked beneath the heavy fall of his boots.

"Lady Viola, do you wish to explain the presence of Dira Mbtai-Joro? Has she any reason to be here? Despite certain mutual interests drawing us together, or her help in Isildi—"

"You ruined my surprise!" Viola cried with a half-joking pout drawing her roses-on-porcelain face into a frown.

"Dira?" I asked. "Dira Mbtai-Joro?" I hadn't thought about

the Equatorial woman since Alba had penned and I had signed an unanswered letter asking for assistance. I hadn't expected aid from the Equatorials—though they were strong allies of a united Galitha, and their formidable military would have stood by any foreign invasion, they had little interest in dabbling in our civil strife. At least, until now.

"One and the same."

"I shall summon Theodor and Kristos, then, if—"

"Not so fast," Viola said. "Dira wished to speak with Sophie first."

"Alone? Viola, that sounds—" I bit back my suspicions before they could tumble out. Viola knew the dangers of intrigue and politics, perhaps, in an academic sense, but no one had tried to assassinate her recently, either.

"Equatorial conventions. Women on social or business calls meet with the ladies of the house first." Viola's smile crooked into a grin. "You should see what she thought appropriate to wear to Galitha in winter." I followed her to the formal receiving parlor, where our guests waited.

Dira arranged her skirts around her ankles, the voluminous cotton poorly suited to the cold parlor. The man beside her, a Pellian in outdated Galatine clothing, inched closer toward the fireplace, where a weak fire played on a few half-burned logs.

I tended first to the fire, coaxing the coals into a full blaze, before turning back to Dira. "I am not entirely sure it's me you want to discuss your business with," I said. "And not Kristos or Theodor."

A smile played on her lips. "But why should we not, Sophie Balstrade, discuss matters of state? It is not our gowns that concerns you, is it?" She paused. "I would be willing to change into a suit if you've any lying about."

"Fair enough," I said. Dira was fully capable of representing her interests, and, I squared myself with a confidence I didn't feel, I had to represent ours.

"I come with a proposal," she said. "It concerns alliance."

I gaped. "But the Allied States—they have only ever supported Galitha in maintaining peace, in neutrality."

"That is true," Dira replied. "But the Allied States are not interested in a military alliance. Not with the Reformists, not with the Royalists."

"Then I'm afraid I don't understand," I said, glancing from Dira to the Pellian man and back again.

"I should make introductions," Dira said, as though it were an afterthought, but she was too meticulous for that. "This is Artur Hysso, chancellor of the Pellian Chamber of Delegates."

"Pleased to make your acquaintance," I said, beginning to rise. He stood and bowed, holding a hand to indicate I should remain seated. Unsure of proper social protocol with foreign dignitaries, I complied.

"The chancellor is the position in government most akin to heading the Council of Nobles," Dira explained. "Except that he is elected and does not report to any king."

"Oh," I said, suddenly feeling I'd committed a terrible breach of etiquette allowing him to bow to me, if he was, in effect, the most powerful man in his government.

"We are come to persuade you in considering alliance," Hysso said, confident in the concepts but stumbling a bit on the pronunciation.

"We—we sent letters," I said. "Months ago. Inquiring as to your...disposition. Yet at that time you were not inclined to help us."

"In that time," Dira supplied, "there have been some rather drastic changes in the state of Pellian affairs. One of the princes of the Allied States, in an effort to secure his own island's and

family's fortunes in these...shifting times, has attempted a par-
tial annex of Pellia."

"Annexation of Pellia?" I asked. "Do you mean—that he's
conquered part of a foreign country?"

"Not in name. He has not attempted to change the governance or the title of the place, if that matters. But he has assumed
control over certain...resources. Resources of a magical nature
that it seems are becoming quite valuable, as the Galatine Civil
War has revealed to us. The Pellians are not able to offer much
resistance," Dira added coolly.

I glanced at Artur Hysso, who did not react to this assessment of his nation. "Resources? Do you mean Pellian citizens?"

"I mean precisely that."

"But the Allied States," I pressed. "They're permitting this?"

"They are willing to let Lairn Ani-Fyn make this gamble
for them. They see the turning of the tide. For centuries—
millennia!—magic is a superstition, a rumor. At best, an uncertain aid. And then this summer, it blazes like a meteor, like a
comet portending disruption, alteration, rebirth even. Everything has changed."

"Because of what I've done?" I asked, cold despite the roaring fire.

"Don't oversell yourself. The Serafans have been influencing
policy all along. What the Serafans did was possible for them
only through secrecy. Without their secret?" She bit her lips into
a thin line. "They have clearly decided that the better gamble
now is to engage the full range of possibility in their magic. It
is quite clear to us now that the Serafans' casting can influence
military engagements. Then we heard rumors that your gifts
were not as...rudimentary and frail as we had been given to
understand of casting."

"Everything has changed." Our war had fractured more

than Galitha. It had shaken the foundations of every nation on the map.

"Yes. And also, no." She leaned forward. "It is the changes we have not yet seen that we know might be the most influential. This may be only the beginning of what casting might do. The first man who honed a knife didn't envision a line company in a bayonet charge."

"The Equatorials came to Pellia. They first offered alliance, but the terms—" Hysso shook his head. "We will not allow our people to be so used. Not for another's wars. But the Equatorials, they are more powerful than we. They did not need to ask. They are powerful enough, they can take." His face drew taut. "And so they did."

I began to understand, slowly, horrified. "This—this prince *took* Pellian people? To the Allied States? Without their consent?"

Dira's mouth constricted as though she had tasted something sour. "He will not admit it. But there is no indication that they left Pellia willingly." She swallowed. "Bondage is against all our traditions and ethics. Which is why the country looks the other way. But it feels necessary to match this new weapon of our potential enemies. Which is why the country allows it to continue."

"But what does he expect the Pellians to do?" I asked. "They know traditional methods, traditional casting only— which is what you understood, a simple boost in fortune. One clay tablet at a time. Not the methods the Serafans use. Not what I've done."

Dira watched me a long moment. "I wonder if any of us knows, to the full extent, what you have done," she mused. I didn't reply. "Ani-Fyn believes even the most rudimentary of casting is worth investing in. But he also believes, I am sure, that they can be trained to match the Serafans' prowess."

"If this continues," Hysso added, "it will not be long before the Allied States simply conquer all of Pellia. We cannot stand against it alone."

We couldn't defend Pellia, I thought with silent desperation. Even if incursion by the Allied States was wrong, if they had engaged in slavery, an abomination of all our ethics. "I am not sure that we have the ability to offer what you need," I began, readying myself for Hysso's disappointment.

Dira smiled. "I think you have the ability to accept precisely what Pellia would like to offer. A conquered nation has no rights, can be made slaves. But a nation who willingly joins another?"

Hysso held up a hand. "We are independent, in the face of great nations like Galitha, like Serafe, for centuries. We are small, but we are proud. Yet a new Galitha—a democratic Galitha—could be a home for us. And in exchange, we will provide troops to serve in your army."

I exhaled, thin and shaky. We needed men, needed them more than ever. And what better way to protect the Pellians from incursion by other, newly magic-hungry neighbors than by bringing them under our wing? Pellia could be a Galatine province, equal to the other Galatine provinces. With their men, we could pursue victory in Galitha City. With our influence, they could ward off new threats. The negotiations could begin immediately.

I had learned enough to ask one more question first. I turned to Dira. "Why are you brokering this alliance?"

Her eyes glinted with amusement. "Ah, you've learned much," she said. "Everyone has their reasons, do they not?"

"And what are yours?" I tried to keep my voice light, calm like hers, but I worried, mired in a game I only half understood.

"If Lairn Ani-Fyn is favored, and given positions of accolade for such action, my own family will be out of favor, and the only way to regain favor will be, it seems, ethically unsavory methods. I would rather maintain our position the way my family always have."

"Which is?"

She grinned. "Forming alliances with our neighbors. If we aid Galitha's Reformists in their time of need, I am sure you will remember us. And if the Allied States are in dire need, disadvantaged without magic of our own, there will be a nation now doubly strong in charm and curse, willing to aid us. And the Mbtai-Joro family will be your connection."

"Very well." I stood, firm resolve in my motion hiding my panic at what I was doing, acting on behalf of a nation that existed only on paper and on a battlefield. "We have the beginnings of an agreement."

47

I BURST IN ON THE OFFICERS' MEETING, MET BY ANNOYANCE THAT turned quickly to excitement as I explained the turn of events. Kristos immediately convened the council to review the charter for any possible problems, Sianh cornered Hysso to discuss his troop strength and promise of additional recruits, and Theodor formally presented himself to Dira. The council found no objections to the proposal, and entered into negotiations with Hysso, with the aim of adding Pellia as a member equal to the rest of the Republic of Galitha, with equal voice in the Council of Country.

Theodor, Kristos, and I oversaw the vote, overwhelmingly in favor of the unification. A few voices protested, loudly, that Pellian inclusion was anathema to Galatine history and culture, but pragmatism outweighed these concerns. Many of our council members, in truth, had worked alongside Pellians in the fishing and shipping trade, and two pragmatic southerners were Pellian immigrants themselves. "Fools act like they've never met a Pellian," a council member from the southern coast muttered near me. He glanced at me and blushed, but I nodded in agreement with him.

Pellian troops began arriving just as the first flurries

supplanted autumn's rain. Pellia's army was not large, but they dedicated most of it to our efforts—with the understanding that we would meet and excel that commitment once the war was won, were Pellia threatened. Better, they had been a standing army, and were trained, meticulous, and needed little instruction to adapt to Galatine methods. New Galatine recruits arrived, as well, many of whom were fishermen who filled out Annette's ranks of sailors.

"By winter's end we will have a full army again," Sianh said, reviewing the troops maneuvering on the parade ground of the school. With the exception of the Pellian marine units, who were Pellia's version of elite forces and badly needed on Annette's ships, he had combined and reworked the regiments yet again so that the troops were fully integrated. Cohesion on the field, he said, could only be achieved through discomfort in drill—and discomfort he served in droves. Unfamiliar comrades, increased maneuvers, longer sessions of bayonet and firing drills, all with winter bearing hard on Rock's Ford.

"And by day's end we'll have a redrawn map of Galatine electoral districts with representation fairly distributed to include Pellia." Theodor heaved a contented sigh, smoothing his mussed hair before putting his hat back on. It sat perfectly askance over his brow, giving him a dashing military bearing. "Hysso knows his business, and Dira has proven a keen arbiter."

"Any word from Niko?" I asked.

"Nothing. The electoral districts fairly include Galitha City. They can elect representatives like the rest of the country, and we'll sort it out then." Theodor's grim monotone told me he anticipated it wouldn't be so easy.

"I am, as always, grateful to be your military advisor and not involved in your politics," Sianh said with a shake of his head, never taking his eyes from marching maneuvers.

"Politics! Remember when that meant a talk about a Melchoir essay in the salon, Theo?" Viola sailed toward us, a silk quilted petticoat bouncing in an icy wind.

"Yes, before Reform Bills turned into bayonet charges," Theodor said.

"It turns out a cabal of women gossiping in parlors can effect great things." Viola laughed, winking at me. "They haven't changed much for us, have they?"

Theodor tensed. "That can come later. Once the structure of governance is in place, the laws themselves will be subject to constant reevaluation. And change."

"You'll tell us 'later' until we're all doddering and gray," Viola said. "I'll confess, it rankles me, this part of 'progress.' As a noblewoman, I at least had some agency, some power. And now I must lose it all—more than the men because they at least still have the right to vote."

"Vivi, be patient," Theodor began.

"Honestly, Theodor, I think we've all been rather patient," I countered. "You have women sewing your shirts and tending your wounded and doing your laundry not because this army pays well—it doesn't—but because they believe in this cause as much as the soldiers do."

"As I said," Sianh murmured, "I am very grateful I am not involved in your politics."

Before Viola could snap at Sianh, Fig dashed up to us. My stomach lurched—usually when the diminutive messenger was out of breath, he was the bearer of bad news.

"Penny! She's had the baby," he panted. "Kristos's there now but wanted Miss Sophie to come, too—"

"She's had the baby?" Viola's eyebrow angled upward. "I think you must be mistaken, she was at breakfast not six hours ago, and these things take time."

"No, ma'am, she was in a hurry to be born, Dr. Oglethorpe said."

"She!" I caught Theodor's hand. "A girl."

Kristos and Penny and a tiny bundle wrapped in soft white linen were safely ensconced in their room in Westland Hall by the time I tumbled through the door. Penny had the tired yet triumphant look of a boxer who, despite taking a few knocks, had won the bout by a mile, while Kristos looked proud and happy and thoroughly dazed.

Penny grinned and beckoned me over. "Here, hold her. Isn't she pretty?"

I took the bundle in my arms. She was red and wrinkled with a shock of dark hair, and her tiny eyes squished themselves shut against the bright afternoon light. "She's beautiful," I said. It was the truth. My little niece—my brother's baby, my blood, new little citizen of a new Republic of Galitha—was beautiful.

"And you're all right?" Theodor asked, blushing. "That is— childbirth is—I mean..."

"She's a rare one, to be so quick with the first and do so well," Hamish said gruffly despite his broad smile. "But she is fine as fine can be. She could like as not use a nap, though."

"Is it all right?" I whispered, still holding the baby. Penny nodded, and we stepped out of the room.

"I'll let the others know Fig isn't telling tall tales," Theodor said. "Say, does she have a name?"

Kristos started. "A name? No, not yet—we hadn't decided on one," he replied, dazed.

Theodor nodded and trotted off. "Penny is doing well," I said, "and this little button is grand as anything, but what about you?"

Kristos's lips twitched into a faint smile. "Me? I hardly know what to do with myself. She's—she's real."

I laughed quietly. The motion jostled the baby and she stirred, then fell asleep again. "Babies do tend to be real, Kristos."

"I mean, I knew she was coming and I knew she was going to be—real—but..." He sank onto a delicate bench upholstered in pink silk. "But she's *real*. And this is real, and I'm a father now. A real father."

"You'll be a fine father," I said.

"I've no idea what to do, what to expect."

"Did you know how to lead a revolution?" I joked. I traced the tiny fingers gripping the edges of her wrapping. There were fingernails—perfect little ovals. Why hadn't I thought to realize she would have fingernails? I wondered.

"But this is a person, a little human with needs and—oh, hell, someday she'll have hopes and ideas and dreams—"

"Every man and woman who followed the Red Cap movement did, too," I said quietly. "And every man and woman out there encamped in the cold. They're all people and you led all of them. Surely you can be a good father, too."

"I think that might be what scares me," Kristos said. "I—I could look at the Red Caps and then the Reformist army and still see the ideas, the concepts, the new ethical government writ large before all of them. I can't look at her and see that. I just see—her. Her perfect little mouth and—that's Penny's chin. I think she's got your hands, sort of long and square."

"She has your ears," I said quietly. "It's not a bad thing, Kristos, to see people first, before ideas. To love before you think."

"I know. I—I see that now." He tucked a loose end of the linen swaddle back in place, but it came undone, and the baby began to cry. "Have you any idea how to wrap one of these?"

"None," I said. "But I think we can figure it out together."

48

—◆—

"A NEW BABY! I THINK THIS DESERVES SOME SORT OF CELEBRATION, don't you?" Viola said as we gathered on the cold portico of Westland Hall, watching the troops march back to their quarters after evening inspection.

Sianh eyed the petite Galatine noblewoman suspiciously. "A celebration? In the midst of war?"

"Just a simple supper party! We held them all the time during the winter social season in Galitha City. Dinner and polite conversation and maybe a punch if we can manage it." She paused. "Not too much punch. I know how army officers can be."

"Trust Viola to think of a party at a time like this," laughed Theodor. "But I confess I agree. We have welcomed Pellia, rebuilt an army and—sweet mercy!—we finalized a country charter, all without a proper celebration. And now we've a new arrival—and everyone will want to know, have they settled on a name yet?"

"Not yet. Kristos is getting all sentimental and wants to wait through the end of the first one hundred days like Pellians do." I laughed. "I suppose she's the only baby around, so there shan't be any confusion."

Sianh agreed, for once, to raid the finer stores of our army's provisions, given that a fine dinner could show our diplomatic guests that we were not ready to succumb to starvation. "It never pays to look desperate, even if the ink is dry on the contract," he muttered to me as I reattached a loose epaulet before the party.

I didn't have my own closet at my disposal, of course, but Westland Hall still held a sizable portion of Theodor's mother's and sister's wardrobes. Both women were smaller than me, petite Galatine women with dainty builds like songbirds. In the back of a musty closet, I found a dark gold gown of his mother's in the outdated "flying" style, loose shoulders and an open front. Likely it was set aside to be remade, but a war and fleeing her home had put a stop to any sartorial planning. I looked, and felt, like a dowdy aunt invited last minute to a supper party, but I made the gown fit.

We gathered in the private family dining room of the estate; the formal dining room, a larger and more stately space, had been taken over as part of the field hospital. Even so, candles blazed in sconces and from silver candlesticks on polished cherry sideboards, illuminating full sets of silver and finely painted china. Penny wasn't ready to be out of bed yet, but Kristos came down with my niece long enough to present her, to a deluge of well wishes. She slept soundly through the entire parade around the room, oblivious to the coos and congratulations.

"And in red and gray!" Dira smiled. "She is a little patriot, is she not?"

"A beautiful child," said Hysso.

"In Serafan, we say *Hya'tin Fia*," said Sianh, "which means 'due welcome, small stranger.'" He bowed and presented his sword to the slumbering infant, which earned some laughter from the gathered regimental officers, but I saw the glint of a tear in the corner of his eye before Kristos returned the baby to Penny.

Viola had rustled up stewards from the corps of former Rock's Ford military school students. As nobles' children, they were used to being served rather than serving at a table, but despite my worries they would appear sullen or reluctant, they were eager to be given even a minor role of honor. A young man with sun-kissed skin and neatly clubbed black hair held my chair for me, and another poured wine.

We passed trays of cheese and stuffed figs, as though this were a perfectly ordinary Galatine dinner party. Kristos returned and engaged Hysso in a lively conversation about historical Pellian philosophy, and its influences on first the Red Caps and now the Republic of Galitha. Dira watched with bright curiosity, tasting each cheese and sipping her wine.

"Do you like the figs?" I asked as she tried one.

"They are surprising—with honey! Rather sweet, are they not?" she said. "Like dessert. But we do not take to sweet foods at home, for the most part."

"This is your first time in Galitha, then?" I said.

Dira nodded serenely. "It is. I hope to return when the atmosphere is a bit calmer. I find that the scenery is quite interesting."

"A toast, then!" Theodor cleared his throat and stood, a scanty glass of wine in hand. "To a renewed Republic of Galitha, to our citizens both old and new, and to our friends and allies." He lifted the glass as a signal for us to join him. The sunset outside the lead glass windows danced through my wineglass, casting a shadow like a smear of blood on the nearest wall. "We hang on the edge of a great—"

The door swung open with a crack like thunder, and the officers serving as stewards put their hands to their swords. Sianh had his sword out and at the ready, and was on his feet and in front of me in one motion. As I peered around him, blocked into my chair by his thick legs, I saw that the intruder was a rail-thin man accompanied by two of our officers, his hair overgrown and disheveled and his clothes marred with old and fresh stains.

It was Ambrose.

Theodor's brother was pale as snow, his lips cracked and gray. I rose from my chair and silverware clattered to the floor as I jostled the table. Sianh stepped aside as Theodor rushed toward his brother.

"Ambrose!" Theodor said as he embraced him, but he swayed under the weight. Theodor ushered him to a chair. "What's happened to you?"

"A few months in a jail cell in the Stone Castle," he said, "followed by bombardment of the city by the Royalists and a rather uncomfortable trip to get to you."

"Jail cell?" I looked at Ambrose and then at Kristos, who hung back from the tableau unfolding before him. Dira and Hysso watched with polite but intent interest.

"I was an enemy of the Galatine people," he said, glancing at Kristos as though assessing him, too. "Anyone of noble lineage or—what did Niko Otni call it?—guilty of 'excessive consort' with the nobles, that's right."

"But you were in the city? All along?" Theodor said, and I spoke at the same time, "I was there, I asked—"

"I know. The names of those jailed weren't made public. I think the idea was to quietly dispose of us later—I'm not sure, maybe I'm being uncharitable. But Otni couldn't afford public trials and disagreements over what should be done with nobles who stayed—sweet hell, especially not nobles who stayed and helped."

"You did help, didn't you?" I said. "When they stormed the Stone Castle, you opened the secret door from River Street."

Ambrose's tired eyes lit up. "How did you know?"

"I heard that the Stone Castle was breached, and that someone opened that door," I said. "Someone who knew it existed, how to open it—I didn't think Otni did." I shook my head. "Of course he was happy to take the credit for it."

"Of course he was," Ambrose repeated in a tired echo. "Yes, the uncomfortable fact that the victory over the city had something to do with the interference of a noble would have come out if he did anything public with me. And several others, I might add—a dozen of us from the university alone were actively assisting the efforts of the Reformists in the city. But Otni wants to start fresh, I think." Silence settled around us.

"He can't start fresh," Kristos said finally, through gritted teeth, "by killing people united under the banner of the Republic of Galitha."

Ambrose's brow creased, then shot up in surprise. "Republic of Galitha! Brilliant! I can see it in the history books now. The formation of the great nation of—" He broke off in a fit of coughing.

"Damn Otni's eyes, Ambrose, you're ill."

"Not important." Ambrose coughed. "There are plenty who agree with you, Balstrade. While the city was under bombardment, the first time the Royalists got within range to strike at the city center, the Stone Castle took some slight damage—nothing serious, but we didn't know at the time that the whole place wouldn't come down around our ears. Some of the guards decided they didn't want our corpses on their consciences."

"It's bad in the city, then." Theodor stood slowly from beside his brother and paced toward the opposite wall, sharing a glance with Sianh. "The bombardment has begun in earnest."

"It's begun, and I don't mind telling you that you had better get there before it's ended in earnest."

Sianh swore. "Why has this Niko not sent word?"

"I thought he must have," Ambrose mused. "He's not a great enough fool to think he can outlast them."

"He's not?" Theodor snapped.

"Divine Natures, I hope not." Kristos sighed. "I suppose it's possible his messengers didn't make it through."

"And Theodor's consumptive brother did?" Viola said. "No offense, Ambrose."

"It's plausible," Ambrose said. "I left the city immediately—clearly I had no good reason to hang around and see if I was going to get arrested and imprisoned again. And I know the countryside."

"No," Kristos said slowly. "I know Niko. He sent Fig, and Fig made it. He's sent letters, when he wanted, and those made it. He could have sent someone. He thinks he can hold the city on his own. And he thinks if he does he'll be able to leverage his way on giving Galitha to the Red Caps to govern."

"He is mistaken," Sianh said. "Whatever fool thinks he can withstand bombardment and blockade on his own is a fool indeed."

"He has always been bold. Too bold. It doesn't matter," Kristos said. "We have to go north. Now. March on the city. Now."

"Our troops are ready," said Hysso. "Ready for this—history with Galitha."

"Well put," Theodor said, burying any reticence he felt. "And we are ready, as well."

"But in winter," Gregory said. "It's against every military manual out there."

"Perhaps so," Sianh said slowly. "But it is perhaps not unwise. One," he ticked off, "the Royalists will not anticipate it. We may in fact surprise them, at least to some degree. I would venture that they have made their encampment outside Galitha City to overwinter and will therefore be massed there, which means that, two," he counted, "they will not be a great impediment on the move northward. And finally." He swallowed. "We either win this campaign or we lose the war. If we fail, it is over. We shall spend winter on prison barges or in the ground."

"We'll all hang together," I murmured to no one but myself.

"Then we move now," Kristos said. "Galitha City is where it started, and Galitha City is where it's going to end."

49

THE SPEED WITH WHICH THE ARMY COULD PACK UP AND MOVE surprised even Sianh, who watched in the pale gray before dawn as the lines of men moved northward, the wagons of supplies and gear trundling on behind. "I am very grateful we were able to requisition oxen," he finally said.

"Pastoral Galitha has its advantages," I replied. He smiled in reply. It was the last time I saw him smile on the march toward the city.

Scouting troops cleared our path of any belligerent Royalists, and we rejoined them as we marched, our numbers gathering strength as we approached the city. We all knew, with fear and excitement fusing our thoughts with our nerves, that this would be our final battle. There were only two outcomes. We might win a victory here, and though skirmishes and rebellions might follow the war, we would effect the surrender of the Royalists.

Or we would be defeated. Summarily, once and for all. The Republic of Galitha would die before it had even really begun.

The day we came within sight of Galitha's towers, Sianh halted us for a short respite before we would march through the night and attack at dawn. The leaders of the army gathered by a small fire, warming hands and finalizing the plans for the morning.

Theodor caught my hand as we walked to join the others. "This is it," he said. I slowed my pace and turned to him. He searched my face, waiting. He wanted a moment of quiet, a moment to mark the importance of what we were about to undertake. Some words, some pledge, some promise.

I found I couldn't give it to him. Stopping the forward motion toward tomorrow meant yielding to the growing panic in my gut that we weren't strong enough, that I wouldn't be able to provide enough magical assistance, that this errand was doomed from the start.

That instead of surrendering to our own deaths, we had dragged thousands into oblivion with us.

"We're expected," I said instead, tugging at his hand.

"Sophie, I—in case we're . . . in case tomorrow—"

"See?" I said, gripping his hand tighter. "You don't really want to talk about it any more than I do. Nothing needs to be said," I added more softly. "I love you. You love me. We will see one another on the other side of this battle."

"But if we don't, I just—I wanted—"

"We will," I said firmly, "one way or another."

He struggled for a moment and then acquiesced, taking my face in his hands and accepting a fleeting kiss as our promise in lieu of long words.

We joined the others by the light of the wan fire. "I could hope that Otni would come to that conclusion on his own," Sianh said. "But hope is not a wise strategy."

"We could send someone into the city," Kristos said. "Someone who knows how to get in and out."

"I'll go," Ambrose said.

"No," Theodor cut him off. "You're hardly of sound enough body to even be on the march with us."

"I'm riding, not marching, thank you very much," his

brother shot back with resignation. "And I could manage getting into the city."

"Even if you did, there are those who would recognize and imprison you again. I'm terribly sorry, brother of mine, but you are a dangerous noble and not to be trusted."

Ambrose laughed, and his laughter disintegrated into coughing.

"How 'bout me?" Fig piped up from behind Sianh.

"*Vimzalet*," Sianh said. "It would be a dangerous gamble for a small bug like you. And yet..."

"And yet he knows how to get in and out undetected. Clearly. The Royalists might not even notice him if they saw him, if he can keep his mouth shut." Kristos studied him. "You can relay a message from memory? If you're caught, you play dumb, because so help me, the Royalists can't get near our plans."

"'Course I can! You take me for some dunce, sitting in the corner after getting the lesson wrong?"

"I take you for someone who didn't go to school a minute longer than he had to." Kristos raised an eyebrow. "Repeat it. What does Otni need to know?"

"You're on your way. You're going to attack, full press, from the southeast approach. They are supposed to wait to leave the city until we've cut the field in half."

Sianh tapped his boot on the hard-packed earth. "And what, *vimzalet*, does 'cut the field in half' mean?"

"Until you've crossed half of it. Taken half of it."

"*Taken* half of it, yes. They should hold inside the city until the Royalists have yielded half of the distance between the edges of their field and the city's wall to us. Then they must join us, so that the Royalists are split, fighting in front and behind their lines." Sianh nodded. "And?"

"The navy will not permit escape by ship. There is a contingent blocking escape by the river."

"Good. Good, in the case that we are successful."

"Well, what am I supposed to tell him in case we're not successful?"

"You tell them to hold in the city if we do not take half the field. And send for terms." He swallowed. "And pray."

Fig repeated the entire message again, and I exhaled a shaky breath as he repeated it perfectly. Too small, too young for such an errand, and yet the best choice. I had hoped, without voicing it even to myself, that he wouldn't be able to get the message right here, and have to stay behind. But no, his memory was flawless.

"Then run for the city," Sianh said. "If you are caught, no heroics. You understand, *vimzalet*?" Behind the teasing I saw genuine affection for his little mosquito.

As Fig ran off, I whispered, low, to Sianh, "We didn't tell him what to do if Niko refuses to aid us."

"He will. His city is under attack and, by all the reports of our scouts, in dire straits. The walls will not hold another week. He will not be so foolish as to risk defeat now that he realizes his plight. It is after victory that you must worry about him."

"And I do," Theodor said. "But not now. Not tonight."

"Take your rest," Sianh said. "Tomorrow comes swiftly."

50

GALITHA CITY, WITH THE SPIRE OF THE CATHEDRAL AND THE ordered roofline of the university, the dark smudge of the Public Archive, the blank space between layers of buildings I knew were the public gardens—it was laid out like a map in front of me. My home. For every man in the ranks around me, Galitha City was a symbol of the country itself, the center of the nation, the seat of its governance. Now it was something more, the final battleground in their war. It was ours, I reminded myself with steely resolve. This fight was ours.

Between us and the city, rows of shining bronze Royalist artillery pieces ran like beads on a necklace down entrenchments dug into the ground. Trees from the nearby forest had been felled and used to build crude redoubts, but even though the fortifications lacked refinement, they would still prove barriers for our troops. In regular rhythm, the guns fired on the city.

Galitha City's walls still stood, marred and cracked in some places, but we were not too late. Sianh, on his unassuming gray mount, began directing the movement of the large wings of troops, and I moved back, out of the way. The regiments all had their orders, and I had mine, but Sianh called to me before I could begin.

"You remember?" He trotted toward me, reining in his horse a few paces from me. "You remember your orders?"

"Of course," I said with a forced smile. "You made them very easy. Find a place to cast, and focus on weakening the artillery and the redoubts. If the riflemen are deployed to the field, turn my attention to them."

"You forgot the most important order I gave you," Sianh said, edging closer. "Do not take risks that would allow you to be captured."

I nodded and climbed a shallow rise, where a dip in the slope provided cover. Then I took a breath, steadying myself, and cleared all the clamor of the troops and the bellow of the guns from my thoughts. I pulled a charm first, and wound it tight around Sianh, burying extra fortitude and fortune into every fiber of his uniform. We needed him. As the battle unfolded, all of the plans we made could be lost in a moment's charge or a flank left open—we needed his lightning-fast insight and decisive orders.

Someone moved next to me, and I jumped, even though no enemy could have breached our lines so quickly. Kristos flopped on the grass next to me.

"Your view is better than mine was," Kristos said with a lop-sided grin. He looked so much like he had a year ago, if I could strip away the lines of worry and the gray-and-red uniform.

"Benefit of the job," I replied softly.

"If this doesn't—if we don't—" Kristos cleared his throat. "I've made arrangements for you. Annette is holding back a ship, she'll meet you at Farrow's Cove, just south of—"

"Kristos," I said, shaking my head. "No. You shouldn't have—we need all the ships."

"Too late now." He forced half a smile. "It was a little clipper, not much good for a firefight anyway. But she'll get you out of the country."

"That's not what we promised," I said with a wry smile. I looked back over the field. The dragoons were readying to deploy. I loosed the charm I held spooled and waiting for my command, settling speed and luck over the dragoons, who began to thunder toward the nearest gun emplacement.

Kristos raised a confused brow. "What did we promise?"

"We promised that we'd all hang together," I said. Lines of troops advanced onto the field, the complicated game of battle begun. "Now—this is where I have to start paying attention. You go run along and—what are you doing? Commanding a wing or some such?"

Kristos laughed. "Babysitting the artillery wagons."

I grabbed his hand and squeezed it, briefly, then began the more delicate work of balancing charm and curse at the same time. Soon dark pockets of jet-sparkle shadow engulfed the redoubts still firing on the city, and I drove needles of curse toward the guns themselves, as though I could spike the touchholes of the guns with magic.

I couldn't, of course—but I could etch the curse into the bronze itself and bury it in the wooden carriages they sat on within the redoubts. They fired, one after the other, and at first I didn't notice a change in the rhythm. I steadied my breath. I knew that curse and charm, both, were not fail-safe spells, but part of me had expected to see something dramatic immediately, like the curse I had flung at the Royalist navy ship. Then, slowly, guns stopped firing regularly. One crew worked at a misfire; another was suddenly quite invested in getting something unstuck from the gun's touchhole. A third crew found itself halved by rifle fire. By the time the blockage was cleared in the first gun, another two guns were misfiring, and finally, one cannon ruptured in a burst of smoke and flame.

I allowed myself a small smile—this was a minor victory, but it was helping. Slowly. I held the dark over the remaining artillery battery, and pressed more light toward the dragoons who closed in on a redoubt. The field looked nothing like I would have expected; the large forces were divided into small-scale skirmishes as units converged and clashed, bayonets flashing and every foot of the field fought for and bloodied.

Section by section, foot by foot, the Royalists yielded more and more of the field. We were pressing them back, but they had nowhere to go; the city walls prevented retreat from one direction. From the direction of the river, unseen from my vantage point but ready, a combined regiment of Pellians and Galatines cut off the only other avenue of retreat.

Then an echoing tattoo of drumbeats broke across the field, and I looked toward the sound, holding the strings of my charms and curses like the leashes of unruly dogs. From the forest's edge, lines of men in Royalist uniforms marched toward the fray. My stomach sank—we thought we were engaging the full force of the Royalists, but they had held what appeared to be a dozen companies in reserve, and now they challenged us, forcing our men to split and fight in both directions at once.

I scanned the lines of advancing Royalists, but I didn't see any Serafans. I had doubted they could be used here; the fight was too close, too tightly packed together for their casting to influence only one side or another. But behind the advancing Royalists I heard the wan shadow of music. Serafan pipes. The Royalists were marching away from the influence of the musical casting, but they would be fortified with additional luck, courage, and energy for the first vital moments of engagement.

Then, from the thick wall of forest hedge, coarse brambles not thinned by winter, I saw something else. Rose-pink uniforms. The riflemen.

I knew where my attention had to go, what I had to do, even

as it turned my stomach. The riflemen were the most dangerous strategy that the Royalists could deploy against us. Trained to pick off officers, dragoons, even the musicians whose drumbeats relayed orders, a few well-placed shots could throw our troops into chaos. Fortunately, their finely tuned rifles took over a minute to load per shot. And that gave me time to work.

With a bracing exhale, I pulled fresh dark magic from the ether, thicker and deeper than I had ever attempted to draw out before. Black, dim, and veined with flashes of jet-like sparkle, it surged with a life of its own, a force unused to being manipulated. Still, it yielded to my direction, and I sent it in wide bands across the field to where the rose-uniformed riflemen were taking their positions along the tree line.

I snipped a length of curse from a band like clipping thread from a spool, and wound it around the first rifleman, then another, then the man next to him, all down the line. The magic fought against constraint, but I pressed it into the fibers of uniforms, holding it fast in wool and linen and felted hats. I forced back revulsion in myself as the curse magic began to affect them, one man clapping a hand to his befuddled head like a caricature of confusion. Yet most of them continued to press on, working their recalcitrant hands on weapons that now seemed to rear against them. One man sliced clean through his thumb with his flint, blood staining his coat cuffs as it poured down his wrist.

I found the next rifle unit, and repeated the process, and again, but it wasn't enough. The first unit, even cursed, continued working, and the first rifle shots, louder and sharper than the musket fire, echoed over the field, making my heart constrict in my chest. I couldn't see if they had hit anyone, not yet. But I pulled back to the first unit I had laid curses on, and not only strengthened the magic, but tightened it, sinking it into rifle wood, sinking it deep into cloth until I could feel the resistance of skin and muscle to the invasion of curse magic.

I turned away from the painful horror at what I was doing and pushed deeper.

The first of the riflemen clutched his head in visible pain. His neighbor vomited into the high weeds. Tears streaked my cheeks and nausea rose in my gut, but I continued, tightening the ring of curse around each man, hoping against my own fear that my control was good enough to incapacitate them.

The sharp cracks of the rifles grew sporadic and then disappeared, but I held firm to the darkness, not allowing it to grow any stronger, to siphon any more ill luck out of the ether that could begin to encroach on our own men. I teased it back, thoughts of decaying lilies in cursed water sticking thick in my memory.

Then a shout from behind me, several rapid footfalls, and something broad and solid made contact with the back of my head. I saw black.

51

—–ᨠ––

THE FIRST THING I NOTICED WHEN I WOKE WAS A ROAR OF PAIN, nothing like the needlepoint tapestry of headache after casting too much. I inched a hand up the back of my skull, locating an exquisitely tender egg. I opened my eyes. I was in a tent—no, an officer's marquee. My fingers closed over the blanket beneath me—fine cashmere, not coarse wool.

"They weren't supposed to harm you."

I started, and the pain increased to the point of nausea.

"Help her sit." The voice was familiar, pale and feminine and elegantly precise. Someone stood beside the bed, and I craned my head carefully to see her. A girl in a pink worsted wool gown and large pinner apron—sturdy hands and sun-browned nose, and certainly not the speaker. She looked at me sympathetically as she offered an arm. I waved her off and struggled upright on my own.

Polly sat at the foot of the bed. She watched me impassively, wide blue eyes neither remorseful nor hostile. She wore a riding habit of deep, rich blue, slim gilt braid winking at the seams and buttonholes. The bright flash of sun on her gold buttons made my eyes water.

"Dicey, you can leave. The patient appears at least acceptably recovered." The girl dipped a curtsy and scurried from the tent as quickly as she could.

"What happened?" I asked. I furtively checked myself—still dressed in my gray-and-red traveling suit, not harmed beyond the goose egg on my head.

"Isn't it clear? You were a threat to the Royalist enterprise, and so you were taken captive. A brilliant maneuver by the Third Light Infantry, I'm to understand, undercut your men's defenses at the base of your hill and had you in hand before any resistance on the other side."

"But they weren't supposed to harm me," I repeated with more than a little cynicism.

She met my eyes, level and honest. "I think someone was a bit concerned to have to fight a witch."

"I'm—" But I couldn't make that argument anymore. I had been harming men, directly, with my magic. Did Polly know? Surely by now they must have worked out that the sudden illness of the rifle companies wasn't coincidental.

"Someone will, I am sure, be disciplined. Father didn't want violence on a woman, even a curse-casting Reformist, even in the midst of battle. It felt unseemly."

Polly shifted in her seat, and I realized, with thick foreboding settling in my stomach, that the guns had fallen silent. The field was quiet. No musket fire. No reports of cannons. No shouts. There was no way we were so far removed we could not hear the echoes of battle, if battle still raged. No, silence had descended on the field.

"You didn't go to Serafe."

"No, I did not go to Serafe." Polly's smile was absurdly apologetic. "I feared you would set men to follow me to my father, were I honest about my plans."

"I hadn't even considered it," I said.

"I am in no way surprised you hadn't. Now. I do wish you weren't trying to have this conversation through what I imagine is a wretched headache," Polly said, "but it's imperative we speak of your immediate future."

"With you?" I pressed a hand against my throbbing temple. "That is, you're...authorized to...what is this, a negotiation?"

"The Royalist leadership has given me the authority to open these negotiations with you, given that everyone else is occupied with far greater concerns at the moment."

Carefully, deftly spoken. Nothing revealed about the outcome of the battle.

"What do they want to negotiate? I'm in no position to accept your surrender." The attempt at bravado was weak and I felt its absurdity. No point in bluffing or even joking. I had no leverage here—or did I? Why negotiate with me at all? "What is there to discuss?"

"Your defection." I started, but Polly merely smiled. "Come, you must have considered the reality, that your skill set would benefit anyone who possessed your loyalty."

"There is no way for the Royalists to possess my loyalty," I retorted. "I—I've only employed my skills for the benefit of a cause I believe in."

"Is that so? Because I'd understood you to be rather lukewarm on the subject of revolution until quite recently. Only after my brother took up the cause. You were never a Red Cap alongside your own brother."

"I didn't want my brother to be hurt! I was never in favor of violence. I believed in reform. Is that truly so impossible to comprehend?"

"No. But I suggest something else, that your loyalty is not only to a cause but to people you care for. Your brother. Theodor." She narrowed her eyes. "It's not so easy, always, to speak only in terms of ethics, to act only in the service of causes. Is it?"

My fingers worried the soft weave of the blanket under me. "No, it isn't."

"I think we understand that better than most, you and I." She sighed. "But now. The subject of your loyalties. We would be willing to consider a bargain. You know full well that the lives of your Reformist leadership are forfeit, traitors under the rule of rightful law. Spoken plainly, Theodor and Kristos will both be sentenced to an ignominious death by hanging, to be carried out quite promptly."

Now it was my turn to stare at her impassively, not letting the yawning horror in my gut speak plainly across my face.

"Unless." She leaned forward. "We would give them parole, to leave Galitha immediately, of course, if you pledged your loyalty to the Royalists and to the Galatine Crown."

"You want me to fight for you?"

"In the immediate future, yes. We anticipate difficulty routing the last of the revolutionaries from the city, and in that you would promise to aid us. But after that—no, I don't think your talents are suited for overseas deployments and defensive maneuvers. You would be granted lodging, access to any library or assistants you needed, and given charge to develop casters for the Crown, for Galitha. To rival any adversary."

I wanted nothing more than to spit in her eye, but my dry mouth wouldn't allow for that, and I knew it was unwise, regardless. If Polly and I were here, at parlay, clearly the battle had been won—

I stopped. Had it? The guns were silent, but that did not mean that the Royalists had won. It didn't mean *anyone* had won. Parlay. Perhaps the two sides had merely come to parlay.

If I agreed to her terms, I would be loosed on my countrymen. That much was clear—she and her fellows would hold the lives of my brother and my beloved over me until I had spun enough dark magic to effect a surrender. They had Serafan casters who could confirm my work, who I would likely work alongside. But—the thought crept in, I could be deployed against the city and never know who held the field.

Still, insidious and ugly—if the Reformists had been beaten on the field, refusal meant the lives of those dearest to me. I took a shaky breath, knowing the gamble I had to take.

52

"I'M SORRY," I SAID WITH A TREMBLING VOICE, "BUT WE ALL promised to hang together."

Her breath hiccupped slightly, surprised, and before she could recover, I knew—I had guessed correctly. The Royalists had not won, and their gambit was to not only remove me from the battlefield calculus but turn me against my own.

"Well. If that's your choice, I'm sure you'll get your wish. But you might reconsider—"

"I won't. The guns will recommence momentarily, I imagine. Unless your brother and mine have accepted the surrender of your father."

The carefully controlled mask cracked, and she scowled. "You are cleverer than I gave you credit for. No. We have not surrendered. This was merely a parlay—well, the gambit failed. They'll try the same shoe on the other foot, of course, if it comes to it—see if they're willing to accept some forfeit for your return."

"They won't," I said, confident. I could trust Sianh to stay strong in that regard even if the others buckled. "Tell me honestly, who has the upper hand now?"

She stood and shook out her deep indigo skirts. "You. But

you're counting on the participation of the men still inside the city walls." She didn't wait for confirmation. "You won't get it." She plucked her hat from a finely carved table, its balance wobbly on the uneven ground. "Perhaps you would be interested in watching," she added as she perched the petite tricorne on her rolls of fair hair.

I hesitated, but the rumble of the guns resuming convinced me. The war still waged. I couldn't play my part unless I stayed present and ready.

I swung my legs over the side of the bed and let the tent swim around me for a moment as I regained my bearings. Then I followed Polly outside.

I quickly ascertained our position—encamped between the advancing Royalists and the city, but closer to the sea than the battlefield. If the Reformists took the day, it wouldn't matter; Annette's ships were closing in on the harbor and would not permit retreat. But Polly didn't know that—none of the Royalists did.

"Our best view would be from a bit higher up," Polly said, her crisp, conversational tone returned as though she were welcoming dignitaries to tea instead of escorting a hostage. "But I think that unwise—it would be in view of the fracas back there, and in view is in range." She essayed a slight smile. I eyed her, suspicious of her courtesy. Did she still think I might abandon my decision and fight for the Royalists?

Not likely, I ventured. This was the game she knew well, a game of polite faces and silent deception, a game of cordial words and hidden blades. I kept my distance, even though I felt sure another attempt at knifing me was unlikely. She didn't usually have to bloody the weapons herself, and I doubted it benefited her now.

"There. The harbor." I saw it, not too distant, the water

reflecting golden sunlight as the day arched across the sky. Packed with Royalist ships, ready to fight or to flee. I didn't smile—even though they didn't know that they were lying in a trap.

"You already know what our Serafan allies can do," she said. "But we have not yet shown the Reformists in the city. We felt it best to save that, to hold it in reserve."

"We?" I asked. "Do you help make the martial decisions for the Royalist army?"

She tugged her skirt away from a fallen branch with a sharp jerk of her hand. "No, we don't need women and nuns to do that." I felt the keen knife-edge of grief—and knew Alba could have leveled Polly with one look. "Or disgraced Serafans—I heard he was a prostitute. Is that true?" She turned to me with a sardonic smile.

I returned it with a pert grin. "He was. Quite highly sought after. Excellently talented," I added, letting her color around the ears. *Go ahead and try to embarrass me*, I bid her silently. *I grew up among the trash bins and gutters, I can win that game.*

But then a faint echo from the harbor stopped any words in my throat. Music. Serafan harp and violin, their tones thicker, wilder than Galatine instruments. We could hear only the echoes, only the remnant of the music they plied, but I knew full well— it was rife with curse magic, and it was bombarding the city.

I searched it out, trying to pinpoint which ship carried the curse casters. I found the black cloud of glittering magic emanating from a space in the center of the harbor. "They must be on a very small ship," I said.

"A little skiff," Polly confirmed. "Who would have guessed that the most powerful weapon on the seas would be borne by Admiral Merhaven's personal sailing vessel?" She laughed, white teeth showing like pearls.

"Is it the same?" I asked. "As before, as at Hazelwhite? The physical disorientation, the illness? Or are they trying something different?"

"Can't you tell?"

"No," I said. "Perhaps if I studied their methods more, but I'm no expert in their version of casting." I was barely an expert in my own, I felt, still experimenting and testing, failing as often as I succeeded.

"Interesting. I don't know." She essayed a sly glance in my direction. "I don't suppose the promise of studying with the Serafans, learning their methods, would entice you any more than what I've already offered?"

"Afraid not."

"Pity. Galitha needs someone like you, you know. The world is changing. I can't imagine any country can ignore casting any longer, after what you've done. Even Kvyset," she added lightly.

I ignored her, and pinpointed the space where a single sail, stowed but gleaming white, bobbed in the harbor. I couldn't see the deck of the ship itself, and of course couldn't see the instruments, the musicians, or the amplifying device they had used on us. It was far away, much farther than I had ever been from a successful target.

Still, the cloud of curse magic was clear, and had a clear source. I flicked a bit of charm magic from the ether, and drove it toward the curse magic. If I could bisect it, as I had done during the Battle of Rock's Ford, perhaps I could lessen its effects on the city, perhaps even divert it entirely. I pushed it onward, farther, but sweat began to bead on my forehead. The hard-driven line began to unravel and spread back into the ether.

I was out of range, and utterly incapable of altering the Serafan casting.

Polly watched me with a quirked eyebrow. "You tried, didn't you?"

I didn't bother replying.

"You did! Would that I could see it, could see what you see." She met my eyes. "Yes, I am a bit jealous. I'm allowed—you can not only see but manipulate the strings of fortune binding the world." She looked back toward the harbor, the minute white sail her only indication of the source of the Serafan magic. "It won't be long, I imagine, until they capitulate, and if they don't—well, they'll be easy enough to rout."

"You have to win on the field first," I said, cold fear trickling through my confident words. The riflemen were probably picking off our officers even as I spoke. We had counted on reinforcements from the city, for the gates to open and Niko's men to flood the field—but only when we had successfully gained enough of the field for them to take that gamble. "You have to breach the walls."

"We will," Polly said. "Eventually."

53

DESPITE POLLY'S INSISTENCE THAT THE ROYALIST VICTORY WAS near at hand, the sun crested past noon and the guns didn't abate. She grew tired of watching the harbor, where a cloud of curse she couldn't see sustained an assault on the city, and directed me to return with her for luncheon.

"You're being absurdly polite to a hostage," I said as we returned to the tent that I now realized were her campaign accommodations.

"I'm merely treating you as I might a high-ranking officer." Polly called for Dicey, who hurried to her mistress with a flagon of cool water and a pair of glasses. "Lunch please. Some of the smoked cheese, and the leek pastry, if there's any left."

"Someone here is making leek pastry?" I snorted. "Not exactly eating as a common soldier, are you?"

"Dicey is worth her weight in gold. She can cook almost anything using just a brazier." Polly poured me a glass of water, and Dicey returned with a platter of cold ham, cheese, and half of a galette that smelled heavily of onion.

I hesitated over the plate Dicey served me, and Polly laughed. "I won't poison you. That would be very stupid." She broke off a piece of cheese with her delicate fingers. "Think of it our way.

You have to either join us—yes, I know, that's very unlikely, thank you for disappointing me yet again—or be fairly tried and hanged. As a criminal. Otherwise we're the horrid war criminals who murdered a prisoner of war with a leek tart."

"Fair enough," I said, nibbling at a corner of pastry. Polly was right—Dicey was a culinary genius. But I wasn't hungry, not with the echo of the guns and the dark magic seeping through the city.

There was little point in conversing with Polly. I was not going to change her mind, nor would she change mine, like parallel rivers running close but never coming to a confluence. A battle raged without us, all the words and pamphlets and arguments and laws Galitha could produce coming down to shot and steel, to bloody ground yielded and gained.

"Do you ever get tired of it?" I murmured.

"What?" Polly set her fork down next to an empty plate. I wasn't sure how she managed to eat, but I'd learned that the nobility of Galitha had stomachs of iron when it came to managing their nerves. They could pretend blithe contentment at the buffet in the midst of a firestorm.

"Waiting. Waiting for this battle to end, waiting for the council to vote on a measure, waiting for someone else to do something when you'd damn well rather just do it yourself?"

Polly smiled, faint but honest. "All the time. It's why I'm here instead of holed up in Serafe with my mother and Jonamere. At least here I can do something. Maybe not as much as you," she said with residual spitefulness fading, "but something. It was my idea to remove you from the battle."

"Well, thank you very much for that."

"Come now, you can't blame me. Father and the others still don't, I think, appreciate just how much you could do. How much I can presume you were doing."

"And you do?"

"I speak better Serafan than they do, and I understand the magicians they've brought here when they say that what you've done is beyond their abilities." She smiled as I started. "Yes, they admit as much. They want to know how you've done it."

I fell still, forcing my face into an impassive mask. I had feared this. "It's not something I can teach," I hedged.

"I don't know your abilities as a teacher, but their ability to learn is not dependent on that. It's something you could write about, something you could record. Something others could study." A slow shadow of understanding crept over her face. "You're afraid of it, aren't you? Of what you can do. Are you afraid of being powerful?"

The question slapped me like a dash of cold water. It was incisive, reaching past the recent months of necessity and into who I was, a seamstress, a charm caster, a Pellian girl trying to make a name for herself in Galitha City. I had never imagined power for myself. "I'm afraid of what this can do," I answered instead, "in the wrong hands."

"As were the men who invented gunpowder, too, I'm sure, and cannon, and fast ships. I imagine if we trace it far enough back, the first man to whittle a blade from flint said, 'Ah, but can I trust all of my neighbors with one of these?'"

"And it takes very little study to prove his concerns correct."

"Not unfounded, no. But impossible to avoid. The world marches on, Sophie, and either you can accept the power that comes with what you've discovered, or someone else, someday, will."

Shouts from the hilltop overlooking the city interrupted us. A runner, then another, raced past Polly's tent, and she followed them. I began to stand, but a man in the brown uniform of a City Guard stopped me. A member of the Royalist army now, and utilizing his skills perhaps gained in the prisons of the Stone Castle to guard me.

"What's happening?" I asked.

"I couldn't say," he said, with a slight shake of his head that told me he was reading nothing good for the Royalists in the bustle in the center of the encampment. "You just stay put there. And don't..." He clamped his mouth shut.

"Don't try any of my witchcraft on you?" My mouth twisted into a wry grin. "But how would you know?"

"Now then! You give me any reason to think it's so, and I'll—" He pressed his lips together against the unsavory thought of shooting a woman point-blank. "I've a musket right here." He held it out as though to prove his point.

I sat down, weary. "I have nothing to gain in harming you," I said. There was a time I would have said that I wouldn't, that I couldn't harm him. That time was gone.

He positioned himself nervously by the flap of the tent. Dicey stepped toward me, and I started. "Are you done with that?" she asked, pointing to my plate.

"Yes, I—it was very good, but I have no appetite, I'm sorry."

"I haven't, either," she said. She had freckles across her sun-tanned nose, and bright blue eyes. "Do you want tea? I've ginger tea, if your stomach is all knots."

"Thank you, but no." I sighed. "May I ask—why are you here?"

She shrugged, rattling the plate of uneaten leek tart. "You mean why am I with the Royalists and not the Reformists?"

"Or with anyone at all, yes."

"I was in Galitha City when the Red Caps staged their coup." She swept a few loose crumbs off the table. "We—my family—wanted nothing to do with it. Didn't want that kind of death on our doorsteps."

"I can understand that," I said, hoping I sounded less jaded than I felt.

"But it came anyway, and my brother got caught up in the street fighting. Took a blow to the head—we don't know who did it, and I don't care. He doesn't, either. Never woke up. He died a few days later." She straightened. "The Red Caps and the Reformists after them can't keep the peace. Can't keep things from turning to riot and rot. When Niko Otni and his horde took over the city, I fled. Plenty of people did. Plenty of us came here. We've been safe here."

I hesitated. There were a thousand arguments I could make—Kristos's impassioned appeals for basic liberty, Theodor's dogged determination on the importance of a rule of law, Niko's confidence in the commoners, my own realization that stability could only be bought so long, and at a high price. But I found I couldn't voice any of them. Not now.

"I'm sorry about your brother. I hope your family is safe."

"Damn your eyes!" Polly sailed back into the tent, the guard following her, bayonet fixed. "What did you do?"

"Me?" I stood, reflexively backing away under the scrutiny of a bayonet pointed at me.

"In the harbor. Whore's ass, I shouldn't have shown you, you did something, but I can't figure how—"

"I have no idea what you're talking about," I said, forcing my voice to be as level as I could, even as I quaked with fear under Polly's anger and the guard's steel. Dicey had wisely slipped away.

"How did you manage to send the message, that's what I don't understand."

"I truly," I repeated, "do not know what's happened."

Polly watched me a long moment, and finally made up her mind. "You don't, do you?" She gestured to the guard. "Come with me."

54

WE CLIMBED THE LOW HILL AGAIN, OUT OF VIEW OF THE BATTLEFIELD but with eyes on the harbor, and I knew immediately what had infuriated Polly.

Black smoke rose from the harbor, thick and curling, and under it, flames lapped what rigging and sails I could see. I strained to make out the Serafan casters' ship, but I couldn't pick it out in the hazy chaos of destruction.

"Mercy," I whispered. For once, I was thankful I couldn't see more clearly. Sailors and marines were probably leaping from ships for their lives, caught in a crushing melee of broken hulls and flames.

"No, you didn't know." Polly swallowed. "Tell me, is the casting still holding over the city?"

She had no way of knowing. The Serafan casters had all been deployed, on the field and on that ship in the harbor. I answered honestly anyway. "No. It's gone. It doesn't last past casting it, not long anyway."

"So the city is freed from its effects."

"If my experience with the 'effects' are any indication, yes." I exhaled, still shaky, still very aware of the cruel steel of the bayonet mere yards away from me. "How did it happen?" I ventured to ask.

"How?" Polly's voice raised a pitch. "Fire ships, that's how. Whatever pitiful excuse you have for a navy managed—we should have known. It was a dreadful mistake to mass our navy here. Damn it all." Her voice seethed with anger but her body remained motionless, her face stone, watching the destruction of the strength of the Galatine navy.

Annette. The thought soared, and then crashed into itself, faced with the death and pain surely overtaking Galitha City's harbor. It didn't matter that those men would have had me killed in an instant; I couldn't rejoice over their deaths. But Annette! Against the massed Royalist navy we had held out some hope she could delay or complicate their retreat, but she had managed something far more effective.

A roar rolled from the battlefield and across the Royalist encampment, rising up the hill. Free of the curse casting, Niko's men within the city had begun their foray from within the walls. That meant—my eyes went wide at the thought—that even without my help, even without the benefit of additional charms hung over the Reformist soldiers or curses disabling the riflemen, we had breached past the midway point on the field.

We had pushed the Royalists back and now the rest of the Reformist army would clamp them in a pincer, between two advancing lines, and we would have our surrender.

"It won't be long, will it?" I asked.

Polly's mouth was a hard line. "From what I understand, no. Becoming trapped between the two halves of your army was our worst-case outcome, but even then...even then we anticipated being able to retreat around the city to the harbor. That is now impossible.

"I could have you killed," she said quite suddenly. My chest constricted around her words. "Perhaps I ought to."

"I'm not a bargaining chip?"

"Yes, you are." She turned away, finally, from the burning harbor. There were glints of tears in her eyes, but she blinked them quickly away. "And whatever else, I would rather Galitha—even a perverse Galitha—have you and your abilities than leave us defenseless in the face of the Serafans, should they ever deploy their casting against us."

I softened slightly. Polly, Lady Apollonia, loved her country. She loved it badly, twisted her love for it to suit her and her desires, but she loved it.

"We are both for Galitha, whatever else might be between us," I said. "And I—I can't promise anything, but I will advocate for the right treatment of all prisoners."

"I know you will." Polly sighed. "You proved that well enough when, sweet fool that you are, you let me go after I tried to assassinate you."

"You're a very bad assassin."

Polly hiccupped a bitter laugh. "I am. Would that I had succeeded, perhaps this day would have been different."

"I do not think so," I said. "What role I played was far less than what the common people of Galitha effected."

"So you say." Polly pulled her shoulders back and smoothed her dark blue skirts. "I imagine we have a parlay to attend, and soon."

I didn't expect to be included in the parlay that led to the formal surrender of the Royalist troops, but the king decided I was worth at least something as a bit of theater to bluff with, so sent a runner to have me brought to them under guard, with bound hands and, ludicrously, blindfolded. Pageantry, I guessed, for the benefit of anyone who thought I might dare to cast a curse over the proceedings.

Though I couldn't see where I was shepherded, the shade and the breeze told me we were under a pavilion erected near the battlefield. A marquee top, perhaps. *What a ridiculous affectation*, I chided whoever had wasted time in putting up a sunshade for the proceedings. As though someone had expected a painting to be done of the great surrender at Galitha City, and the artist was even then sketching from life.

I sobered—it was likely a scene that would be painted and displayed, many times over. And here I was, trussed like a pig at market and with a blindfold.

I heard the arrival of the Reformist contingent. My heart was in my throat, pressing against my breath, waiting to hear a voice, any voice I recognized. Terrified that one might be absent.

"You could take the blindfold off her, you know." Kristos. Cocky, self-assured, slightly inappropriate even now. I exhaled in shaking relief. "She doesn't have to see you to curse you."

"It stays." The resonant voice of the king himself. "Well. It seems you have bested our efforts here."

"We have bested your efforts completely." Theodor. My knees felt suddenly weak, buried fears that he wouldn't survive the battle resurfacing now that safety gave them voice. Tears dampened the interior of the blindfold. "We demand unequivocal surrender."

"You demand?" That was Pommerly.

"That is, is it not, the correct term?" Sianh's careful, clipped diction. I smiled—all three of them, safe.

"No, it's the correct term," Kristos said. "He's hoping he can bluff us out of pressing the fact that they're completely surrounded and have no means of retreat."

"Enough." Regardless of his current tenuous position, the former king of Galitha commanded attention. "We mean to offer surrender. But there are terms."

"You're in no position to demand terms," Kristos said.

"But we will make our requests. We do hold a prisoner of some value." I stiffened, but I tried my best not to look concerned. *Whatever they say*, I begged silently, *don't give in. We've come this far.*

"You'll give us all safe passage and protection," a new voice said. Merhaven. "You will not take us prisoner, no executions. And in return for that goodwill, we will return her."

"No prisoners," mused Kristos. "No executions. That sounds very well indeed."

"Then we have struck a bargain?" Merhaven was too eager.

I could almost sense the deep breath Theodor took before he began to speak. "We can be persuaded to allow the soldiers and officers of the Royalist army to remain free, under the good faith of parole, under no penalty, provided of course that their loyalty remains to Galitha. Whatever government Galitha enacts, they shall serve it, or they leave the service of the army immediately and return to their homes."

There was a stifling silence under the pavilion. "We can discuss the army separately," Merhaven finally said. "We require such for those nobles leading this army."

"I thought I noticed a strange emphasis on *we* in that first statement," Kristos said. "Surely you aren't attempting to negotiate solely for yourselves and your highest-ranking officers?" I could imagine his face, half a grin lilting across it, his eyes sparking. "That would not look well, willingness to abandon an offer of parole for your entire force, in favor of protecting your own flesh. Tsk, tsk."

Merhaven had never, I imagined, encountered anyone quite

like Kristos, and I could imagine the red tinge spreading over his ears and cheeks. But it was the king who spoke instead. "Theodor, you must think reasonably. It would be barbarous to imprison your own father and sister."

"It was barbarous to bring war to your own countrymen because you didn't like laws passed in their consideration." My heart ached for Theodor, for the control in his voice, for the dearth of emotion I knew must have been painful for him to achieve. "We will accept your surrender. Your army will have parole, under the limitations we've discussed. But you and the commanding officers of this army will stand trial before your countrymen for your crimes. That is the offer we make."

"Then we will execute the witch we captured," Pommerly interjected.

"You will return my sister, or we will rescind the offer of parole for your army," Kristos half shouted.

"No, you won't," Merhaven said. "Because that wouldn't look well." Kristos had set himself up perfectly for that, I thought with withering hope. "So the witch dies, unless you are willing to grant us the same protection as the army."

"No." I started at Polly's voice. "No, she does not. What laws has she broken?"

"Lady Apollonia, this is not a good time to—"

"To what, Father? To remind everyone that we are bound by certain conventions, certain laws, and that this woman hasn't broken any of them?" She laughed lightly, exemplifying that control I wasn't sure I could ever muster. "If you want a law against casting, I suggest one be enacted. But she was a combatant in this battle, the same as any man-at-arms captured. See?" I felt her light fingers on my arm, on the red wool trim of my gray riding habit. "She is even in uniform." I felt her hand tremble slightly over mine.

The silence was oppressive, beating against my ears as the darkness assaulted my unseeing eyes. "Very well," the king finally said. "We've played our hand, and it turns out that both of my children carry trump cards of laws and ethics. Would that I had raised them poorly." Yet even then, in the face of crushing defeat and the end of life as he understood it, there was a faint spark of pride when he spoke of Theodor and Polly. "You have our surrender."

55

SIANH REMOVED THE BINDINGS FROM MY WRISTS A MOMENT LATER, and I tore the blindfold from my eyes and ran to Theodor and Kristos. I flung myself at both of them, surprised to realize I was sobbing even as I laughed.

"Slow down, there," Kristos said as he half tumbled into a tent pole and the entire pavilion shook. Theodor caught my hand and I saw that a coarse bandage wrapped Kristos's calf.

"Oh! Oh you're—"

"Nothing serious, shot just grazed it a bit."

"Your brother bleeds like a hog," Sianh said.

"I think you mean 'stuck pig,'" Kristos said. "And yes, I don't do anything halfway. It's fine," he reassured me, but I swiftly pulled a charm from the ether and embedded it into the fibers of the bandage, imbuing it with health. The effort on top of the rush of emotion made me light-headed, and the edges of my vision faded toward light.

"Steady," Theodor said. The trio of Royalist leadership, and Polly, had already been marched away under guard, and three coffee-colored camp chairs they had set up like thrones for the interview remained. Theodor guided me toward one, and Kristos, with a grunt, gratefully settled into another.

Theodor quickly related the ending of the battle. "We crossed the halfway mark, and Otni did not deploy. I assumed Fig didn't make it through. It was close for a while, but suddenly they all poured out of the main gate like a flood."

"It wasn't Fig's fault," I said. "The Serafans were casting on the city, from the harbor. We couldn't have seen it from our position, even if I'd been there," I added. "If Annette hadn't sent in the fire ship, I don't know if they could have been stopped."

"Sweet Galatine Divine," murmured Theodor. "It was never a strategy we discussed, but I suppose I always knew it was an option. A desperate one—if we wished to retain the Galatine naval vessels for the Republic. All of those ships, destroyed?"

"Enough of them, surely." Sianh's mouth was set in a firm line. "There is an expression in Serafan. 'Better to drown than burn, better to burn than drown.'"

My mouth was dry. "Are all your expressions that depressing?"

"I could not say." He shook his head. "But what a terrible way to perish."

"Let's not discuss it any longer," I whispered. "Is it over? Really and truly?"

"The Royalist army is secured," Theodor confirmed, "and we're in the process of combing the area and searching near the harbor. Everyone is being kept under guard and arms requisitioned. We will have to figure out exactly how to—what? Muster them out?"

"They have terms." Kristos shrugged. "They'll need to decide if they're loyal to a new Republic of Galitha or if they want to find other employment."

"We shall not send our troops home quickly," Sianh cautioned. "Until we are assured there are no holdouts, no southern lords ready to fight."

"You expect that?"

"I expect many things that never happen," Sianh said with a grin. I finally felt the wash of relief I didn't realize I'd been waiting for at his smile. The grim battlefield demeanor was gone, and he was, though still engaged in serious matters, lighter. "But for now, there is a city to march into in triumph."

Sianh secured horses for all of us; his mount and Theodor's were not fresh and, as he said, deserved a rest and some oats. There were no sidesaddles to be had, so I was obliged to hitch my skirts awkwardly around my legs. The wool molded against my legs like a pair of unattractive breeches, and I would have cared less that I looked like a country bumpkin riding the family mule to market if we weren't about to parade in front of the entire population of Galitha City.

I rode between Theodor and Kristos, at both of their insistence. Sianh, along with a few officers selected by him for exceptional service, rode behind us, and the First Regiment quickly martialed itself to follow while the rest of the soldiers took on the work left in the wake of the battle—securing prisoners, locating the injured, aiding in the field hospitals. I felt exposed on my mount, on display along with the leadership of the army of the Republic of Galitha, but as we took a steady pace across the battlefield, I suppressed any argument. I had fought here, too. I forced myself to look at the battered redoubts, bodies still lying where they had fallen, at the artillery pieces, abandoned at the last minute by Royalist soldiers but with curse magic still clinging to the places where I had sunk it into wood of carriages and emplacements.

I turned my face away from the field. I knew the death we had wrought here. It was impossible to deny, to forget. It pressed itself into my memory, that I dealt out loss just as the cannons and muskets had. With a heavy sigh, I looked instead toward the open gate of Galitha City.

I had seen my city thousands of times, the gate we rode through as familiar as a corner of my house or the shape of my own fingernails. I had seen it in summer, winter, and every weather, but I had never seen it from horseback, lined with cheering and weeping citizens.

I looked over the crowd gathered to watch as we rode toward Fountain Square, where I knew Niko's headquarters had been and where ours would, at least temporarily, be. Most looked weary, worn to their cores, and pale, but with the first blush of revival sweeping their cheeks and underused smiles creeping over their faces. They were thin, most of them. Clothes needed mending. Buildings needed repair. There were certainly logistics of feeding and housing all of these people to address—the larders of the besieged city were sure to be scraping thin, and many houses were uninhabitable.

For now, for today, I could only smile, joy, relief, and real, tangible hope breaking across my face like sunrise. The people lining the avenue felt the same, I knew. The storm was over. Morning had broken, finally, clear and promising. And so many people! As though all of Galitha City had gathered, united in celebration that, if nothing else, tomorrow had finally come and it had not brought death and destruction.

We spilled into Fountain Square. We were met by not only more crowds of cheering citizens but by a bloc of Niko's red-capped army. Niko Otni stood at their head, a polished spontoon in his hand. Beside me, Kristos and Theodor slowed, and Sianh ordered the regiment behind us to come to a halt.

Niko took two paces forward and met first Kristos's eyes, and then, briefly, mine. There was still a dark determination there, as though this battle was not over. I clenched my fists around the reins, and my horse skittered backward, sensing my anxiety. Readying to fight, I knew as I felt the muscles tense and spring beneath me, and I took a steadying breath and forced myself to relax.

Niko broke into a wide smile and lowered his spontoon. Kristos dismounted and embraced him, then Theodor. I dismounted last, but did not approach him. I glanced at Sianh, who had taken the reins of Kristos's horse. He nodded once, keeping his eyes on Niko.

"We must begin to settle this split army into one whole. I will find someone to take the mounts," he said.

"We're meeting in Otni's headquarters now," Theodor said, joining us. "We need to decide—"

"Many things," I said quietly, laying my hand on his arm.

56

"I say we execute the lot of them," Niko said. "They would have done no less for us."

"Be that as it may, that doesn't mean executing regular troops is within the conventions of war," Theodor said. "Nor the terms of the surrender we negotiated."

"Sod your conventions! And I wasn't present at your negotiations," Niko said. "What's to stop them from mustering against us again if we just—what? Let them go?"

"The regulars are paid to fight," Kristos countered. "They're not going to take up arms without that. And we control the treasury now, remember?"

"We control some of it. Too much of it is still tied up in noble estates," Niko said. "But fine. We'll shelve discussing what to do with the soldiers."

"No," Kristos said, "we're done discussing it. We have to conduct ourselves as a legitimate government moving forward, and that means honoring our treaties and pacts." Theodor nodded in agreement, and Annette slipped quietly into the room.

I caught her hand in relief—we hadn't had bad news out of the harbor, still simmering with smoking ships, but that didn't reassure me until I saw her in person. Her hair was a disheveled mess beneath her cocked hat, and there were scorch marks on her wool coat. I asked my question without speaking—was she all right?

She forced a small smile, but there was a haunted hollowness in her eyes, and I saw—she had made the decision to send the fire ships into the harbor and knew already, knew in her deepest core, that she would have to live with that decision for the rest of her life.

"Your treaty is less important than the larger question anyway," Niko said.

"Which is?" Kristos waited patiently.

Niko was almost enjoying this, I thought bitterly as he unrolled a large map. All of Galitha spread over the table between us, the southern coastline and eastern forests, the mountains and the rivers cupping broad plains between them. Marked in reds and golds across the map were, I realized as I squinted, noble estates.

"As I said." Niko cleared his throat. "The nobles still own most of the land producing grain and, ultimately, gold. How do you prevent another insurrection when they have every advantage?"

A sour silence permeated the room. "I suppose you had something in mind," I said.

"As a matter of fact—"

"But it's not your choice," I said.

"The hell it isn't! It's not yours," Niko shouted. "You and your prince don't make the rules here."

"Never said we did," I replied. "But you don't, either. We have a Council of Country. Properly elected. Now that we've combined with the forces here, your men will elect representatives from their ranks to fill the rest of the seats. And then they can make the decisions."

Niko narrowed his eyes. "How do I trust that this council isn't seeded with nobles?"

"Oh, never fear," Kristos said. "We've got a couple."

"What!" Niko slammed his hand on the table. "Of all the gall. I believed it of your simpering sister, Balstrade, I certainly believe it of that crown prince buffoon, but—"

"They joined the Reformist fight willingly. They earned their voice."

"A voice to drown the rest of us out," Niko said.

"They're solidly in the minority," Kristos said. "There's no way they can swing the vote toward their interests." His voice lowered, almost dangerous. "And they fought and died for us, too."

"We can't have any left. None. What they did—damn your eyes, Balstrade! You saw that field, flooded with the blood of our countrymen, and you'd forget already that the nobility did that?"

"I'd be hard-pressed to forget that," Kristos replied tersely. "But we built an army of Reformists, not just Red Caps. Most of them aren't going to take kindly to—what, Niko? You want to slaughter everyone with a noble bloodline in the country?"

Niko clamped his jaw shut but stared at Kristos, his answer clear.

"I'm not going to institute some sort of purge, a slaughter. That's not what this army fought for."

"Then what are you going to do?" Niko demanded.

"We're going to let the elected council do its job," Theodor said, his tone confidently deployed to end the argument.

"You!" Niko snorted. "You don't have anything to say here. You don't have a role in this play any longer. Take your princely costume and get the hell off the stage."

"He's wearing the same thing I am, Otni. And he absolutely does have a role here," Kristos shouted. "He led this army as much as I did, and he's not any less entitled to his place here than you are."

"That," Niko said, ice in his eyes, "is a matter of opinion."

"There's a more pressing concern, anyway." I spoke softly, but it echoed in the silent room. "We're holding the leadership of the Royalist army prisoner. Per the terms of surrender. Merhaven, Pommerly, several other nobles in the highest roles of leadership. And the king."

"What of the queen? And their children?" Niko shot back.

"Most of their children are Reformists," Kristos replied. "Their youngest son is but a child, too young to be held accountable. He and his mother are in hiding, probably in Serafe somewhere. I'm inclined to pretend we don't even know that and let them escape. We are holding Lady Apollonia."

Theodor's mouth was a taut line, and he gripped the edge of the table with white knuckles. "I believe," he said carefully, "that it would be right for the elected representatives to decide their fate."

"There ought to be a well-documented trial conducted as tightly within your legal framework as possible." Sianh hadn't said a word as we'd quarreled, but now that a clear direction was reached, he added his guidance. "This is the beginning. It must be clean."

"Clean." Niko snorted. "Nothing about this has been clean, Serafan."

"I know much of war. I know it is not clean. But you, as governors, must be."

"Governors. I rather like that title," Kristos said.

"Don't get too attached," I said. "The council will be deciding how long you're keeping it."

"And," Niko said with his cockeyed grin, "how long the nobles and royals in our custody keep their heads."

57

THE COUNCIL OF COUNTRY CONVENED THE NEXT MORNING IN THE open hall of the Public Archive to deliberate over the first major decision of the new Republic of Galitha: what was to be done with the leaders of the Royalists. I watched the debates, Niko's impassioned oration in favor of swift execution, several more cautious arguments about the lack of precedent for executing surrendered enemies, an extremely dull exposition on the history of treason trials in Galitha from a lawyer named Maurice Forrest, and an earnest appeal to justice from Vernon Harrel, the southern soldier I had last spoken to in Hamish's field hospital at Westland Hall.

By late morning, all the members of the council who wished to have a voice in the debate had done so. There were tentative forays into legal debate and confident assertions of pragmatic concerns. I had promised Polly that I would offer some advocacy for the fair treatment of the prisoners. As individuals. I took a shaky breath. I had no vote, but the council would entertain opinions from the gallery before proceeding to a vote.

I stood. "Governors, permission to speak."

Kristos started, surprised not that I was there, but that I would add my voice to public debate. A lot had changed since the last time we had that opportunity, I thought ruefully. "Granted," he said.

"I'm not a lawyer. I don't know the laws or the legal precedent for executing prisoners of war. But then again, most of you aren't, either," I said. This earned a few light chuckles. "I'm not a soldier. I didn't fight on the field of battle with you. But I've risked my life alongside you, and I knew that I wouldn't be granted even the consideration we're giving the Royalist leadership now." Nods from the more fervent Red Caps.

"This is the first thing that this council is going to do, and it is how you'll be remembered. You will build the laws of Galitha on the back of this choice. Will it be clemency, or justice?" I paused. "Or does cowardice pass for clemency, or vengeance pretend to be justice?" That earned a few sour looks from across the range of men assembled. I pressed on anyway. "We should be governed not by our basest qualities. Clemency is not weakness when granted fairly in the face of evidence. Vengeance is not justice when meted out to anyone who's offended you. Consider the crimes of the individuals and judge them from there."

"What are you saying?" Niko demanded.

"I've heard these debates consider all of the prisoners as one unit. But they're not. The crime for which execution is the prescribed sentence is not 'fighting against us and losing.' It's treason." I waited to see if Niko, if the assembly gathered, understood what I was saying. "Merhaven, Pommerly, and the king conspired to undermine the laws of the land as passed by the then-ruling-body, the Council of Nobles. That was, in my estimation, treason. The other officers currently held prisoner may not have been involved in that conspiracy. Neither was, from the evidence thus presented, Lady Apollonia." I swallowed the half lie. I knew Polly had been actively complicit, but no one else needed to know the extent of her treachery unless it came out in a trial.

"They still sided with a treasonous government," Niko said.

"Yes, they did," said Kristos, "but the reasons and rationales of the individual become far more varied at that point." He looked at me and smiled faintly.

"Call the vote." Niko smacked his hand on the table in front of him, dismissive.

The first proposal on the table, the one that had been debated, was summary execution for all the prisoners. It failed, by a large margin. I exhaled a shaking breath as a new proposal was swiftly made and seconded, to try each of the prisoners individually, and this passed by an even larger margin than the first had failed.

Noon crested the sky and the councillors recessed to scrounge something to eat, still being served communally out of Niko's system of provisions. I wasn't sure why I left the Public Archive and made my way to the Stone Castle, but I did. It was just a short walk across Fountain Square, a strangely familiar set of steps across now-pockmarked cobblestones, beside the scarred and burned fountain.

No one stopped me; the guards recognized me, or if they didn't, they knew the uniform of the Reformist army and the woman wearing its colors must be the magician, the witch, the consort of the Rebel Prince—whatever character I played in the story they wrote for themselves of the Galatine Civil War. We were all still writing it, I reminded myself. It wasn't over, not yet.

Not while the king and the others were held in cells below my feet.

"Take me to Lady Apollonia," I said to the sergeant standing guard over the desk.

"Has that been authorized by the governors? I mean to say, no offense, but I've orders not to allow the prisoners access to visitors. Except when authorized."

"Would I be here if it wasn't?"

"Suppose not." The unclear balance of power worked to my advantage this time, but I would have to consider, in future, where I would require the permissions of an ordinary citizen, and where I would walk as an assumed leader. I almost laughed—a year ago I would never have presumed I would be considered an exception to any rule, law, or polite suggestion. "All right, Cortland, you take her down there."

Lady Apollonia was held apart from the men; the Reformist army guards running the place kept up the tradition of male and female wards, despite only having the handful of prisoners. I was familiar with the cells, having spent an uncomfortable day in their damp, close confines a year before. I couldn't sneak a blanket out of the communal storerooms without someone asking what I was doing, but I had a pocketful of brown bread and an apple.

Polly sat on the floor in the corner of her cell, posture as regal as when she had received us in the parlor at Westland Hall. She still wore the blue-and-gold suit; it was stained with mud along the hem, and her hat was missing.

The guard, Cortland, edged back but didn't leave. "You needn't wait," I said. "I can find my own way out."

"I should stay," he replied. I shrugged. If he was going to stop me from giving Polly food, so be it. I reminded myself that she wouldn't have done as much for me.

"I thought I wasn't to be permitted visitors," she said pertly, though she didn't stand.

"I'm allowed a bit of leeway," I said to Polly, ignoring the guard's shadow behind me.

"Ah, and so power corrupts already," Polly said, but without the bitterness I had expected. I offered her the food. She stood and crossed the cell in three graceful strides, accepting the bread and wrapping it in a corner of her blanket. "Forgive me, but I fear I may be hungrier before I am relieved of that concern."

"So you believe you're for the gallows, then?"

"Is there any doubt?" She watched me with clear eyes. "There is, then. I hadn't held out much hope. Despite you keeping your head."

"It's hardly a matter of tit for tat," I said. "My head wasn't payment for yours."

"No, I hadn't expected that."

I waited, but Polly didn't offer what she had expected, if anything. "They're going to try you all individually."

"So we drag out this torture longer, very clever."

"I thought you'd be pleased to learn you're likely to keep your head."

"Am I?"

"If they'd wanted it that badly they could have voted for it already." I paused, not sure what I had expected. Gratitude? That would have been foolish, and Polly didn't know—might never know—I had spoken for her. "Tell me," I finally said, "if you were freed, where would you go? What would you do? You, your father, the others."

"I can't speak for them," Polly said with a shrug.

"You must understand," I said, frustration building, "that you do speak for them. At least...would they foment insurrection again, do you think?"

"I couldn't say." She cut off my impending retort with a flick of her wrist. "But I doubt it. Your new system will doubtless deprive us of our ability to do so. As for me? I suppose I actually would go to West Serafe this time, live in exile. I certainly wouldn't want to live *here* any longer."

I sighed. I wanted something, some inkling of remorse from her, a hint that she saw the errors she had made, but I had to accept that, as she stood before me in a stained, resplendent Royalist blue suit, she had in her estimation made no errors. Lady

Apollonia was not going to apologize. She had nothing to apologize for.

I turned to leave.

"Thank you." Her voice was clipped, polite but terse, but I detected a glint of honest gratitude.

I turned back. "You're welcome," I said. "I—I have no reason to want you to suffer," I added.

"I know," Polly replied. "Despite everything else, I do know that." She gave me a long, strange look. "I assume you did something. That you had some hand in this small bit of clemency."

"I did," I replied simply.

"I thought you would." She shrugged, and sat down again, rolling her apple from one hand to the other. "That, if nothing else, you would be useful."

"Useful?"

"Far more useful *alive*." She tossed her apple in the air and caught it. "I find I'm hungry after all. Please do leave me to my luncheon?"

I swallowed, hard, and beckoned Cortland to lead me out of the cells. Of course—Polly speaking on my behalf, saving me from the noose, hadn't been in kindness. She had read me well enough to know I was a better chance at leniency for her than even her brother was. I wanted to be angry, but strangely, I wasn't. We both played our hands and we were both still alive. What was there to begrudge any longer?

58

THE TRIALS COMMENCED IMMEDIATELY, UNDER A COURT SYSTEM enacted to imitate the old Galatine judiciary but newly staffed with elected, not noble, judges and fitted out with juries levied from the common people of Galitha City. I had no part to play on that stage any longer, unless someone called me as a witness, which I very much hoped no one would. I was tired. I didn't want to see anyone else dead, even if it was lawful and right, and I most certainly didn't want to be a part of condemning anyone. Even by telling the truth. I preferred to remain silent.

Instead, I began to search the city for my friends. Alice, Emmi, and Lieta had all worked for the Reformists in the main compound when I had last been there, but the city was turned inside out as the bulk of the Reformist army set up encampments around and in it. Wounded poured into the hospital within the city, the storehouses were overwhelmed with requests, and already tensions strained between the city's Red Cap main force and the mixed group of Reformists who arrived with our army. A brawl broke out within a day of victory, several of Niko's officers picking a fight with noble officers from the Sixth Regiment.

After a few rabbit trails leading me to defunct addresses and a burned-out block of the quarter our shop had been in, I finally found Alice. She was still sewing shirts, set up with a small company of seamstresses and tailors to serve the army in what had been an upscale haberdashery. I saw her before I entered the building; she sat cross-legged on a table pulled next to a large window that had somehow survived all the fighting intact. In the wide swath of sunlight, she rapidly stitched a hem into a shirttail.

"I don't suppose you have any of your cousin's burned scones with you?" I asked as I walked inside.

Alice started, dropping the shirt and jumping off the table with a heavy thud. "Sophie!" She gathered me into an uncharacteristically enthusiastic embrace. "I heard you were captured, but then I heard you were all right, and then my sister said she saw you in Fountain Square, and—oh, this is a relief."

"I'm fine, of course I—" I stopped myself. There were no blithe assumptions that anyone was all right, not now. "And you?"

Her jaw settled into a hard line, and she glanced around the bright shop. "I'm taking my break," she said loudly. A man in a red cap nodded, his lips curled under in a perpetual scowl that might have been habit or might have been an old injury.

I followed her outside into the chilly sunshine. "It's a cold winter this year." She clapped her hands together and then wrapped them in her apron. "I ought to have taken my cloak but no bother about that now."

"You don't want to speak in front of them?"

"They're loyal to Niko Otni, to a fault."

"Has Niko—or these men—treated you badly?"

"Not just me. We're still required to work for the army if we want to eat—at least, if we want a share of the food Niko confiscated. When we were under siege, it made sense. Now?" Her exhale was a stream of white. "Now people need to go back to tending their families and trying to get their businesses running again. Those of us who can't fight he gives half rations even though we work twice as hard. No work, no rations. My mum and I are sharing mine."

"I didn't realize—I'll make sure this is addressed right away."

She nodded, as though she didn't believe this was possible. "Well, frankly, Niko has no right to be in charge of all of us any longer."

"Only if he's chosen by the council as one of the governors."

"And if he's not? Some of these lads won't take to that easily." She pursed her lips. "They're set against Theodor ruling, in any way."

"So is he, I would say." I began to laugh, but it died on my lips.

"I hope it's that easy." Alice shook her head, her cheeks reddening in the chill of the wind. "But it isn't just Theodor. It's all the nobles. They're—the Red Caps won't be happy if the nobles aren't routed out of Galitha completely."

"I don't think," I said deliberately, "that anyone will be completely happy with the decisions that stand. That's how we'll know we have a good compromise."

Alice essayed a smile. "That sounds about right."

"Where are the others—Emmi?"

Alice's face drew taut. "Emmi is working in the hospital. Any Pellian who can charm cast was summoned there, under no uncertain terms."

"To cast charms for the patients?"

"Otni heard that you had some luck doing so down south."

"Yes, but—" I sighed. "I had different methods."

"The Pellian methods won't work?" Alice sighed. "Poor Emmi, working all that time for no reason."

"It should work, but I can do better," I said. "And I'll see you soon."

Evening was already falling, so I hurried home instead of to the hospital, feeling a bit chagrined that I hadn't thought to go there first and see what I could offer. Everyone I thought of clamored for my help, for my hands and eyes and, often, magic. They hung from me like weights. I shook my head—no, I was lucky. I could help, I could give more of myself. Unlike so many in this city, I hadn't lost everything.

Theodor's old townhouse had survived the worst of the barrage, and he and I, along with my brother, Sianh, Annette, and Viola, took up lodging there. Any intention of moving into separate houses had never been mentioned; we gravitated without needing to say anything toward one another. I lifted the latch and found everyone already gathered in the parlor, warming themselves by a roaring fire in an otherwise sparse room. Much of the furniture had been taken in Theodor's absence, but we contented ourselves with pillows and bolsters on the floor as though we were in a Serafan reception room.

"There is no other way," Kristos said. "We have to requisition the noble wealth if we're to allow the people to recover. If," he added with emphasis, "we are to take away Otni's stranglehold on the food and supplies in this city."

"As long as his Red Caps control the storehouses, we can't very well expect fair governance," Theodor agreed.

"Why can't the council just order him to give them up?"

Theodor sighed. "Gentleman's agreement. Well, as gentlemanly as Otni can be. We did form a government without his input, as we were forced to, under the pressures of war. He stockpiled and controlled supplies, under pressures much the same. So we rather grandfathered in both systems with the understanding we won't revolt against one another. Eventually—soon—we'll get rid of the storehouse system and Galitha City will get seats on the council."

"Lovely," Annette said. She twirled a pocket watch on its chain between her fingers. "So what now—you requisition noble lands, money, silk, and gold? Viola won't be keen on giving up her jewelry."

Viola laughed and snatched the watch from Annette. "If it means knocking that smug look off Niko Otni's face, it's worth it. I won't repeat what he said when I installed those portraits of you four in the council chambers."

"He can eat his shoe," Kristos said. "Those were most excellent portraits. And we're not brutes. We'd requisition land and bank assets only. Wouldn't dream of taking their personal effects. It would flood the pawnbrokers' market with ugly suits and gaudy jewelry, anyway."

"There's simply no other way," Theodor said reluctantly. "Not only for ending Niko's stranglehold on our goods here, but we can't allow the nobility to retain the means of production— the means of wealth, really—and expect any sort of democratic system to work. But…"

"But taking it from them will certainly cause some strife as they've no real means of livelihood," Kristos filled in, not bothering to wait for him to complete the thought. "We've been over it before. I'm not sure, frankly, that I care about their pedestrian difficulties, but what do you propose?"

Theodor sighed. "I don't know—perhaps let them keep their homes and some pittance of acreage—fifty, perhaps?"

"Fifty acres is more than anyone else would have," Kristos retorted.

"And it wouldn't take long for them to buy up neighboring acreage," I added. "If they have the means to build their estates back to what they were, soon we're in the same mess as before."

"I know!" Theodor spat. "I know. I just…"

"You don't want to imagine your family home overrun by peasants?" Kristos asked blandly.

Theodor's mouth went taut. "I said no such thing. Galatine

Divine. I never even expected to see the place again." His eyes closed, briefly—leaving Rock's Ford and Westland Hall meant he might never set foot in his childhood home again. I knew he felt that pain deeply, even if he didn't say anything about it.

Especially now, with the trials concluded. His father, Pommerly, and Merhaven were all sentenced to hang, alongside most of the noble officers. Polly was spared the noose but exiled from Galitha.

Viola tapped her graphite pencil on the pad of paper in front of her, her sketch of the fire-gutted building across from us paused. "What do they do? The nobles."

"They deal with a little unfairness," Kristos muttered.

"That's not what I mean—literally, what do we want them to *do*? Become tinkers and tailors? They're not exactly skilled labor. I could hire myself out as a portrait artist, of course, but most of them are utterly useless."

"I think that's something we have to accept that we'll work out later," I said softly. "I know. These are people you know, people you care about. But...but we can't care about their troubles to the detriment of everyone else, can we?"

"If any have skill with a sword, perhaps they can try their luck with the Serafan army," Sianh said. "They seem to like Serafans, given how many of them have run to West Serafe of late."

"Now, that's a fair offer." Annette shared a sly grin with Viola. "Our families have both inquired as to the state of our villa in Port Royal."

"They were quite content pretending we didn't exist until we had a nice house away from all this nasty democracy business," Viola interjected.

This earned a laugh, but Theodor quickly slipped back into pensive quiet, his brow furrowed with unspoken concerns. "Perhaps," I said, "we should have a game of cards."

"We could play snapdragon!" Kristos said with an impish grin.

"I am not," Annette said, "falling for that again." Setting things drenched in alcohol on fire was Kristos's favorite tavern pastime, but Annette had been unimpressed with burning her fingers for sport fishing flaming raisins from a dish.

"Burning Skies?" he suggested.

"I do not know what that is," Annette said firmly, "and I do not wish to find out. Don't you play anything civilized, like dominoes?"

"Perhaps he would be amenable if we set the tiles on fire," Sianh said with a smile. "Come, Kristos, I will play this snap-dragon with you."

Despite the warmth of the parlor and the chorus of laughter as Sianh and Kristos squared off in their game, Theodor stayed so quiet that I almost didn't notice when he slipped away to our bedchamber.

59

FIRST THING THE NEXT MORNING, I HURRIED ACROSS THE CITY toward the temporary hospital set up to accommodate the wounded of both sides of the battle for the city. The Lord of Coin's offices were still imposing, but the façade was now hung with gray-and-red banners as though signaling that it had been taken, officially, from noble control.

"Sophie!" Emmi shouted across the crowded ward, earning sharp looks from the surgeons on staff and several of the nurses. She didn't notice as she trotted across a floor cluttered with pallets, blankets, bandages, and bodies to bowl me over in an embrace. "You're here!"

"Yes," I said, grinning despite myself. "And so are you."

Her smile faded, though she fought to keep it bright. "It's—we're trying, Sophie. We really are. I wish I'd learned more from you."

I surveyed the ward. This wasn't even the worst of the cases, I knew—they were taken to the offices and anterooms of the old Lord of Coin's establishment, not this open room. Still, the misery was written broad across the floor, as wounded and ill men bore patiently their pain or gave way to quiet moans or sobbing. Bandages binding heads, faces pale and sticky with fevers, red edges on the linen wrappings on shoulders and limbs, bodies absent arms and legs.

What could a few clay tablets do against such suffering?

"Get the others," I said quietly. Swiftly, Emmi fetched Lieta, Venia, and Parit from corners of the room where they had been working. I waited, trying to avoid catching the scents of death and dying that settled in pockets and were borne on every puff of wind or passing nurse's skirts.

They greeted me briefly, but I cut our embraces short. "I know you're doing your best," I said, "but I think if we work together we can do more, in less time, for all of these men."

"How?"

"I—there are ways of casting we didn't learn from our mothers," I said with a faint smile.

Lieta's brow constricted. "You found new ways of casting?"

"Of course she did—our mothers didn't teach us to sew with charms," Emmi said.

"Not just that. I can't explain now, but I will." I bit my lip. Part of me didn't want to spread this knowledge, to expand who had access to the power I had uncovered. But what gave me the right to withhold it, to hoard it for myself? "For now, just hold hands." I took Emmi's hand in my left and Lieta's in my right, and each reached out their free hand to Parit and Venia.

I began to pull a thick cloud of charm, and I felt the energy of the women next to me building alongside it, surging as they saw the golden haze swelling above us. Like handling a fat fistful of carded wool, I drew threads of light, twisting them to strengthen them and then driving them into blankets and bandages, embedding them deep in the fibers. I worked like the machines in Fen, keeping multiple threads whirring at once, mechanized in rapid clockwork like the gears of those hulking iron looms.

Beside me, Emmi gasped, and Lieta's face shone with amazement. Parit went ashen, and Venia gripped Emmi's hand so tightly her knuckles were bone-white. She reached a hand for Parit, and they closed the circle. The power around me surged, and I caught it, magnified the cloud of charm above me, stabilized it. Within a half hour, every shred of fabric I could find was worked through with charm, glowing golden to our eyes only.

"Sophie," Lieta said softly. "What miracle is this?"

"It's what you do, grandmother," I whispered, struck reverent by the power of charm casting shared. "But carried out a little differently."

"But all of us together—you can do it alone?" Emmi asked, incredulous.

"Yes," I said. "But I wouldn't have been half as quick, nor the charm as powerful."

"How did you find out how to do this?" Parit asked, half-inquisitive, half-accusatory.

"I knew I could draw it without the needle and thread once I saw how the Serafans use music."

"We know all about that," Venia said with a sardonic smile. "I've never been that ill before, except maybe on a particularly bad day of morning sickness."

"So I knew that you don't have to handle a material, don't have to work a charm into it by hand. That you could cast directly. I just combined that with what I know about charming materials," I said with a shrug.

"By all our ancestors, Sophie." Lieta shook her head. "You make it sound so simple."

"We should tell the head nurse," Parit said. "So maybe they'll let us take a break."

Emmi, Venia, and Parit went off in search of the ward mistress, but Lieta hung back. "Sophie, I—do not take offense, please. But I had heard rumors of your casting. I did not believe them, but now that I see you know things I did not think possible, I must ask."

My stomach felt hollow, and I knew what Lieta would ask before she voiced the question. "Yes, you can do the same with curses."

"I thought as much, that one *could*. The Serafans certainly did. But, Sophie—can *you*?"

I hesitated. "We all did a lot of things we wish we didn't have to," I said. "But yes. I cast curses." The weight of those words was heavy, heavier than I had believed it could be.

"Oh, Sophie." Lieta's face fell.

"I'm sorry, I know I've disappointed—"

"No, no, my dear. I am sorry. To do harm with one's gift—it was not taken lightly, I am sure, but it will not leave you lightly, either, will it?"

"No," I confessed. I thought of the riflemen, bodies doubled over as they were wracked with pain, of the soldiers enveloped by the darkness at Rock's Ford, of the screams of dying men on the Royalist naval ship as it was engulfed in flame in the Fenian ocean. That was all done at my bidding, under the darkness I commanded.

"And yet." Lieta sighed. "And yet many others have caused pain as well. Many others have dealt out death like so many hands of cards."

"I suppose," I said, "that it's only the lucky ones who haven't done something they'll regret."

"I suppose you're right. And I fear we aren't finished yet."

60

"FIRST ORDER OF BUSINESS," KRISTOS SAID, "IS THE SLATE OF nominations for the election of Galitha City's councillors." I sat in the gallery of the council chambers, what had once been the archive's large reading room. Now the shelves of books were rearranged against the back walls so that the open space, with benches and a podium for the governors, could host the official business of Galitha. Including mine. I fidgeted as I waited for the housekeeping portion of this session to be completed so that I could raise a grievance against the council—the continuation of Otni's wartime work-for-rations system. Alice and my casting friends had all confirmed as I'd visited with them in the past weeks that most of their families didn't get enough to eat under the system and couldn't find a way to bring in more approved work. My palms were damp against my wool skirt; despite the late winter cold outside, the room was warm with the press of bodies, but I had chosen to wear my Reformist army riding habit quite deliberately.

"Anyone with the requisite number of signatures may have their name included on the ballot," said Maurice Forrest, who had taken a position as adjutant for the temporary governors. He read the names thus far included, heavy with Red Caps and early agitators of the movement. I nodded—it was fair, for them to be represented in some or all of the five seats on the council open to the city. "This is now the final opportunity for additions to the ballot," Forrest said in conclusion.

"There is one more." A voice sailed over the heads of the gallery and the assembled council in front of it, followed by a blur of dove-gray silk and lavender wool cloak.

"Miss Snowmont." Forrest gave a stiff little bow in greeting. "You are bringing forward a citizen's signature petition?"

"Indeed I am," she said with a bright smile. "My own."

A murmur from the crowd quickly accelerated into a torrent of objection and curiosity, and even a few hearty laughs. I assessed the three temporary governors presiding over the session; Niko scowled, Kristos allowed a little smile to play about his lips, and Theodor looked exhausted.

"Surely," Niko said, "you must be joking."

"Certainly not," Viola answered with mock astonishment. "Who would joke about something so serious, so vitally historic, as our first elections in Galitha City?"

"Viola, I appreciate your enthusiasm," Theodor said carefully, "but you must know that you are not permitted to run for a seat on the council."

"Am I not?" Viola's voice leveled and she met Theodor's eyes. "I am lately a citizen of Galitha City. There is no law, of which I am aware, which would bar me from running. Nobles are permitted to run provided they have complied with the requisition of their property, which I have. You may all recall," she said, gesturing delicately, "that I assisted in such efforts with the property of those nobles within the city." She paused, as though considering more points to levy at the objections, though I was sure she already had them well-rehearsed. "There are in fact several nobles, of minor houses, already serving on the council, who were elected by their peers in Hazelwhite."

"Despite my concerns regarding noble inclusion on the council," Niko said icily, "that is in fact not my objection."

"Oh! Well, I did collect the requisite number of signatures." Viola handed the stack of papers to Forrest, who dutifully began to scan them. "More, in fact, than requisite."

"Significantly more," Forrest muttered.

"You're a woman!" someone yelled from the council's benches.

"Very astute," Viola replied without missing a beat.

"Miss Snowmont," Kristos said, still fighting back a smile, "it appears that your sex is, in fact, the objection."

"My sex!" Viola laughed. "There is no law barring my sex from running for the council." She paused. "There is a law barring my sex from voting in the elections. But not from being voted for, as it were."

"You can't be serious." Niko stood. "We can't be seriously considering this. We have more important matters to attend to than indulging this former noble in her delusions."

"Hold on a moment." Maurice Forrest had a heavy stack of papers and was leafing through all of them, back and forth in a dizzying display of fanned pages. "Definition of nomination—yes, citizen—and citizen definition—yes—does not include sex within the definition of citizen." He looked up, blinking. "The only requirements to occupy a seat on the council is to be a citizen in good standing with the law, selected by means of a legal election. Our legal documents do not define citizens as male."

"They don't, do they?" Kristos said. I gaped at him. "Well, something for the council to take up another time if they so desire."

"Another time?" Theodor said.

"We can't take it up right now, it's a charter matter, which means it must be added to the agenda two weeks in advance and with a written notice." Kristos shrugged. "Can't go against our own charter. Miss Viola Snowmont, consider your name added to the legal ballot of the elections for the Council of Country." Kristos nodded once, and Viola returned it with a dainty curtsy, then sat down next to me.

"Kristos knew, didn't he?" I whispered.

"He and Ambrose may have helped me check into the legality of the whole thing, yes. And Kristos suggested it needed to be quite public so that I wasn't simply ignored." She smoothed her silk skirt.

"And what if you actually win a seat?" I whispered.

"Wouldn't that be grand?" Viola grinned. "Didn't you have something you wanted to say?"

I glanced around, noting the still-muttering councillors and Niko's palpable dark mood. "Oh, excellent timing."

"That's hardly my fault," Viola whispered with a shrug. "Go on, now."

"Governors," I said as I stood. "Permission to speak."

"Oh good gory offal, you're not running, too," a man nearby shouted.

I ignored him even as another man replied, "We'll have the Tea Party Council before long."

"It will have to be renamed the Quilting Assembly," someone in the gallery suggested, to more laughter.

I cleared my throat. "Governors? On a matter for the council."

Niko glared at the chatter and then at me. "Well, go ahead."

I spoke louder than the whispered jokes around me. "There is some concern about the wartime system of rationing still in effect in the city. We have requisitioned the financial and estate assets of the city's nobility and are in the process of doing so for the rest of Galitha. Our ability to pay our soldiery will there-fore soon be independent of any stores left within the city. Our trade networks will be opened and running as before—at least, as normally as can be expected."

"It's a fair system," Niko retorted. "Those who work are paid in what they need."

"It was a very good system for a city under siege," I replied. "But this city is no longer under siege. There are people who cannot work under your system who go hungry, and their fam-ilies have no way of making additional income or buying addi-tional goods."

"That's nonsense." Niko waved his hand.

"Wait, it's not nonsense, really." A man with dark hair clubbed with a red leather tie stood nervously. "My sister has a newborn, husband died in that last battle, she can't work, and my rations don't do well enough for all of us."

"So we'll amend the system—"

"No," Theodor said, cutting Niko off. "The system as it stands puts too much power in the hands of the government. Just as the noble system before it did. It's time it ended."

"The nobility were tyrants," Niko shouted in reply, to some agreement among the council and the gallery.

"Many a system of governance," Theodor said firmly, "can create tyrants. We do not wish to become what we fought and died to overthrow."

"What we died to overthrow—as though you're not the prime specimen of what we fought and died to overthrow!" Niko slammed his hand on the table in front of him, staring Theodor down in a clear challenge, but Theodor stood stoic, refusing to give voice to a duel of insults. His bearing was dig-nity personified, I thought with a swell of pride, but he looked tired.

"Governors," Kristos said quietly, "this is a matter for the full council to debate, not governors, and temporary governors at that. I suggest we table it until the city's elections are concluded." He met my eyes and nodded. The gentleman's agreement had been challenged, and publicly. Soon we could move forward.

61

"YOU DON'T HAVE TO GO," I SAID QUIETLY, AS THEODOR COMBED clove-scented pomade through his hair and gathered it into a queue. "Everyone would understand."

"I am a temporary governor of Galitha. I am the Reformist army's commander. It is my duty."

"I think the circumstances a bit unusual, this time."

"If I am not there, it will be taken as a statement and that statement will be broadcast by Otni and his followers. That I'm still a sympathizer to the nobility."

"It's your own father," I said. "Your own father on the gallows."

"I know!" His hands trembled as he tied a dark charcoal ribbon around the leather holding his queue. "Divine Natures, Sophie, I know. In every inch of the law, in any law, this is the due course of action. I cannot afford—we cannot afford—to imply anything but complete acquiescence to and respect of that law."

I took his shaking hand silently. I was dressed in my gray-and-red riding habit again, freshly brushed and pressed and the buttons shined. I wondered when I could put it off for good.

We walked to Fountain Square, cleaner and in better repair

than it had been when we first rode in after the Battle of Galitha City, but still bearing deep scars. The ugliest was a gallows erected in the center of the square next to the fountain, which was neither running nor frozen but emptied of water. I accompanied Theodor to the platform set aside for the council members overseeing the proceedings, joining Kristos and Maurice Forrest in its center. Maurice was no charismatic personality, that was sure—but he shook Theodor's hand gravely and I saw empathy in his soft smile.

"Excuse me." The voice preceded a parting of bodies and polite head tilts as Viola and Annette stepped through the crowd of councillors.

"You didn't have to—" I whispered as Viola embraced me.

"No, but it seemed only right. To be here next to Theo. He's stood by us often enough," Annette said. She was paler than usual, dressed in a dark gray riding habit trimmed in black. Viola's gray silk gown was covered by a black mantelet. The councillors had worn dark clothing, too, and all the square looked as though it were the site of a massive funeral. It was, in some sense—today we buried, in symbol, at least, the end of the nobility and monarchy of Galitha.

I stood as close as I could to Theodor without imposing on his image of governor of Galitha, and I noticed that Viola and Annette did, as well, forming a semicircle of silent support around him as the three prisoners were led from the Stone Castle to the gallows.

I scanned the scene, eyes narrowing as I realized that Niko was nowhere to be seen. As a governor, he ought to have been on the platform with us. I caught Kristos's eye and mouthed the single-word question. *Niko?* His brow furrowed and he shook his head slowly, answering, *I don't know.*

My eye caught a brief flash of light—not physical light, I saw instantly, but charm. I tensed, but it was only Emmi, standing next to Parit, Venia, and Lieta near the stairs of our platform. Emmi held up a simple linen banner embroidered in Pellian weeping hearts and sunrises—the designs used for funerals and naming ceremonies, respectively. An ending and a beginning represented in fabric, the threads glittering with faint magic. I swelled with pride in her—she had learned to cast in stitching without any more tutelage from me. I could have cheered out loud, any other time, but instead I gave her a small smile in acknowledgment.

The trio of condemned men ascended the platform. Silence reigned across the square; I had wondered if there would be mockery, cheers, shouts of acclamation or condemnation, or if the people of Galitha would bear the weight of this moment quietly. We had treated Westland, Pommerly, and Merhaven well, I was relieved to see—their clothes were clean, and they had been given at the least soap and water as they all looked well-kempt. Yet they were broken, too, without bearing any bruises or wounds, in a quiet submission to their fate.

They had chosen it, I reminded myself. Time and again, at each juncture, chosen to deny the common people any rights, and even when the law had demanded their compliance, they had rebelled against it. They had rebelled, I reminded myself. They were the traitors.

Theodor stood still as a post in front of me, and I knew he was repeating this rehearsed speech in his own mind, to keep out the simple fact that one was his father.

Before the pronouncement could be read, a clamor broke out from the quarter of the square nearest the Public Archive. I turned, stomach falling like stone, to see a crowd of men in red caps and red sashes, bearing banners and led by Niko Otni in a new scarlet frock coat. Many of them carried long knives or clubs—whether intending to use them or in show of force, I couldn't tell. Kristos's mouth clenched into a thin line, and most of the councillors rustled, concerned, among themselves.

Niko and his men marched through the crowd to the center of the square and took positions in front of the gallows, facing them, in lines and columns like soldiers.

"Sweet Sacred Natures," Viola whispered in condemnation as they stood in rank and file like a military parade. "They've made it about *them*."

Niko stared up at the former king of Galitha with an unnerving grin. "You thought to take on a country, to take on the people of Galitha. We're stronger than you, even with all your money and all your power."

"Oh hell," muttered Kristos. "He shouldn't be allowed to talk."

Theodor and Maurice shared a glance. Theodor couldn't be the one to speak, not now. With the weight of the role of adjutant of the council bolstering his slight frame, Maurice mustered his largest voice and called across the square, "There is a proper order for these proceedings. Please allow the pronouncement to be read and—"

"We've got our own pronouncement!" Niko yelled. "That hanging is too good for these men. Still wearing their silk suits, their good shoes—why, are those jewels in your buckles?" He laughed, insouciant, at Pommerly.

"Please allow the pronouncement to be read and the proceedings to continue," cried Maurice Forrest, but he was quickly drowned out in shouts and jeers from the Red Caps. Now the composure on the gallows was beginning to crack—Pommerly was sweating and Merhaven swallowed, rapidly, eyes darting from the Red Caps to the platform. What did they intend to do, drag these men from the gallows and beat them to death? Sunlight glinted from a scythe in reply.

This wasn't the answer. Maybe the former king and his traitorous confidants deserved a painful death at the hands of those they had oppressed. But the people of Galitha didn't deserve rule by mob. We had fought to give them something better than that, to give them fair laws and real justice.

Silently, I slipped back into the crowd of council members, the press and swell of their bodies swallowing me. I found Emmi in the crowd by her banner, the white linen and the faint charm glowing dimly.

"Take my hand," I whispered urgently. Emmi threw the banner over her shoulder like a dishrag and motioned to Parit, next to her, to come closer. I inhaled deeply as I centered myself and reached for the charm magic. Dark magic danced nearby, almost nipping at me with its intensity, and I knew—its presence was a byproduct of fear, drawn by my own lack of control. I knew I could bury curse magic quickly in Niko's scarlet coat and incapacitate him almost instantly, but that would only cause more serious problems later. Instead, I pushed the darkness away with a steady, deliberate hand, and focused on the light.

I felt when Venia and Lieta joined the chain of hands as the charm I had pulled surged in strength. I wove a net of light, pulsing with goodwill, patience, love—anything that might cool hot tempers and quiet angry minds. Anything that might turn them away from violence. Emmi squeezed my hand tighter as I settled the net across the backs of the Red Caps first. It was impossible to tell if there was any change in their intentions, but I doubled the loop of neighborly goodwill around Niko, tightening it as I pressed it deep into the red wool of his coat.

"Here, now," Kristos said, hopping down from the platform in a nimble jump, "we're a nation of law, not a government by riot. We've earned that." His voice rose—he wasn't speaking only to Niko or even all of the Red Caps but to the

entire crowd. This was about keeping their faith, not just dis-
suading Red Caps from riot. I turned the charm toward the rest
of the crowd, enveloping all of us, myself included, with bright
fortune.

Kristos strode toward Niko confidently. The charm driving
outward over the crowd constricted and tensed as I cut it off and
started another, a new charm for safety, ribboned first around
Kristos. "We've earned the right to try these men, and to judge
them, and to carry out a sentence. We don't have to resort to
shouting in the streets any longer, to brandishing pitchforks and
scythes."

"Come now, Balstrade," Niko said, voice lowering. "It's not
over and done so easy as hanging a few men. You know that as
well as I."

Charm pulsed over the whole crowd, but nothing compared
to the fire in Niko's eyes or the confidence in Kristos's voice.
"You're right. It's far from over and done. We have work to do.
Right over there." He gestured to the Public Archive, where the
council had been meeting. "We have elections to hold. We have
laws to write. We have a city to rebuild, and I say the sooner the
better. Put this aside and then we can get back to work."

Murmurs of assent buoyed Kristos's words. I didn't know,
would never know, if my charm had effected the openness
toward peace and the refusal of violence, but I slowly uncurled
my hand from Emmi's. I could see Niko's plans pivoting. If he
pressed ahead with a demonstration of retribution, too many of
the crowd would turn on him and his Red Caps. He glared past
Kristos toward the platform, toward Theodor and the women
flanking him, and then shot a pointed look at me.

"Then the Red Caps will witness the end of what we started.
And never forget," he said, "that we started this."

Theodor stared straight out over the crowd, face like stone

and taut as a spring. I rejoined him as the brief pronouncement was read. I don't think any of us really heard it, though we knew what it said—treason, rebellion against Galitha's laws, death. Death in every word of it. I couldn't be sure, but I thought Theodor's father searched for his son's eyes, to meet them to say some final farewell that we had denied him in speech.

I closed my eyes when the trapdoors opened and the men fell. I couldn't help it, but I still heard the creak and rattle of the wood and the rush of weight, plummeting downward, unchecked. The cumulative breath that the crowd sucked in and held, for a long moment. Next to me, Theodor made no sound save a tiny, choked sigh.

62

THE WEEKS FOLLOWING THE EXECUTION HUMMED WITH A QUIET industriousness. Across the city businesses reopened, and crews of citizens employed by the council began repairs to the pockmarked roads and crumbling buildings. Ships sailed into the harbor for the first time in months, bearing goods from southern Galitha, the Allied States, and Fen. The city's elections came and went; to Theodor's surprise, but not mine, Viola was elected a councillor alongside three prominent Red Caps and one bookish printer with nervous, rabbit-like mannerisms and startlingly anarchist opinions.

"We needed at least one solid anarchist," Kristos said as we gathered at the council chambers for the swearing in of the final councillors. "He used to print our broadsides, back when we were just the Laborers' League."

"Oh, how far we've all come," Annette said with a laugh. "Viola looks well." I'd made her a tailored gown for the occasion, working together in the firelight of the parlor after my long days of helping Hamish and the charm casters in the hospital. The charcoal gray was cut like a man's double-breasted frock coat in the front but swept into a gown's long skirts. I thought,

with a pang of nostalgia, about the pink gown she had first com-
missioned from me. How far we'd all come, indeed.

"A word?" Niko's dark eyes blazed and he stood too close for
my comfort. "In private." He glanced to Theodor and Kristos,
who stood talking with Maurice Forrest and Hamish Oglethorpe.

I stiffened. Next to me, Annette laid a hand on my arm,
protective. Though she had eschewed her admiral's sword, I
knew she carried a slim naval dagger under her skirt. I laid my
hand over hers.

"Privacy will be difficult to find here, I'm afraid." I inclined
my head toward one of the archive's windowed alcoves. No one
stood in the curve of the window itself, though plenty of councillors stood nearby, consulting a map of southern Galatine port
cities. "That might be the best we can do."

"Very well." He marched toward the window, then whirled
to face me before I had a moment to even think what he wanted.
"I know what you've done."

I stepped back, afraid of the intensity in his eyes. "What did
I do?"

"You know damned well. Your casting."

I swallowed hard, remembering the deep gold I'd woven
through the crowd at the hanging. I had expected Niko to find
out from someone who could see the charm, eventually, and I
had anticipated his fury. "What of my casting?"

"How else did that noble bitch get elected, save your
meddling?"

Fear broke like a soap bubble and I almost laughed—but
then it settled like a film over my relief. It didn't matter that I
hadn't—that I wouldn't—use my abilities to affect political outcomes. Niko believed I had. And if he believed it, who else did?

"I didn't do anything, Niko. She won the seat on her own."

"Whore's ass, she did." Niko shook his head. "It's not right.

You can seed whatever you want with no one knowing, make people...do things."

"I can't do anything of the sort," I bristled, but I couldn't forget the Serafan methods of influence, of weaving magic and reality together to make friend and foe alike react however the caster chose. I had, in some immeasurable way, affected the crowd in Fountain Square, pushing them away from violence and toward benevolence. "And I certainly wouldn't."

"I don't feel like listening to one of your treatises on ethics, Sophie, so let me simply say—I won't stand for it. I'll figure out how you do what you do and I'll put a stop to it."

I stared back at Niko, squaring my shoulders. "Viola won her seat fairly. Just as those three Red Caps and the anarchist did."

"So you say. But so help me, Sophie, if you interfere with the selection of the governors. If your noble-born fiancé takes the rightful seat of one of our people—"

"If he does, it will be because the council feels it is in this nation's best interest that he take a large role in leading it!" I took a steadying breath. "Besides, I can't simply make people do what I want. It doesn't work like that, especially for an election."

"So it does work like that, sometimes."

"No!" I sighed, exasperated. "If it concerns you, I will remain absent for the nomination and confirmation of the governors."

"It does more than concern me. That this has gone unchecked, that you continue to bolster your noble friends, that you're like as not a traitor to the new Republic." He leaned closer, so that I could smell that morning's sausage and onions on his breath. "It concerns me gravely."

"I don't have to stand for these sorts of insults. If I were a man—"

"If you were a man I'd have finished this already," he said flatly.

I turned on my heel and returned to Annette, who was now joined by Kristos and Theodor. "We're going to have to do something," I said through breath that began to shake, "about public perception of charm casting at some juncture."

"I'll have to find a new printer," Kristos joked quietly, but he took my hand and watched as Niko strode back toward the councillors' platform.

The five new councillors were sworn in and presented promptly with a full agenda, including the nomination of governors to supplant the temporary positions we'd created during wartime. Annette and I left quietly, and I saw Annette sneak a last look at Viola as she rose to address a question about the ledgers of seized noble property. Annette smiled to herself.

I spent the day with Alice inventorying the wartime fabric reserves in preparation for decentralizing Niko's storehouses, and came home with a head swimming with yardage and broadcloth widths and numbers of bolts of linen. Shortly after, the rest of the household arrived home in a chorus of laugher and shouts as they burst through the door.

"Meet the official, not temporary, fully vetted governor of Galitha!" Viola cried.

"*The*, as in singular?" I smiled. "Which one of you?"

"Theodor," Viola said, beaming. "Voted near unanimously to nominate him."

"Told you they'd pick you as one of the governors," Kristos said. "As sure as I always win at dice."

"I beat you at dice last night," Theodor said with a weary smile. "I don't know. I wish..." He paused. "I shouldn't have accepted the nomination."

"But you are more qualified for the position than anyone else. They know that. They know they need someone who has led before. Who understands how laws work," Sianh said.

"Kristos didn't accept his," Theodor said. "He was nominated, Sophie. Nominated first, before anyone else."

"And declined." Kristos shrugged. "As it turns out, I'm excellent at political theory but actual politics? I can let someone else take the reins. I'd rather write the first pamphlets and books of the new Republic."

"You can't stand people disagreeing with you." I laughed. "If you write books, you don't have to listen to what people say about your ideas."

"I can't stand people with bad logic disagreeing with me and having equal say as I do," Kristos said. "Theodor has the patience of a nursemaid for putting up with them. You should see him— he can manage to wrangle them like a sheepdog among goats."

"And I now have a five-year term herding the goats," Theodor said, disquiet deepening the wrinkles around his eyes.

"I say this deserves a celebration!" Viola said. "I'll bring up a bottle of sparkling wine from the cellar—it's still there, isn't it, Theo?"

He opened his mouth to protest, then simply nodded. "There's still a case of the Urusine and a few of the sparkling Lienghine."

I caught his hand. "Would you like to step outside for a bit? While Viola whips a party out of a bottle of wine and some old prunes?"

Theodor nodded with a grudging laugh, and we walked out into a bright winter afternoon. It was perhaps curiosity and perhaps nostalgia and perhaps a bad idea that drove us along the road toward the public gardens. Tents and brush shelters skirted rosebushes and fountains, temporary shelter for an overwintering army. The only space where the rows of wedge tents were absent was the labyrinth of boxwood, and I wondered if its paths and dead ends would soon hold canopies of pine branches for those still lacking shelter.

"The last time we were here," Theodor said slowly, "was Viola's party for the passage of the Reform Bill."

"We thought it was over then." I sighed.

"We were inimitably stupid." Theodor stopped and watched several men coax a thin blaze out of the coals of their campfire. "Perhaps we still are, if we think it's over now."

We rounded a bend in the path, and I saw it—the greenhouse. "I wondered if it would still be here," I confessed. "I didn't want to say anything, didn't even really want to hope that it survived." Tentatively, I pushed on the door, partially blocked by a shattered flowerpot, and stepped inside.

Sunset etched bright hues into the glass walls and ceiling, bringing color into the garden plots inside, though most of the plants had withered without watering. I gently touched one exception, an East Serafan cactus blooming with tiny yellow flowers.

"I don't imagine I'll have much time to bring it back to its former glory." Theodor pulled his penknife from his pocket and sliced the stem of a dwarf rosebush. "No sap at all, she's dry as kindling."

"It's all right to be disappointed," I finally said, his search for live plant stock yielding little more than cacti and sickly olive trees. "The losses of this war—they're not just on the field. Kristos says that the archive had books stolen—rare ones, valuable ones. We won't get those back. The scholars at the university have certainly stagnated of late. We won't export much grain this year, I'll wager, and our wine and cider exports will be hurting even longer."

"Our new government is a tower of matchsticks ready to collapse, people lost their livelihoods and, worse, their families, and our economy won't recover for years. And my houseplants died," Theodor snapped. "That's hardly worth the notice."

"But you care," I said quietly.

"I oughtn't to care! How many thousands killed, wounded, lost limbs? How many will struggle for years to come, widows and orphans? How many businesses destroyed? And my hothouse flowers died, well. Let's erect a monument to my prize dwarf crystal hydrangea, shall we? I am a governor of Galitha and I have deeper hurts to consider on behalf of my country."

I struggled to find the right words, to acknowledge that even in the face of death and destruction, loss could also be measured in hundreds of minute ways. In families split and friends no longer speaking, in books stolen and in ciders unpressed, in children's birthdays missed, in a rare cultivar dead from neglect. "It will take a long time to recover what this war took from many people. It took the gift you worked so hard to give Galitha."

Theodor sank onto a bench, a rusty trowel clattering to the floor beside him. He kicked it away. "There are better gifts I ought to have given her."

"And you yet will. But first you gave this one." I sighed. The building was still sound, and the tools at the ready to rebuild what he had created, once, in a simpler time. No, not simpler, I acknowledged. The simplicity that allowed for his study and development of his art was a false peace, made by ignoring the deep fault lines cracking the country's very foundations. Not simpler, not really, nor better, but I held to the hope, fervently, that we could return to peace. "We'll need places like this again, someday."

"We never did need them." Theodor turned an empty ceramic flowerpot over in his hands.

"Of course we need archives and gardens and universities— what in the world is the point of a free country governed by its people if its people can't invest in beauty and knowledge and art?" I snatched the flowerpot away from him, turning it over and brushing dirt away from the drainage hole at the bottom. "This? This flowerpot without a plant is about as satisfying as having nothing beyond bread and barley to think of. It's..." Laughter bubbled in my voice without my permission, but I recalled Sianh's phrase in Serafan for a useless thing, a hopeless case. "It's a cup with a hole in it, Theodor."

He looked up, confused, and then broke into a rueful smile, remembering. "It *is* a cup with a hole in it."

"Galitha won't always be at war or setting up a new government or struggling to rectify the mistakes of its very recent past. It's going to need places like this again."

"I suppose I know that, if I make myself think about it. But after this is over..." He took the flowerpot back and set it carefully on a saucer. "I can't really believe that I'm going to be filling my days with gardening again. I don't know what my place will be."

"I don't, either," I said quietly. I sat next to him. "We're going to have to figure that out together."

63

WINTER BEGAN TO SOFTEN AROUND THE EDGES, THE SNOWS receding from the lawns and the icicles melting from the eaves, and the frozen stalemate between Niko's contingent and the rest of the council began to abate, as well. Niko still made his vehement distrust of Theodor clear at every turn, and I noticed more than one unflattering broadside tacked up around the city. Even so, Niko's barbed insults didn't seem to snag on Theodor any longer, and Theodor seemed almost content with his work. I fell into a comfortable routine of assisting Hamish at the hospital, meeting with my Pellian friends and with Alice, and playing occasional hostess to the new political elite of Galitha. We had even begun to talk, in vague notions not yet fully coalesced, of a wedding.

I was readying for tea with Maurice Forrest and his family when I was interrupted by a brisk rap on the door. Annette stood on the wide portico, framed by a contingent of Kvys nuns. Not just Kvys nuns, I saw as I scanned their faces, but members of Alba's order—the ones who could cast. Tantia shyly raised her hand in greeting. I raised an eyebrow in return, but before I could ask, Annette stepped in front of Tantia. "I found these ladies looking for you," she said. "They were held up by the officials at the port."

"Looking for me?" I asked. "Didn't the letter reach them about Alba?"

"They're aware of what happened to Sastra-set Alba, but their main aim was to find you." Annette ushered the sisters inside.

I offered a half smile to the silent huddle of nuns, and gestured toward the parlor. They moved in a single unit away from the door. "Thank you for bringing them—do I need to sign for them or some such?"

"As though they're import goods? No, I don't think so. The officials took the good word of the Lady Admiral that they were on the up-and-up."

"Are they?" I whispered.

"Too late to worry about that now," Annette said. "But I'll stick around. Not that I'm much good in a fight, but then again..." She craned her neck to see the front parlor, where the sisters waited patiently. "I don't suppose they are, either."

"You might be surprised," I muttered.

I joined the sisters in the parlor, while Annette hovered by the door, hand on her hip where her petite rapier had hung on board ship. "Welcome to Galitha City," I said. "What brings you to us?"

Tantia stepped forward, the default representative of the group, speaking the most Galatine. "You bring us to Galitha."

"I—there may have been some misunderstanding?" I said. "I didn't ask you here."

"No, that is not my meaning." Tantia shook her head. "We come to find you. We come to work with you. To learn. To continue."

I hesitated, their aim slowly becoming clear. "You want to continue learning to cast."

Tantia nodded. "To learn from you."

"I see," I said slowly. "What about your order?"

"Order is—what is the word?" She conferred with Immell, who stood beside her. "*Hurcuthi.*"

"*Hurcuthi-set,*" Immell replied. "Is like mess. Mess of garbage."

"After Alba left," I guessed. "The leadership is undermined? Compromised? Fighting?"

"Fighting, yes. No," Tantia said, holding up her hand. "Not in the open. Behind doors, whispers. But we fear. If some win, we are—are crime."

"What you did was illegal by Kvys laws, and religious laws," I supplied. "We would say 'you are criminals' in Galatine." I sighed. "Excepting, of course, that in Galitha, we have no such law and would say no such thing."

"Is more than doing illegal thing," Immell said. "Is that *we* are illegal."

I caught Annette's eye across the room. She studied the sisters intently, as though their stoic posture or plain gray gowns and white veils might reveal something more for her to read.

"If we stay, we fear—we fear—" Tantia struggled to find the words, tugging at the blackwork cuffs of her fine linen shift.

"You fear they will kill you," Annette said bluntly. "Execution. You fear execution. Simply for having your abilities." I started, but Tantia dipped her head, grateful for the right words, grateful someone else had said them. Immell bit her lip. Her shift was worked in black embroidery at the cuffs, too, but the edges were frayed and her boots scuffed and battered. The other sisters, despite carefully starched veils, had similar wear in their appearance—torn hems and stained collars, holes in the soles of boots and dusty skirts.

I turned to Annette. "They're refugees. Political refugees."

Annette crossed the room in three long strides and answered in my ear, low and rapid so that the Kvys couldn't hear. "We're a newborn nation knee-deep in our own troubles at the moment."

"I know." I looked back at Tantia and Immell, their modestly clasped hands growing white at the knuckles.

"They are here because they have violated whatever archaic laws the Kvys still maintain. That isn't our doing."

"They are here because of me and because of our war, Annette."

"The Serafans may see this as consolidating some sort of magic army. The Allied States may be suspicious of our motives. And who knows what questions this raises with Kvyset."

I caught Annette's arm, steadying both of us. "I know. But there's nothing we can do to stop them from raising those questions now. The Kvys casters came here. The questions are already raised."

Annette pressed her rosebud lips together. "We have to protect Galitha first, Sophie. We can't—"

"It's not our decision. My only choice right now is whether to offer them tea or supper, and then commend them to the council."

"I suppose you're right." Annette backed away from me with a wary look toward the Kvys nuns waiting silently for my answer.

"I'll have tea ready in just a moment," I said, a barely audible tremor in my voice. "Please make yourselves comfortable."

64

—∿—

"Niko is absolutely apoplectic," Kristos said, landing in his chair at the dinner table with a resounding thud. "He's convinced you've invited them to form some sort of cabal of magical influence."

"It doesn't," Annette said judiciously, "precisely *not* look like that." She cut a thick slice of oat bread and handed it to Kristos. Despite the elegance of eating on the polished wood table of a former noble's dining room, our meals were more rustic than sumptuous. I didn't mind; there was something comforting about split pea soup and meat pies and porridges, like those I had made in our shabby kitchen to share with Kristos, long ago.

"But it isn't factual, and that is what matters," Theodor fumed.

"We both know that isn't true," I replied.

"Perhaps you *should* form a cabal of magical influence," Viola said, delicately spooning some ham and bean soup. "Then at least they would have a real reason to be worried."

"That's not funny," I replied. Viola shrugged with an impish smile.

"It's not funny, but it's also not a terrible idea," Kristos said.

"No, not the secret underhanded part. I mean some sort of cabinet post or committee overseeing Galatine magic use."

"It might just be the most valuable angle we can play—with Pellia as part of Galitha and the Kvys refugees seeing us as the natural place for practitioners of casting to go, it gives us a certain cachet." Theodor raised an eyebrow at me. "We will eventually need to develop some legal framework around that."

"Lovely," Viola said with a light snort, "you've only just recognized that casting is anything more powerful than an old wives' tale, and you're going to form a bureaucracy around it."

I shook my head. "There will be time enough for that eventually. But for now—what does the council say we do with the Kvys nuns?"

"They can stay, provided they are not found to be attempting to 'influence' our politics—in any way, including magical. From what I knew of Alba, I'm more worried about them lining pockets or making alliances, frankly." Theodor stirred his soup. "I don't know that anyone likes the idea of playing host to ousted nuns, but most of the council felt we couldn't refuse without looking as though we're incapable of accommodating them."

"And we wouldn't want the Serafans to think we're weak," supplied Annette. "Ah, well. I hadn't considered that side of it."

"Or the Allied Equatorial States. Dira only represents her own interests, not the whole nation, and plenty in the States are watching carefully to see whether we can stand on our own two feet before they commit to any alliances or trade agreements." Theodor shrugged. "Back to politics as usual."

"Are you telling me that you dragged me through that horrid Five-Year Summit and we're back to square one?" I teased.

"To some extent." Theodor grimaced. "All those agreements were made before we were the Republic of Galitha—sweet

Sacred Natures, that probably means we're going to have to rene-gotiate the Open Seas Arrangement." He groaned into his soup.

"At any rate," Viola said, clearing her throat. "Speaking of arrangements. I think it's time that Annette and I were out of your hair. Penny should be making her way to the city soon enough, Kristos, and I figure we'll have a spring wedding for these two," she added, waving a lithe hand at Theodor and me. "Time for the birds to make their own nests, I think."

"You're still quite welcome, even if we—when we—" I stumbled. It was so close, so real, something I had never thought possible. I smiled. "Even when we're married."

"What are you waiting for, anyway?" Kristos prodded.

"It's been a bit busy, between the war and founding a nation," Theodor said. "And in truth, the Office of Records only offi-cially opened a fortnight ago, and they're quite swamped."

"You and Penny aren't married," I shot back.

"We have a baby," he retorted. "That is even more binding a contract. You could do that, instead."

Annette and Viola exchanged an amused glance. "Viola has a dozen commissions already, for paintings, and the Office of Naval Affairs is paying me quite well as an advisor at the moment. So we have enough, we think, to rent a little town-house or the like." Annette compressed her brows. "I think. If I understand rent contracts correctly—perhaps you want to look at our agreement, Sophie?"

I laughed. "Of course, I'm quite facile with rent agree-ments. Though of course, things have changed a bit, now that it's citizen-owned property."

"Well, a toast then, to new homes and new beginnings," Kristos said. I raised my glass of weak small beer alongside the others, exhaling deeply with a strange, most welcome optimism.

"As pleasant as this all is, I've a meeting with Forrest at his house in—hell, less than an hour." Theodor grinned. "If you open any of those bottles from the cellar, you save some for me," he said, planting a kiss on my head as he made for the door. I stood to clear the table. As Viola assisted me, she kicked something under the table.

"Isn't this Theodor's?" she said, holding up a leather portfolio.

"Yes," I sighed. "And I imagine he's going to need that if he's meeting with Maurice. I'll chase him down," I added, catching the portfolio when Viola tossed it to me.

I swung my mantelet over my shoulders as I hurried down the street. Theodor's quick stride had already put him a block ahead of me, on the other side of the street, nearer the river. I took the foray as a pleasant surprise. We hadn't had much time alone, and it would be nice to walk together to Maurice Forrest's house, on the other side of Broad Street, alongside the river, which rolled with swift-flowing eddies as it swelled with snowmelt. Perhaps we could even discuss plans for a wedding—something small, a simple party at the public gardens with our friends.

Before I could catch up enough to call out, I saw another figure walking toward him, purposeful and direct. I squinted— it was Niko. He must have been coming to see us, I thought, to discuss—who knew. Yet another argument about the liquidation of the wartime storehouses, about sending the army home, about something. But he didn't turn toward the house. He kept his sights set on Theodor.

I slowed, unsure if I should interrupt. It seemed quite possible they had some sort of business with one another, or that Niko would take advantage of finding Theodor alone to try to persuade him privately of one of his views. What Niko lacked in Kristos's silver tongue he made up for in dogged determination, and this could be like any other chance meeting or open session in the council. Except for one thing.

Niko held a pistol in his hand.

My heart seemed to stop, and my legs turned to putty, but I surged forward anyway. I called out, but neither noticed me.

Niko cocked the pistol and lifted it, leveling on Theodor's chest. He seemed to move through layers of filmy organza, hazy and indistinct, though I knew precisely what he was doing, what was going to happen. I couldn't move as quickly as my mind worked, couldn't reach out and change the tableau unfolding before me.

The pistol fired.

Theodor dropped to the ground.

Niko was gone even as the report echoed up the street, over the river, tearing everything apart in its wake. I ran to Theodor's side, my knees scraping on the hard stone as I dropped beside him.

It felt like it could have been me, life bleeding into the cold stone, seeping rapidly into oblivion. My hands scrabbled for his, for the wound in his chest, for something to hold on to, to tie his life to this world, somehow. His eyes found mine, recognition blooming. He tried to speak; all he could manage was a choking rattle. I gripped his hand tighter, willing life, willing health. Charm magic sparked around us, and I drove it toward him, enveloping him in light. He smiled, faintly, and squeezed my hand in return.

For a moment I believed I could save him.

Then he exhaled a bloody breath and slipped away, eyes losing focus, or perhaps focusing on something else, far away, something that I couldn't see.

He was gone, and I was left in a pool of blood and charm magic sinking slowly into the dank stone.

65

I MUST HAVE BEEN WAILING, BECAUSE KRISTOS FOUND ME WITHIN minutes, my voice hoarse. He pried me away, my gown slick with blood, and wordlessly led me back to the house, putting my recalcitrant body into Viola's arms. Her eyes widened with shock but she simply lowered me onto the nearest couch and began to unpin my bloodied gown.

"Who?" Kristos said. His eyes were dark coals in the long evening shadows. "Who?"

I shook. "He ruined everything."

"Who?" he demanded.

I trembled as I looked at him, knowing the price of naming the guilty man. Knowing it meant rending the fabric of the new country before it had even been fashioned into a government. I could have said nothing, pretended I found Theodor already wounded, already dead.

Kristos knew better.

"Niko," I whispered.

He turned and plucked his sword from where it hung with the coats and cloaks, a martial interruption to the homely woolens lining the wall. Wordlessly, Sianh followed him, looping his sword belt over his coat.

I lurched forward. "No, you can't—"

"They'll be safe," Viola said, pressing me firmly back against the settee.

"But if they—if Niko—"

"Don't concern yourself over it." Annette's soothing voice skimmed over a tremor of fear, like a mother fussing over a sick child. "Let them take care of it."

Sianh and Kristos strode out into the night, the door closing behind them with hollow finality. Viola motioned to one of the men stationed in our house as a clerk and gave him concise directions in a low timbre I couldn't hear. I remained motionless, my vision centered on the door, as though I could bore holes through the wood to the settling darkness beyond, could follow Kristos and Sianh.

Annette brought me tea. I pushed it away. "Drink it," she said, kind but firm. "You'll thank me later."

I thought it a strange thing to say, but after I'd drained the cup, sleep pulled heavy on my eyelids. I slept and woke in dazed starts, through velvet darkness and the glimmers of daylight, and into twilight again, losing track of time until I woke to sunshine in my eyes and my arm asleep under my head.

It was cruel waking to memory, even as the sun poured bright through the window of the room where I had been put to bed. Not the room I'd shared with Theodor—Viola and Annette were wise enough not to make that error—but still, he was there. The furniture he had chosen, the dove gray of the walls, a painting of a brilliantly blooming tropical plant across from the bed. My voice gouged my throat in wordless agony and I buried my cries in a pillow whose case smelled like his preferred laundry soap.

I wasn't as silent as I'd hoped, because Kristos tentatively shuffled into the room a few minutes later. I stared at him, looking like a madwoman with eyes rimmed red, I was sure, and with fear churning my gut.

"How long was I asleep?"

"Two days." Kristos swallowed. "Annette thought it best to save you the shock to your nerves by lacing a cup of chamomile with nightbloom poppy. Naval trick."

"If anyone ever drugs me again, I'll—I'll—" I found I couldn't verbalize the word I had begun to say in jest: *kill.*

"I'll be sure to tell her that."

I waited, not wanting to ask, terrified of the answer, but I finally whispered, "What did you do?"

"We took him into custody," Kristos said. "Some of his sycophants thought to put up a fight, but Sianh disabused them rather quickly of that idea. He didn't seem particularly well supported, in any case."

"You arrested him?"

"Of course. He needs to stand trial. He doesn't deny anything, for what it's worth. He said ridding the country of noble and magical influence was necessary." Kristos sank onto the bed beside me. "Necessary. I hate that damn word. It doesn't mean what men like Niko think it does."

I stared at the painting of the blooming flowers, the colors bleeding into each other as tears lined my eyes. "I was afraid you had carried out the sentence yourself. And that I would wake and find the city at war with itself. And yet…a trial could tear us apart, too."

"We will survive that. Due process, proper order, equal application of the law—" Kristos stopped, and I knew what we were both thinking. That was what Theodor would have said.

I closed my eyes. "I wanted to kill him."

"If it's any consolation," Kristos said, "he feels the same way about you. Shit." He exhaled. "I'm sorry, it's not the time for jokes."

"He said as much to me, once." I sighed.

"He suggested he expected to find you both together. He had a brace of pistols on him when we arrested him. He distrusted your casting, he was convinced you had orchestrated Theodor's election and had brought those nuns in, too. I—" Kristos broke. "If he had taken you, too, I couldn't—I wouldn't know what to do." He straightened and wiped his eyes. "No, I'm sorry. This is your quiet fortnight, not mine. I don't get to harass you with my problems."

"We never really were much for old traditions at the best of times," I said. "And now? There's too much each of us needs to do to take a quiet fortnight."

"No, not you. You—you don't owe anyone anything. It's your right."

I didn't care about traditions or rights or any other rationale for why it would be acceptable for me to lock myself in this guest room in my dead would-be-husband's home. I only knew that I couldn't imagine standing up and getting dressed and going out of doors to meet a world without Theodor in it, not yet. I had remade myself to fit Theodor in my life, unpicked the old seams and let them out, and now there was too much room. My life didn't fit any longer, and I didn't know how to refashion myself again.

I stayed silent a long time, and Kristos didn't press me to speak. "Kristos?" I finally said.

"Yes?"

"I don't want to stay here."

He didn't question it. "I'll find us a different place."

"Ask Alice to come stay with us. And—maybe Emmi."

Kristos nodded and left me to the silence.

When I came downstairs the next morning, Alice was knitting in the parlor. "I made tea," she said, matter-of-fact, as though she had lived in this townhouse her whole life and we had only just discovered her. "Your brother is hiring the porters to move to the new house now."

"Already?"

Alice shook out her knitting and rolled it around her yarn ball—a sock, I saw, as she stabbed her needles through it. "There's a house requisitioned from the nobility, nice place overlooking the river, perfect as one of the governor's houses. They've got three houses near one another, close enough to the city center for official business when needed."

"But then the governors will need them—"

"Of course, you didn't know." Alice paused. "Your brother is one of the governors now."

"Kristos! He—he refused the nomination."

"Yes, but…" Alice cleared her throat. "After what happened," she continued with deft avoidance, "with two vacant seats, the council asked if he would reconsider. So that at least one of the army's earliest leaders would be one of the new Republic's governors."

"I see." I let out a shaky sigh. It should have been Theodor. Anger surged at the stinging injustice of what Niko had done, taking Theodor not only from me but from Galitha. "I think I'll take that tea now."

66

WITHIN A MONTH, ALICE HAD OBTAINED A PERMIT TO REOPEN the shop I had given her. She insisted I take it back, at first, but I refused. It was hers by rights both legal and ethical, and I found when I considered taking up shopkeeping again that the prospect leeched too much memory into it. Even a new shop, a new location, and new wares would have been haunted by my old life. She moved into the apartment over the shop, as proud to have her own business as she was to have a better home for her and her mother.

More, I didn't care to leave the apartment I'd carved out of my brother's house. Every corner, every coffeehouse and tavern, every broadside churned out of the bustling printers across the city thrummed with gossip about the trial of Niko Otni. The evidence was exceptionally clear, but the political drama of it jolted through the city. A few loyal followers held tight to Niko's cause, but the assassination didn't have the effect he had hoped. He might have guessed as much—what gossip I couldn't avoid suggested that no one else had been willing to take the pistol in their own hands.

"It was like an opera," Sianh said as he took dinner with me in my sitting room the evening after Niko insisted on testifying in his defense. "Serafan opera. All stabbings and impassioned orations as to why the blood was a necessity and the blade a friend."

"You said I would enjoy Serafan opera," I said, pushing a ruby-red radish around my plate. It left a deep pink stain on the white china and I stopped abruptly. "I don't think you're selling it very well."

"One does not attend the opera for the plots," he said. "The music brings life to even the most wooden of stories. Otni saw himself as singing an aria, I think, but it lacked a certain... believability."

"You think he was lying?"

"Hardly, no. I think he had attached himself to a falsehood so completely he thought it was the truth—that a man of noble birth could not possibly lead a new Galitha." Sianh paused and set his knife and fork down, balanced with gentle precision on the rim of his plate. "I do not think it likely the jury will find him innocent of the charges."

Hanging, then. And another man would be dead, a casualty in the Galatine Civil War. Even if hanging was just, even if the guilty verdict was well-earned, I wasn't sure I could stomach any more death. I nudged my plate away from me. "I would rather not talk about it any further."

Sianh complied with the dexterous conversation that had made him a success in the Warren in Isildi, though I would never have told him that. He produced a set of silver dice from his pocket and taught me a simple game of wagers, and kept me distracted enough until late in the evening that gallows and juries were the furthest thing from my thoughts. The next day, I started a new gown from fabric Kristos had left for me and had the bodice nearly complete before I thought to wonder if the jury had come to a decision late in the afternoon. When I met

Kristos at the door, he didn't need to say anything—the painful peace in his bearing told me Niko was guilty.

Penny finally made her way into the city, wearing the still-unnamed infant in a neatly wrapped cocoon as she bustled around the house. She threw herself into making it as homey as possible. Though a grand estate in the classical Galatine style, and far larger than anything Penny, Kristos, or I had ever lived in, it was a victim of the war, too. Its three stories were almost bereft of furniture, the curtains had been torn down for fabric, and several rooms' rich wood floors and silk walls were marred with claw marks and stains where a pack of dogs had gotten inside.

Penny prodded me into helping her with friendly jokes and frequent nagging, though I didn't tell her that the main reason I consented to leaving my rooms was because I felt guilty watching her try to strip wallpaper and polish floors while tending the infant.

"I wonder who lived here," Penny mused as we tore down a ruined panel of silk. She teetered on a stepladder but refused to stay firmly on the floor. The baby slept soundly in a basket nearby.

"One of the Ladies Pommerly," I said, ripping a section of the silk as we fought with it. "Which is why I don't feel badly at all living here," I added.

"The Pommerly family was one of the worst, wasn't it?" Penny rolled a length of stained fabric around her arm. "Along with—oh, what was that admiral's name?"

"Penny, you just lived through the single most historic event in centuries of Galatine history, and you can't remember that admiral's name?" I laughed. It felt strange, rusty and thick, yet welcome. "Merhaven. His name was Merhaven."

"That's right." She hopped from the ladder. "Well, they certainly left in a hurry. The larder is a mess."

"The dogs didn't leave much," I said. I didn't add that I knew that this particular member of the Pommerly family had not escaped the city.

"What are we going to do once we get this down?" Penny asked. "We haven't the same fabric lying around, I'm sure."

"No. We'll have to have the walls painted. Maybe verdigris," I said with a sly smile.

"I don't care how stylish it is, that green is far too bright for indoors! It would make a fine calash or pair of shoes, but to be surrounded by it? Ugh!"

"Alice specifically suggested verdigris," I said, another laugh working its way to the surface.

"She did not!" Penny giggled.

The baby roused and began to cry, her little face red with the exertion of so much sudden volume. "She'll be hungry again," Penny said, deftly lifting the little bundle and pulling her breast over the top of her gown in one motion. "Greedy little thing," she cooed as the baby latched hastily.

"She's nearly a hundred days old. Isn't it time she had a name?" I asked, gathering the scraps of soiled wall covering into a bin.

"We were thinking about that," Penny said softly. "We'd like to have a little party here for her naming, the way Kristos said Pellians usually do."

"Kristos has never been interested in what Pellians usually do before," I said. Perhaps having a baby changed that, and now there was something about himself he wanted to capture and save for her, before it was too late. "Emmi could help with the arrangements, if you like. Oh, Lieta would be over the moon to come, too. She loves babies."

"That would be wonderful," Penny said. She paused, then pressed on. "We picked a name, but I want your blessing. If it's not all right with you, we'll pick something else."

I stopped picking up stray bits of silk. "Of course," I said, confused.

"Theodora," Penny said quietly. "We'd like to name her Theodora."

The room looked suddenly tight, too bright and too condensed, and I realized it was because my eyes were overflowing with tears. "Yes," I said softly. "That would be perfect."

67

WE MANAGED TO PAINT THE FRONT PARLOR AND THE FOYER IN time for Penny and Kristos to hold a naming party for Theodora. Emmi spent all morning in the kitchen with Penny, teaching her to make sweet almond pastry and *gami*, which translated roughly as *glop* in Galatine but was a fragrant paste made of herbs, nuts, and oil that Emmi paired with dainty charred flatbreads.

"This is delicious," I said, wiping some *gami* from my chin. "To think, I never liked Pellian food. I'm beginning to think my mother didn't know how to cook."

"She definitely never made anything like this," Kristos agreed. "Remember that spinach pie?"

"That was terrible." I laughed.

"She probably didn't salt and towel off the spinach," Emmi said. "Here, have a pastry."

"The baby would like to eat again," Lieta said, finding us in the kitchen. She had spent all morning holding the infant, who took to Lieta's bony arms like she'd been born there. "And your first guests are arriving."

Penny took the baby to nurse once more before the party, and Kristos and I greeted Viola and Annette, who arrived early with arms full of gifts. More guests arrived, from the council members Kristos felt obligated to invite to the old friends from the dockyards he used to work alongside. Lieta had coached Kristos and Penny in the simple ceremony, and now sat keenly attentive to the proceedings.

Penny presented the baby, whom she had changed into the red silk gown I had made for the occasion, its long skirts hanging to Penny's knees when she held her. A matching quilted cap tied under still milk-damp double chins. She slept soundly in her mother's arms.

"This is my daughter," Kristos said, for once stilted formality taking the place of his easy banter. Lieta nodded, encouraging.

"I have named her Theodora," Penny said, to a quiet murmur of appreciation from the gathered crowd. I saw Annette wipe her eyes and Sianh swallow, very deliberately.

"It is a good name," Kristos recited, his eyes bright and his voice quavering. The rote words of the simple ceremony finished, they paraded her around the room, introducing her by name to each guest.

We then gathered around a simple table of food, and Sianh cracked open a bottle of Serafan spirits. "We toast with a strong drink for a baby, so that she might grow strong, too," he said.

Theodora woke, cried, ate, and slept again like clockwork, much to the delight of everyone gathered, and consented to being held by stranger after stranger, some more adept at bouncing a baby than others. After a couple of hours grazing on Emmi's delicious food and sips of Sianh's exceptionally strong drink, the guests began to leave, one by one.

"I've something to ask you," Kristos said, when only we were left gathered around the remnants of the food. Kristos slathered *gami* on his flatbread, scraping up the last bits remaining in the crystal dish.

I sighed and passed my flatbread to Penny, who lobbed her plain flatbread at Kristos's head.

"What was that for?"

"Next time let the mother of your child have the last of the *gami*," I suggested.

"I didn't realize!" Kristos hurriedly offered his bread to Penny, who passed mine back to me.

"What did you want to ask?" I prodded. "If it's sharing this almond pastry, you're out of luck."

"I wouldn't dream of asking," Kristos said. "No, it's the council. Remember we said that we were going to have to have some legal framework for casting? We need your help."

"I suppose I can offer my expertise," I hedged. Reentering the fray of politics filled me with apprehension. Without the partner I'd had in Theodor, I felt lost.

"Yes, good, of course. But there's more, too. The council thinks it would behoove us to open some sort of office not only for policy but for training. They'll give you space out of the university. It would be combined with a sort of advisor to the council position, I believe."

I nearly dropped my pastry. "What gave them the idea I would ever consent to that?"

"What?" Kristos said around a large bite of flatbread. "It made sense, given the circumstances. That is, you don't have an official role any longer."

I stared at him, involuntarily wavering between rage and weeping. "A lot of things made more sense a month ago," I finally said, tears spilling over my cheeks.

"Damn it, Kristos," Penny said, scooting her heavy chair closer to me. It made a terrible noise as the legs dragged on the floor, but she doggedly pulled herself close enough to grab my hand.

"I'm sorry, I'm not trying to be insensitive." Kristos stared at his food as though realizing it would be uncouth to continue wolfing down his pastry while his grieving sister sobbed into her skirts.

"But you are being insensitive," Penny hissed. "Honestly. She can take as much time as she needs to—"

"No," I half shouted. "No, I can't. I can't just sit here in my brother's house for the rest of my life like some dotard aunt."

"I was looking forward to having an auntie here," Penny offered, a little too eagerly. "You'll be such a help with Theodora!"

"The governor of Galitha can hire more help than you could ever need, I'm sure," I said with a smile. I knew Penny was after the same thing her decorating projects had been aimed at—making me feel useful again. "You two will want to get married and make this a proper—what? Governor's Mansion, is that what we'll call them?"

"Who said anything about getting married?" Kristos said, blanching as he received the full extent of one of Penny's worst glares. "What? It's a joke, of course."

"You are intolerable," Penny said, glowering at him as he ducked his head and nibbled on his bread.

"You're right, Kristos," I finally said, wiping my wet cheeks with the back of my hand. "I don't have an official role any longer, and I don't have a shop to go back to, and I don't have a house of my own to maintain. But I never said I was interested in being a government official, or even that I'm able to."

Kristos groaned. "Not this shrinking violet stuff again, Sophie. You're more than capable."

I held back a torrent of anger I had done very well to bind up and put away—that Kristos had no right, ever, to criticize what I used my gifts for. "I need to think about this." I cut him off from further argument, raising my hand and standing up. "I need some air."

68

~~~

I STRODE DOWN THE STREET, NOT ENTIRELY SURE I KNEW WHAT direction I was walking until I found myself near Fountain Square. The cathedral had been restored to a place of worship and contemplation after having been pressed into the service of the Galatine Civil War. I still didn't have any compulsion to seek solace in the meditation on the Galatine Divine and her Sacred Natures, but I did seek quiet. I tentatively opened the great front doors. No placard announced any services in progress, though a clutch of reverent women sat in an alcove filled with lit candles, praying, and several parishioners still sat in the pews.

I walked the perimeter ringed with stained glass depicting the Sacred Natures, the sea and sky and wide plains of Galitha rendered in colors more saturated than life. Carefully laid piecing of the glass suggested the movement of grain and waves in the images as though some divine breath washed over them, imbuing them with life. I sank onto a bench in front of a great sunburst of glass pierced with the light of the last of the sunset.

"I told him you would not like the idea."

I started as Sianh sat down beside me.

"Did you follow me?" I hissed.

"No, I was observing a service in celebration of the Sacred Nature of the Galatine Fields. Agriculture, yes?"

"I wouldn't know," I replied, distracted. "Why were you watching that?"

"It is instructive, if I am to stay in this country. To know what its people believe."

"Some of its people." I sighed. The fractured light from the sunburst window scattered red and orange and gold on my hands. "You don't seem surprised to see me."

"I was preparing to leave when you entered. I am not surprised to see you distressed, no, though I did not realize you took to prayers in times of distress."

"I don't," I said. "I just—it's quiet here. Usually," I said with a pointed glance at Sianh.

His smile was soft. "Yes, and you wish to have quiet, so I will take my leave." He stood.

"Wait," I said, impulsive, and he sat next to me again, close enough to speak in hushed tones that didn't echo among the high arches of the cathedral. "Where are you going? I mean, now that your contract is over."

"I was promised retirement, remember? A pension."

"And I'm sure it's been given to you."

"Yes. And a land grant, for a bonus. A part of the Pommerly estate near Rock's Ford."

"You're going to take up farming?" I laughed, a hard, bitter noise breaking on the muffled quiet of prayers. "Forgive me, but the thought of you trading a sword for a plow is..."

"It is an unlikely image, yes. I believe I will raise horses, not crops. I have also been asked to take a position at the Rock's Ford Academy."

"They're keeping that open? I would have thought, with the abolishment of the nobility, that it would be closed."

"It is a great resource for Galitha, and now it can serve her greatest resource—her people. Anyone may enter, if he has a will to work and the capacity to excel."

"You sound like you've become an idealist all of a sudden."

"A man cannot run against his own current forever," Sianh murmured. "You have given me a second chance at a life with some meaning."

"I didn't—"

"Yes, you did. You and whatever fate compelled our meeting. It was your word that gave me a place among this company. I am grateful."

"No, we are grateful. We would never have succeeded without..." I shook my head.

"That," Sianh said with a lilting grin, "is likely true. But now. I will be leaving for Rock's Ford within the week. And you?"

"And me?" I stared at my hands, the shadow colors of the dying sunset fading swiftly away. "I don't know. I loosed something on the world and now I suppose it's my responsibility to wrangle it. But, Sianh, they don't—they don't know what they're asking."

"What do they ask?"

"They want me to train others to cast as I do. To bring that power under their control, to wield it—but they don't understand." I met his eyes, surprised to see them fixed steadily on me as I spoke. "But you do, don't you? They want you to teach men to kill each other, and you will. Even though you know what that looks like."

"I will. Even though I carry with me every life I have taken." He said it simply, without pain, without pride. A fact only, though perhaps the most profound fact that defined him. "You do not need to do as I do. But they will learn, one way or another. Once humans know what is possible, they reach and pull and claw to get it for themselves. For my part, if I teach them to kill, I may also teach them duty and responsibility and respect. Another might not. But I will." He didn't press me further, but I took his meaning. I was a more responsible acolyte for the discoveries I had made than others would be.

"It's this—this going forward," I whispered. "Going forward alone. I miss—" I choked on his name and buried my face in my hands, words impossible.

Sianh didn't speak, or even move, except to lay his calloused hand on my shoulder. I leaned against him until weeping had spent me and my eyes were dry. "I'm sorry," I whispered.

"Why? Why do you apologize for the most natural thing, the most true thing that you might do? We do not respect grief as we should," he said, "if you apologize for its presence."

"He would have known what to do," I said.

"It seems to me," Sianh said slowly, "that very often, Theodor said he did not know what to do and you were the voice who spoke through his confusion and doubt. I am not at all doubtful that you would know very well what to do if he were asking you for advice."

"He said that?"

"Only every day." Sianh handed me a white linen handkerchief. "If it were anyone else, what would you tell them?"

I wiped my eyes with the handkerchief and refolded it carefully. "I would remind them that Galitha needs all of us more than ever," I said. "And that we all have our talents and knowledge that no one else has. But I also—I also would have rather this all stayed hidden."

"Such things cannot stay hidden forever. I even suspect that, in the end, it will be for the best. No more subterfuge. No more hidden casting. Do you fear your own power in effecting that new world?"

I started—Polly had asked me the same thing, but I bristled

at the question all the more, coming from a friend. "I don't want it. I don't deserve it."

Now it was Sianh's turn to break the silence with a snort of laughter. Several praying women turned and gave him sharp looks, but he didn't seem to notice. "If you don't deserve a place among the victors, no one does. It hounded me that you would be relegated to your brother's house, forgotten."

"I figured I was a cup with a hole in it." I smiled wanly as Sianh started at the old reference. "My use was over. I suppose...I suppose maybe it isn't."

Sianh shook his head. "Far from it. I foresee your resonance in the world only just beginning."

69

—ᴍᴍ—

"Don't eat all of those plums yourself!" Viola swooped between a basket of fruit and Kristos's outstretched hand, earning a playful swat to her shoulder for her trouble.

"I was getting another one for Penny," he countered, swiping three golden plums so ripe I expected them to burst. Penny laughed as he tossed her one, catching it with one hand as she let a squirming toddler down to run to her father.

"Thea, don't play in the dirt," Penny chastised her. "Auntie Sophie just finished that dress, don't muss it all up."

"There's a reason I made it in white cotton," I answered with a grin. "It might get dirty, but it can be laundered into the ground, too."

"Now, don't you take the rest of my plums!" Viola protested as Thea plucked a plum from the basket with her plump, sticky fingers. She looked like Kristos, with a mop of dark curls and a winning grin that she deployed on Viola at that moment, earning herself another plum.

"Where is Sianh with the lemonade?" Annette asked, scanning Fountain Square as though assessing the waves from the prow of a ship. The sun pelted down on all of us, heating the crowded square that pulsed as though alive with the press of people. Republic Day, celebrated to commemorate the passing of the Reform Bill, had become a settled rite in Galitha in the three years since the Civil War. It was fitting that the Galatines should choose to celebrate, not a divisive war or its bloody battles, but the moment that it tried to effect change peacefully. Of course, that meant the national holiday was near Midsummer, and the heat was worse than it had been in years.

"He's there," Penny said. "Just past that big tree." She sat down on one of the few chairs we'd set up, visibly relieved to be off swollen feet brought on by her second pregnancy. She fanned herself with a napkin so hard that the fat pearls hanging from her ears bobbed in the breeze.

"Aren't you glad we're in the shade?" Kristos asked, handing her a metal cup beading condensation. More than merely being in the shade, we had a reserved pavilion along with the rest of the Galatine government. "Being a governor has its perks."

"Yes, but we have to listen to one of your speeches, don't we?" Penny laughed. "I'm not sure it's worth it."

"This one will be short, I promise." Kristos handed me a cup of water as well, flavored, I saw with appreciation for Kristos's ever-refining palate, with mint.

Sianh schlepped a keg of lemonade toward us, and Thea clapped her hands with delight. "She is not excited to see me, I know better," Sianh said as he set the lemonade down on our table. "It is either the lemonade or that I promised her she might pat the horses I brought north for the races."

"It's the lemonade," Kristos said, clasping his hand as if meeting again for the first time in years, though we had spent the last week together. The Republic Military School was closed for the weeks surrounding the national holiday, and he had come north to try his horses at the first annual National Races.

I poured myself a glass of lemonade and sat on a blanket

in the shade of a sprawling flaxwood poplar. A strand of seeds settled in my cup, and I plucked it out. Thea dashed toward me, intent on the lemonade. Instead, I drew a charm from the ether and strung it in front of her. She laughed and grabbed at it, letting me twine it around my fingers and then swing it between them, dancing like a marionette of light.

Annette and Viola dealt a hand of Pepper with Artur Hysso, now a representative for Pellia in the Council of Country. Kristos and several councillors toasted with cups of lemonade some accomplishment I couldn't hear. Sianh sat next to me, watching Thea tug at strings of light invisible to him.

"She is gifted as you are," he said.

"Sometimes I wonder how many of us are, if only we trusted ourselves to see it." I pulled the strands of light and crossed them as though playing cat's cradle with string, and Thea giggled. "And these little ones trust what they see better than grownups do."

"It may be. Or it may be you are still unwilling to accept the unique nature of your gifts. Even after—what? Teaching dozens of pupils, writing influential Galatine policy on magic, effecting international accords on the use of casting? And all in three years as special advisor to the council?"

"Three very long years," I said. "Pass me a fig?"

Sianh obliged and took several for himself, as well. "I have much I want to discuss with you, on matters of teaching and pedagogy in our unusually utilitarian fields. And you must meet my horses—fine Galatine beasts."

"I should like that." A wadded napkin pelted the side of my face, expertly lobbed to fly under the brim of my hat, and I looked to Annette, who jerked her thumb toward the podium.

"I take that to mean we are to silence ourselves and pay attention to the speeches," Sianh said.

"I believe so," I said, passing the napkin to Sianh with a narrow-eyed nod suggesting its next target: Annette's feather-trimmed hat. He nodded and tucked it carefully away, saving it for an opportune moment.

The governors faced away from us toward the open expanse of Fountain Square, crowded with people whose voices dimmed and silenced as the first of the three governors took the podium. Hamish Oglethorpe, tired of criticizing the missteps of political function, had run for a vacant governor's seat. He and Kristos butted heads nearly daily, as Hamish had an uncanny habit of pinpointing the precise weaknesses in Kristos's ideology-rich and pragmatism-poor proposals, but Kristos respected him. They balanced one another, in some of the same ways Kristos and Theodor had.

Sitting behind the governors meant that we couldn't hear most of what they said. I sat politely, the sun growing stronger as it traced its arc over the city and the shade of the flaxwood poplar next to me shifted. I watched Thea play with her doll, carved of wood and named, inexplicably, Florence. I had made the poppet a complete ensemble out of remnants from Alice's shop, and anticipated teaching Thea to sew by helping her make more miniature gowns and petticoats.

There was a burst of applause and cheers from the crowd, and Hamish paused. Even if I couldn't hear his speech, I knew it was a summation of our successes in the past three years since the conclusion of the Civil War and an optimistic view toward addressing the challenges we still faced. The government was secure, between the regional councils and elected mayors throughout the Republic of Galitha, and the national Council of Country in Galitha City and its three governors. Though we had been plagued by practical challenges to voting policy, resulting in riots during the first elections after the war, the subsequent elections had run smoothly. After long arguments, that right was extended to women, as well, and I had cast my first ballot alongside Emmi and Alice.

More, international trade and relations were nearly restored to prewar confidence, even with West Serafe, which had grudgingly committed to treaties on the use of magic that I had taken no small part in writing. Fen's workers' strikes continued, but we tactfully threw our support in the form of trade agreements behind those *rylkfen* who had come to amenable terms with their workers. Money spoke clearly, and more and more mill owners and factory investors pressured the government to codify workers' rights.

More applause for Hamish, and I caught snatches of what he said—discussing the sewer system of Galitha City. I laughed— improving the health and sanitation of Galitha City had been his pet project, and it was well underway. Already there were fewer outbreaks of ague and dysentery, which he insisted had to do entirely with improved flow of water. Commerce continued to progress in the city, with renewed energy and democratic efficiency for opening new businesses. I allowed myself a contented sigh. So much destruction and death, but it had made way for this—a country with a bright future.

Sianh mistook my sigh for boredom and raised an eyebrow. "Kristos said that the speeches would be short."

"He said *his* speech would be short," I said. "Hamish made no such promise."

Sianh laughed quietly. "Apparently not. He is—what does one say in Galatine? Long-winded. Though to be honest, I could appreciate some breeze right about now."

I passed him a glass of cool lemonade as Hamish finally concluded his speech to cheers and shouts from the crowd. Emmi, Parit, Venia, and my other Pellian friends were likely there somewhere, folded into the crowd. With the too-familiar pang of loss, I remembered Lieta, absent in our gatherings since early spring, when she had passed on peacefully in her sleep. I still met with the others, now inviting them to my too-large offices at the university. I had expected Emmi to want to keep working for Alice, but she had come to me to be included in tutelage in casting alongside the Kvys sisters and others from Galitha, and eventually, West Serafe as well. She was not as gifted as some of the others—Tantia had a remarkable ability for casting strong magic into solid material, and the nuance of some of the Serafans was extraordinary. Still, Emmi was eager to learn and now held an assistantship under me in my post at the university.

The inclusion of Pellia as a province of Galitha had made for uncertainty among some Galatines at first, but I had noticed a change recently, accepting our Pellian immigrants to Galitha City with more generous attitudes than before the war. There would still be challenges; I was sure Hamish had skipped mentioning the small but vocal Galatine Nationalists who had sprung up from disaffected Royalists and Red Caps alike, their newfound political alliance formed on rejecting the inclusion of Pellia. They circulated pamphlets and ran, typically unsuccessfully, for office, but did not seem inclined to disrupt national peace to further their aims.

Kristos took the podium. Sianh made a show of taking his pocket watch from his waistband, marking the time Kristos began to speak. I hid my grin at his joke behind my hand as Kristos unexpectedly hopped down from the podium and began to cross a corner of the square. The crowd parted for him as he strode toward a raised platform next to the new statue that had been placed in the square a week prior, carefully covered and wrapped in layers of tarps.

Now the tarps were loosened, tied only with a large gray

swath of linen around the middle. Kristos made a great show out of gesturing to the statue, but I couldn't hear anything he said. Still, it must have been important, because the crowd was as still and silent as a service in the cathedral. He tugged at the linen swath, and by some impressive engineering, the tarps fell away from the new statue.

It was Theodor. Rendered in deep gray granite, with one hand on a sheathed sword and the other resting on the trunk of a young sapling as though he had just watered it. My breath caught in my throat with a sharp, joyful, grief-spiked, "Oh." Sianh looked to me quickly, assessing in an instant that I was not upset, only overwhelmed. Kristos met my eyes across all of the people between us in the square, and I nodded with a growing smile. Theodor was where he should be, overlooking the heart of the capital of the country he helped to build. The country he never gave up on.

A cheer grew from one corner of the crowd and rippled across the square. I exhaled and a tear slipped down my cheek. The hole he had left in my life was no longer raw and painful at every glancing touch but had grown flexible and accommodated the joy of his memory as well as the loss. With the statue permanently fixed in the center of the city, a small part of what had felt undone by his murder was rectified—he would be here for the growth and change he should have helped to shepherd.

Slowly, the crowd dissipated, meandering toward the riverbank or the newly christened city parks or the public gardens for picnics. Viola and Annette opened boxes of honey cakes and ham and biscuits and cucumber rolls filled with goat cheese, and Sianh poured out more lemonade. Through the bustle of passing plates and clinking glasses, Thea clambered over laps to reach mine.

"Light?" She turned her big brown eyes up toward me expectantly. "Auntie?"

"Of course, sweetness." I drew a thread and let her twine it around her fingers. She giggled as I wound it around her hands, then nestled her dark curly head into the crook of my arm to reach for the strands of charm magic. As the conversation around us dipped into weather and horses, parties and politics, I watched the shadows play on the granite statue across the square and the light play across my lap. With a contented yawn, Thea fell asleep.

Acknowledgments

When I started writing a book about a seamstress, I wasn't sure anyone but me would want to read it. And yet, here we are, three books later—I'm humbled and honored and blown away to have been able to share this story with you all. I certainly wouldn't have been able to, however, without the support, expertise, and work of many talented and wonderful people.

Jessica Sinsheimer, my incredible agent, thank you for your encouragement, guidance, and optimism.

Everyone at Orbit, your talent and enthusiasm are an absolute joy to work with. My editors, Sarah Guan and Nivia Evans, each more brilliant than the other—thank you both. Ellen Wright, Laura Fitzgerald, Paolo Crespo, and all the publicity folks, thank you for your work. I thought I had the most beautiful covers before, but this one—damn. Lauren Panepinto, it's utter genius, and Carrie Violet of Memorial Stitches, the embroidery is breathtaking. Tim Holman and Alex Lenicki, thanks as always for your support.

Thank you to my patient and understanding family—my husband and partner, Randy, and my two daughters, to whom this book is dedicated. You share me with imaginary people and made-up worlds and print on a page, and I know that isn't always easy.

Mom and Dad, thanks for your encouragement of young me and for your support now, including babysitting duty during editorial calls.

For all the support from friends, community, fellow sewists and readers and history nerds—thank you. Especially my friends, too numerous to list, in the living history community, where a culture of enthusiastically seeking and sharing knowledge makes even the most obscure primary sources accessible—research for this book owes quite a bit to your efforts.

So much gratitude to all the fellow creators giving me inspiration every day. I will miss many of you as I attempt any list at all, but in particular, Alexandra Rowland, Marshall Ryan Maresca, Tasha Suri, Melissa Caruso, Asha Brogan, Eileen O'Connor Ramsey, Cass Morris, Amy Carol Reeves, Evie Skelton, Lynn Graham, Mike Chen, Erica Huffman, and so many others sharing their gifts and joy with the world. Thanks for letting me nerd out with you.

Finally, to you, readers, who picked up a book about a seamstress and followed her story to the end (or, really, to another beginning). I am grateful to each of you.

extras

orbit

meet the author

Photo Credit: Heidi Hauck

ROWENNA MILLER grew up in a log cabin in Indiana and still lives in the Midwest with her husband and daughters, where she teaches English composition, trespasses while hiking, and spends too much time researching and re-creating historical textiles.

Find out more about Rowenna Miller and other Orbit authors by registering for the free monthly newsletter at www.orbitbooks .net.

if you enjoyed
RULE

look out for

THE OBSIDIAN TOWER
Rooks and Ruin: Book One

by

Melissa Caruso

As the granddaughter of a Witch Lord of Vaskandar, Ryx was destined for power and prestige. But a childhood illness left her with broken magic that drains the life from anything she touches, and Vaskandar has no place for a mage with unusable powers. So Ryx has resigned herself to an isolated life as the warden of Gloamingard, her grandmother's castle.

At Gloamingard's heart lies a black tower. Sealed by magic, it guards a dangerous secret that has been contained for thousands of years. Until one impetuous decision Ryx makes leaves her with blood on her hands—and unleashes a threat that could doom everything she loves to fall to darkness.

ONE

There are two kinds of magic.

There is the kind that lifts you up and fills you with wonder, saving you when all is lost or opening doors to new worlds of possibility. And there is the kind that wrecks you, that shatters you, bitter in your mouth and jagged in your hand, breaking everything you touch.

Mine was the second kind.

My father's magic could revive blighted fields, turning them lush and green again, and coax apples from barren boughs in the dead of winter. Grass withered beneath my footsteps. My cousins kept the flocks in their villages healthy and strong, and turned the wolves away to hunt elsewhere; I couldn't enter the stables of my own castle without bringing mortal danger to the horses.

I should have been like the others. Ours was a line of royal vivomancers; life magic flowed in our veins, ancient as the rain that washed down from the hills and nurtured the green valleys of Morgrain. My grandmother was the immortal Witch Lord of Morgrain, the Lady of Owls herself, whose magic coursed so deep through her domain that she could feel the step of every rabbit and the fall of every leaf. And I was Exalted Ryxander, a royal atheling, inheritor of an echo of my grandmother's profound connection to the land and her magical power. Except that I was also Ryx, the family embarrassment, with magic so twisted it was unusably dangerous.

The rest of my family had their place in the cycle, weavers of a great pattern. I'd been born to snarl things up—or more like it, to break the loom and set the tapestry on fire, given my luck.

So I'd made my own place.

At the moment, that place was on the castle roof. One gloved hand clamped onto the delicate bone-carved railing of a nearby balcony for balance, to keep my boots from skidding on the sharply angled shale; the other held the wind-whipped tendrils of dark hair that had escaped my braid back from my face.

"This is a disaster," I muttered.

"I don't see any reason it needs to be, Exalted Warden." Odan, the castle steward—a compact and muscular old man with an extravagant mustache—stood with unruffled dignity on the balcony beside me. I'd clambered over its railing to make room for him, since I couldn't safely share a space that small. "We still have time to prepare guest quarters and make room in the stables."

"That's not the problem. No so-called diplomat arrives a full day early without warning unless they're up to trouble." I glared down at the puffs of dust rising from the northern trade road. Distance obscured the details, but I made out at least thirty riders accompanying the Alevaran envoy's carriage. "And that's too large an escort. They said they were bringing a dozen."

Odan's bristly gray brows descended the broad dome of his forehead. "It's true that I wouldn't expect an ambassador to take so much trouble to be rude."

"They wouldn't. Not if they were planning to negotiate in good faith." And that was what made this a far more serious issue than the mere inconvenience of an early guest. "The Shrike Lord of Alevar is playing games."

Odan blew a breath through his mustache. "Reckless of him, given the fleet of imperial warships sitting off his coast."

"Rather." I hunkered down close to the slate to get under the chill edge that had come into the wind in the past few days, heralding the end of summer. "I worked hard to set up these talks between Alevar and the Serene Empire. What in the Nine Hells is he trying to accomplish?"

The line of riders drew closer along the gray strip of road that wound between bright green farms and swaths of dark forest, approaching the grassy sun-mottled hill that lifted Gloamingard Castle toward a banner-blue sky. The sun winked off the silver-tipped antlers of six proud stags drawing the carriage, a clear announcement that the coach's occupant could bend wildlife to their will—displaying magic in the same way a dignitary of the Serene Empire of Raverra to the south might display wealth, as a sign of status and power.

Another gleam caught my eye, however: the metallic flash of sabers and muskets.

"Pox," I swore. "Those are all soldiers."

Odan scowled down at them. "I'm no diplomat like you, Warden, but it does seem odd to bring an armed platoon to sign a peace treaty."

I almost retorted that I wasn't a diplomat, either. But it was as good a word as any for the role I'd carved out for myself.

Diplomacy wasn't part of a Warden's job. Wardens were mages; it was their duty to use their magic to nurture and sustain life in the area they protected. But my broken magic couldn't nurture. It only destroyed. When my grandmother followed family tradition and named me the Warden of Gloamingard Castle—her own seat of power—on my sixteenth birthday, it had seemed like a cruel joke.

I'd found other ways. If I couldn't increase the bounty of the crops or the health of the flocks with life magic, I could use my Raverran mother's connections to the Serene Empire to enrich our domain with favorable trade agreements. If I couldn't protect Morgrain by rousing the land against bandits or invaders, I could cultivate good relations with Raverra, securing my domain a powerful ally. I'd spent the past five years building that relationship, despite muttering from traditionalists in the family about being too friendly with a nation we'd warred with countless times in centuries past.

I'd done such a good job, in fact, that the Serene Empire had agreed to accept our mediation of an incident with Alevar that threatened to escalate into war.

"I can't let them sabotage these negotiations before they've even started." It wasn't simply a matter of pride; Morgrain lay directly between Alevar and the Serene Empire. If the Shrike Lord wanted to attack the Empire, he'd have to go through us.

The disapproving gaze Odan dropped downhill at the Alevarans could have frozen a lake. "How should we greet them, Warden?"

My gloved fingers dug against the unyielding slate beneath me. "Form an honor guard from some of our nastiest-looking battle chimeras to welcome them. If they're going to make a show of force, we have to answer it." That was Vaskandran politics, all display and spectacle—a stark contrast to the subtle, hidden machinations of Raverrans.

Odan nodded. "Very good, Warden. Anything else?"

The Raverran envoy would arrive tomorrow with a double handful of clerks and advisers, prepared to sit down at a table and speak in a genteel fashion about peace, to find my castle already overrun with a bristling military presence of Alevaran soldiers. That would create a terrible first impression—especially since Alevar and Morgrain were both domains of the great nation of Vaskandar, the Empire's historical enemy. I bit my lip a moment, thinking.

"Quarter no more than a dozen of their escort in the castle," I said at last. "Put the rest in outbuildings or in the town. If the envoy raises a fuss, tell them it's because they arrived so early and increased their party size without warning."

A smile twitched the corners of Odan's mustache. "I like it. And what will you do, Exalted Warden?"

I rose, dusting roof grit from my fine embroidered vestcoat, and tugged my thin leather gloves into place. "I'll prepare to meet this envoy. I want to see if they're deliberately making trouble, or if they're just bad at their job."

Gloamingard was really several castles caught in the act of devouring each other. *Build the castle high and strong*, the Gloaming Lore said, and each successive ruler had taken that as license to impose their own architectural fancies upon the place. The Black Tower reared up stark and ominous at the center, more ancient than the country of Vaskandar itself; an old stone keep surrounded it, buried in fantastical additions woven of living trees and vines. The stark curving ribs of the Bone Palace clawed at the sky on one side, and the perpetual scent of woodsmoke bathed the sharp-peaked roofs of the Great Lodge on the other; my grandmother's predecessor had attempted to build a comfortable wood-paneled manor house smack in the front and center. Each new Witch Lord had run roughshod over the building plans of those who came before them, and the whole place was a glorious mess of hidden doors and dead-end staircases and windows opening onto blank walls.

This made the castle a confusing maze for visitors, but for me, it was perfect. I could navigate through the odd, leftover spaces and closed-off areas, keeping away from the main halls with their deadly risk of bumping into a sprinting page or distracted servant. I haunted my own castle like a ghost.

As I headed toward the Birch Gate to meet the Alevaran envoy, I opened a door in the back of a storage cabinet beneath a little-used stairway, hurried through a dim and dusty space between walls, and came out in a forgotten gallery under a latticework of artistically woven tree roots and stained glass. At the far end, a string of grinning animal faces adorned an arch of twisted wood; an unrolling scroll carved beneath them warned me to *Give No Cunning Voices Heed*. It was a bit of the Gloaming Lore, the old family wisdom passed down through the centuries in verse. Generations of mages had scribed pieces of it into every odd corner of Gloamingard.

I climbed through a window into the dusty old stone keep, which was half fallen to ruin. My grandmother had sealed the main door with thick thorny vines when she became the Witch Lord a hundred and forty years ago; sunbeams fell through holes in the roof onto damp, mossy walls. It still made for a good alternate route across the castle. I hurried down a dim, dust-choked hallway, taking advantage of the lack of people to move a little faster than I normally dared.

Yet I couldn't help slowing almost to a stop when I came to the Door.

It loomed all the way to the ceiling of its deep-set alcove, a flat shining rectangle of polished obsidian. Carved deep into its surface in smooth, precise lines was a circular seal, complex with runes and geometric patterns.

The air around it hung thick with power. The pressure of it made my pulse sound in my ears, a surging dull roar. A thrill of dread trickled down my spine, never mind that I'd passed it countless times.

It was the monster of my childhood stories, the haunt of my nightmares, the ominous crux of all the Gloaming Lore. Carved through the castle again and again, above windows and under crests, set into floors and wound about pillars, the same words appeared over and over. It was the chorus of the rhyme we learned in the cradle, recited at our adulthood ceremonies, and whispered on our deathbeds: *Nothing must unseal the Door.*

No one knew what lay in the Black Tower, but this was its sole entrance. And every time I walked past it, despite the unsettling aura of power that hung about it like a long bass note too low to hear, despite the warnings drilled into me since birth and scribed all over Gloamingard, curiosity prickled awake in my mind.

I wanted to open it—anyone would. But I wasn't stupid. I kept going, a shiver skimming across my shoulders.

I climbed through another window and came out in the Hall of Chimes, a long corridor hung with swaying strands of white-bleached bones that clattered hollowly in a breeze channeled through cleverly placed windows. The Mantis Lord—my grandmother's grandmother's grandfather—had built the Bone Palace, and he'd apparently had rather morbid taste.

This wasn't some forgotten space entombed by newer construction; I might encounter other people here. I dropped my pace to a brisk walk and kept to the right. On the opposite side of the hall, a slim tendril of leafy vine ran along the floor, dotted irregularly with tiny pale purple flowers. It was a reminder to everyone besides me who lived or worked in the castle to stay to that side, the safe side—life to life. I strained my atheling's sense to its limit, aware of every spider nestled in a dusty corner, ready to slow down the second I detected anyone approaching. Bones clacked overhead as I strode through the hall; I wanted to get to the Birch Gate in time to make certain everything was in place to both welcome and warn the envoy.

I rounded a corner too fast and found myself staring into a pair of widening brown eyes. A dark-haired young woman hurried toward me with a tray of meat buns, nearly in arm's reach, on the wrong side of the corridor.

My side. Death's side.

Too close to stop before I ran into her.

if you enjoyed
RULE

look out for

THE RANGER OF MARZANNA

The Goddess War: Book One

by

Jon Skovron

Sonya is training to be a Ranger of Marzanna, an ancient sect of warriors who have protected the land for generations. But the old ways are dying, and the Rangers have all been forced into hiding or killed off by the invading empire.

When her father is murdered by imperial soldiers, she decides to finally take action. Using her skills as a Ranger, she will travel

*across the bitter cold tundra and gain the allegiance of the only
other force strong enough to take down the invaders.*

*But nothing about her quest will be easy. Because not everyone is
on her side. Her brother, Sebastian, is the most powerful sorcerer
the world has ever seen. And he's fighting for the empire.*

1

Istoki was not the smallest, poorest, or most remote village in
Izmoroz, but it was close. The land was owned by the noble
Ovstrovsky family, and the peasants who lived and worked there
paid an annual tithe in crops every year at harvest time. The
Ovstrovskys were not known for their diligence, and the older
folk in Istoki remembered a time when they would even forget to
request their tithe. That was before the war. Before the empire.

But now imperial soldiers arrived each year to collect their own
tithe, as well as the Ovstrovsky family's. And they never forgot.

Little Vadim, age eight and a half, sat on a snow-covered
log at the eastern edge of the village and played with his rag
doll, which was fashioned into the likeness of a rabbit. He saw
the imperial soldiers coming on horseback along the dirt road.
Their steel helmets and breastplates gleamed in the winter sun
as their horses rode in two neat, orderly lines. Behind them
trundled a wagon already half-full with the tithes of other villages in the area.

They came to a halt before Vadim with a great deal of clank-
ing, their faces grim. Each one seemed to bristle with sharp
metal and quiet animosity. Their leader, a man dressed not in

armor but in a bright green wool uniform with a funny cylindrical hat, looked down at Vadim.

"You there. Boy." The man in green had black hair, olive skin, and a disdainful expression.

Vadim hugged his doll tightly and said nothing. His mother had told him it was best not to talk to imperial soldiers because you never knew when you might say the wrong thing to them.

"Run along and tell your elder we're here to collect the annual tithe. And tell him to bring it all here. I'd rather not go slogging through this frozen mudhole just to get it."

He knew he should obey the soldier, but when he looked at the men and horses looming above him, his whole body stiffened. He had never seen real swords before. They were buckled to the soldiers' waists with blades laid bare so he could see their keen edges. He stared at them, clutched the doll to his chest, and did not move.

The man in green sighed heavily. "Dear God in Heaven, they're all inbred imbeciles out here. Boy! I'm speaking to you! Are you deaf?"

Slowly, with great effort, Vadim shook his head.

"Wonderful," said the man. "Now run along and do as I say."

He tried to move. He really did. But his legs wouldn't work. They were frozen, fixed in place as if already pierced by the glittering swords.

The man muttered to himself as he leaned over and reached into one of his saddlebags. "*This* is why I'm counting the days until my transfer back to Aureum. If I have to see one more—"

An arrow pierced one side of the man's throat and exited the other side. Blood sprayed from the severed artery, spattering Vadim's face and hair. He gaped as the man clutched his gushing throat. The man's eyes were wide with surprise and he made faint gargling noises as he slowly slid from his saddle.

"We're under attack!" shouted one of the other soldiers.

"Which direction?" shouted another.

A third one lifted his hand and pointed out into one of the snowy fields. "There! It's—"

Then an arrow embedded itself in his eye and he toppled over.

Vadim turned his head in the direction the soldier had been pointing and saw a lone rider galloping across the field, the horse kicking up a cloud of white. The rider wore a thick leather coat with a hood lined in white fur. Vadim had never seen a Ranger of Marzanna before because they were supposed to all be dead now. But he had been raised on stories of the *Strannik*, told by his mother in hushed tones late at night, so Vadim knew that was what he saw.

"Get into formation!" shouted a soldier. "Archers, return fire!"

But the Ranger was closing fast. Vadim had never seen a horse run so swiftly. It seemed little more than a blur of gray and black across the white landscape. Vadim's mother had said that a Ranger of Marzanna did not need to guide their horse. That the two were so perfectly connected, they knew each other's thoughts and desires.

The Ranger loosed arrow after arrow, each one finding a vulnerable spot in a soldier's armor. The soldiers cursed as they fumbled for their own bows and let fly with arrows that overshot their rapidly approaching target. Their faces were no longer proud or grim, but tense with fear.

As the Ranger drew near, Vadim saw that it was a woman. Her blue eyes were bright and eager, and there was a strange, almost feral grin on her lips. She shouldered her bow and stood on her saddle even as her horse continued to sprint toward the now panicking soldiers. Then she drew a long knife from her belt and leapt toward the soldiers. Her horse veered to the side as she crashed headlong into the mass of armed men. The Ranger's blade flickered here and there, drawing arcs of red as she hopped from one mounted soldier to the next. She stabbed some and slit the throats of others. Some were only wounded and fell from their horses to be trampled under the hooves of the frightened animals. The air was thick with blood and the screams of men in pain. Vadim squeezed his doll as hard as he could and kept his eyes shut tight, but he could not block out the piteous sounds of terrified agony.

And then everything went silent.

"Hey, *mal'chik*," came a cheerful female voice. "You okay?"

Vadim cautiously opened his eyes to see the Ranger grinning down at him.

"You hurt?" asked the Ranger.

Vadim shook his head with an uneven twitch.

"Great." The Ranger crouched down beside him and reached out her hand.

Vadim flinched back. His mother had said that *Strannik* were fearsome beings who had been granted astonishing abilities by the dread Lady Marzanna, Goddess of Winter.

"I'm not going to hurt you." She gently wiped the blood off his face with her gloved hand. "Looks like I got you a little messy. Sorry about that."

Vadim stared at her. In all the stories he had ever heard, none of them had described a Ranger as *nice*. Was this a trick of some kind? An attempt to set Vadim at ease before doing something cruel? But the Ranger only stood back up and looked at the wagon, which was still attached to a pair of frightened, wild-eyed horses. The other horses had all scattered.

The Ranger gestured to the wagon filled with the tithes of other villages. "Anyway, I better get this stuff back where it came from."

She looked down at the pile of bloody, uniformed bodies in the snow for a moment. "Tell your elder I'm sorry about the mess. But at least you get to keep all your food this year, right?"

She patted Vadim on the head, then sauntered over to her beautiful gray-and-black stallion, who waited patiently nearby. She tied her horse to the wagon, then climbed onto the seat and started back the way the soldiers had come.

Vadim watched until he could no longer see the Ranger's wagon. Then he looked at all the dead men who lay at his feet. Now he knew there were worse things than imperial soldiers. Though he didn't understand the reason, his whole body trembled, and he began to cry.

When he finally returned home, his eyes raw from tears, he told his mother what had happened. She said he had been blessed, but he did not feel blessed. Instead he felt as though he had been given a brief glimpse into the true nature of the world, and it was more frightening than he had ever imagined.

For the rest of his short life, Vadim would have nightmares of that Ranger of Marzanna.

Follow us:

f /orbitbooksUS

🐦 /orbitbooks

▶ /orbitbooks

Join our mailing list
to receive alerts on our
latest releases and deals.

orbitbooks.net

Enter our monthly
giveaway for the chance
to win some epic prizes.

orbitloot.com